Praise for the novels of Adele Parks

"I'll drop anything for a new Adele Parks: she nails it every time."
—Lucy Foley, #1 *New York Times* bestselling author
of *The Paris Apartment*

"Absolutely gripping, this is revenge lit at its best. Provocative and compelling. I was left breathless at the final twist"
—Lisa Jewell, *New York Times* bestselling author of *The Family Remains*

"Whip-smart protagonist, immensely satisfying."
—Karin Slaughter, *New York Times* bestselling author of *Girl, Forgotten*

"An astonishing achievement, Parks gets better and better."
—Gillian McAllister, *New York Times* bestselling author
of *Wrong Place Wrong Time*

"As always with Adele...this is an absolutely gripping read."
—Richard Osman, *New York Times* bestselling author
of *The Thursday Murder Club*

"Adele Parks is the queen of the domestic drama."   —Sally Hepworth

"Serves up the perfect dose of escapism laced with tension and darkness."   —*Cosmopolitan*

T0191184

THE
IMAGE
OF
YOU

ADELE PARKS

/|\MIRA

ISBN-13: 978-0-7783-8744-2

The Image of You

First published in 2018. This edition published in 2024.

Recycling programs
for this product may
not exist in your area.

For questions and comments about the quality of this book, please contact us
at CustomerService@Harlequin.com.

TM is a trademark of Harlequin Enterprises ULC.

Mira
22 Adelaide St. West, 41st Floor
Toronto, Ontario M5H 4E3, Canada
MIRABooks.com

Printed in U.S.A.

For my friends Colleen LaFontaine and Tara Pinches

With love

PROLOGUE

What do we even call this decade?

The seventies, eighties, nineties, etc. were simply defined, the noughties had a special something, but where are we now? I'll tell you where. The teenies? A decade that sounds like a close relation to that annoying kids' programme that used to be popular when I did a lot of babysitting. It's demeaning. I'm living through the decade where I hope to reach my emotional, professional and sexual prime and its name puts me in mind of life-sized purple, blue, yellow and orange puppets with lisps. Horrible. This decade is a vicious, cruel debacle of a decade. It is. Shall I tell you what's wrong with it? Besides its name. Yup, I'm going to. I have a list.

1. Open-plan offices; no one can have any secrets, not even a secret nibble on a chocolate bar.

2. Communication is 90% text/email/social media messaging; communication is therefore at least 50% misunderstood. That is a conservative estimate.

3. Facebook. It makes us neurotic and deceitful; I mean, really, is everyone else having so much fun, and so many babies?

4. The lack of personal responsibility and the rise of the suing/blame culture. For goodness' sake, own your disastrous life!

5. People talk in cinema and theatres. They sometimes leave to go to the bathroom or, worse still, they take off their shoes. Yuk! Standards, people, standards!

6. And that thing people do. Post a profile picture of themselves taking a picture of themselves in a mirror, so the phone is in front of their face. Why?!

This list is by no means exhausted, but your patience probably is, because:

7. People are not as patient as they used to be.

Anyway, you get my point.

On the plus side, this has been the decade when wearing onesies became OK. That's something, a saving grace maybe, because really there's never been anything more comfortable, more wonderful, to wear when curling up in front of Netflix than a soft, baggy onesie.

And do you know what the absolute worst thing about this decade is? The one that kills me. No one, and I mean *no one*, has the expectation that they will meet anyone because their eyes collide across a crowded room. It. Does. Not. Happen. Not anymore. We meet online and I think that's sad. I'm thirty-one and have been so very, very good all my life; not so much as a flirty text sent to one guy whilst I was with another. I'm faithful first and foremost. I think loyalty is all, it's the backbone of all relationships—nay, the very oxygen—but that is not the case with men. No, madam. They are faithless, selfish, reckless, heartless bastards, every last one of them. I promise you.

Unless, of course, they're wet. Just saying.

The hairs on his body stood proud. As though they were trying to desert him. He felt sweaty, clammy yet icy cold. He put his hand out to steady himself. The flat of his palm against the mirror. His hand in her blood. A perfect print. Fuck. He reached for the water glass where not long ago toothpaste and a toothbrush might have sat. This was surreal. This couldn't be happening. He filled it with water from the tap; it was lukewarm. He swallowed it back but still his throat was dry. Closed. It was like swallowing sand. He sank down on to the bathroom floor; his arse was in her blood. The wetness seeped through his trousers to his skin.

This sort of thing didn't happen to someone like him. He was a good guy. Or at least a good-enough guy. That's what he'd always thought.

But he was also the sort of bloke who lied on dating sites to worm his way to a thoughtless shag; he had fast and dirty sex in hotel rooms, in alleyways and toilets.

He didn't know what sort of bloke he was. Maybe this kind of thing did happen to guys like him. Not-good-enough guys. They did. You read it in the papers. Sleazy, chaotic people ended up in sleazy, chaotic situations.

There was so much blood. His thoughts wouldn't sharpen or clarify, they squelched around his head. He could smell the iron of her blood. He stared at his hand. Covered with it.

It wasn't some sick joke. It was real. He knew. Somehow he just knew. He felt it: she'd gone. He scrambled to his feet, turned to the basin that was smeared with her blood, and threw up. The trendy little basin with its small plughole wasn't designed for this sort of waste. His vomit settled in the bowl; he could see remnants of the evening's supper. Spinach. Carrots. How could it be that he was still digesting a meal they'd eaten together but she was gone? He had to push his waste away with his fingers, run the taps. With-

out thinking about it he started to splash the water around the basin, cleaning away her blood too.

He didn't have any choice. He was a man who had swiftly fallen from having too much choice, to no choice at all.

ONE
Anna

Zoe laughed her head off when she read Anna's online dating profile. Well, she would, wouldn't she? She was so cynical. Sometimes her cynicism could be frustrating. Hurtful even. 'You can't say that. You just can't,' she screeched, hysterically. Her voice travelled from far away yet rang loudly in Anna's head, blocking out everything else.

Sometimes Anna regretted contacting Zoe. If she didn't get in touch, would Zoe ever get in touch with her? Anna pushed the thought away. She wasn't up to examining the intricacies of their relationship right now. Everyone knew families were complex, tricky. Anna firmly believed you had to carry on regardless. You can choose your friends but you can't choose your family. You still had to love them. Those were the rules.

Instead, she asked, 'Why can't I say that? It's how I feel.'

'Feel.' Zoe repeated the word, throwing a whole host of contempt into it.

Some people are born romantic and manage to stay that way but they're very few and far between; most have it slowly eroded away through a series of cancelled dates, dreadful dates, white lies, black lies—they turn cold. Zoe was simply born hard. Granite. Sometimes it was difficult to believe that she and Anna came from the same seed, the same womb. In fact, they were monochorionic, monoamniotic twins. The rarest sort, only occurring in one per cent of twin pregnancies. Just a step away from conjoined. Their closeness was a scientific fact: they shared the same amniotic sac, the same placenta. There was only one afterbirth. Anna told herself that they were each other's yin to yang. They balanced one another, but at this exact moment in time she didn't feel balanced, she felt swamped.

'You should say you're twenty-nine,' Zoe insisted.

'But I'm not. I'm thirty-one. I don't like lying.'

'Face facts. Men like younger women, Anna Baby.' Zoe argued with an air of feigned regret.

'I know, but will two years make a difference?'

'Yes, when you're the wrong side of the big Three O. Alarm bells. Panic stations.'

Whilst Zoe was arguing for Anna to hide this fact, age was not something that bothered her personally, not in the slightest. Zoe was not hostage to the sound of the ticking of her biological clock; she couldn't even hear the chimes. The baby-making business wasn't something she'd ever shown any interest in. By contrast, Anna thought about it a lot. She'd always been happiest playing with her dolls, whereas Zoe was forever climbing trees or dashing off on her bike at breakneck speed, not even bothering to put on her helmet. Anna wanted to stay at home, make a home; Zoe rushed at escapades and loved to take risks. Yet Zoe was the one who always had men in her life. They fell at her feet whilst Anna seemed to be singularly unsuccessful in affairs of the heart.

It shouldn't be this hard, all she wanted was to meet a good man—a faithful, kind, perceptive man. If he was handsome and funny that would be a bonus. If he wanted a Kardashian-size family that would be amazing although as long as he wanted at least two, then Anna was happy. Wealth would be awesome, but she wasn't greedy; if he earned a modest amount yet ticked all the other boxes, she'd still be delighted. Her main concerns were that he was a decent sort; that she'd be able to trust him.

Anna knew exactly what constituted the perfect wedding day. The dress had to be a big romantic, lacy number, in at the waist, with a flowing skirt. Kate Middleton nailed it—what was more 'princess dress' than an actual Princess's dress? You couldn't go wrong with tight white roses. Six bridesmaids looked amazing, plus two flower girls. She'd have the menu printed on a doily, she was planning on fireworks, doves, a string quartet and a live band. Nina Simone's 'My Baby Just Cares For Me' would be their first dance. The children would be called Freddie and Maggie.

She could see it all. The proposal, the anniversaries, the births and the first days of school.

She just didn't know what the groom looked like. Or what he was called. Or where he was. But he had to be somewhere on this planet, didn't he?

As far as Anna was aware, Zoe had never, ever thought about her wedding day. Well, at least not beyond commenting that marriage was patriarchal enslavement and she'd rather chew off her own left hand than slip a ring on her finger. Safe to say, Zoe was the one who called the shots, broke the hearts.

'Don't you ever worry about being lonely?' Anna probed.

'No. There's a big difference between being alone and being lonely. Besides, I've got you. Haven't I?'

'Absolutely.'

'We always have each other. Always and for ever.'

The thought was somehow comforting and daunting.

'It's just seems wrong to lie about my age. What sort of start is that to any relationship?'

Zoe laughed her slightly manic, quite pitiless laugh. 'What? Lying to a bunch of online losers on a dating site seems wrong? I'd have thought it was de rigueur.'

'Excuse me? Losers? Do I have to remind you I'm about to add my profile and join their ranks?'

'I'm sorry, did I say losers? I meant to say strangers. Look, Anna, none of them ever tell the truth. The guy who says he's six foot one, he's five foot eight. The guy who says he likes hiking, skiing and mountain-bike riding has never done anything more physical in his life than the missionary position. Actually, scrap that, he wouldn't even crawl on top.'

'Stop it, Zoe. Can't you be a bit supportive?'

'I am being, by advising you to lie about your age. If you want to be successful at this, then you'd better learn how to play the game. Newsflash: Men prefer younger women.'

A huffy silence ensued for a moment or so. Anna was counting to ten, trying to keep her patience, Zoe was probably just wondering how to word her next criticism.

'And you cannot begin your profile with the words, *my friends say I'm romantic, thoughtful, trustworthy, honest.*'

'But they do say those things.' Or they had. Her American friends.

The truth was Anna didn't have that many friends here in the UK. Even with Skype, FaceTime, Facebook and emails it was hard to stay close to those she'd left behind in New York two years ago. Oddly, whilst she was the one that had moved away, her friends in Manhattan seemed to be the ones that had moved on. They were no longer running around the city wearing heels, drinking *mojito*s. Most of them had married in the past few years. They'd fast-tracked from proposal, to wedding list, to ceremony, to pregnancy and were now participating in nursery interviews. It left her dizzy, the speed with which these women had achieved so much. Dizzy and—well—jealous. She did her best to supress her jealousy. Jealousy wasn't very 'nice girl' and she was a nice girl, she really was. Twice, at great expense, she'd crossed backwards and forwards over the Atlantic to attend wedding ceremonies; she posted seemingly endless gifts for engagement parties, weddings and baby showers that she couldn't attend; she facetimed her friends and watched them spoon mashed sweet potato into the little pink mouths of their firstborns. She had tried, but it became increasingly difficult to stay interested in the endless, exuberant (exhausting) emails about the colour of bridesmaids' dresses, the colour of baby poop.

She'd once confessed as much to Zoe, who shrugged and muttered something about ceremony, pregnancy, nursery, alimony. 'Only when they hit alimony do they become decent friends again.'

Anna scowled. She didn't want to see any of her friends divorced. She didn't want to think about that side of things. No matter what the statistics were.

Unfortunately, making new friends here in London hadn't been as easy as she'd hoped; Londoners, she found, did not welcome their new neighbours with baskets full of cookies and muffins. She remembered when she and Zoe were just nine years old and her family emigrated to Bridgeport, a city one hour's drive north of New York; they'd been overwhelmed by the generous welcome neighbours, keen to be friends, had laid on. They were inundated with home-baked produce, orthodontist recommendations, tips about drycleaners and hair salons, as well as invitations to barbecues, supper parties, pot lucks and spit roasts. Even then, Zoe had been the sceptical sort. She'd insisted that people were just excited by the novelty of their Mancunian accents, impressed by their parents' prestigious jobs, or fascinated by identical twins, and that their interest would eventually wane. However, she was wrong. The Turner family made firm friends with the positive, purposeful and gracious American neighbours. For over twenty years now, those friends had shared fat turkeys and thick-crusted pumpkin pies at Thanksgiving suppers; together they'd watched fireworks dazzle and fade into the hot, black nights every July 4th; the twins and the other neighbourhood kids had trailed door to door, scooping up handfuls of sticky treats on Halloween, and dipping into cool outdoor pools throughout the long summer vacations.

These friends had been there throughout the bad times too. The traumatic and horrific times.

By contrast, since Anna had moved to London she'd been living in a third-floor flat on the edges of Tooting Bec. She shared landing space with a similarly aged couple, but they'd yet to make eye contact. She'd hoped for a dinner party invitation but their interaction had been limited to embarrassed shuffles around the recycling bins. The truth of the matter was that making friends took time, energy and commitment. Anna had all three, in spades, but she tended to spend them on her work and her campaign to meet a potential husband. There wasn't much room left for friendships. Besides, she had Zoe. And whilst Zoe didn't actually live in England, she took up so much space.

Anna tried to defend her profile. 'But my friends do say I'm romantic, thoughtful, trustworthy, honest.'

'Yes, they do. More's the pity.'

'Well, I'm not going to say sexy, ambitious, pushy. That would be your profile.'

'I'm not disagreeing with the adjectives exactly—although I don't think they're the most captivating traits for this particular sort of project—my objection is starting with the words *my friends say*. It shows a lack of confidence. You ought to know yourself better than anyone. You ought to be able to present yourself without the prop.'

Anna shrank from the idea. How could she write, 'I'm romantic, thoughtful, trustworthy, honest?' It sounded so conceited. It left her so exposed.

Zoe continued, 'And I'm not sure about this next bit either. *I like long walks (especially along the beach!), I really enjoy watching movies (everything from blockbusters to art house!) and there's nothing I like more than a lazy Sunday of reading papers and enjoying a pub roast lunch.*'

'What's wrong with that?'

'Well, for one, you're a vegetarian so it's a lie. Rather cancelling out the claim that you're honest.'

Anna blushed. 'It's not really a lie. I do like going to the pub for a nut roast but adding the word 'nut', well it changes everything.'

'Yes, you're right about that, at least. You absolutely do not want to say you're vegetarian. Only skinny, pale guys will respond. My point is that you might as well say *I watch too many romcoms and absolutely believe in the happily ever after. I love the montage part when the couple are seen doing this sort of overtly romantic thing.* It's actually scary.'

Anna was stumped. She did believe in the happily ever after and the montage. 'Well, what would you write?'

'I don't know. Maybe, *I like being tied up and whilst I've never tried three in a bed, I'm curious.*'

'Zoe! Be serious.'

'I am being. Besides, I promise you I'd get a stack of responses.'

'Yes, but from the most awful people.'

'People who like sex are not awful people, Anna.'

Anna didn't know how to respond. Sex frightened her. Well, not frightened exactly, but certainly it confused her. She'd had lovers, three to be exact, and the sex had been fine, once she'd got used to it. Quite pleasant, some of the time. But her favourite bit was always the cuddling that happened afterwards, if she was lucky. She didn't even enjoy the foreplay because, well, it was so obviously leading somewhere. *There.* And it made her anxious.

She was pretty sure she wasn't very good at sex. She just wasn't that into it. Which was a disaster considering the time she'd been born. She was sure her shyness, which manifested itself in a distinct lack of imagination in the sack, would have been an attribute, a veritable selling point, in the Victorian era when all that was required was for the woman to lie back and think of England. Nowadays, women were expected to be confident, adventurous, dirty. She was certain there was a secret knack—like being able to play tennis; a matter of knowing how to hold the racket and when to swing—she, unfortunately, did not have the knack. And it wasn't like you could go to a club and ask for lessons in sex. At least, she didn't think you could, could you? No, surely not, and even if such a service was available she was far too shy to avail herself of it. She'd tried reading *Fifty Shades of Grey*, convinced everyone else was getting encyclopaedic knowledge and she was missing out, but it only intimidated her further because *that* Ana was enjoying multiple orgasms when Grey simply looked at her. How? *How?* She'd had to read a number of reassuring online book reviews to discover that a lot of other people thought that was ludicrous too.

She'd been a slow starter. She'd attended an extremely academic all-girls school. Her mother had driven them to and from school until they were eighteen, so opportunities to meet boys had been few and far between. At least they had been for her. Somehow, feral Zoe managed it. Anna had followed the rules, happy to concentrate on getting great grades and confine her longings to some unobtainable singer in the latest popular boyband.

Luckily, in her college sorority there were quite a few girls who were pretty religious and didn't believe in sex before marriage. Zoe argued this was just a ruse, to pique men's interest further, 'Everyone loves a challenge.' Whatever, it gave Anna a crowd to hang out with who did not expect to have a dozen sexual partners before they'd graduated. 'Hang out with? Hide away with, more like,' chastised Zoe.

Then, she fell. Hard. She couldn't eat, couldn't sleep, could barely talk when she was near him. When he noticed her, things just got worse. They dated. She couldn't believe her luck. He'd chosen her. He had a wealth of choice, unlimited, and yet he loved her!

For a time.

Then he didn't.

Even now, the thought caused her to blink, an attempt to bat the pain away, keep the tears at bay.

When he split, a killer rumour was put around. People said she was just not that into it. Someone quoted her ex as saying it was like making love to a firm pillow. The shame. Recalling the conversation still made Anna's ears burn. Her eyes sting. Her heart beat too fast. That's why he'd left her. Obviously. Crippled with an acute sense of inadequacy,

Anna struggled to get back on the horse, as it were. It took a long time and she didn't even much like the next guy she dated, although everyone else did: her mother, her father, her friends. Not Zoe. Zoe never thought anyone was right for Anna. It lasted far longer than it should have, went a lot further than she intended. She hated to think of it. A waste of her time, her soul and spirit. It was torturous. It ended. Yeah, he was unfaithful. What a surprise. Not. Fuckwit. That's what Zoe called him. Thoughtless, careless, useless fucking fuckwit. Anna sometimes could see that there was a very genuine attraction to letting the expletives rip, although she tried not to herself.

She was abstinent for so long that Zoe argued she'd have 'grown over'. Lovely. These past few years she'd been dating again, but confidence issues led to trust issues; she always wanted to wait a couple of months before getting into anything physical. By that time, more often than not, she'd found texts on her boyfriends' phones to and from more willing and enthusiastic women. No one could blame her for looking at their phones, or checking their emails, she had trust issues and her fears were invariably borne out. Suffice to say, she'd had a lot of short relationships. A lot. Yet not much actual experience.

If she had been a bit better at *it*, then perhaps her three lovers and various other lesser boyfriends, who never made it to lover status, wouldn't *all* have turned out to be two-timing rats. *All* of them. How awful was that? What a brutal fact. She had only ever dated men who ultimately cheated on her. It had to be her own fault. This deep-seated insecurity and self-consciousness was too personal to articulate. This dreadful feeling of blame and failure too shameful to share. Even with Zoe, *especially* with Zoe. As close as they were— and in many ways they were inseparable—Zoe wouldn't understand. She clearly had 'the knack'. She'd had it since she was fourteen and first started seducing boys. Anna found her twin exasperating and admirable all at once.

'I suppose you're going to laugh at the next bit too, aren't you?'

'Which bit?'

'The bit where I say my friends and family mean the world to me.' Anna was intimately acquainted with Zoe's bluntness, which often bordered on meanness, and although Zoe always insisted she was only trying to toughen Anna up before someone could smash her up, it was sometimes hard to take. Anna often tried to brazen it out, take the mick out of herself before Zoe had a chance to do so. 'You're going to say it's a meaningless phrase and that everybody values their friends and family, unless they're a complete psychopath, therefore I shouldn't waste my precious word count on stating the obvious.'

'No, actually. I rather like that bit,' replied Zoe.

Always full of surprises. Absolutely. Always and for ever. 'Oh.'

Anna was just languishing in a rare moment of having secured Zoe's approval when Zoe snorted and added, 'But that last bit is ridiculous. *Looking for a meaningful, long-term relationship. Love rats and two timers can walk on by.* Pleeeease!'

TWO
Nick

'So why internet dating?' Nick asked as he picked up the bottle of wine (an excellent rich white, Pouilly-Fuissé Le Clos 2012); he preferred red wine on the whole, but he'd recently had his teeth whitened at quite some cost and wanted to avoid staining. He tilted it in the direction of her glass, waiting for her nod. She gave it, he poured. The internet dating question, though inevitable, wasn't the first thing he asked her. He'd established her accent was American (with very faint North England undertones), she'd travelled here by tube (the line had been mercifully, surprisingly uncrowded), she'd rather hang on to her coat than hand it in at the cloakroom (because she always mislaid the ticket that was needed to reclaim it) and, yes, the wet, dark, late February evenings were a pain, she couldn't wait for spring. Now to business.

'You do it too, so you know,' she flashed him a shy, small smile.

He understood that she wasn't challenging him but simply looking for some empathy. He shrugged, a deliberately ambiguous gesture. He was unwilling to offer up his reasons because doing so would be detrimental, probably fatal, to the health of the evening. For him internet dating was a convenient way to a thoughtless shag; he very much doubted she'd want to hear that. For some months now, he'd had an active online profile on two or three dating sites, plus he was on Tinder; he found these sites an efficient resource. You could glide through fifty potential targets in a few minutes; it took hours to do that in a bar. A man had his needs. Women did too, he was pleased to say. Plenty of them. It was a misconception that all the women on these sites were looking for deep and meaningful; many made it very clear that they were looking for fast and fun. They wanted to go to expensive restaurants, loud clubs, hot and heaving bars; then they wanted recreational sex. Everyone's a winner.

However, this vision of loveliness obviously was not in it for the fun. Her profile was quite explicit. He'd had a bit of a shock tonight when, just before leaving his flat, he'd finally got around to properly reading it. Typical of him to be mugging up so late in the day; he was careless when it came to relationships. He'd never do the same at work. There, he was so much more thorough and dedicated; he'd never risk reading briefing notes just before going into a meeting. He should have researched her more thoroughly before asking her to dinner; he'd simply clicked 'wink' because she was so hot. Having read the profile, he'd thought about cancelling however they had a reservation at Villandry St James's, one of his favourite restaurants, and a man had to eat.

Besides, she was quite especially cute.

He didn't send the blow-out text. OK, she was looking for romance, possibly marriage and two, maybe three kids. Not his scene. One day, yes. Today, tomorrow, within the foreseeable future? No. Still, there was no harm in hooking up for dinner. It was just dinner.

The thing he was struggling to get his head around was why she needed to resort to online dating to kick-start that whole shebang. Pretty, smiley, seemingly clever; surely she had enough friends of friends to do this the old-school way, and he had a hunch that's what she'd prefer. True, it had become increasingly common and acceptable to look for (and even find) long-term partners online, the statistics were mind-blowing. He liked numbers. Found them easy to recall, comfortable to live with. Over nine million Britons had used online dating sites, which hauled in an estimated cheerful

£300 million per annum for the UK economy. The Chancellor must be so very grateful to all those lonely hearts, there ought to be more tax breaks for singletons (although Nick believed that a fair few of the men on these sites weren't single). Theirs was a generation of tech-savvy individuals who regularly used devices to keep in touch with friends and relatives; online dating was a natural next step.

Even so, he couldn't get past the thought that it was really a last resort for the desperate or a ruthless way in for the smutty and slutty.

He fell into the latter category. Was she the former?

'Well, yes, I know *my* reasons,' he persisted. 'Although I'm puzzled about your motivation. I mean you're so—' He decided to just go for it. Why not? Make her evening. 'Beautiful.'

She smiled again, a broad delighted beam. It surprised him to note that he wasn't even giving her a line. Gentler than the women he usually met. More thoughtful, maybe. She looked as though she wasn't wearing any make-up, other than some lipgloss. That couldn't be true. He knew enough about women to understand that even the most natural beauties wouldn't leave the house without slapping on tinted moisturizer and mascara (still, they'd swear on their mothers' lives that they were au naturel).

'I'd've thought you had to beat men off with a stick.'

'Sadly, not the right type of man.' She let out a small, shallow breath. Not quite a sigh.

'You have a type?'

'Well, if I do, I'd say I'm fatally attracted to two-timing rats.' She took a sip of her wine and watched his reaction.

'I see.'

'I want something different.'

'Understandably.'

She looked at him, head cocked to one side, curious. It was obvious that she was trying to weigh up what sort of man he was exactly. He held her gaze, hoping she wouldn't.

Not *exactly*. He fell into that category, the two-timing-rat category. Not always but certainly sometimes.

The waiter interrupted them and asked if they were ready to order. Glancing at the menu for just a few seconds, she efficiently ordered two courses; he did the same. He was glad she wasn't the sort to mess around asking about ingredients, insisting on substitutes and wanting to know where the chef had trained, etc. He was so bored of women who said they had allergies to carbs or couldn't eat red food, or needed to eat a minimum of five exotic spices each day to stimulate their memory capacity. He'd have been happy to accommodate specific dietary requirements if these women were hostage to genuine allergies or if they just fessed up and said they were hoping to shift a couple of pounds. He understood that women were forever being pressurized into dieting, a doomed pursuit to gain a figure like Mila Kunis, but they wouldn't—couldn't—admit it, so instead they made up allergies. This Anna woman cut through all that crap, which was refreshing. When the waiter left them in peace, Nick nodded, urging her to continue.

'Online dating makes sense. I've stopped hoping to find the love of my life hanging around in noisy bars or nightclubs or even through friends.' She blushed, probably regretting using the 'L' word. She might as well have arrived with a placard declaring: *I'm looking for The One, no time-wasters*.

He grinned, as if to say, 'That's OK, I'm not fazed by commitment.' He wasn't exactly trying to mislead her, not exactly. It was more that he couldn't help trying to charm her. Habit. She rushed on in her explanation, no doubt hoping he hadn't noticed her gaff.

'I mean I thought there was a chance at college. People do, undeniably, meet other people at Yale however it just didn't work out for me.'

Had he heard her correctly? Yale? Wow. Good for her.

'Well, I thought it had actually, for about two years and two semesters, then I discovered the man I'd given my heart to was freely putting about other parts of his anatomy with pretty much every other woman in the student union, student bar and library.' She tried to laugh but he could tell it still smarted.

After all this time. Imagine. He clocked as much. Warned.

Damaged, complicated women were not his thing. Then she straightened her back, jutted out her chin and he felt something slip inside his belly. Sort of melt. She was plucky. Besides, he couldn't help but be fascinated by the fact she couldn't bring herself to say cock, dick or even penis. 'Parts of his anatomy.' Sweet.

'I confronted him.' She was trying to make the point that she wasn't a pushover.

'How did that work out?'

'He made me feel naive and prosaic,' she admitted, shrugging. 'He insisted that we'd never talked about exclusivity. He behaved as though *he* was disappointed in *me*. I thought it was a given. Nearly three years.'

Loud and clear, he was hearing her. Warning number two. Still he didn't feel the need to text his mate, Hal, the number 8. That was their signal; then Hal would call with some fake emergency and Nick would apologize, tell his date she could call a friend and they could order whatever they wanted to eat, that he'd pay, but he had to leave, his mate needed him. It was a foolproof exit strategy and Nick had used code 8 a few times when his date turned out to be a psycho, a bore or a moaner. Hal grumbled about getting involved in what he rather quaintly called 'skulduggery' nonetheless he always came through; Nick prided himself on the fact he'd never just pretend to be going to the loo and leave the annoying date high and dry, as some men did.

'And after uni?'

He was testing her. She looked the sort to have read all the dating books and whilst he hadn't read any, through an almost inexplicable process of osmosis Nick had gleaned that the books advised against giving too much detail about one's dating history when on a first date. It was a passion killer, sitting with all those ghosts of relationships past. It showed unequivocal signs of fucked-upness. What would she do? Was she on the normal scale of regretful or was she mental and resentful? He was strangely relieved and certainly pleased when she breezed over his question.

'Of course lots of people date colleagues but that's never been a route for me. Then, if you're busy at work—and who isn't nowadays?—well, there aren't many other opportunities to meet people simply through happenstance.'

He nodded approvingly. Glad she hadn't lingered. He too understood the importance of not dipping his pen in company ink, that was something he always avoided.

She continued, 'I had other things to focus on. Then suddenly, everyone seemed to be internet dating and I thought, why not? I buy loads of stuff online. Books, shoes, food, even jeans.'

'Even jeans. Do you?' He raised his eyebrow playfully, to show his surprise. Just one—channelling James Bond.

'Yes, even though getting a decent fit with denim is the very devil,' she said, grinning.

'Indeed.'

'You have to try on dozens and dozens of pairs before you find the right one. I'm always returning stuff. I'm on first-name terms with the man at the Post Office counter. Maybe I should date him.'

He laughed at her joke, the correct amount, not too heartily, that would have been offensive.

She carried on, 'I suppose if I can get jeans that fit, via online, then…'

'Why not a man?' He finished off her sentence, helpfully.

'Exactly.'

'You get a wider choice of everything online; why would I leave something as important as finding love to chance?' she asked.

He should probably run a mile. The 'L' word twice in five minutes. They wanted different things. She was clearly husband hunting, and he wasn't ready to settle down. But if he was, he supposed he might look for a sweet girl, who blushed and charmed. Someone who made his stomach flip when she straightened her back and jutted her chin. He sat firm.

Shyly, she looked at him from under her eyelashes. He smiled back, warm, hazy. To be fair, he had to admit, she wasn't out to trick anyone.

'What about you, Gus?'

'Me?' Gus? Yes, him obviously.

'What made you try online dating?'

Nick hesitated as he tried to think of something more impressive than the truth. The waiter arrived with their first course, which bought him a moment.

'Oh, the usual, my friends thought it was a good idea,' he replied, evasively.

'Worried about you, are they?'

'Something like that.'

'Are you—' She stopped herself. 'Oh, it's none of my business.' She waved her hand, as if trying to bat away the half-articulated thought, yet it sat between them alongside the bread basket.

'Go on. You can ask me anything.' Because he didn't have to answer her.

She cocked her head to one side again. She somehow reminded him of the King Charles spaniel he'd had when he was a boy. Coco, such a sweet little dog. Not that Anna's tongue was hanging out. Her lips were moist, inviting, sensual. On someone else Nick might have identified them as blow job lips, but this woman emitted a particular freshness that negated any such thought. She smelt of fabric conditioner and (he was probably imagining this) butter icing.

'I just wondered whether you've recently been in a relationship.' Her face collapsed, mortified. 'Sorry. Crazy thing to bring up. I just thought, with your friends being concerned, that maybe you'd just had your heart broken.'

He had pressed 'wink' on Anna's profile because she had

big brown eyes that smouldered and big round boobs that beckoned;there was more to her than that. He could tell as much already. She was sincere and hopeful.

It was a bit off-putting.

Well, not off-putting exactly. Overwhelming.

Actually, shame-inducing.

After all, he hadn't even used his real name online, whereas she was an open book. She was clearly searching for someone to trust. He felt a bit sorry for her, internet dating sites weren't the place for that. He also felt a touch protective of her, suddenly irritated by all the lying cheats out there who fictionalized their profiles in order to seduce. Including himself. He felt shoddy.

'I don't know about broken.' He picked up the bottled water, glad they'd bought Evian rather than requesting tap; she was a mineral water sort of girl, worth that extra bit of effort. 'Bruised.' It wasn't true but it was what she wanted to hear. If he said that his heart was numb, not through pain or disappointment, but due to boredom, he doubted she'd react well.

'I see.'

She nodded and it amazed him, how such a slight movement, just a commonplace everyday gesture meant that he had a need to swallow, to run his tongue around his teeth. His mouth was as dry as a desert.

'Don't be embarrassed, Gus, I'm twenty-nine, you're thirty, it would be impossible to reach this age and not have experienced some level of disappointment in the arena of love.'

Really? The arena of love? He wanted to laugh. Not at her, though. With her. She was obviously nervous, and that was sweet.

She picked up her napkin and buried her face in it. 'What is wrong with me? Who in the history of humankind has ever used that expression without irony? Or at all?' she sputtered. He gently tugged at the napkin; laughing, she relinquished it, then quickly reached for her wine glass, took a sip and added, 'I've experienced some level of exquisite happiness too—of course.'

Briefly, intermittently? He was suddenly curious. Who had made her happy? How? Her beam widened a fraction further, he hadn't thought it feasible. He couldn't in that moment imagine any man ever hurting her, bruising or breaking her heart, cheating on her. Why would they? Reading his mind, she filled in the blanks on her romantic history.

'Sadly, it's been my experience that men just can't keep it in their trousers.'

He nearly choked on his drink.

'Not that I'm suggesting they shouldn't get it out of their trousers *ever*. I mean if they're in a relationship, then they most certainly should. I'm not celibate or anything,' she added hastily. 'It's just that I'm looking for a one-woman guy and—you know what?—I'm pretty fearful that they are as rare as unicorns.'

Nick shifted in his chair. He liked to think of himself as a faithful sort of guy but he was not *absolutely* so. No, not really. The fairest way to explain it was that, occasionally, there had been a blurring of the time frames around the beginning of one relationship and the end of another. And sometimes, a bit of a misunderstanding when it came to the exclusivity clause whilst casually dating. Look, he didn't demand it; so why should he offer it? He didn't think he was the worst guy in the global history of sexual relations. Men did tend to cheat. He thought there was probably something in the theory that it was a genetic thing. Men were supposed to sow their seed widely and all that, it was for the good of the human race. Monogamy was unrealistic. Why would the internet have been invented if men were supposed to be monogamous? However, looking at Anna's huge puppy-dog eyes across the table he didn't know if that was true. Or at least fair. It felt a bit sordid. Daft.

For a moment or two they both concentrated on their food, making small approving noises and chewing carefully.

'And how has it been working out for you? Have you been on many dates?' he asked. It wasn't just politeness that drove him to inquire.

'A few.'

Clearly none of them had been an earth-shattering success. She was here with him, wasn't she? She hadn't found Prince Charming yet.

'Any especially notable ones?' He was fishing.

'Not really. I'm very familiar with the menu in Starbucks.'

He pulled a face, showing his disappointment with the lack of originality of a date in a coffee-shop chain.

'I've also met one guy for a wander around the National Portrait Gallery, I played mini-golf with another, and I've been on the London Eye.' She shrugged and smiled at the same time; he believed the shrug the most. 'I'm seeing a bit of London.'

'What was wrong with those guys?'

'Nothing was wrong exactly. It was more a case that they were just not right enough.'

'Score?'

'I'm sorry?'

'Out of ten.'

'Oh, I see. I thought you meant, did I—' She didn't finish the sentence.

He smiled to himself, glad that her mind was wandering in that direction.

'Most of them would score a five or a six out of ten.'

He pulled his face into an exaggerated grimace. It earned him a giggle.

'No chemistry?'

'Exactly. And you?'

He'd had dozens of dates on the back of Tinder and the other sites. Lost count. Most of the time he scored. Literally. Obviously, sex at the end of a date meant the metaphorical score was at least seven out of ten, because sex was sex; some of the women had been so hot and willing he would have to rate them nine. Naturally, he couldn't say so.

'Same thing, really,' he mumbled. 'Have you had any disasters?'

'No axe-wielding psychopaths as yet. I'm pretty choosy about who I decide to meet up with. From their profiles and the pre-texts it's relatively easy to rule out the weirdos and jerks. Of which there are very many.'

'There are?'

'Oh yes.'

'Tell me about those,' he encouraged, mischievously. Recalling disastrous dates had to have the effect of throwing a flattering light his way.

'There was one guy who said he had a thing about feet and couldn't wait to smell mine.'

'No!'

'Yes. Then there was the one who wanted to comb my hair with the brush that once belonged to his mother.'

'Weird.'

'She was dead.'

'Fuck.'

'Quite. Then there was the guy who asked if he could bring his mother along to meet me.'

Nick started to chuckle. He couldn't tell if she was teasing him. She seemed in earnest.

'One bloke told me that he was wearing women's knickers as he texted me because it made him feel empathetic towards me.'

Nick couldn't help but laugh out loud now.

'Another sang the whole of George Michael's 'I Want Your Sex' the first time we spoke on the phone. Hardly subtle. Tuneless to boot.'

An enormous, genuine guffaw. She was playing with him. Surely. She took a sip of wine, batted her eyelashes and beamed right back at him, neither confirming nor denying.

'You know, I have something I need to tell you straight away. A confession.'

'Oh.' She looked instantly wary.

'My name isn't Gus.'

'What?'

'I'm not called Gus.'

'You're Angus? It's short for Angus?'

'Well, yes, Gus is short for Angus. And it is my middle name. I'm actually called Nicholas. Nick, really, to my friends. Nicholas Angus Hudson.'

'Your friends call you Nick?'

'Yes.'

'So why did your profile say Gus?' She paused, fork halfway to her luscious lips. She looked sad. Disappointed.

He shrugged, ashamed. 'I don't know. I guess I didn't want people I know knowing I was looking online.'

'People you know? Like a wife you mean?'

'God no!' He said it loudly, other people in the restaurant turned to stare. He moved his head closer to hers, locked eyes and tried his very best to look sincere. Suddenly it was important to him that she believed him. Even if he was telling a lie. 'I mean the guys I work with, clients, my boss. Those sort of people.'

'Your boss is on AllThat dating site?' She arched her eyebrows.

He allowed himself a smile. 'Maybe, you never can tell.'

'There's no shame in it.'

'No, I see that now. But you said yourself that you've met more weirdos and jerks than normal guys. I didn't want people judging me.' He'd actually always gone under the name Gus because it was harder for women to track him down afterwards if they were so inclined. However, it wouldn't be the worst thing in the world if Anna looked him up afterwards. In fact, he rather hoped she did want to stay in touch. He couldn't explain it.

She stared at him, weighing him up. Eventually she murmured, 'You're neither weird nor a jerk. But then, you're not normal either.' He looked perplexed, then relieved when she admitted, 'I think you might be quite special, Nicholas Angus Hudson. I do.'

THREE
Anna

He didn't try for sex?' Zoe sounded astonished.

'No. He just kissed me on the cheek and said goodnight.' It was a warm, soft kiss. He had good lips. Not too sloppy or wet, or dry, or nippy. Just right.

'And he was outside your flat?'

'Yes, I told you, we shared a cab but he didn't get out of the cab, he took it on.'

'Did you ask him to come up for coffee?'

'Oh, come on, Zoe. You know that's not my style. That question cannot be delivered innocently, at least not after a date. I might as well have said the crop, mask and condoms are upstairs.'

'Are they?!' Zoe sounded excited, almost impressed.

'No, of course not. I'm joking,' mumbled Anna, a tiny bit sulkily. 'Not unless there are any stashed away after your last visit.'

Zoe sighed and then pronounced, 'I don't think he can be that into you.'

'That's not a very nice thing to say.'

'Well then, is he gay?'

'No.'

'You seem confident. Was he a bad dresser?'

'No, actually very stylish. Smart.'

'Smart!' Zoe repeated the word with so much disgust Anna wondered whether she had just inadvertently said 'herpes'. 'Just a bit of a drip then? Did he have a limp handshake? Sweaty palms?'

'No. A firm, dry handshake.'

'Well, what other explanation can there be?'

Anna sighed. 'I think he's a gentleman.'

'They don't exist, at least not outside Doris Day movies. How can you still believe in all that crap?'

But Anna did believe. She believed in gentlemen, knights in shining armour, The One, love at first sight and everlasting love. The whole hog. Admittedly, of late, her belief had been tested to the limits. It was difficult to stay eternally optimistic in the face of such mounting evidence to the contrary, although last night, meeting Nick, well, it had given her renewed hope.

It had been a perfect evening. Ten out of ten. She wasn't an especially vain woman, far from it, but she thought that Zoe was wrong, he *was* into her. She was almost confident enough to be certain. They'd really hit it off. They hadn't stopped talking all evening and they'd had three courses plus coffee. He wasn't one of those who just talked about himself either; they talked about her a lot too. He wanted to know what she did for a living. Usually, when she told someone that she worked for a drop-in day centre for the vulnerable and homeless, she was greeted with one of two reactions. Most people said she must be a saint, they gushed that it was wonderful that there were places for 'those type of people to go, so reassuring', but then they commented that they could never do it personally and, following that, they always seemed embarrassed to admit to their own line of work, especially if they worked in anything fun or frivolous. Ironically, her job—which her parents thought of as a poor reflection of her education level and intellect—intimidated people. The other common reaction was that people remarked that it couldn't possibly pay well and that anyway, really, there was no need for homelessness, 'Not down here in the south, at least. I see signs in shop windows all the time advertising jobs. Work, pay your bills, look after yourself. Simple.' She knew it was hopeless and pointless trying to explain the complexities of mental health, the pressures of susceptibility and the overwhelming feelings of helplessness to this sort of character—the sort who thought that everyone ought to be able to tough out the bad times—and yet she never could quite stop herself from trying. Again, ever the unequivocal optimist. Not that her arguments on social deprivation, trauma, domestic violence or lack of opportunities ever made a difference. Quite often, announcing what she did for a living stopped the conversation altogether; people assumed she was a holier-than-thou, vegan, tree-hugging crunchy.

He'd shown the exact right amount of interest. 'What goes on there then? On a day-to-day basis, I mean. Talk me through your average day.'

'Well, we offer practical support including subsidized meals, access to healthcare and laundry and showers. Basic yet essential stuff that the rest of us take for granted. Not that there's anything wrong in taking it for granted,' she'd added hurriedly. 'That's actually my dream, that one day we get to a point where everyone *can* take this stuff for granted.'

He'd nodded, understanding and encouraging her to go on.

'A big part of it is offering housing and benefits advice too. We have our own welfare officer who comes in to do that and to assist with court appeals. That sort of thing.' She wondered whether it was all sounding a bit heavy. 'There's also a bike club offering affordable bicycles and maintenance that's staffed by a volunteer.'

'What's your role?'

'I'm the administration manager, sort of front of house. When I'm not dealing with admissions, volunteers or staff issues I help out wherever I can. In the kitchen, cleaning, lending an ear, making calls and writing letters. Whatever is needed.' A lot was needed;she could only do her bit. She was learning to accept that. She couldn't fix everyone and everything. Although she wanted it all to be better. 'The centre is a much-needed base for many of the homeless in the local community and the local oldies who live alone. It's shocking to think when there's all this,' she'd paused and gestured around the restaurant full of stuffed suits, 'just a few miles down the road, there are people without food and basic shelter.'

'Sobering thought.' He'd taken a sip of his wine and she could tell he was thinking about the issues but he wasn't cowed by them.

It could be overwhelming if you allowed it to be. The trick was not to allow that. You were no help to anyone if you became despondent or emotional.

She smiled again. 'It's very rewarding. It's called Drop In. Our guests are always making jokes about it being a drop-in for drop-outs. You have to have a sense of humour, right? What about you?'

'I work in the city. I'm one of the loathed investment bankers you hear so much of. I work for Herrill Tanley. You've probably heard of them. One of the world's top ten investment banks.'

He'd passed the test. Not cowed then, or embarrassed by his ambition. He was strong and proud, and she liked that.

'And what does your day entail?'

Of course he said it was too boring to go into. All bankers said that but she couldn't agree. It had to be fascinating, didn't it? Moving all that money around; making more money or losing it. Thrilling. Just because she spent her days in a drop-in centre full of the old and vulnerable, none of whom had two pennies to rub together, it didn't mean she couldn't appreciate extreme wealth. She resisted stereotypes. She did not despise the wealthy just because she chose to do a job that exposed how much poverty there was in the city. She didn't blame individuals; she didn't even blame the system. She didn't think there was much point in blaming at all. She preferred to just get things done. She told him so and persuaded him to go into more detail.

'What does an investment banker do, exactly? Go on, educate me.'

'You went to Yale; I doubt I'm qualified to educate you.'

He'd clocked her brief reference to her university, and he was obviously impressed by it. That was a nice change. Many men were overawed when they heard where she'd studied. Still, to be on the safe side, she'd chosen to flatter him. She didn't want to make him anxious.

'I did a liberal arts degree. I'm pretty useless when it comes to economics.'

He'd launched into an explanation. 'Well, corporate investment bankers provide a range of financial services to companies, institutions and governments. They manage corporate, strategic and financial opportunities. You know, such as mergers, acquisitions, bonds and shares, lending, privatizations, IPOs?' He'd paused and looked at her hopefully, clearly wondering if she was keeping up.

'IPOs being initial public offerings?'

'Yes.' He looked surprised.

She nodded encouragingly.

He'd plunged on, 'Corporate investment bankers also advise and lead management buyouts, raise capital, provide strategic advice to clients, and identify and secure new deals.'

She really had wanted to get it, but discovered she didn't care that much after all. It was a teeny, tiny bit boring. Not as interesting as working with people. Money was simply money at the end of the day. It was never broken, it never needed to be fixed. Maybe that was the attraction. Still, she'd shown willing. 'And what area are you in?' she asked vaguely. They had to specialize, didn't they?

'I'm in equity capital markets. I advise clients on how much capital to raise, from where and when, through research and analysis of products and markets.'

'Oh.' Whatever made him happy. That was her philosophy in life.

Besides work, they talked about their friends, holidays, movies they'd seen or missed, books they loved or loathed. They both enjoyed music, although she was keen on classical concerts and he was more of a festival fan. They talked about their exercise regimes, agreeing they could do more, it was a matter of time. All the usual things.

Except for families.

It was Anna's experience that men rarely talked about their siblings unless probed, which she had no intention of doing. They sometimes spoke of their parents in passing but most working men who'd moved out of the family home focused on their careers or social life for conversational fodder. This was fine by Anna. Indubitably, if she and Nick dated and became serious about one another, she'd have to introduce Zoe one day, but she was reluctant to give her room at such a convivial table. Zoe always soured things. She didn't mean to. She just couldn't help herself. It was also tricky to mention her parents without mentioning Zoe. Her relationship with them (which was strained) was coloured by their relationship with Zoe. Anna had been having such a lovely evening, she just didn't want to get into any of that.

He was handsome and funny. Few men could really own the adjective handsome. He could. Dark-eyed, rugged, masculine. He'd held his knife and fork properly, closed his mouth to chew. He didn't get drunk or make sexist or racist jokes. She did not believe that the fact he had not pounced on her in the taxi was because he wasn't into her, she thought it was because he respected her. He'd said he'd call in the morning. He was that specific. She decided not to mention as much to Zoe now. She'd only spoil things. Find fault with him, sow doubt into Anna's mind.

'I'm tired. I need to go to bed. What time is it for you?' Anna never could keep the time difference in her head.

'Seven.'

'Did you work today?' It was never a given.

'Yep, I did some work for a glossy brochure.'

'What sort of brochure?' Anna asked, unsure whether she wanted to hear the answer. Work was work but sometimes Zoe took on modelling jobs that Anna felt were a little racy. Swimwear was one thing. Underwear another. Adult novelty toys altogether a different story.

'For a high-end furniture store.'

'That's great!'

Zoe made a sound that communicated she thought the work was anything but great. She wanted to be an actress, not a model at all, if she had to model (and she did if she wanted to pay the rent) then she felt catalogue or brochure shoots were not where it was at. She thought she should be *a face*. Zoe was nothing, if not confident.

Anna was impressed with Zoe's modelling job, even if she was just in the background of some marketing litera-ture for a furniture store. She knew that the chances of Zoe becoming the face of a skincare product or a luxury label were practically zilch, considering their age. If that was ever going to happen for Zoe, it would have by now. There had been a period of time when it had been possible, but Zoe self-sabotaged. Burned her contacts, damaged her looks. Anna thought Zoe was lucky to get any work at all now. Especially work where she kept all her clothes on. This was exciting! Anna could never get over the fact that Zoe was a model, actually paid hard cash just because people wanted to look at her. It was a weird enough concept if you thought about it in relation to a stranger and all the weirder because Zoe and Anna were identical twins. Anna had never said so, but logically, if people thought Zoe was beautiful enough to be a model, then she must be too. They had the same big brown eyes, the same broad forehead, high cheekbones and cute, pointy chin. They even wore their hair the same length at the moment, just past their shoulders; Anna did so because it was a good length to scrape back into a practical ponytail yet could look pretty after a blow dry. Zoe wore hers that length because her agent instructed her to: she could add extensions or fashion a fast up-do, depending on what the stylist required.

Anna had never actually voiced her thought that as they looked identical, in theory, she too could be a model, because in her heart Anna knew they were totally different. Their features were the same but everything else was different. Zoe had something about her…confidence, sex appeal, a manner. Anna couldn't quite name it; she certainly didn't possess it. She supposed the French might shrug and say Zoe had a certain *Je ne sais quoi*. Whatever it was, it was the difference between being the administrator at a day care drop-in centre and an actress-cum-model in New York. It was the difference between being someone whose favourite part of sex was cuddling and someone who felt threesomes were foreplay.

'It was a drag, actually. The shoot overran significantly. I was supposed to be like out of there by four but it was obvious that they hadn't got what they needed and I'd have to stick around for a couple of hours extra.'

'Was that your fault?'

'My fault?' Zoe sounded stunned and uncomprehending.

'I just thought, if they hadn't got what they needed, it might be because—'

'No, it was not my fault,' Zoe snapped. 'It was the photographer's idiot assistant. He hadn't brought a reflector to bounce light so he had to go back downtown to get it. Everyone's patience was frazzled. When they finally set up I demanded that they pay me overtime or I said I'd walk out and leave them in the lurch.'

'But you wouldn't have done that.'

'I certainly would have.'

Anna told herself that it was admirable that Zoe knew her own worth and was prepared to ask for reasonable remuneration. There were always articles in the glossy magazines encouraging women to ask for pay rises, still Anna wasn't totally convinced that Zoe demanding more cash to do a job she'd already agreed to was the same thing at all. Those articles were directed at women who'd detected a gap between the remuneration they earned and the payment their male co-workers received, not stroppy wannabe actresses who were paid well for having defined cheekbones.

'What happened?'

'Not surprisingly, they pleaded poverty, said there wasn't any cushioning in the budget.'

'Oh well, at least you asked.'

'I made them give me some of the furniture they were photographing. I explained I was doing them a favour. If their poxy pieces are seen in my flat everyone will want one.'

'Is the furniture poxy?'

'No, although it's not to my taste. I'll sell it on eBay. I could make some good money.'

Anna knew she had to end this conversation and get some sleep. Speaking to Zoe was draining; sometimes she thought it was near to depressing, but she'd never say as much. She couldn't. She certainly didn't want to listen to any more of Zoe's aggressive entitlement, not tonight. She wanted to go to sleep and think about Nick. Perhaps, if she was lucky, dream about him. Nicholas Angus Hudson. Mr Hudson. Mrs Hudson. Anna Hudson. OK, she was getting ahead of herself. Still. She yawned ostentatiously, then said her good-byes. She hoped her subconscious would play ball and push Zoe from her mind and deliver up Nicholas Angus Hudson.

FOUR
Nick

Late April and spring had finally pushed its way into the dirty, neglected streets and into the grateful, receptive minds of Londoners. There was occasional sunshine, and determined buds, which quickly sprouted into leaves, grew on the trees. Nick thought the clement weather was a good omen. He had called her the very next day, like he'd said he would. And the one after that. They got together three times in the first week of meeting, and that regularity was sustained in the weeks that followed.

Unprecedented.

'So is she your girlfriend then?' asked Hal.

Nick and Hal had only known one another eighteen months however as their workstations were side-by-side they felt they knew each other pretty well. Neither had a secretive nature but, even if they had, the open-plan stations eliminated the possibility of privacy. Nick could get along with most people, he was a charming man, still he was glad Hal was the bloke he sat next to every day of his life, from 6 a.m. to 7 p.m., and often later. Hal was also a charming man and, as such, knew the effort required to be so; with each other they relaxed. They could be quite un-charming, if the mood took them, and there would be no fallout.

'I haven't labelled it.'

Nick kept his eyes on his screen; they both did. This wasn't male embarrassment at discussing emotions, it was just that taking their eyes off the screen could cost a couple of hundred thousand in a heartbeat.

'It?'

'Us. I haven't labelled us.'

'Why not?'

'Because I don't have to. She hasn't asked me to.'

'She hasn't?' Hal could not hide his surprise.

Neither of them were used to coming across women who actively oozed laissez-faire. This century tended to produce women who, when on the dating scene, were guarded, damaged, uptight or simply defeated.

'No.' Nick grinned at Hal.

On the surface the two men were quite similar. Suited, booted, young, healthy, wealthy; they had it all going on. They both dated with the sort of regularity that would have earned them the title of 'womanizer' in a different generation. Each man assumed that part of his life plan was to have a wife, kids and a house in the country. The difference was, Hal actively sought a wife who would be the catalyst to this ambition. He was sometimes secretly envious of his married friends, of the comfortable closeness and automatic solicitousness that flowed between husband and wife. He wanted a cheerleader. Whilst Nick had only ever thought it was something that would happen at a vague, unidentified point in the future.

Then along came Anna.

It was a slow day on the markets; if things had been busier Hal wouldn't have had time to give a crap about Nick's affairs.

'You've seen a lot of her.'

'Yeah, I have.'

'How long is it now? Six weeks?'

'Two months.'

'You seem as though you're really into her.'

He was, possibly. Probably. Almost certainly, but who said that out loud? 'She's cute.'

Hal nodded. 'Are you seeing anyone else?'

'No time, mate.'

'She takes up all your time, does she?'

Nick paused. It wasn't that she took up all his time, he just couldn't imagine wanting to spend time with anyone else. 'I guess.'

'Sounds like a girlfriend to me, loser.'

Hal suddenly started to hit his keyboard with some level of ferocity, Nick scanned his own screen so see what he was missing. Nick knew Hal didn't actually think men with girlfriends were losers. The opposite. It was just how they spoke to one another; casual insults were scattered around the office like pellets at a paintball party. Loser was one of the mildest uttered, some would scar a sailor. They were bankers, they had a duty to behave like arses; the general public expected it from them. Unquestionably, if Nick was in a relationship his mate was going to have to take the mick.

Was he? In a relationship? Generally, when he dated, he avoided the word and everything that went with it. He tried not to meet parents, or even friends, he did not see a woman two or three nights on the trot, he never left his toothbrush at hers. He didn't want to give the wrong impression. Yet he couldn't deny that this thing with Anna was different. He hadn't met her parents, but that was because they lived in America. They'd had drinks with some people she did a Spanish evening class with. He was now the proud owner of two electric toothbrushes, so was she. It was easier than carting one backwards and forwards between their flats.

Hal took a sip of his coffee and then winced because it was cold. 'I thought you were only ever looking for an uncomplicated shag.' His eyes continued to scan his screen.

'Yes. I was, initially.'

'This is not an uncomplicated shag, though, is it? I mean you went all the way to Stratford to see *King Lear* on Saturday. There're easier ways of dipping your schlong than driving to the River Avon, sitting through several hours of incomprehensible auld English, watching some actor pretend to go mental.'

Nick hadn't thought of it that way. 'We went boating too,' he pointed out.

'And the sex? How is it?'

Nick knew that all Hal was expecting was a number. That's what they usually did. These grown men—with their tertiary-level education, a six-figure salary, mothers and sisters—usually reduced women to a score. He could just pluck a number out of the air and be done with it. Hal might change the subject then. But what would that number be? He had no idea. He couldn't give her a mark out of ten. That wasn't right for Anna. It was demeaning.

It was not what he'd been expecting. Well, he hadn't been expecting anything in particular, not above and beyond his initial hope of an uncomplicated shag, as Hal so rightly pointed out. He wasn't into all that projecting, imagining and hoping bollocks, that was for women and blokes who struggled to get enough. Even if he had indulged in a bit of 'what if?' he'd never have imagined a scenario whereby the shag didn't happen until the ninth date; he couldn't have imagined that he'd stay interested that long. That long and beyond. At first he assumed that he'd hung about because the more she demurred, the more his interest increased. It had to be that, had to be. Everyone wanted what they couldn't have, he more than most. It was like being a teenager again. Kissing, kissing with tongues, his hands on her breast over her clothes, her top and bra off. Yes!! Then his hands brushing her thighs, his fingers slipping the lace of her panties aside. She wasn't teasing him. It didn't seem like a game or a strategy. She just needed time.

The surprise was, he gave it to her. Time and attention and understanding.

He couldn't possibly have foreseen that the shag, when it was eventually delivered up, wasn't a shag at all. It was something significantly more complicated. More—and he hesitated to use this word but could really think of no other—more *meaningful*, he supposed. He couldn't put his finger on it. Truthfully, technically, it wasn't the best sex he'd ever had. Far from it, she wasn't filthy or adventurous; he'd sort of got that message in the eight dates leading up to the deed. However she was honest, intense, intelligent, and somehow that permeated the sex. It was…remarkable. She was fairly reserved and evidently not very experienced but he was pretty certain he could help her relax, grow her confidence in that area. He certainly wasn't complaining. There was something about her reticence that made it quite unique, they weren't swinging from chandeliers—or the modern equivalent, which was making movies and sexting— the sex was simple. Not simple as in boring. Simple as in uncomplicated. Simply good. Not good as in 'not bad'. Good as in—yes, he was back to that word again—*meaningful*. It had a particular and peculiar passion to it.

Hell.

'Come on, mate,' Hal urged, keen to hear the racy details.

Nick shook his head. The thing was, it didn't even matter that much to him—the number, the score—because sex was only part of it. 'It' being whatever they were. There was also the fact she was funny, kind and a great conversationalist. Yeah, that came simply too. Also not boring, also meaning-ful. He thought her job was interesting and she wasn't overly needy. If he couldn't see her one night because he was work-ing late or wanted to sink some beers with his friends, then she simply nodded and busied herself doing something of her own; there was always a gallery she wanted to visit or someone she wanted to meet up with. She was not the sort to hang on his every word. He liked that about her.

Hal raised his eyebrows, knowingly. No doubt he'd pushed Nick to exactly this point of realization on purpose.

'And how was the *Lear*?'

Nick felt more confident about answering this one. 'Excel-lent! A production of verbal lucidity and visual solemnity.'

Hal looked blank.

'They played it with northern accents, and the everydayness of the tones lent an almost soap-opera feel to the family conflict. You know, we recognized these people,' he enthused.

Hal was beginning to snigger.

Indignant, Nick pushed on. 'Brilliant, really, that a four-hundred-year-old story about domestic disputes and regal power struggles can still hold our attention, because of the wonderful combination of poetry shot through with laughter and suffused with—dare I say it?—spirituality.'

'Is that what Anna said?'

Nick started to tap his keyboard frantically, giving the impression he was very busy.

FIVE
Zoe

My gut reaction to this Nick guy? Dislike. Sorry, however there it is. I'm pretty sure he is a Class A bullshitter. For one, most men are. For two, *all* of Anna's boyfriends are. For three, his online dating profile starts with the line, 'I'm pretty new to this, but here goes.'

Yes, I looked him up. For sure. Anna can never see these things clearly. She's pathetically romantic, never learns the lessons. I decided to join the dating site when Anna did. Not that I need to hook guys that way (I still believe online dating is for losers—sorry, but I do). I just want to keep an eye on who Anna is dealing with. There are risks and Anna is barely capable of looking after herself.

Just that first line told me everything I needed to know about this asshole. That self-effacing crap is so layered. It's patronizing. Offensive. By saying he's new to internet dating he is really saying, 'Wow, what am I doing here? I'm so fucking hot, who'd have thought I'd end up on a site like this? Normally, I meet people the regular old-fashioned way.' Clever, I suppose, because probably everyone on these dating sites is surprised to find that's the way the world turns now. Surprised? Shocked? It's a strong opener, an effective way of lulling others who feel self-conscious into a false sense of security. For all of Anna's bravado I know she hates the fact she hasn't met anyone the old-fashioned way. Absolutely she does, she's a traditional sort of girl. She'd kill to just spot someone at a party, or a bar somewhere, eyes meet across a crowded room and then fall: crash, bang, wallop. Fool. Anna is forever saying dating sites are the way forward, that they are practical, sensible, but the truth is she finds them humiliating; I know she does. Anna is definitely the sort to fall for his pseudo-humility bullshit.

It's crap, obviously. With a bit of digging I found out that his profile has been up for months and on various different sites, yet he hasn't changed the wording. Clearly, he is forever trying to catch fresh meat. Oh, Anna. His profile is still up, by the way. Not on the site where he met Anna, he's not that stupid, but on Tinder and some of the others. Wanker.

He is fucking hot, though. That much is true. All the more reason to be suspicious. Why is he on a dating site? He could turn heads in bars. And isn't he a banker too? Come on, hot and rich, how can he possibly have problems getting women to date him? The online stuff can only be a backup. Nothing more than a booty-call database. I read on.

'I'm a glass-half-full kinda guy and I love laughing.' No shit, Sherlock. Who doesn't love laughing? Even if it's laughing at other people's misfortune. He has to be some sort of psychopath to write that twaddle. Plus, he's missed the point, so maybe not that clever after all. Profiles are supposed to be conversation starters. No one can say, 'Oh, I see you like laughing, that's really interesting because I go laughing every Wednesday at this little bar I know, some people just go for a low-level chuckle although I'm a full-on guffaw. Would you like to join me?' If he'd said he liked comedy or, better yet, if he'd had the balls to name a few comedians that he favoured, then I might have had more respect. 'I guess I'm here for some good banter.' Well, that should have been a red light to Anna. A line like that means, 'I'm not looking for anything too deep. I'm here to have fun.' Basically, he's a commitment phobe.

I want to pull my hair out with despair as I read the bit that made Anna go weak at the knees and decide how well suited they both were: 'My family and friends mean a lot to me.' Absolutely fucking hilarious. Well, there you go, that was a startling USP if ever I've seen one. Not. I'd love it if just one of these idiots had the guts to say, 'My parents disowned me after I persistently broke the law and their hearts when I became addicted to heroin. The only friends I have are other scumbag users.' Now that would be interesting.

Although, a bloke could write that and Anna would probably still press the little 'wink' button and start up something. She loves a hopeless, helpless case.

It's actually great entertainment reading these profiles. I had thought about going out tonight. A club, maybe, to dance with wild abandon and to drink vodka. However, I've ended up staying in, laughing my ass off at the hopeless profiles that people are stupid enough to post. Don't they understand? They're supposed to be selling themselves. This is their moment to set the world alight, to show that they are unique little snowflakes with the power to make an avalanche. I've counted nine men who claim to like, 'Going out and staying in.' Fuck me, how exciting is that? They like *existing*. Bland, bland, bland, bland. Then again, those people aren't quite as offensive as the hipster bloke who claims not to watch any TV. Oh pleeeeease. He might as well have written, 'I consider myself devastatingly hip and uncompromisingly original.' He probably knits or listens to sixteenth-century choral music. Who doesn't want to talk about *Game of Thrones*? I'm also suspicious of the handsome guy with a neat moustache who says he loves attending lectures at the V&A and has ambitions to be a cordwainer. Come on, Princess, do yourself a favour and get out of the closet. You're batting for the other team, I cannot make you happy. Which, let me tell you, breaks my heart because I like to think I can make every man happy.

I stretch down the side of my bed and find a bottle of vodka. I unscrew the cap, delighting in the sound of the metal scraping against the glass. I take a swig; it burns the back of my throat. Confession, I don't actually like the taste of vodka, but I never let that stand in the way of me and oblivion. You have to be kidding, for real? 'I'm looking for a partner in crime.' If only they meant it. They don't, though.

They mean the opposite. 'Oh, I'm a jolly bloke, just a normal Joe Schmo.' I reach for my cigarettes. Every time I do so I can almost hear Anna gasp.

These dopes are depressingly easy to mock. Sitting ducks. I just don't understand them. I get dates whenever I want a date. I have no qualms about asking men out directly, they rarely say no. Which man is going to pass up the opportunity of wild sex with a model who talks dirty? And, as I've no desire for them to call me back—like, ever—I'm never disappointed; if I think they might call and want to see me again, I give a false number.

I think I have some sort of masochistic tendencies. These profiles are offending me and yet I can't close my laptop. I mean look at this. 'Genuine guy wants to meet genuine girl.' Pass the bucket. Why is everyone so obsessed with being paired off anyway? Why don't they want to go out into the word and create, or even destroy; somehow make an individual impact? Why does everyone just want to do what everyone around them is doing, everyone before them has done, what everyone will do until the end of time?

Procreate.

Weird then, that this commonplace desire is so poorly expressed. It appears that most people have a limited vocabulary, they're unable or unwilling to express what they want romantically, and I know for a fact very, very few men dare say what they want sexually.

I have access to Anna's profile and history so I know who she's winked at, who she's had conversations with and who she's actually dated. I persuaded her to share her password on the grounds of safety, rather than admitting to an insatiable curiosity. This way, at least someone knows who she is meeting up with. You hear about people going missing. Bad things happen. I'm only trying to keep Anna safe.

I don't like him. Don't trust him.

I will not let him hurt Anna. It's my job to protect her.

SIX
Anna

Cinema?

Anna looked at the text and smiled. It wasn't the most eloquent or verbose invitation but it was part of a longer conversation about what they should do tonight; they'd both been pinging suggestions back and forth to one another all day, even though Nick shouldn't be using his personal phone at work and Anna generally tried not to be on her phone too much when she was at the centre.

To see?

Within just a couple of minutes Nick sent a list of movie suggestions and times: an action thriller, a courtroom drama and a romcom. She texted back her preference for the romcom.

That's on at The Electric. Near you. Pick you up? I'd like to see where you work.

It was time he saw the place. Usually the centre closed at 5 p.m. and she knew Nick wouldn't be here until at least an hour or so after that, but she had enough paperwork to keep her busy. Anna was always discreet about who visited Drop In. There wasn't a legal confidentiality clause the way there was between lawyers and clients, or even a moral one the way there was between doctors and their patients, but there was an unwritten agreement that the people who availed themselves of the centre's services could expect a high level of discretion, therefore it wasn't the sort of place you invited friends to pop by. It was a shame really, because Anna was incredibly proud of Drop In. She knew it provided an invaluable service. There honestly wasn't anything more uplifting than a relaxed afternoon spent in the company of the visitors, playing board games, chatting, drinking coffee or listening to one of the guest speakers that she or her boss, Vera, from time to time arranged. She was pretty sure Nick would love it and be proud of her. On the other hand, if he arrived on a day when they were delousing a visitor or cleaning up emotional or physical crap, she doubted he'd be that enamoured. She wasn't criticizing Nick; most people would struggle with some of the nitty-gritty tasks that she and Vera performed as a matter of course. No doubt it was much better that Nick's first visit to the centre was when no one else was around.

She expected the day to drag, in fact it flew by. She was kept busy helping two Syrian women write letters to their local council about an exploitative landlord. Anna picked up her pen, fired with righteous indignation and armed with an impressive vocabulary.

Vera left at five on the dot. 'You happy locking up?'

'Totally.'

'I wish I had the time to hang about and meet your Mr Right. He seems pretty fly for a white guy.'

Anna giggled. 'How long have you been waiting to use that expression?'

'Since the moment you told me about him.'

Anna appreciated that Vera was making an effort to be delighted for her. As a single mum of two rowdy boys whose father had turned out to be unspeakably disappointing (he had a deep and meaningful relationship with the Child Sup-

port Agency but not with his sons), it was hard to be unequivocally positive and hide her weary cynicism when it
came to men. The way Vera saw it, Nick was a man so he
was bound to be trouble, although Anna seemed happier,
more content since they'd met. Grudgingly, Vera accepted
he couldn't be all bad, although she probably wouldn't actively trust him until they celebrated their Golden Wedding
anniversary. Anna didn't let it bother her; Vera's concern
came from a good place.

'I have some filing to do and I'm going to tidy up the
library corner. If I run out of things to do I have a novel
with me.'

'I can't imagine you running out of things to do in this
place.'

It was true that fighting the good fight was never-ending.
Both Anna and Vera were excellent at their jobs because they
worked like crazy during office hours yet had developed
an ability to, more or less, switch off once they'd closed the
door behind them. They had to, otherwise they'd be overwhelmed by the struggles and pain that they witnessed daily.

Having completed the filing, Anna settled herself in the
library corner and stared out of the window. She watched the
day's tempo change; suited daytime workers scurried to the
tube, evening revellers began to emerge. The street wasn't
a posh one but, as with so many London streets, it was vibrant, with at least four eateries in view. The surrounding
scents swaggered between cinnamon doughnuts and over-
flowing bins that need attention. At six twenty, Anna saw
Nick approaching; she jumped up and grabbed the keys,
rushing to the reception door, preparing to throw it open
and welcome him. Then, she spotted Ivan striding towards
her from across the road. He was twitching violently. She
quickly unlocked the door.

'Fuck off,' yelled Ivan, and he jerked his head.

'OK, Ivan. What is it?'

'Fuck off,' he repeated and again threw his head with some violence.

'Do you want a cup of tea?'

'Fuck off,' he repeated.

'Hey! Now, mate, that's enough.' Nick had heard Ivan's expletives and he ran forward to intervene, anger and disgust written all over his face.

Anna wasn't sure what his impulse would be: to cover her ears, as he considered her quite the princess, or to thump Ivan. By the look on his face and the way he was puffing out his body to fill his entire six-foot-one frame, it looked like he was erring towards throwing a punch. Ivan responded by cowering, twitching with increased violence, whilst yelling, 'Fuck, fuck, fuck.' Anna stepped between the two men.

'It's OK,' she insisted, firmly holding Nick's arms at his side. Over her shoulder she said, 'Come on, Ivan, what do you have to do?'

He stared at her, confused and angry. 'I'm OK.' Reaching for his wallet, his body still convulsing, he pulled out a card and, without making eye contact with Nick, he passed it over.

Nick took a step back, but still held his body rigid. As he read the card, Anna saw his shoulders relax. 'You have Tourette's.'

Ivan nodded. 'Fuck.' Another jerk.

'What's shaken you?' Anna asked, rubbing Ivan's shoulders.

Stammering, he explained, 'Another fucking refusal. Fuck.'

'Ivan's applying for jobs,' Anna explained to Nick. 'So, Ivan, this is my—'

'Boyfriend,' prompted Nick.

'My boyfriend, Nick,' Anna confirmed with a smile.

Ivan dragged his eyes up to reach Nick's face.

'Pleasure to meet you,' said Nick. 'Sorry to hear about the knock-back. What was the job?'

Ivan took Nick's outstretched hand and shook it. 'Office

cleaner. Fuck.' Again he jerked his body but Nick didn't flinch in response.

Anna was proud of him. So many flinched. Even the regular visitors to Drop In sometimes misinterpreted Ivan's complex neurological condition and assumed he was aggressive and threatening. People were prone to snap judgements. How could they not be? Living in a world where news is mostly received in 140 character bulletins from Twitter.

'Shall we all go inside and have a cup of tea?' suggested Anna.

Ivan nodded, and to Nick's credit he didn't even glance at his watch, although a cup of tea meant there wasn't a chance of them getting to the trendy cocktail bar he'd earmarked for them to visit before they went to The Electric cinema.

Instead, he asked, 'Have you any biscuits?'

'We might have some Rich Tea.'

Ivan and Nick shared a look. 'Fuck,' they chorused.

'I'll nip out and get some chocolate Hobnobs,' offered Nick. 'That's a proper biscuit.'

SEVEN
Nick

When he was with her, he found he wanted to show her a good time, he wanted their dates to be memorable, impactful. Perfect. It was important to him that she had the best views, that her seat wasn't near the draughty door, that he carried an umbrella, opened taxi and restaurant doors for her. The whole nine yards. OK, so they'd started with the safe meal in a restaurant but he'd made an effort to mix it up since. They'd been bowling and visited London Zoo. She'd taken him to a classical music concert at the Royal Festival Hall; it hadn't been awful. He'd taken her to a rugby match at Twickenham; she'd done her best to understand the rules. He suggested hip hop karaoke in Portland Street, she suggested an evening learning to make gourmet sushi in Wimbledon. He reserved a table at Sexy Fish, arguably the most OTT restaurant in London where people went to be seen, she introduced him to a curry house where you brought your own drink, sat on a communal bench and ate whatever the chef had prepared, no menus. They'd had equally brilliant nights at all these places. There were no tests or tantrums, no demands or ultimatums. She was refreshing.

He understood women were equal to men—obviously they were, he wasn't a moron. His mother and sister were very intelligent, admirable women, and he'd studied and worked with countless women who were better than him at something or other: deal making, working a room, running the London marathon. Truthfully, he couldn't think of a single thing he could do that some woman of his acquaintance couldn't do better. Women were amazing. He sincerely believed that, sadly it had been his experience that women didn't believe it quite so much. It seemed that they rarely liked themselves.

Insecurity could be crippling. Many had an annoying habit of dismissing or underplaying their achievements. It bored him because manners dictated that he had to then bolster the perfectly adequate human being, pointing out her merits—merits that should have been obvious and a source of pride. It was a waste of time. It struck him that whilst he'd dated incredibly intelligent, passionate and beautiful women in the past, he hadn't dated incredibly sensible ones. Anna's sensibleness was novel and welcome.

He'd been expecting nothing; but this, well, this was possibly *something*.

This morning, ever since Nick had told Hal about spending the evening with Ivan, rather than going to the movies, Hal had amused himself by humming 'Here Comes The Bride.' Ha ha, very funny.

She'd been amazing last night. So calm, so reassuring. He'd noticed that it was not just when he was with her that he thought of her, she came to mind when she was nowhere about. The truth was, she was always on his mind.

Nick drew breath. Had he just had that thought? Had those words formed that exact sentence in his mind? Oh crap, he'd started to think in song titles! He'd even go so far as to say he was beginning to have some understanding of the lyrics, and he didn't mean the songs he heard thrashed out in the bars and clubs he visited—the songs about bitches and asses—he meant the sort of sentimental stuff he'd heard dolloped around his own house when he was a very young kid. The revelation hit him like a blow.

He was falling in love. No? Yes? Hell.

Obviously, Nick had been in relationships before. A number of times. He was thirty, not thirteen, but none of the experiences had been especially scarring or especially momentous. Clearly, falling in love was a thing, there were endless books, films, songs and plays devoted to it. People drank themselves sick because of it, gambled, made themselves jobless or homeless, some people went totally mad for love; he just hadn't felt the impact. His mother joked (somewhat desperately) that he'd been born without the necessary part of the brain that permitted a functioning, mutually beneficial, loving relationship. It was fair to say that he'd always found it quite overwhelmingly difficult to imagine sharing everything from his Krups coffee pods to the thoughts in his head, his bank account to his bed. Or, more accurately, he found it difficult to imagine doing that with just one person for the rest of his life. He knew his mother longed for grandchildren, and whilst she only allowed herself to admit it once a year (at Christmas, after a glass too many), she made it clear she couldn't understand why there was no sign whatsoever that Nick might provide them one day. She worried less about his sister, Rachel, who was not dating at the moment but had at least had serious boyfriends in the past.

'Your father and I have done our best to set a good example,' she'd mutter, nonplussed. 'It hasn't always been easy, but nothing good comes easily. We've stuck at it and that's what counts.'

She had no idea that this annual speech was part of the reason why Nick felt falling in love was a con. As far as he could gather, his parents appeared to exist in a state of wearied forbearance, rather than in everlasting ecstasy, which after all was what was promised.

When his friends announced they'd found someone special that they might want to move in with, possibly even marry, he'd always understood they'd been compelled by practicalities—shared bills, that sort of thing. No judgement. Obviously companionship was a motivator for some, just not for him. He was surrounded by people 24/7. Gobby, greedy, pushy, noisy people, much like himself. He liked alone time. He needed space. He also appreciated that some blokes met domestic goddesses, and that held an attraction. Those women filled the fridge, sorted out a bloke's wardrobe and threw impressive dinner parties but Nick liked visiting restaurants and he earned enough to have all his shirts picked up from his home, laundered and delivered back to him. His domestic arrangements were fine, thanks very much, and they weren't tied up in any way with sex or feelings, which was a bonus. OK, admittedly, he couldn't procreate on his own still he wasn't in a rush.

His private mobile buzzed. He glanced at the screen. It was his father.

He opened the conversation in his usual way. 'Hello, Dad. This is not really a good time to talk.'

'Right, son. Yes, yes, of course. Course not.' His father sounded miles away. Distracted.

Were they on holiday? Had Dad lost track of the time difference? That would explain him calling during office hours.

'Sorry, Nicholas, sorry to disturb you at work. But it's your mother. She's had a fall. She's, they say—It's not good.'

EIGHT

Zoe

It's hard. There's always a residue of guilt. The fact is, I was doing a lot of drugs and drinking when Anna first had her heart snapped at Yale. John Jones. That bastard's name is etched on my soul almost as deeply and clearly as it is on Anna's. John Jones. Such a boring, predictable name. He really oughtn't to have had the impact he did.

He broke Anna.

Not just her heart. Her mind, her self-respect, her self-esteem, her ideals. All that was smashed to smithereens too. Even her moral compass started to spin uncontrollably; without the belief in a happily ever after Anna didn't know how to negotiate her way through the world. It was messy, ugly. A waste. She trusted him entirely. She'd mistook high cheekbones, attractive eyes and floppy hair for something profound and momentous when really it was just a matter of a fortunate gene pool. It was humiliating, so very public. No wonder Anna felt she couldn't complete her degree. With the benefit of hindsight (now older and, if not wiser, then certainly more experienced) I can, I suppose, see that the man was not evil.

He was just thoughtless, careless.

She went back home, crawled under the duvet and gave up. Not just her degree (although that was bad enough— you should have seen our parents' reaction to that news) but for a time, a long time, she struggled to hold anything together. The days when she brushed her teeth and hair were seen as wins. She buried herself away. It took three years before she'd even go on a date with anyone else. And that is a whole other story (equally crap and gory). She found herself a little office job in a carpet cleaning company. It wasn't what we'd hoped for.

Look, I'm not big into regrets but I do sometimes feel bad I wasn't around much. Maybe, if I had been, I could've nipped it in the bud earlier—her excessive grieving for him. Look, maybe there was nothing I could've done. She's always been overly sensitive.

There's a widely accepted way to figure out how long someone should pine for an ex. You have to divide the duration of the relationship by two, not double it. Anna did not abide by those rules. Did not. Could not? I accept that the formula is a bit facile. I mean there ought to be some variance, reflecting how into him she was in the first place and the fact he was the guy who bagged her virginity (that was a huge deal to her) and that it ended when she walked in on him screwing someone else *in her bed*.

Even I accept that's got to sting.

So she couldn't keep to the lamenting schedule that suggested she'd be back in the game within eighteen months, tops, and that just depressed her more. She felt guilty and pathetic for feeling how she did, way after everyone else had expected her to move on. Honestly, to most people her grief for the relationship just seemed self-indulgent. Her friends stopped calling. They were busy getting on with their own lives. Yeah, they sent cards to mark the holidays but somehow they just made her feel worse because the holiday cards were stuffed with cheer and news about promotions, engagements, babies, progress. I guess she was pretty lonely. But, hey, I'm not her babysitter. I had my thing. We're not conjoined. Being the person who is closest to her in this whole world, it might seem brutal when I say that I found her reaction exhausting and disproportionate. However, I do sort of understand it.

Anna is deep.

Extreme.

People don't get that about her. They're fooled by her good manners and outwardly cheerful demeanour. That's her role. I'm the pain in the ass. People tend to be lazy, see what they want to see. Idiots. Fact is, she's not so simple. She's complicated. They left her to her heartbreak, pretended it was normal, pretended she'd get better. So it solidified into depression and ultimately manifested as bat-shit madness, by which I mean she went out into the world with a renewed and heightened zeal for finding The One; her one true love, her knight in shining armour.

Everyone thinks *I'm* the crazy one but, fuck, I'm not the one who believes in this fantasy.

I still think that if anyone had put in a bit of time and effort, like Ma and Pa for instance, or some of Anna's supposed friends, they might have guessed she'd never be the same again. She remained upset about the break-up for—oh, I don't know—for ever. She turned into the sort of person who couldn't be expected to handle any more bad stuff ever. Of course, there's always bad stuff. That's why she needs me now. I look after her now.

I read this study from the University of Berkeley to try to understand what she was going through. It said that when you are in love (assuming you believe in that toss), then your brain is wired for reward, the reward being interaction with the object of your affection. When you split up and stop seeing your lover the reward isn't coming but that doesn't stop your brain from wanting it, from trying to get it. Can be a nasty thing, the brain. Quite the adversary. I guess she experienced some painful withdrawal. I get that.

I suppose it felt like her cold, dying heart was pumping gritty, grey ashes throughout her body, poisoning her bloodstream with disappointment and despair.

I guess.

NINE
Nick

In the time between his father calling him and then him getting through to his mother on the ward, Nick googled the injuries. He'd been told she had various cuts and bruises, a concussion and a fractured hip. The fractured hip was the thing that concerned him the most. His father said she had a break in the top neck of the femur, inside the socket of the hip joint. 'They'll need to operate today,' he'd muttered fearfully. Nick was left to imagine plates, screws, rods, cement. Pain.

When he finally did get through to his mother she, quite predictably, insisted that he didn't need to worry or fuss and that he certainly didn't need to drive all the way to Bath to see her.

'You're a busy man, Nicholas darling. I won't hear of it.' Her words were determined although her tone didn't match up. She told him that she was seeing all the best doctors, consulting with experts. No, he certainly didn't need to make inquiries in Harley Street; she was getting the most marvellous care available, right there in Bath.

He wasn't reassured, he knew that she'd never make a fuss and her needs always came quite far down the list of priorities if she was the one drafting the list. A nurse was holding the phone to her ear. She hadn't broken her arm but she was in too much pain to move even her upper body.

'They're operating in the next hour or so.'

'A *general anaesthetic*?'

'No, darling, a spinal *anaesthesia*. You know, an epidural, like they sometimes give you if you're having a baby.' She tried to laugh but the sound was shot through with discomfort. Nick hated the thought. It sounded risky, dangerous. 'They tell me an epidural has less chance of complications.'

Her bravery impressed and horrified him. He didn't want there to be a need for her bravery. 'What were you thinking, Mother?' He normally called her Mum but shock and concern made him aggressive.

'Well, the gutters needed cleaning. We thought there was a nest.'

'Why didn't you get someone in, or wait until I came to visit?' If he was honest with himself, it was a hollow offer. He had no idea how to clean gutters; he'd never once helped his parents with an odd job around the house or garden. It wasn't that he was unwilling to do so, it just hadn't ever occurred to him that they needed him in that way. They were *his* parents; they did the looking after. When did they become vulnerable and unsure?

'Your father and I have always managed.' His mother sounded irritated. Possibly with herself, possibly with the entire ageing process. 'He holds the ladder and I climb.'

Nick couldn't understand what had possessed his normally sensible parents to stubbornly insist on doing this for themselves.

'Maybe we should have got someone in. But, well, you read such awful things, don't you? About men coming round with their ladders yet they're not clearing out the gutters as you're paying them to do, they're sizing up the place. I've read about it, in the local paper. Tricksters.'

Nick would have preferred that the house was emptied of every stick of furniture than have his mother end up in this state. He felt awful that she and his father had been hostage to these miserable tales about conmen. He dreaded reaching the time of life when he'd not only see a threat at every turn but also feel unable to conquer it.

His mother pushed on, valiantly. 'The doctor said that prompt surgery and a tailored rehabilitation programme, which starts as soon as possible, can significantly improve a person's life.'

He wondered, what did that mean? 'Improve a person's life.' It meant that the quality of her life was in doubt.

The bloody internet. What he read about hip fractures just sickened him. Left him feeling queasy. The internet informed Nick that hip fractures were depressingly common amongst the elderly, in fact they were classed as a major public health issue due to the ever increasing, ageing population. He didn't find any solace in the statistic that around 75,000 hip fractures occurred in the UK each year. He felt indignant, cheated. His mother was only sixty-two; the average age for this sort of fracture was eighty. He'd read that recovery was precarious, slow. He'd read about the risk of infection, blood clots and pressure ulcers.

One in three people die within twelve months of fracturing their hip.

He rang off and then called Anna. Quickly, he brought her up to date.

She listened without interrupting. Only when he'd explained the entire situation did she ask, 'So are you setting off now?'

'Well, Mum is insisting that I don't take time off work. She doesn't want me to make a fuss. She says I'll just be in the way.' He waited a beat.

'Do you want me to come with you?'

'Yes, please.'

Nick picked up Anna outside her flat. She was waiting for him because they didn't want to waste time trying to get parked. She swiftly flung her small suitcase on the back seat and hopped in. He appreciated her efficiency.

She leaned towards him and put her hands on either side of his face. 'It's going to be OK. I'm right here by your side.'

It wasn't just her efficiency he valued; her tenderness was comforting.

The traffic on the M4 was predictably, agonizingly slow and Nick drummed the steering wheel with impatience. Throughout the journey he tried not to imagine his mother sedated, lying on a trolley under the glaring lights, the surgeon's cold, sharp knife, yet he thought of nothing else. Anna walked the tricky line between making decent, cheering conversation and allowing him to stay lost in his thoughts.

Nick hadn't had many difficult times in his life. He was a middle-class boy born to two adoring parents, George and Pamela. He and his younger sister, Rachel, attended the local comprehensive school, which was listed as outstanding by Ofsted. He'd been Sports Captain, a position that guaranteed him popularity, and he'd always had a gift for maths and the sciences, so he did well in his exams. There'd been a frustrating point when, despite this, three of the five universities on his UCAS form turned down his application without even interviewing him. (His mother blamed the fact he hadn't completed his Duke of Edinburgh awards and had refused to take up a musical instrument.) Despite everyone assuring him he only needed one offer, he'd felt like a failure; all his friends were being offered places in exciting, faraway cities. He locked himself away in his room until, at last, an envelope arrived inviting him to interview. He eventually secured a place at the London School of Economics. A very prestigious uni; indeed, his first choice. It had all come right in the end. However, this early disappointment set a pattern. From then on, Nick always had the same reaction to any period of uncertainty or poor luck; he would lock himself away, ride it out alone. If the markets dipped, or if a sport's injury lingered, he didn't want the well-meaning (often giddy) assurances that people always seemed to offer up. 'You've got to take the rough with the smooth', 'It's all for the best in the long run', 'Chin up'. Empty responses based on false assumptions. He preferred to be alone.

Until now.

Now, he found solace in Anna's company. He kept glancing to his left and when his eyes fell on her smiling face and intelligent eyes, he felt fractionally better. Her perfume filled his car, something floral and old-fashioned; he liked it. He wanted to breathe her in.

They drove directly to the hospital and arrived in time to catch the last half an hour of official visiting hours.

He and Anna swiftly walked through A&E, wound their way through the corridors, looking for the correct ward, encountering some palpably confused patients, drifting about, searching for a bathroom or vending machine. He felt grossly uncomfortable. He preferred to surround himself with gorgeous, flourishing, robust people. He worked hard in the sort of industry that entitled him to sumptuousness, excess and pleasure. He didn't know how to process the skinny, hardback plastic chairs, the endless tubes attaching people to machines and the distinct smell of disinfectant trying to erase infection and dirt.

He knew he was lucky. His mother could have killed herself. But he didn't feel lucky, he felt terrified. Like a lost child. He just wanted to get to his mother's bedside. 'This is an awful place to bring you,' he muttered to Anna.

'No, not at all. I'm glad to be here to support you. That's what it's all about, after all.'

He looked at her questioningly.

'In the end, isn't it?'

He didn't dare ask her exactly what she meant by that. He supposed she must mean dating, sex, friendship. In the end, it was about looking for someone to share it all with. Share life. And death. She squeezed his hand, he wasn't alone. He squeezed hers back.

When they first approached the bed his mother had her eyes closed. Even so, he could tell she wasn't sleeping; her body was not relaxed enough to suggest sleep. The wizened old lady who lay flat in the hospital bed, a pillow between her legs to keep her hips in place, looked nothing like his sprightly, energetic mother. He was assaulted by an old memory of the time when he and Rachel found a baby bird that had fallen out of its nest in their back garden. It lay bald and struggling on the soil. They'd scooped it up and taken it inside, determined to feed it and make it better. The bird didn't live. He was annoyed with himself for thinking about that. The image of the baby bird tumbling from its nest crashed into his mind, even though he'd never actually seen the fall. Then he saw his mother, legs and arms flapping, falling through the sky in slow motion. He heard a crack as she landed. And broke. Felt it. He shook his head. How was it that a race that had put man on the moon, created theories of relativity and quantum mechanics, couldn't control subconscious thoughts?

He wanted to hug his mother but didn't dare, in case he hurt her; he didn't even dare take hold of her hand as one was bandaged and another had a needle stuck in it, with a tube trailing out. He plonked himself in a chair by her bed.

Her eyes fluttered open, she saw him staring at the tube and shrugged, 'Just a painkiller, Nicholas. Very effective. I'm beginning to understand why people do drugs.' She smiled at her own joke, desperate to cheer him up; ever the mother. Her skin was normally soft and pink; today it was grey and waxy, except where it was purple with bruises. 'Darling, you didn't need to come all this way. I told you not to,' she scolded, although it was obvious her heart wasn't in it.

He could tell she was secretly relieved to see him. His sister lived in Edinburgh and worked as a schoolteacher. She couldn't get to Bath until the weekend.

'Where's Dad?'

'You've just missed him. I sent him home. He's very tired. Been here at my side all day. Will you be staying at home tonight? Have you let him know he should expect you?'

'No, probably not, we're likely to take a hotel.' The word *we're* alerted his mother to Anna's presence. Carefully, she tilted her head. 'Who's this?' she asked with a warm smile.

Anna immediately scooted around the other side of the

bed and sat down. Then, with infinite tenderness, she took hold of his mother's bandaged hand. 'I'm Anna Turner, Mrs Hudson. A friend of your son's.'

'A special friend, I hope,' said his mother with a totally inappropriate twinkly laugh. Obviously, she was assuming her dramatic fall and dreadful injuries were a valid excuse for appalling unsubtlety.

Anna blushed and grinned. 'Can I get you anything to drink? How about some water or a nice cup of tea from the cafeteria? I bet they offered tea at about six p.m. but you'll have still been out of it.'

His mother laughed. 'Spot on, and I'm parched now. How did you know that?'

'I'm intimately acquainted with hospital procedures,' Anna replied light-heartedly. 'We'll ask the nurse if you can have one. Are your feet cold? Would you like me to put on a pair of socks for you?'

'Oh dear, I couldn't ask that of you.'

Anna was already out of her seat, rummaging through the bedside table. 'Has someone brought socks? Ah, here we are.' She deftly moved to the end of the bed, untucked the sheets and blanket and began to gently, oh so carefully, ease a sock on to Pamela's right foot.

His mum looked relieved, 'Could you go and ask about the tea, Nicholas? Leave me to get to know your lovely friend.'

'Bring it in a proper cup, Nick. No one enjoys drinking tea from polystyrene,' added Anna.

Nick was impressed with Anna. Blown away, actually. Obviously, it was her training at work that made her so practical and simply sensible. Or maybe that was her personality and the reason why she'd been drawn into such a caring industry in the first place. He didn't know which came first, the chicken or the egg. He did know that he was exceedingly grateful for her empathy and cheer.

They stayed all week, right through to the weekend. In

the end they did decide to sleep at his family home rather than go to a hotel; Anna suggested his father might need the company and support, as his mother was likely to be in hospital for a while, and he wasn't used to being on his own.

Nick knew they'd be put in separate rooms; it was just the way it was with his parents. He'd be locked away in his old room, a shrine to his boyhood, filled with rugby trophies and posters from gigs he'd attended. She'd be in the spare room. He felt sad about that; it surprised him to note that it wasn't the sex he'd miss at night, it was holding her. His body wanted to spoon hers. He craved it enough to risk his father's displeasure. Like a teenager he sneaked from his room into the one where Anna was sleeping. He lifted the duvet and she scooted over. No fuss.

TEN
Anna

Anna thought Nick's parents were almost as adorable as he was. She'd had a perfect few days. Of course the circumstances of their meeting were unfortunate nonetheless every cloud had a silver lining, she'd always believed that. If poor Pamela hadn't fallen off the ladder it might have been months before Nick felt comfortable with asking Anna to meet his parents—possibly years! Pamela was on the mend now, and Anna had been useful, there was no doubt about that. She was almost in her element; hospitals, caring for people, it was her thing. Zoe had brought hospitals into her life. At first, Anna had been afraid of them—it was the peculiar smell of sterilizer and fear—but then her parents explained that hospitals were where people went to get better. Usually. She'd had to trust them.

Anna felt very at home with the Hudsons. Nick's mother was brave and grateful, easy to talk to and full of that commodity Anna so admired: an ability to be chipper when things were awkward or difficult. Anna's own parents did not do cheerfulness; all their merriment had been knocked out of them. They did deep retrospection and regret; they had quite a line in recriminations too. Nick's father was quieter than his wife, yet he still had an air of determined optimism. He had been very handsome once, you could see it in his bright twinkling eyes and his long noble nose. He walked tall, not stooping, refusing to bend to his age. Anna couldn't help but think that Nick was likely to look similar at around that age. Dignified. Attractive, in an old man sort of way.

The only fly in the ointment was Nick's sister, Rachel. Rachel didn't seem overjoyed that Anna was here helping out. If Anna was a less positive person she might go so far as to say that Rachel resented her presence. Rachel was stiff and formal with her, although she seemed reasonably pleasant with others. Anna didn't want any trouble so she ignored Rachel's coolness; at least, she silently clocked it but decided not to draw attention to it. Mentioning it to Nick wouldn't help matters. The problem of difficult sisters was one that had to be approached with caution; she knew that better than anyone. Besides, the Hudsons had enough on their plates; they didn't need any sniping, it was far better to continue being bright and breezy. Anna knew that Zoe would not be so tolerant; she'd take instant umbrage with Rachel and then, no doubt, have a showdown of some form. Zoe wouldn't see that Rachel's manner was the result of shock or fear at her mother's accident, she'd see it as a tussle for Nick's affection and loyalty, a declaration of war. Offended on Anna's behalf, Zoe would fast make an enemy of Rachel. She was a bit overprotective that way.

However, Anna felt bad for Nick's sister. Things had careered off on the wrong path from their very first meeting, and that was all because Rachel had missed the Saturday morning visiting period and felt frustrated, thwarted. All she wanted was to see her mum; Anna understood that, on some level, Rachel resented her because she'd spent time with Pamela when Rachel couldn't.

They first met in the busy hospital corridors. Nick immediately pulled his sister into a big hug and, as they broke apart, he beamed, 'Rachel, this is Anna, my girlfriend.'

'I assumed as much.'

Anna was used to hugging the senior Hudsons by then so she threw her arms out wide, ready to embrace. Stiffly, Rachel stuck out her hand, clearly showing she wasn't on for anything more intimate. She looked frazzled. Rachel obviously only had her mind on her mother and had clearly grabbed the first thing she could lay her hands on to wear. Her T-shirt was yellowing under the arms and her jeans stretched across her bum and tummy. She was nothing like her brother. He was lean, hard-bodied; he worked out, it was important to him. Even this week he'd found time to go for a run whilst Anna was making breakfast.

'How's Mum?' Rachel had directed her question at Nick. But since Anna had now linked her arm through his and was standing so close to him they looked like they were practically zipped together, it took a certain amount of determination to blank Anna's existence, and yet blank it Rachel did. 'They won't let me in to see her, they said I had to come back at two p.m.'

'They're quite strict about visiting hours,' pointed out Anna, with a sympathetic grimace. 'We've been here since nine. So she's had plenty of company, you don't need to worry about that.' Rachel appeared not to have heard Anna; maybe Anna was speaking on a different frequency, one that Rachel simply didn't pick up. She carried on, regardless. 'Visiting hours are nine until midday and then two until five thirty. Then you can come back anytime from six thirty until nine in the evenings.'

Rachel didn't acknowledge this helpful information at all. Instead, she asked Nick, 'How is she?'

'Well, a fractured hip isn't good news, as I said on the phone. Still, the operation went as well as we could possibly have hoped.'

'Is she comfortable?'

Anna tried to lighten the atmosphere with a little joke. 'She's getting hooked on the drugs.'

It was as though she hadn't spoken. Rachel kept her eyes trained on Nick. 'How long will she have to stay in hospital?'

'She can come home on Tuesday afternoon. Then she'll

have almost daily appointments with physios for quite some time.'

'How will Dad manage driving her backwards and forwards to these appointments?'

'Will you be able to take any time off?' Anna asked.

It seemed she had finally got through, Rachel glared at her. 'No. I'm a teacher. I break up for half term in a few weeks' time. I can spend nine days down here then but I can't get any leave during the term.'

Having been on the receiving end of one of Rachel's hard frowns, Anna now felt she'd be happier being ignored altogether.

Turning to Nick, Rachel said, 'You'll have to take time off work, Nick.'

Nick shrugged apologetically. 'I'm not sure that can happen. I've already had three and a half days off. I have to go in on Monday. I'm close to completing on a big equity capital deal. I suppose we could hire some help.'

'Pamela won't like that,' pointed out Anna. 'Nor George.'

Nick nodded, sadly.

'I could stay the week. I could look after them,' Anna offered.

Both the Hudson siblings turned to her in surprise. Nick's expression was full of admiration, Rachel looked more irritated.

'That's very kind but don't you have to get back to your work too? You do work, don't you?' Rachel's tone somehow suggested she believed Anna was the type of woman who had a daddy that paid for everything, until a husband would.

'Anna works at a drop-in centre for the vulnerable and homeless,' said Nick, somewhat triumphantly. He clearly wasn't oblivious to the implication behind his sister's comment.

Rachel's expression shifted slightly, she looked grudgingly impressed. 'Oh. Well, since you've been here most of the week already, it strikes me that your employers have been extremely understanding as it is.'

'True, they have. I told them it was a family crisis,' said Anna, smiling brightly.

'But you are not family,' Rachel snapped, almost choking on her indignation.

'No, but I am the one who can get time off.'

Rachel stared at her shoes.

Nick pulled Anna into an enormous hug. 'God, you are a marvel! If you're sure.' Nick turned to his sister. 'The parents love her. You have to see it.'

'I can imagine,' Rachel muttered.

'That's settled then.' Nick nodded, relieved. 'Thank you, Anna. Thank you so much. I don't know what we'd do without you.' He leaned in and kissed her long enough to make Rachel feel the need to turn away for the sake of decency.

That night, Anna waited for Nick to sneak into her bedroom as had become his habit. She totally respected his parents' wish for them to have separate rooms but she loved the fact that he broke the rules for her. On cue, at 11.45 p.m. he gently nudged the door open. She scooted to one side of the bed and lifted up the duvet, invitingly.

'I feel like a teenager,' he whispered as he slipped in beside her.

'You did this sort of thing when you were a teenager?' Anna couldn't quite keep the shock out of her voice.

'I was a really bad boy.'

'I don't think I want to know the details.'

'Really? You won't find them sexy?' He started to gently kiss her ear, her neck.

'More likely, disturbing.'

'Cute pyjamas by the way. Are those actual kittens on them?'

Anna couldn't tell if he was teasing her. The pyjamas weren't what anyone would call sexy. Pale-pink kittens on lemon clouds. They were the sort of things that a girl should only wear at home, on duvet days, whilst eating a tub of ice cream, in an ironic-recapturing-of-childhood way.

'Yes,' she confessed.

'Sweet yet surplus to requirements.' Nick started to undo the buttons.

Anna gripped the neck of the pyjamas.

'Dad is fast asleep if that's what's worrying you,' he murmured as he landed kisses on her collar bone.

'Your sister is the other side of this wall,' replied Anna in a hiss-whisper.

Nick grinned. He didn't seem too concerned about the proximity of Rachel. He edged his hand up under her pyjama top and cupped her right breast; gently, with his thumb, he circled her nipple.

'Look, Anna, I'm sorry Rachel seemed a bit off with you today.'

'Was she? I hadn't noticed,' Anna lied.

The cool start in the corridor had turned distinctly icy later on. Anna wasn't sure if Nick had been aware—he had a lot on his mind—but she was relieved to receive his reassurances. Rachel had practically stipulated that Anna did not return to the hospital, either for the afternoon or evening visiting sessions. She insisted that Anna and Nick ought to take some time off and dawdle around the shops in Bath, perhaps have afternoon tea at the Spa tea rooms. On the surface it was a thoughtful, generous offer however Anna had dealt with Zoe for many years and whilst she wanted to believe in the apparent kindness, she couldn't help but think Rachel had an agenda; she wanted her mother to herself. Understandable, of course, Anna reminded herself. Not wrong at all. Besides, she and Nick had had a lovely afternoon. Hand in hand, they'd wandered along the cobbled streets, poked around the pretty little independent shops. Nick was extremely generous; it became impossible for Anna to pass comment on anything nice because he'd offer to buy it for her. A beautiful, chunky silver necklace, a trendy suede jacket, a pretty floral teapot. Needless to say, she hadn't let him; she didn't need a thank-you gift for helping out with Pamela. It was her pleasure.

Whilst Rachel and George were visiting Pamela this evening, and Nick had been catching up on some work emails, Anna had made dinner for everyone. She'd pushed the boat out, as it was the last night before Nick had to head back to London, so she wanted to make it special. She prepared beef in a red wine sauce, which she'd planned to serve with creamy mash. She thought that when George and Rachel returned home at nine thirty, they'd be starving. As it happened, when Rachel arrived home she'd declared that she was going to make a sandwich and eat it in her room; as a consequence the others had eaten in a silence that couldn't be described as anything other than uncomfortable.

'She was unforgivably rude this evening.'

'Maybe she really was exhausted and simply couldn't face making conversation,' offered Anna.

Nick stared at her with open admiration. 'How come you're so understanding? She behaved like the basic bitch. I don't know why she's being so difficult.'

'Is she? Well, there's a lot going on.' Anna didn't want to believe there was any issue between her and Rachel. She liked Nick. A lot. She didn't want the first trustworthy, sexy, kind and thoughtful man she'd met since, well *ever*, to come with any ifs or buts attached. She pushed the thought to the back of her head. These things were often mind over matter. 'Anyway, you don't have the monopoly on difficult sisters.'

'Hmmm?'

'No.' Anna sighed. 'The behaviour your sister demonstrated, for the record, that wasn't even on the scale of 'difficult'. Not on the scale as I see it.'

He propped himself up on his arm, interested. 'You have a sister?' Nick was obviously sideswiped.

She could see his eyes flicker left to right, trying to recall.

Wondering whether they'd had that conversation. The one where you each asked about the other's family. She smiled at him and decided not to acknowledge the fact that he was clearly, desperately trying to recall. Maybe. Maybe not. If they had, the details were hazy. Perhaps they'd had it on that first date when they drank too much wine, which was why he couldn't quite remember.

They had not had the conversation.

She hadn't known how to tackle the matter. Surely dripping Zoe's existence into his was the safest way forward. The truth was they had a lot to learn about each other. It was the strangest thing; they were so comfortable with one another, she sometimes forgot how new their relationship was. She felt she'd known him for ages and that he knew her well too. He knew she liked to drink her tea black, that she was good at doing accents, that she could do a perfectly executed cartwheel, that she always read the last page of a novel before she began because she liked to know where things were heading, that she liked him to blow on the back of her knees. But there was more to discover.

'Did I know you had a sister?' he asked.

'I think I've mentioned her although I may not have. I find it's hard to talk about.' Anna refused to catch his eye. 'She's—It's complicated—' She broke off.

Actually, she really didn't want to talk about Zoe. She didn't want to bring her into this warm and cosy room, she would mar their lovely day. Nick was lying next to her, delicious, in nothing more than underwear. She leaned towards him and kissed him gently. He was pretty easy to distract. He kissed her back gently at first and then with firmness and passion. His lips were warm, soft and solid by turn; they fitted. He gently touched her cheek and his fingers trailed down her neck, to her collar bone. She felt anchored, safe. He moved his hands over her, carefully but assuredly. Anna allowed herself to relax a bit. Things were getting better, easier.

For a time, they both forgot about their sisters, his parents, thin walls, kitten pyjamas and impending physio appointments. They forgot about everything other than each other. He swept her up in an unusual, but very welcome, wave of desire. Nick was different from the other men she'd encountered. She was sure of it. He was thoughtful, truthful, wonderful. He wanted to please and pleasure her and she wanted to please and pleasure him. She found the experience to be considerably better than it had ever been with her previous lovers. Importantly, he seemed to like it well enough. He grunted, groaned and moaned at what she assumed to be the appropriate times.

Afterwards, he held her tight. She put her hand on his chest and felt his breath calmly pour in and out, in and out. He seemed to be quickly drifting into a deep slumber. His ability to find easy, contented sleep encouraged her to ask the blackness, 'Did you enjoy that, Nick?'

'Of course,' he murmured, and he squeezed her closer.

'Was it, erm—Was it good? Good for you?'

He kissed the top of her head, tenderly. Then she felt his mouth on her ear. He whispered, 'Don't worry. These things sometimes take time. It was lovely.'

Lovely? These things sometimes take time? Don't worry? Anna froze. That couldn't be good. Could it? No, it couldn't. *Don't worry?* Well, of course she was worried. She watched as his eyelids closed heavily and his breathing steadied a fraction more, fell a fraction deeper. How could he sleep? He'd as good as said that sex between them was terrible. A disappointment. That *she* was terrible, a disappointment! Restless and mortified, Anna stared at the ceiling, sleep eluding her.

'I'm going to make a phone call to my sister, let her know my plans to stay here another week,' she whispered.

'Now?' he murmured, barely conscious.

'She lives in the States. This isn't late for her.'

Anna crept downstairs. She didn't bother putting a light on because she didn't want to disturb George or Rachel.

'You need to watch your back around that sister of his. She sounds like a bitch,' snapped Zoe.

Anna immediately wished she had the ability to keep more to herself; Zoe's take on everything was always so soul sapping. She'd stupidly hoped that Zoe would tell her Rachel was simply tired, that there was nothing to worry about at all.

'You're staying there for another week? An unpaid home help?'

'I'm doing them a favour.'

'You're a mug.'

'I'm just doing what any girlfriend would. Besides, his parents are nice. I like being around them.' Anna looked around the Hudsons' front room. Even in the dark she could make out the highly polished furniture, the numerous colourful throws and cushions, and the outline of countless photo frames that housed images of the family.

'Weird, since you couldn't wait to put distance between you and our own parents.'

'Well, that's different. They're different.' Anna went quiet, she didn't like talking about them, she didn't even like thinking about them. She couldn't believe Zoe had brought them up. They hadn't exactly been friends to her. Normally, she was vitriolic about them. Suddenly, Anna felt tired. She didn't know why she was wasting her time down here, talking to Zoe, when she could be snuggled up in bed next to Nick. She wished she didn't feel so compelled to check in with Zoe. She longed for more independence. She no doubt needed it.

'How's the sex?'

'Oh, Zoe.'

It really was as though she had direct access to the deepest recesses of Anna's mind. The most fearful shame. The most shameful fear. Anna wished she hadn't. Honestly, some things ought to be allowed to remain private. 'Fine, thank you,' she said firmly.

'Fine?' Zoe's voice was full of scorn and pity.

Anna reached for Nick's word. 'Lovely.' It sounded hollow. As hollow as it had sounded when he'd said it to her. 'It's lovely,' she insisted.

'You just keep telling yourself that, Anna.'

'Besides, everything isn't about sex all the time you know, Zoe. Other things matter too.'

Zoe let out a sound that was meant to be somewhere near a laugh and yet, at the same time, was deliberately nowhere near at all. It was a hollow, almost cruel, bark. 'Yup, just stick to that. One day you might convince yourself.'

ELEVEN
Nick

Pamela was encouraged to get up and walk about as quickly as possible after the surgery. Initially, she felt quite some discomfort, her legs and feet were swollen. She was given an injection to help prevent *blood clots*, and *antibiotics* to help prevent infection. A chirpy *physiotherapist* taught her some gentle exercises to help strengthen the hip and she was given instructions on how to bend and sit. Once everyone was reassured that Pamela would make a good recovery, albeit a slow one, the trip to his family home had turned from one that was shot through with panic and tragedy into something not unlike a mini-break.

Anna's presence had undoubtedly been a godsend. The attributes that Nick had already glimpsed now shone. She was cheerful, practical, uplifting. She instinctively knew how to blend in and make herself at home with the Hudsons so that they didn't feel the burden of entertaining at this tricky time, but simultaneously she saw the invisible boundaries and did not assume over-familiarity. She accompanied Nick to the hospital in the morning, then left him and his dad to go on their own in the evenings, so that they had time to discuss medical cover, the *physiotherapy* assessment and rehabilitation programme. Anna stayed at home and prepared hearty, delicious meals; shepherd's pie, lasagne and toad-in-the-hole. Since Pamela was in hospital Anna could take over in the kitchen without stepping on anyone's toes.

Nick understood that his father was dealing with the

shock of a near miss. George was not the sort to make a drama out of a crisis yet the couple had been married almost thirty-nine years and it was impossible to shrug off the incident easily. On the drive home from the hospital on Sunday afternoon, Nick's last visit before he returned to London, Nick noticed his father was being particularly quiet.

George kept his eyes firmly on the road, monitoring every manoeuvre Nick made, watching for cyclists or foxes that might behave unpredictably and dart in front of their vehicle. He muttered, 'I can't help it. I keep thinking of what might have happened. If she'd been just a few rungs further up the ladder.'

'But she wasn't,' replied Nick.

'I've worked out she'd have fallen on the patio, perhaps even through the glass roof of the conservatory.'

'Dad, don't think like that. It doesn't do any good.'

'It was only because she fell on the lawn that it isn't worse.'

Nick turned to his father and was shocked to see he had welled up. He'd never seen his father cry. Conscious of as much, George turned to look out of the passenger window. They pulled up at traffic lights. Nick pressed the button to wind down his window; the urban afternoon air drifted into the car, chaotic and hopeful at once. Next week it would be May. Couples, eager for summer to start, sat outside pubs on benches; their laughter and cigarette smoke wafted through the air.

'I couldn't do without her, Nicholas. That's the thing. I couldn't imagine life without her. Do you know what I mean?'

Nick didn't know how to answer, so he stayed silent. He wished Anna had been in the car with them. She'd have known what to say to his dad.

Neither man spoke for the rest of the journey, caught up in their own thoughts about the women in their lives.

It was a relief, when they opened the front door, to be

greeted by a delicious smell, a beautifully set table and the tunes of Duke Ellington. Anna had discovered that George was very fond of jazz and had once seen Duke Ellington play when he was a young man himself, on the sort of youthful holiday that was unforgettable; Ellington had long since been George's favourite.

It was just what they needed.

TWELVE
Alexia

I remember when I was first told I was having twins as though it was yesterday. It was late January. A miserable time of year. We lived in Manchester then and I did, and always will, love that city. Friendly, buzzy, great shopping, however it doesn't look its best in late January—nowhere does. I recall killing time before the scan appointment. I dragged my heavy body from shop to shop, unfairly angry with myself for already having a tummy at this early stage of pregnancy. The shops appeared drab and defeated. Tatty, single sale racks were all that was left; the spring season offerings looked unconvincing, silly, overly optimistic. There was little joy to be found at work either. My students were all miserable: broke, moody, aware that sunshine was a long way off and, before then, they had to get through their exams. I'd known I was pregnant about a day after conceiving—at least, that's the way I remember it. I'd suffered dreadful morning sickness from the get-go. I was looking forward to the first scan because it meant I was closer to the wonderful twelve-week mark, when people promised me I'd start to feel more human again.

Twins. Wasn't expecting that.

Two little beings, not unlike sea horses, bobbing about inside me. I did not feel excitement. I was frightened. Preoccupied with the thought, *how are they going to get out?* One baby was scary enough, but two! In my opinion, it's pretty unfair, the whole baby-making process. It beats me how the most natural and necessary thing in the world is as inconvenient and excruciating. It starts so sexily, simply and beautifully and it ends so messily, painfully. Sore. David was delighted with the idea of twins. Unequivocally. But then he wasn't the one who was going to have an experience equivalent to crapping a watermelon—twice—was he? Like I said, the whole thing is unfair. I wonder what would happen to the world's population if there was a rule that we had to take turns in giving birth; first child gestates in the mother, second in the father, and so on. My guess is there would be a lot of only children—and absolutely no families of four.

In the end, as it turned out, the birth wasn't too traumatic. Because Zoe was breech the obstetrician recommended a Caesarean; I jumped at the chance. Most twins don't go to full term; mine went to thirty-six and a half weeks. It was fine. Anna was born first, five minutes ahead of her sister, exactly six pounds; Zoe was five pounds seven ounces. They needed a bit of time on the prem unit although nothing too frightening or dramatic. There's a story people like to hear about that time. At first, they were put into little incubator cots, right next to each other, and as Anna hit a good weight, they quickly sent her back to me; everyone wanted to get on with the breast feeding. But then Zoe suddenly became agitated. They checked the tubes, the drip, her meds. Nothing amiss, yet nothing would settle her. It was as if she sensed her sister's lack. So, on a whim—gut instinct, if you like—I asked the nurses to take Anna back into the prem ward and lie her next to Zoe again. As soon as they did so, Zoe immediately calmed down, her heart rate went back to normal. After a while, they took Anna away again, in case the timing of Zoe settling had just been a coincidence, but once again Zoe began to struggle and mew distressingly. Again they put Anna back in the cot; silence, calm. The same thing happened a third time. They didn't try a fourth. No one likes to see a baby suffering.

David was delighted, practically bouncing on the balls of his feet. He kept saying, 'Science can't explain that!'

I was glad someone had been able to comfort Zoe but I wished it had been me. It was then, when they were less that twenty-four hours old, that I saw that my babies would never need me the way other babies need their mothers. A mother should be the most important person in a baby's life. I was not. I was less important to either of them than they were to each other. They needed each other more. More than anything. I tried not to feel pushed out. Left out. I tried to accept that no one would, or should, ever come between them. But, well, it was difficult.

It's pretty scary being a mum of twins; scary and exhausting. I can't find the words to describe the depths of tiredness that I felt those first few months. David did his best. His architecture firm was generous about him taking time off to help. He took two weeks; that was considered lavish paternity leave in those days. They'd have allowed him more, I think. In truth, he wasn't keen. His excitement about the twins was mostly theoretical. He said I had my mother to help me. David is not a chauvinist, not at all. He's wonderful around the house; he respects my opinions on everything from movies, to politics, to how to change a tire on a rainy highway; he's actively delighted if I bring in a bigger pay packet than him. It's just, he wasn't very suited to looking after small babies. I wasn't either, actually, but I wasn't given a choice. I'm an academic. I like books, reason, debate. I had no interest in small babies. I remember my lovely mother's face when she saw them! She was full of awe—absolute, unadulterated reverence. She kept calling them 'angels', 'darlings' and commenting on their utter, utter cuteness; she was literally gasping, giddy with joy. When I looked at them I saw nothing other than overwhelming responsibility. I saw scrawny, needy charges. They made me feel inadequate and guilty.

Don't get me wrong, I loved them. Passionately but in an animalistic, instinctual way, not with any rationale or reason, and I struggled with that; I'd always depended so heavily on my reasoning. I was a fish out of water. Before and since, I've read a lot of books on the subject of mothering twins, a *lot*, and I understand that it's not unusual for an overwhelmed new mum to have difficulty bonding, especially when faced with a multiple birth. I mean it's just a constant round of screaming, feeding, changing, soothing, screaming, feeding, changing, soothing, screaming—. You get the picture. With two of them there's no time available to just sit and be.

I've often thought back to those times and wondered whether I damaged my girls in some way. Whether they felt a lack. A lack neither of them have ever grown out of. It's a dreadful thing to carry around. Awful. Could I have changed things? Could I? Because if I could, I would. You have to believe that. I'd do anything. Give anything. I've talked about this a lot with various therapists over the years and the universal opinion is always, 'No!' I did not cause this by failing to bond in those first few weeks. They tell me, 'Don't blame yourself. Don't beat yourself up.' Yet who else am I to blame? I'd never blame the twins themselves.

Anyway, things change so quickly when they are young, don't they? You think they'll never sleep through a single night, that you'll go mad with sleep deprivation, or that you'll disappear under an avalanche of dirty nappies, or that you'll scream out loud if you have to get your boobs out in public just one more time to push your nipple into a hot, insistent little mouth.

Then they do sleep through. The next thing is they're up and running, out of nappies, eating real food and delighting in it. Zoe's little face when she tasted banana! Anna's when she tasted chocolate! In a blink of an eye they are developing their own personalities, becoming little people. That gave me something to work with. My love changed. Thickened. It flowed not just from my gut but from my heart, soul and head.

David adored them too. We were good parents. Or at least we thought we were. We did our best.

It just wasn't good enough.

THIRTEEN
Pamela

Every time Pamela clapped eyes on Anna she said to herself, 'Sweet girl, very sweet.' Nick hadn't brought enough girls home for his mother to make an accurate comparison between Anna and his other girlfriends; she had to be assessed on her own merits, no bad thing. When he was younger, Pamela sometimes encountered girls in the hallway, as he was rushing them in or out; some didn't even make it out of the car, he'd insist they wait in the passenger seat whilst he dashed in to change his shirt, pick up some more cash. None of them lasted long enough to make an impression; they were, on the whole, interchangeable. They were always giggly, smiley, eager to please. She pitied them. She wanted to explain to these hopefuls that the usual rules did not apply, that there was no sense in exerting effort to ingratiate themselves with her, the mother, because he, the son, would do what he liked. Initially, she hadn't been concerned about the lack of discernment, she'd been sure that someone would come along, cut through, but then he'd turned thirty and had still not nudged towards a show of preference. Pamela had begun to wonder what it was exactly that Nick was looking for. Whether he'd ever find it.

Then Anna. What a surprise. Far more serious than Pamela might have predicted, and simply far more pleasant. Really rather lovely! Pamela had known that her son would pick a beautiful woman, that was a given, but she'd thought he might be drawn to a bit of a diva. It wasn't what she'd wanted for him, obviously, it was what she had feared. The truth was, he liked a challenge and had a tendency to veer towards the imprudent. She'd fully expected him to pick a tough, tricky, testing type. Most of the women on his Facebook account fell into that category. Lots of front, literally and metaphorically. He had over a thousand friends on Facebook. It astounded her! How could he possibly know that many people? They all had straight, white teeth, glossy hair, universally big chests (the men and the women!). Pamela sometimes checked her children's Facebook accounts when she hadn't heard from them for a week or so. Rachel's was always reassuring; she had about a hundred friends, many of whom Pamela recognized. Rachel posted educational reports from the *Guardian* and photos from Outward Bound weekends. Nick's profile, not so much. His impossibly glamorous photos of women with plunging necklines and young men holding beer or champagne bottles were often accompanied by captions such as 'YOLO, call me!' or 'Got your back, Bro.' She thought he probably selected these shots to suggest a life of glitz, success and affluence. As his mother, she saw only turbulence. Anna was a pleasant surprise. Predictably lovely to look at and also lovely to be around. Pamela felt proud and relieved that her son had more wit than she'd feared.

Offering to stay in Bath and oversee her recuperation was a wonderfully generous thing for Anna to do, and it was impossible not to enjoy the attention. Pamela was more vulnerable and shaky than she wanted to admit; she was grateful for Anna's breezy, efficient and kind presence. She saw to it that they attended appointments, she noticed things like whether the bedside light was bright enough to read by, or whether the tea had sat too long and stewed. She was almost too good to be true! The week following Pamela's release from hospital proved to be pretty hectic so it was all the more wonderful when, on Friday, they managed to spend the morning sitting in the garden, chatting and looking through old photos, whilst George snoozed on a deckchair nearby.

'We haven't looked through our wedding album for years,' said Pamela with an almost apologetic giggle; she wasn't sure if she was apologizing for not looking at it or apologizing for daring to be indulgent and opening it now. She'd only done so because Anna had pushed the issue. They looked like children. They'd married in 1979 when skirts were short and hair was long. Pamela had worn a floppy hat with a wide brim.

'Oh my goodness, you were beautiful,' murmured Anna. 'Not that I'm saying—I mean you're still really—'

Pamela chuckled. 'Oh, my dear, do not trouble yourself. I'm sixty-two years old, I know what I am. And I know what I was. You're quite right, I was beautiful. If only I'd understood the power of it at the time.'

'And so young.'

'I was twenty-four.'

Anna let out a huge sigh.

Pamela understood. At twenty-nine, she believed time was ticking. Pamela didn't agree. Youth went on for ages, if only the young knew it, however she did realize that a woman might begin to get anxious. If she was the sort to want a family, she might start to do a little maths. A year or so courting, a year's engagement, a year or so married and enjoying that (Pamela recommended that time heartily, she and George had waited years before they started thinking about introducing the pitter-patter of little feet or, more accurately, the full-pitched scream of a colicky baby), some time to conceive, then nine months on top of that.

She wanted to pat Anna's hand and tell her there was no rush, but it would be intrusive. Instead, she said, 'It was different then. There are more choices and opportunities now. Nobody feels the need to get married to strike out for independence. In my day the only way you could convince your parents you were an adult was to marry.'

Anna kept her eyes on the album. 'It seems now that co-dependence is the issue. No one seems ready to commit; we're all so good at being self-sufficient that we don't want to let anyone get especially close.' Colour rose in her cheeks. 'At least that's been my experience.'

Pamela was realistic enough to understand her own son fell into the category of commitment phobe.

Anna seemed to mentally draw herself up, shake herself down. 'I think I ought to start making lunch. I've made a quiche,' she offered with a forced smile.

'How lovely. Yes.'

It was a rash whim. Even as she dug in her pocket for her phone Pamela thought that one day she might look back and blame her post-op medication. Still, even as that thought drifted through her mind, she dialled his number. She'd always fiercely stuck by a policy of non-interference where her son's love life was concerned, but was that wise? Was that right? She was his mother after all. She loved him. She wanted the best for him. Time was of the essence. Anna would be back here in a jot carrying a laden tray; if she was going to do this she had to take advantage of her absence right now.

She only managed the barest of preambles, swiftly answering his question about her health. 'Marvellous, darling, I'm being very well looked after. Anna is a treasure.' Then she got to the point. 'Nicholas, darling, I don't often ask anything of you,' she said ominously. 'But I'm asking you to heed this.'

'What, Mother?'

There he was again with the 'Mother' title. Well, at least that showed he had clocked the gravity of the situation.

'I just want to say, don't let such a wonderful woman slip through your fingers, Nicholas. For my sake and your own give this some real thought.'

She could hear her son stifle a laugh. He sounded amused and relieved; presumably he thought she'd rung him with some dreadful news about her health. He coughed. 'Mum, don't worry. There's plenty of time. We've only just met.'

'That's your problem, Nicky,' she rarely used his baby name, 'you always think there's time, however—' She broke off. It was for dramatic effect. 'If the fall has taught me one thing, it's that time can't be taken for granted.' She knew it was a little bit naughty. Verging on emotional blackmail, certainly playing on his fears about how much time she had left on this earth. But she had fears too. Real ones. She loved her son. She didn't want him to be alone. She was only trying to nudge him in the right direction. Just a nudge.

FOURTEEN

Nick

Traditionally, Nick was good at compartmentalizing. He prided himself on it. In the past week he'd managed to obtain a signature on the sizeable equity capital deal, generating an obscene amount of money for his client and a decent bonus for himself. He'd managed not to worry about his mother too much, or think about Anna constantly.

He thought about her a lot, though. He found he wasn't quite able to put her from his mind, he found he didn't really want to. It was wonderful, this thing she'd done, looking after his mother. Above and beyond. He kept thinking of her in his childhood home, imagining her opening cupboards in the kitchen, carrying mugs of tea out into the garden. Ordinary domestic things. Something and nothing. He imagined her grinning when she came across the loo-roll cover; it was a crocheted cupcake. His mother made them and sold them at WI fund-raisers. Her smile, even just the thought of it, made him smile. And her laugh? Well, she had a great laugh; it was surprisingly loud for a relatively reserved woman. It had rung out through the hospital wards, cheering everyone. It had had to be stifled when there was a fear that it would crack through the guest-bedroom walls.

But now all that was going around his head was what his mother had said on the phone.

Where had that come from? What could she be thinking? Well, it was obvious what she was thinking. He'd got the message, loud and clear. His mother obviously adored

Anna. Was she right about him taking time for granted? He was still young. Just thirty. There was no rush. Yet, the lines were blurring. His sex life was no longer entirely separate from his life with his family—not separate at all, actually. Plus, he didn't feel altogether comfortable with that term. Sex life. Not now he was using it to refer to Anna, it seemed too harsh for her. His romantic life? That sounded antiquated. Hal would call it his 'love life', he supposed.

He wasn't himself. It was probably lack of sleep. Understandable. Closing a deal was stressful enough, and his mum being unwell was a whole extra heap of confusion. Not that he felt stressed, exactly. Churned up. That was it. Maybe he was coming down with something. A cold. In May? Maybe not. Hay fever?

Hal had noticed. Just that morning he'd brought in a couple of big, greasy bacon butties and dropped one on Nick's desk, something he did about once a week. The standard joke was that Nick always inhaled his. This morning he'd listlessly picked at it, managed to eat half and then he'd put the rest in the wastepaper basket.

'Are you worried about your mum?' Hal asked; even bankers cared about their mothers.

'No, I don't think so. I mean she's doing well.'

'Then what?'

Nick shrugged.

Hal suddenly looked alarmed, then incredulous. His mercurial face finally settled in an expression of outright excitement. 'My God. It's *Anna*.'

'No. No, it isn't.'

'Not sleeping?'

'No, but—'

'Distracted.'

'Oh, come on.'

'That one wasn't a question, it was a statement of fact.'

'I've probably got a cold.'

'Do you have a temperature?'

'No.'

'Any aches or pains?'

'No.'

'You're in love,' Hal accused, his face breaking into a wide, satisfied grin.

'Don't be an arse.'

Nick made a big thing of studying the screen in front of him, although in all honesty he could not work out the figures. They were jumping around defiantly. Maybe he needed glasses. Yeah, that was probably it. He should get his eyes tested. Her face popped into his head, her voice too. Daft things she said just seemed to float in and out of his consciousness, linger. She was uplifting. What a crazy old-fashioned word, but then it was the perfect one for Anna.

What was that? That wasn't love, was it? Good God, he wasn't, was he?

'How would I know?' he demanded.

'Know what?' laughed Hal, wanting to make Nick say it.

Nick glared. 'How would I know if I was in love?'

'You know when you know,' replied Hal simply.

That was a pathetically uninspiring explanation. Embarrassingly familiar, yet utterly particular.

But.

He thought about his friends who had married. Normal devil-may-care types who morphed into besotted blokes, painfully stammering their way through poorly structured speeches at wedding receptions, intent on trying to convey the depth of their feelings. Not that he was thinking wedding speeches. He was nowhere near a proposal. That would be mental. But. Well. Maybe. The other thing.

He was falling in love. Yes. Wow. Yes. He was.

He knew it because something had slipped into place. He hadn't even been aware that anything was out of place. He'd been busy enjoying his life, pretty sure he'd been served up the best dish available, now it was as though an extra ingredient had been added that made the dish infinitely more appealing. Anna. Everything was glossier, easier, more meaningful since he'd met her. The dish he had been eating, his old life full of casual dates, casual sex, casual lies, was not only tasteless, bland but also a bit repellent.

A/S/L?

Just two tube stops away. Swipe right.

Pic?

No. Lower.

Hey, big boy ;-)

Yes, best ever!!

Text u L8R, Babe.

He was over it.

The plan was for him to work late, catch up on some of the stuff he'd fallen behind on last week, then go to Bath tomorrow. They'd stay there until Sunday, when he'd bring Anna back to London. But he found he couldn't concentrate on the paperwork, he left the office dead on 5 p.m. and called her immediately.

'How's it going?'

'Oh, really well.' He could actually hear her smile. Imagine that, hearing a smile. 'We've all had a wonderful day today. I managed to get your mum comfortable in the garden.'

'Did you? How?'

'Well, you know the Dralon chair that she usually sits in, in the living room? I dragged that outside. None of the deckchairs would have been suitable. No support for her back and hip. The sun was doing its best to peep through but I still put a rug on her legs, I don't think her circulation is what it should be yet. We had quiche and salad. Your dad got a bit merry on cider.'

'Amazing.'

'I'm not saying drunk or anything, just…relaxed. Lunch-time drinking does that.'

He hadn't meant it was amazing his dad was merry; she was amazing.

'We stayed out all afternoon. We've just polished off ham sandwiches and a Victoria sponge for tea.'

'You're making me feel hungry.'

'It was shop-bought.'

'You're good with them.'

'Well, I thought it was important to get her back into the garden as soon as possible. I didn't want her getting a thing about it. I mean she was telling me how much plea-sure they've always got from it.'

'And does she have a thing about it?' Nick would never have thought about any psychological issues following the fall. He was far too pragmatic for that.

'No, not at all. She was really thrilled with the idea. Well, she was once I convinced her that I could drag her chair out-side without hurting myself. It really is a beautiful garden. Then we flicked through old photo albums and chatted.'

'Chatted, about what?'

'They told me the story about how they met. It's a lovely story, isn't it?'

Nick couldn't recall it exactly, although he was aware that it was something to do with a dance hall. He hazarded a guess. 'The Palladium.'

'The Plaza. Your mother was wearing a raspberry-pink jumpsuit. Your gran made it, copied it from a picture in *Vogue* magazine. Your father was wearing flared jeans and a roll-neck jumper. Can you imagine?'

'It's hard to now.'

'I bet they cut quite a dash in their day.' She sounded dreamy. Wistful.

Quite a dash. Who said that sort of thing? Yet he loved her quaint turn of phrase. 'How did they meet exactly? Remind me.' He was pretty sure that he had been told a hundred times, no doubt, but suddenly he cared about the details.

'It was a Valentine's Dance. Your mum hadn't wanted to go, she thought the place would be full of couples, and she was single, so thought it would be depressing. I totally get that,' Anna giggled. 'It's weird to think of parents going through exactly what we go through, isn't it? You know, like uncertainty, expectation, excitement.'

'I guess.'

'Anyway, her friend was desperate to go and so your mum was dragged along. She said it was packed and noisy, even worse than she'd expected. She had a headache and really couldn't be bothered. Normally, she was frequently asked to dance and was happy to do so but that day she hid among the wallflowers…' Anna paused.

Nick guessed she, like he, was imagining the scene. All that possibility swilling around the dance hall, the start of so many romances, families, histories.

'However, your dad spotted her. He said it was the raspberry-pink jumpsuit that did it. 'Couldn't miss her, even if she wanted you to,' that's how he explained it. He said he stared at her until his gaze bore holes into her consciousness.'

'He said that?'

'Yes. Wildly romantic at heart, your dad.'

'I'll take your word for it.'

'Eventually, she looked up at him and just—Well, you can guess what.'

'She stared back?'

'She held his gaze as he weaved his way through the jiving bodies and reached her. He said he just grabbed her hand and has never let it go since.' Anna sighed. It wasn't a sad sigh; it was one of awe. 'Isn't it a great story, Nick?'

'I'm sorry our getting-together story isn't more romantic,' he blurted.

He shouldn't have said that. He didn't want her to feel their start was lousy. It wasn't, it was modern. Or at least, the lousy bit, the bit about him really only looking for a quick fling, was something she'd never know. And OK, their eyes didn't meet across a crowded room but they'd still picked one another from a vast sea of possibilities. Anyway, what did it matter? It wasn't as though they were ever going to be passing their story down to their children or their children's girlfriends, were they?

Or were they?

It wasn't an impossible thought. It was a weird thought. Weeks they'd been together, just a matter of weeks. Well, months, two months and two weeks. Not long at all. Long enough?

'I sort of wish we'd met at a club or in a bar,' he confessed. Suddenly meaning it.

'Do you? Why?'

'I don't know. I think it would've been the sort of story you'd like to have had. I think it would've made you happy.'

Anna giggled, 'I am happy, you dope. The important bit about your mum and dad's story is not how they met but the fact that he's held her hand ever since. Don't you think?'

'I suppose.' He was glad they were having this conversation over the phone because he could feel his skin burn under his eye sockets. He was blushing. Actually turning red. He'd never blushed in his life. Not even as a child. He'd been supremely confident; the sort who only ever laughed at his own mistakes or silliness, never fell victim to crushing embarrassment or shyness.

Anna had an enormous heart but she wasn't messy and emotional, far from it. She was calm and considered. True, she tended to only see things on a myopic level and he was trained to see the big picture, yet somehow they met in the middle, balanced one another. He spent his days making and moving hundreds of thousands of pounds, she sometimes fell to sleep worrying whether the centre would be able to pay the grocery bill at the end of the week. She was straightforward, not mad as a box of frogs, as so many women seemed to be these days, full of neuroses and paranoias. Admittedly, men caused most of those problems still, they weren't fun to deal with. Anna was fun to deal with. She made the most ordinary things into something special. She carried sweets in her bag and cut sandwiches diagonally, every time. His parents' ham sandwiches today would definitely have been triangular. It was a tiny thing but suddenly he couldn't imagine ever eating a rectangular-shaped sandwich again.

Did he actually just think that?

Her world was so different from his, full of damaged and exposed people. That sort of relentless bleakness might make a person hard or cynical, but not Anna; she was gentle, empathetic. Yet strong. He didn't doubt that. She didn't even think her world was bleak; she thought it was a privilege to help. He admired that.

So this is what it meant to love someone. To be in love.

He had to tell her. He had to say the words. Not now, on the phone, because he wanted to see her face react to them. Perhaps hear them back. Yes, surely; she loved him too, didn't she? The possibility that she might not, however slight, slit his gut. He had to know.

He ended the call and then took a tube home. Without bothering to go inside and drop off his laptop, he jumped straight into his car and drove fast, possibly too fast, telling himself that any fine he might pick up would be worth it. He didn't stop to pee or buy coffee, he pushed on, thinking of nothing other than Anna and this new intense feeling he had for her.

As he came within a mile of his parents' house he started to think about how he might tell her. He hadn't said the words before. Well, not unless they were blurted out after especially excellent sex, but he hadn't said them and *meant* them before. He'd have to get her away from his parents. That would be no mean feat; they loved her almost as much as he did. He'd tell her straight away. That would be best. She'd open the door and he'd say, 'Hello, Anna, I love you, do you know that?'

He parked expertly and easily, a blessing those living out of London never appreciated enough, free parking right outside their own house. He rang the doorbell. The front door. That was peculiar of him, he always just walked around the back but, for reasons he couldn't quite straighten out in his head, he wanted the moment to have a certain formality. He heard her yell to his parents, 'I'll get it.'

She swung open the door and, not expecting him until tomorrow, she looked momentarily confused. Then her face cracked into what he considered her signature enormous beam. Hell, she was beautiful. He hadn't got the words straight or steady. He hadn't thought this through at all. There should be a beach, or a sunset, at least flowers. And now, suddenly, he realized he needed a ring too. He had nothing. Nothing other than an impulsive feeling.

He dropped on to one knee and asked, 'Will you marry me?'

FIFTEEN
Zoe

'You've done what? For fuck's sake. Anna, what are you thinking? You hardly know the man.'

Anna stays mute. She can be surprisingly stubborn. And stupid, apparently.

I want to yell at her, 'Don't you ever learn?' I try to temper my shock and outrage so she'll at least respond. 'Well, you're a fast player, I'll say that for you.'

'I didn't play anything,' she insists, no doubt colouring slightly.

Anna blushes about twenty times a day. She blushes when someone farts, or if she drops something, or if someone compliments her. If anyone is ever going to be described as a blushing bride, it will be her. Other people looking at her now might think she's embarrassed, but I know her blushes. This blush is in the hollow of her cheek and actually means she's furious. With me. I don't give a shit. My job, as her sister, is to protect her. And if that means pointing out a few unwelcome home truths, then so be it.

'Anna, seriously, you've only just met this man.'

'Why wait? When you realize you want to spend the rest of your life with somebody, you want the rest of your life to start as soon as possible.'

That's not even her line. 'You just quoted *When Harry Met Sally* at me, didn't you?'

She giggles, unabashed, 'I did actually, yes.'

'For fuck's sake,' I mutter again. I'm not often lost for

words, but she's stretching the limits of my patience here. 'How long have you two been dating now?' I know, I just want to draw attention to it, maybe make her pause for thought.

'Nearly three months.'

That is a stretch of the truth and we both know it. Ten weeks.

'How well do you know him?'

'I know everything I need to know.'

'And how well does he know you?'

'We have a lifetime to discover each other.'

My stony silence is met with her giggles. 'I know, I know. In many ways it's insane but—'

'In *every* way it's insane,' I say, interrupting.

'Except for the fact that he's asked. I've said yes. He wants it. And I want it too.' She pauses and then adds with a voice dripping in longing, 'So much. That's all that matters, right?'

Jeez. I hate it when she does this, when she pleads with me to believe in the crap she believes in. It's awkward, humiliating for both of us. She is a living and breathing Cinderella movie. We both fall silent; neither of us has anything to say that the other wants to hear.

Eventually, in a voice not much above a whisper, she asks, 'Zoe, can't you be happy for me?'

'Nope.'

'But you, more than anyone, must understand that I have so much love to give.'

It takes my breath away. The honesty. The naked longing.

'Maybe you miss being in the States, Anna. Your friends, your family.' I hesitate and then add, 'Me. You're lonely.'

She doesn't like me saying this. The truth hurts.

Rallying, with a bit more force, she retorts, 'The dating scene didn't work out for me in the States. You know that. And yes, I am lonely, at least I was before I met Nick, and now I'm not. I thought you'd be happy for me.'

Her job doesn't help. I question whether it's the healthiest place for a woman like her to work. Surrounded by a lot of people who are practically dead, one foot in the grave. They've lived through their own love affairs—tragic or glorious, fleeting or for ever—now they've nothing better to do than either look back and romanticize them, or stick their noses into other people's affairs. If I had a dollar for every time some nosey old git has asked Anna, 'Still searching for The One, are you, love?' or, 'What's a pretty girl like you doing without a boyfriend?' then I'd be a very rich woman indeed; head-to-toe haute couture. It's not helpful. Why don't people say things like, 'Still searching for the cure for cancer, are you, love?' or, 'What's a clever girl like you doing without a PhD?'

'I don't know what your objection is, Zoe. He's kind, considerate, handsome.'

Yeah, I've said, there's no denying it, he is sizzling hot. That makes me suspicious. 'Why is he single still?' I demand.

'Thirty is young for a man, just not for a woman.'

'Did you really just think that, let alone say it out loud, Anna? Women chained themselves to railings to get you a vote, you know.'

'I'm talking about biology. I'm not making a political point.'

I try to think of some of the obvious drawbacks that there might be. 'Does he have kids stashed away somewhere?'

'No. No previous marriages, no kids, no past live-in partners.'

'No serious exes at all?'

'No.'

I let out a low whistle.

'What?'

'He's a commitment phobe.'

'Well, he clearly isn't. He's just proposed to me. I guess he was just looking for the right girl and now he's found me.'

Anna is trying to sound resolute but I know her as well as I know myself. I can hear the ache and apprehension in her voice, however much she wants to disguise it.

'I hope it's a decent size rock.'

'Oh, it is,' she gushes.

'Well, at least when this all comes tumbling down on your pretty little head you can pawn the ring.'

Anna giggles.

But I'm not joking. Short of ripping the said ring off her finger I'm not sure what I can do about it, so all I add is, 'Well, let's see what Mom and Dad have to say about this, shall we?'

'I'm not a child, Zoe. I'm twenty-nine.'

That almost makes me laugh. 'Hey, have you forgotten who you're talking to? You're thirty-one. Your fiancé is the one who thinks you're younger.'

'Well, whose fault is that?' she asks huffily.

'Whose indeed?'

SIXTEEN
Anna

Telling her parents about the engagement didn't go absolutely brilliantly but Anna comforted herself and looked on the bright side—which was always the best thing to do—it could have been much worse.

She wasn't an idiot, she knew exactly what they'd say; the same as Zoe, and more.

'It's too soon.'

'We haven't even met him.'

'Are you certain?'

'You're not very good at judging this sort of thing.'

She could imagine them taking turns, over and over again, voicing their objections.

'Why don't you just live together, see how things go?'

'No one is in a hurry for you to get married.'

Although they would be wrong about that. She was in a hurry.

'Of course we trust you, it's just that we're concerned.'

She thought it would probably be better to field the inevitable onslaught of incredulity and alarm on her own, even if it meant that she'd feel undermined, dismissed or infantilized, at least that way Nick wouldn't hear any of it. However, Nick had other ideas. He was excited to meet her parents, even if it was through a video call; he insisted they make the announcement together.

'In an ideal world I'd have asked your father's permission,' he pointed out.

'What ideal world is that?' Anna had laughed. 'The nineteenth century?' Although secretly she'd been a little bit pleased that he'd at least acknowledged awareness of the antiquated formality, it boded well for what sort of wedding they'd settle on; one that was steeped in tradition, ritual and romance.

They sat, holding hands, shoulder pressed close to shoulder, as the computer made the little whirling sound promising a connection. Suddenly her mother's face was on the screen. A little surprised (it wasn't her usual day or time to skype), a little distracted. She had a paper in her hand, a pencil pushed into her up-do. Clearly working. She took off her glasses.

'Hello, darling. Is anything wrong?' This was often the first question—and inescapable, since Anna had called out of routine.

'No, nothing wrong,' Anna said soothingly. 'Quite the opposite.'

'Oh.' Unconvinced. Waiting, waiting as always, for the bombshell, the problem, the pain.

For many years Anna had been the one who called her parents to deliver difficult news. Zoe had been in a fight, they were in the headmistress's office, they needed a parent to come and sort it out; she had gone with Zoe and her date to a party, now Zoe was unconscious and the date had vanished, they needed a lift home. As soon as they turned eighteen the girls put one another down as their next of kin on all official forms, so Anna got the calls from the police station or, worse still, the hospital when Zoe was in trouble; then it was her job to call the parents. It was totally understandable that they were often wary when she called. Understandable and sad.

'Who is this?' her mother asked sharply.

Anna wished she could be more charming and affable, but she didn't have it in her. Not any more. Her mother's reserves of patience had been entirely eroded away. Her hope and optimism too, come to that.

'This is Nick. You remember, I've told you all about him.'

Alexia nodded slowly. There was some recognition. Anna often wondered how much attention her mother paid when she called; her mind always seemed elsewhere. Buried in her work or in the past, possibly even in the future, but rarely in the moment. Staying in the moment was the hardest thing of all.

'Pleased to meet you, Mrs Turner. Albeit digitally,' said Nick.

Anna waited for her mother to insist he call her Alexia. She did not offer. She simply nodded at Nick.

'Is Dad around?'

'David, David, Anna is on Skype,' Alexia shouted by way of an answer.

A moment later, her father's face was in the centre of the screen; he beamed at her. No doubt he was also concerned that she'd called, since it wasn't a Sunday evening, but he tried harder to present himself as upbeat and positive. Anna wasn't sure which one of their responses broke her heart more: the blatant apprehension, or the staunch cheer.

'Hello, Princess. How's tricks?'

Anna decided there was nothing else she could do other than dive right in. She held her left hand up at the camera. The diamond took a bow. Anna waited for the rapturous applause, excited gasps, effervescent congratulations. The usual reaction to a daughter announcing her engagement.

Silence. Her mother and father looked at one another and then back towards the screen. Nick squeezed her thigh.

'Is that a—? Is that—?'

'An engagement ring? Yes!' Anna finished her mother's sentence.

'Well.' Her mother's hand went to her throat, eyes the size of saucers. She had lovely fingers. These past few years

Alexia had aged quite abruptly and definitively but her hands remained beautiful.

'I see.' Her father's smile stayed in place, yet his entire face looked troubled.

Nick jumped in. 'I realize this must be quite the surprise.'

'Shock,' her mother stated plainly.

'Unexpected,' her father added, trying to placate.

'We're very happy,' Nick assured them.

'Very much in love,' Anna added.

'Yes,' Nick confirmed.

Anna was practised at managing awkward situations and so she bravely pushed ahead, ignoring her mother's trepidation and amazement, her father's fretful apprehension. She started to talk about Nick's mother's fall, and her decision to stay in Bath to help with the aftercare. She laughed about how they missed one another and spoke on the phone constantly. She relayed the drama of Nick's dash along the M4, his frenzied knocking on the door and then the proposal. Nick chipped in from time to time. They had enough bonhomie between them to carry the call.

'And what are your plans now?' Alexia stuttered.

'We're going to get married,' Anna giggled.

'Well, yes. I understand that's your intention. I mean when?'

'There's no rush. We're just enjoying this moment,' said Nick.

The parents let out a sigh of relief; it was synchronized, therefore loud. Nick and Anna pretended not to have noticed.

'Well then,' said David. Which didn't mean anything much.

For a moment Anna thought the screen had frozen and they'd lost the connection, but then she noticed the telltale twitch under her father's eye shivering. She reached for the bottle of champagne she had stashed nearby in an ice bucket. 'I'm going to open this now. Have you got anything in the fridge, you could toast alongside us, even though you're miles away.'

'It's just gone noon here,' Alexia pointed out.

'Far too early for us to have a drink,' David added.

'Quite early for you, I'd have thought,' Alexia muttered tightly.

'We're celebrating,' said Nick. He threw them one of his easy, charismatic smiles that generally won over clients, his boss, his PA, waitresses and bartenders. It didn't fail him.

Alexia and David raised their coffee cups. 'Congratulations,' they mumbled.

When they disconnected, Nick turned to Anna, winked and said, 'That went well,' in a tone that clearly communicated he thought the absolute opposite.

Anna burst into a fit of laughter. In love, and careless of her parents' disapproval, or concern or whatever it was, they proceeded to get pleasantly drunk on Moët, certain that 5 p.m. was not too early when celebrating something as momentous as their engagement.

SEVENTEEN
Nick

Nick was surprised at how clear-headed Anna was about the wedding preparation. He'd thought perhaps she'd be a tad indecisive; after all, the proposal had been sprung upon her, it wasn't as though she'd had any time to secretly daydream about a wedding. He thought perhaps she might be overwhelmed with choice: church or civic ceremony? Sit-down or buffet meal? Band or DJ? Slinky or flouncy dress? There was a lot to think about. But he was wrong. Anna had a *very* clear idea of what she wanted. Clear, firm, honed. Then it crossed his mind that some women did think about this sort of stuff in the abstract before they'd even met the groom, let alone become engaged. He didn't like the thought—it was somehow impersonal, offensive—so he pushed it to the back of his mind. The important thing was that, happily, her polished plans fell in line with his vague idea of what made the perfect wedding.

They both wanted a big, traditional affair in an English stately home. Morning suits, a string quartet, free-flowing champagne; they wanted the thing done properly. Nick had seen enough friends marry to have learned, through an imperceptible drip, drip, drip of information, that securing the perfect venue for such a wedding wouldn't be easy. They were looking at a year-long engagement, maybe two. He didn't mind. It hadn't just been Alexia and David who had raised eyebrows when they'd made their announcement. Hal and his mother had asked if Anna was pregnant (Hal with astonishment, his mother with more than a glimmer of un-seemly hope). Three of his ex-shags had posted the same question on his Facebook page (they'd gone on to say they couldn't imagine what else might have made such a respon-sibility-resistant, selfish bastard take the plunge; it was quite a relief that Anna had no interest in social media). A long engagement would give them time to prove to everyone how sure they were about one another. Although, this was not something they needed to prove to themselves; Nick hadn't suffered a moment's doubt since he proposed. He was a confident man. A decisive man. And the thing he had most confidence about in the world was his own decision-making.

Tonight, he left the office at 6 p.m. prompt, as he was going to introduce Anna to his old university friends; he was looking forward to it. They'd love her. They were good blokes. They'd be blown away by the news of his engage-ment and wouldn't give a damn if it was hurried or leisurely, they'd just see it as a legitimate reason to down a few extra drinks. He liked being the centre of attention. In fact, until he'd shared the limelight with Anna he'd have sworn that he liked nothing more.

'Hello, my love! You won't believe our luck.' She was breathless and animated when he met her outside the tube station, almost jumping up and down on the balls of her feet, like an excited child.

He stopped her news by kissing her, but once they broke apart it was clear that they weren't going to make it to the pub before she spilt.

'I do believe in our luck, actually,' he said with a secure grin. He put his arm around her shoulders and they started to walk. He could smell her clean hair and her soft floral perfume; he wanted to bury his nose in her hair, snuffle her like a puppy did its owner.

'Do you remember Claydon Manor? That National Trust Georgian house that I showed you online? My favourite venue option.'

'I think so. It's in Surrey, right?'

'No, West Sussex.'

'Uh huh.' He didn't remember it, not exactly. She had, after all, shown him about nine almost identical venues that she quite fancied. It was hard to keep track online; it would be different when he eventually saw them for real, of course.

'Well, I called today, you know, just to inquire about possible dates, and guess what?'

'What?'

'They can do August nineteenth, that's a Saturday.'

'Sounds great.'

'This year!'

'What?' He stopped and turned to her. 'How's that possible? I mean aren't all the good places booked up?'

'They've had a cancellation. They didn't say why. I think I'd rather not know. Clearly awful news for someone but great news for us. Really great.' She was beaming so wide, he thought her face might split.

'But we haven't seen the place. What if it's nothing like the pictures on their site?'

'Well, there are videos online. Three hundred and sixty degrees of every room. They look stunning! I mean, obviously, we'll both go and have a look this weekend, just to check, but I'm certain we'll love it. It really is *the* most beautiful place. So elegant, you know?' She stared back at him, earnest, exuberant.

August. This year. Wow.

It was a bit faster than he'd reckoned on. He did the calculations in his head. Just eleven weeks away. Wow. Eleven weeks.

'Aren't you excited?' For a moment she looked hesitant. Her face puckered with concern, apprehension. Perhaps mirroring his own.

He couldn't bear it; it was like a big, dark cloud blocking out the sun. He did not want to be a big, dark cloud. He *was* excited. He felt it in his chest and in his head. His entire being buzzed. He was going to spend the rest of his life with this woman, they would have a family, they would *be* a family. That was a great thing, awesome. A bit scary. Eleven weeks. But brilliant. Mostly brilliant. This was more exciting than being on a think-tank committee at work, or being the best man at a friend's wedding party, it was really…he hesitated, to let the word form in his head—it was really grown-up.

'Of course I am. It's fantastic news!'

'So you think we should do it? You know, assuming the venue is nice. We should just go for it, right?'

'You think you can get everything organized by then?'

She considered his question. 'I imagine so. Where there's a will there's a way. There's a beautiful little church not too far away. I've already called the vicar and explained I'm from overseas so don't have a local church. He seems really relaxed and happy to meet us. I'm sure he'll do the ceremony.'

'Right.'

'Isn't it great news?'

Yes. Probably. Certainly. 'Then let's do this thing!' He pulled her close and kissed her hard. 'Come on, we need to get to the pub. We have to crack open a bottle of champers.'

Anna had been acquiring quite a taste for it in these past two weeks since he'd proposed. As well as the bottle they shared remotely (and somewhat uncomfortably) with her parents, they'd drunk champagne with his parents (significantly more joyfully, it had to be said) and whenever they were at a restaurant they ordered it; nothing else would do.

'Will they sell champers in a pub?' She looked perturbed.

It was sweet the way she never seemed to take things for granted, but a bit sad too. He hoped one day she'd understand; life was good. 'Yeah, yeah, they will.'

Cai and Darragh, crouched around a small, round and wobbling table, looked stunned when Nick and Anna announced they had set the date and that the date was a matter of weeks away. They'd only just taken in the news of the

engagement; it seemed to blow their little minds that Nick
had finally committed, but they were blokes and so didn't
think it was seemly to get too involved with his decisions.

'You're big and ugly enough to look after yourself, mate.
That's the way I see it,' said Cai. He looked at his champagne glass. He wasn't keen. He'd rather have had a beer.
Champagne was a girls' drink; too effervescent, too short,
too damned pleased with itself. But it seemed rude to say
so; he necked it in one.

'*Your* friends and parents must be flipping out, though,'
Darragh said to Anna. 'I mean a nice girl like you ending
up with this rogue.'

They all laughed, as they were supposed to. Darragh had
been married for nearly three years; he always seemed relieved when friends announced their engagements. Nick secretly believed that Darragh needed his decision endorsing,
shoring up, and saw each man who took the plunge as doing
just that. He used to think it was a bit pathetic of Darragh.
Now he had a much more generous view; of course a married
man would want to see his mates married too. It wasn't a pathetic grasp at solidarity, it was because he knew it was the
best choice and wanted it for his friends. Cai was currently
single, which was his status more often than not. He only
had himself to blame. The barrier wasn't that he was ugly
(although he was no oil painting, but women could forgive
that), it was more that he could often be charmless. Neither
of his mates could keep their eyes off Anna. He watched as
they drank in her sweet, accommodating nature, her infectious laugh, her frankly jaw-dropping sexy-as figure. He
liked their envy; it was hot.

'Where did you two meet then?' asked Darragh, once
they'd caught up on stuff like how things were going at work
and where their football teams were currently languishing
in the league tables.

'Online.' Anna gave a small apologetic shrug.

Nick wondered whether they should have come up with

something different. His friends knew his motivation for online dating. Darragh and Cai exchanged quick grins; it was uncomfortable.

Anna caught them and called them on it. 'What? You think that's shady?'

'No, not at all. We were wondering what a gorgeous girl like you was doing online.'

'Same reason as Nick, regular dating channels had only led to heartache. Weren't you guys amongst those who encouraged him to online date?'

Darragh and Cai looked a bit confused, so Nick leapt in. 'No, not these two in particular. Some of my other friends. Their wives mostly.'

Anna beamed. 'Well, I look forward to meeting them and thanking them for their intervention.' She leaned over and kissed him, a warm, affable kiss that was not inappropriate in a pub or designed to make anyone else feel uncomfortable. 'Right, I'm going to the bar. I'll order another bottle, should I? That one is going down fast.' She grinned. 'Or does anyone want anything else?' She threw Cai the sort of expression that made him confess.

'Actually, I wouldn't mind a beer instead.'

'No problem.' She turned to Nick. 'Miss me while I'm gone.' She blew him a kiss.

All three men kept their eyes trained on her pert backside as she threaded through the busy pub. Nick felt a swell of pride. She was glorious.

Once she was out of earshot, Darragh let out a low whistle. Not a catcalling one, but one that suggested astonishment, 'I never thought I'd see the day.'

Cai simply shook his head, as though also baffled.

Nick grinned. He picked up his champagne glass and took a sip. 'Well, who wouldn't?'

'Cracking girl, no question, mate,' Darragh assured him. 'But—'

'But?' Nick stared at his mate. But? How could there be a but? There were no buts.

Darragh glanced at Cai, nervously looking for backup.

'Fecking speedy,' commented Cai obligingly. 'I can only assume she's an absolute demon in the sack. Like, off the scale, right?'

Nick decided he wasn't going to dignify that question with an answer. It was his fiancée they were talking about. Not some one-night stand. True, they'd collectively had this exact conversation about pretty much every one of their one-night stands, friends with benefits, quick shags, hook-ups and booty calls in the past but, somehow, it now seemed unseemly. Wrong. Besides, she wasn't. Not really. Not a demon. More of a kitten. He didn't want to say so.

Luckily, Cai didn't seem to expect Nick to answer. He continued, 'I mean she's going to have to be, to keep you interested.'

'What do you mean by that?' Nick wasn't being honest with himself here. Who is, all of the time? He caught Cai's meaning.

Cai didn't reply; well, not directly. Instead, he teased, 'Lovely story about how you met.'

Nick shrugged.

'What was that about her thinking we were responsible for you going online to find totty?' asked Darragh, confused.

Sometimes his parlance and cultural references were embarrassingly out of date. Who said 'totty' nowadays? At least, not without a heavy sense of irony. Darragh often seemed a little out of things, a bit behind. Nick, for the first time, considered why his friend couldn't keep up. Was that married life?

'Oh, that. She thinks I was on the dating site because my friends were worried about me, following a tricky and profound break-up,' explained Nick.

'Honesty is so important,' quipped Darragh.

'Oh, come on, are you one hundred per cent honest with Bree, one hundred per cent of the time?'

'I try to be.'

Nick stared at Darragh, challenging him.

Darragh looked up to the right, which is what he always did when he was thinking about something. 'I'd say I'm one hundred per cent honest, ninety per cent of the time,' he confessed.

'What sort of stuff makes up the remaining ten per cent?' asked Cai, interested.

'I sometimes tell her I have work to do on a Sunday afternoon when I just don't want to visit her family. I tell her that I've spent longer in the gym and a shorter time in the pub than I have. Small stuff like that. Stuff that avoids unnecessary rows. It's a kindness.'

'And that's all I did. I avoided upset. Plus, I fully intend to be totally honest at least ninety per cent of the time from now on, probably ninety-five per cent,' insisted Nick.

Neither Cai nor Darragh looked convinced. There was a pause. They sipped their champagne, awkwardly. It didn't seem as effervescent without Anna. Nick wondered if they looked a bit odd, three blokes drinking champagne in a pub without a single woman to even up the numbers.

'So, you're planning on being faithful?' asked Cai.

'Of course.' Nick looked offended, which did not subdue his friends, it just caused them to laugh. 'What?'

'Well, they say a change is as good as a rest,' muttered Darragh.

'Meaning?'

'Meaning you've never been faithful in your life.'

'That's a bit harsh.' Nick threw out a quick, unconvincing grin. They did tend to banter in this way, but it wasn't what he wanted tonight; he'd expected congratulations, geniality. Having spent most of his time with Anna for the past couple of months, he'd got out of the habit of sniping and mickey-taking passing for conversation and companionship.

'Harsh and true.'

'No, not true.' Nick looked from one friend to the other but they appeared resolute.

'OK, tell us when you were last absolutely faithful to someone you dated.'

'Well, it's been a while since I dated in a way that would demand exclusivity.'

His friends sighed, and Nick realized a longer explanation was required.

'Things have changed since your day, Darragh. People date using the American model now. Casually at first, numerous opportunities running simultaneously, and then you might pick one and work towards exclusive status with her.'

'But even when you've had a girlfriend you've always, ultimately, struggled with the fidelity clause.'

Nick's friends knew him well, so he changed the track of his argument. 'That's the point. None of those women were right for me. Anna absolutely is. I haven't so much as glanced at another woman since we met.'

'All of a few months ago.'

'It's summertime, there are a lot of women out there in short skirts, I'm still getting tons of winks on my online dating profile, and I haven't responded to one of them, I promise you, not so much as a peek.'

His friends exchanged sceptical looks.

'What?'

'You still have an online dating profile.'

'I just haven't got around to taking it down.' Nick suddenly wondered why he hadn't done so. 'I've been busy.'

'But you had time to look at it.'

'A big deal at work. My mum's been ill.' He could hear the excuses, lame and exposed. 'Look, it's like Paul Newman said, 'Why fool around with hamburger when you have steak at home?''

'Well, I'm pleased for you, mate. You've discovered fidelity. Congratulations, if you say so, then I believe you,' commented Darragh; he didn't look convinced.

Cai had always been a blunter instrument. 'Well, I don't. It's been just three months, that's no time at all. Do you think you'll manage three years, three decades? With your developed taste for variety, can you imagine never sleeping with anyone else *ever* again?'

Nick found it particularly irritating that Cai had asked this as Cai was single, and yet he went months without sex, years. He didn't get the opportunity often. Could he be jealous? Probably. How hard could it be, staying faithful to a beautiful, kind, clever, sweet woman like Anna? Not hard at all.

He was about to say as much when Darragh chipped in. His tone was undeniably regretful and full of longing. 'Because that's married life, mate. *Never* sleeping with anyone else *ever* again.'

He couldn't be bothered. He wouldn't convince them anyway. Clearly, Darragh had his own issues at the moment; he was obviously bored, feeling the tug of the leash of matrimony, but Bree was pretty bossy and controlling, Nick had always thought so. Nothing like Anna. And Cai? Well, what did he know? Why would Nick listen to either of them? He calculated that the swiftest way to bring the conversation to a close was to laugh it off. Say something laddish and coarse, buy another round.

'Ah, sod it. You're probably right. I'd better not delete those online dating profiles just yet. Lucky they're all under a fake name. This way, I get to have steak on a regular basis but can nip out for burgers when I feel like it.'

'Everyone likes fast food from time to time,' laughed Cai.

'Even if it's bad for you,' added Darragh, raising his glass, as if to make a toast.

They clinked glasses, drained them. The bottle was empty. Nick looked up and spotted Anna heading towards them holding a fresh bottle of champagne and Cai's beer.

'Great timing, my angel. You're without doubt the perfect woman,' he called, gushing with relief that she hadn't been just a moment quicker getting served; if she had been, she'd have heard his treacherous chat.

'What were you guys talking about?' she asked.

'Oh, nothing much.'

'What sort of nothing much?'

'Just meaningless crap.' He put his arm around her, kissed her shoulder.

Thing was, he felt more than a bit guilty, which was stupid, right? They were just words. Stuff he spouted to close down Cai and Darragh; he didn't mean it, but still he felt a bit disloyal. He really couldn't imagine there'd come a time when he'd get bored of Anna. Could he? True, he'd been a bit of a player in the past and, if he was brutally honest with himself—God, he'd never say this to anyone, not even Anna, *especially* not Anna—he would like it if they were a bit filthier with one another in the sack, not always, but from time to time. But that would come, right? Wouldn't it? Of course it would, once she felt a bit more comfortable with him. It was early days. Everything else was so awesome. The conversation, her humour, her intelligence, her kindness, the way his dad and mum wanted to marry her themselves.

Something about the tone of the evening changed. The air seemed to be tinged with the hint of deceit. The guys kept trying to catch his eye, throw him grubby grins when Anna wasn't looking. They weren't interested in the wedding planning and whilst they asked a couple of cursory questions about the couple's plans after the wedding, Anna didn't seem too effusive. Yes, she was going to move into Nick's flat, she just rented at the moment. No, they had not thought about where to go on honeymoon.

'Have you any preferences?' Darragh asked.

She shook her head.

'Europe? America? Maybe a safari?'

'I really haven't given it any thought,' Anna yawned. She did a poor job of hiding it behind her hand.

Nick wondered whether she had taken to his friends; she was certainly quieter than usual. Her reticence, almost silence, made him realize how quickly he'd come to depend on her bright, interesting chatter. He didn't want to linger. He wanted to go home with Anna and make sweet, gentle, reaffirming love to her. Who, exactly, needed reaffirmation, and why, wasn't quite clear in his head. Him? Her? They were out of sync for the first time since they had met and he felt responsible. Before the second bottle was quite finished, he made their excuses.

'But it's not even nine thirty,' Darragh pointed out.

'Early to bed, early to rise,' said Cai with a snigger and a none-too-subtle wink.

It was a harmless enough joke, the sort that had washed over Nick for years, in fact the sort he'd made himself often enough, but it made him flinch. He whispered in Anna's ear, 'I want you to myself.' He tried to gently pull her body closer to his but she stayed stiff and apart.

She stared purposefully at the champagne bottle in the ice bucket. 'I'm still drinking.'

He waited an agonizing five minutes longer whilst she sipped, then he stood up, tugged at her hand; she followed, but with a show of reluctance.

On the walk back to the tube station Anna still didn't say much. He wondered whether it was possible she was having second thoughts about their imminent wedding. The barrage of incredulity tonight might have triggered some qualms. The thought of her regretting her decision to marry in August or, worse still, retracting from the engagement, made Nick feel physically ill. He felt a pain in his gut—no, higher. My God, he felt a pain in his *heart*. He offered to buy some champagne for them to drink at home together. She shook her head, said she'd had enough after all. He felt woozy, adrift. He was very used to handling tricky situations with women, he usually found he was a convenient mix between smooth, sensitive, charming and charismatic; it had always got him by. Then a cold lick of fear ran down his spine. Had she heard him talk to his friends about burgers and steaks and all that junk? He had thought she was too far away, but maybe not, it would account for her reserve. He should just ask her straight out. Like an adult. Apologize. Explain. Beg forgiveness if he had to. Then move on.

He could not.

The words tore in his throat. All he managed was, 'When I'm with my mates, I sometimes say stuff just for something to say. I swear it doesn't mean anything.'

Anna turned to him. Her gaze was cool. Not accusatory but certainly not affectionate. He couldn't quite read her.

'How can what you say not mean anything?' she asked evenly, not revealing whether she'd heard him or not.

Nick was taken aback at the sliver of steel in her voice, he didn't think he'd ever heard anything other than soft, understanding tones or happy, positive notes. Perhaps he was imagining it. His own uncomfortableness was affecting his perception. He should have had the balls to tell Darragh and Cai that he couldn't imagine ever getting bored of Anna. He regretted the nonsense in the bar. In an effort to somehow wipe the slate clean mentally he said, 'Actions speak louder than words, Anna. I've always believed that.' He lifted her left hand to his lips and kissed her finger just near the ring he'd put there only a few weeks ago. The huge sparkling trio of diamonds. 'You know that, don't you?'

Anna sighed. 'Yes, I know that.'

EIGHTEEN
Anna

Anna didn't plan to tell anyone what she'd overheard Nick say in the pub; not Vera, and certainly not Zoe. Zoe would go mental. She'd want to rip him limb from limb, chop off his man parts. She'd demand that Anna call off the wedding. Anna planned on putting the night with Cai and Darragh right out of her head, not giving it another thought. Nick had said it didn't mean anything, that actions speak louder than words.

However, heads and thoughts could be weird things.

Her thoughts had the strength of a Trojan army and they relentlessly marched up on her, assaulting her with disquieting questions. Was he trustworthy? Had she thrown in her lot too early? What did she really know about him? Uncomfortable, unwelcome questions battered her brain all night, even when they'd made love. She hadn't been able to shake them off on the tube ride to work, or even when the centre's visitors started to trickle through the door. Whilst she tried to be her usual cheery self, anger bubbled beneath the surface. She was actually pleased to find an outlet.

'What did you say?' she demanded of the courier as he collected the small package of paperwork that was needed by a barrister in court. She was pretty sure she had heard him properly but wanted to give him the chance to correct himself.

'Just said, don't know how you stand it all day, surrounded by these loons and losers.' He was six foot two, in both directions, hooded, tattooed and bald.

Vera had grown up in Brixton, and considered herself quite the badass, but before she'd even lifted her eyes to give the idiot bloke one of her condemning stares, which worked a treat on her boys and her brothers alike, Anna let rip.

'Actually, the visitors to this centre are amazing. They're fighting demons that you can't even imagine, let alone comprehend.'

The courier was too immature or too stupid to know when to quit; he rolled his eyes, which further incensed Anna.

'Rick, over there, he was a soldier. He took a bullet in his thigh, serving in a country you probably couldn't find on a map. He suffers from PTSD. Have you ever fought for your country?'

The fat courier shook his head.

'Thought not,' said Anna; she rose up out of her chair. She only reached his chest but somehow she towered above him. 'And that woman drinking tea, trying to read, she's dealing with depression, triggered as she's lost one of her kids to osteosarcoma—that's bone cancer to you—and she has another daughter with the same diagnosis. Her husband scarpered, left her to it. The couple of hours she gets in this place are possibly the only feet-up time she gets all week. Do you care for anyone twenty-four/seven? Feed them, bathe them, deal with their meds and hospital appointments?'

The courier guy looked at his feet. Sweat was beginning to bubble on his neck.

'Thought not. And that guy in the corner, playing chess. He's here because he's grieving his wife of sixty-two years. He's lonely. I don't suppose you've ever had a relationship that's lasted sixty-two days, have you?'

He moved his head, something like a shake, the underarms of his T-shirt were dark.

'Thought not,' muttered Anna with grim satisfaction.

'Bet you can't play chess either. You asshole. Get out of here. Get back to your depot, and from now on think about what comes out of your mouth, whilst I think about whether to report you and have you sacked.' Anna collapsed back into her chair. Her chest rose and fell in agitation.

Vera offered to make them both a cup of tea. When she returned to the reception Anna was on the phone. It was clear from her half of the conversation what was happening.

'You reported him?'

'Damn right I did. I have a very heightened sense of just deserts.'

'Are they going to fire him?'

'Yes. He's not on a contract. It's easier for them to let him go than risk upsetting the barrister client, who I threatened to call if they didn't sack the lout.'

'Wow.'

Vera gaped, Anna glared.

'What?' Anna demanded.

'I didn't think you'd take it that far.'

'You can't have liked what he said!' The indignation in Anna's voice made her sound high-pitched.

'No, not at all, but I thought you'd given him a flea in his ear and that would be enough.'

'He was cruel.'

'I'd say stupid. He needed telling, but losing his job?'

'People should be careful about what they say, that's all.'

Vera stared at Anna, sipped her tea. Anna tried to look busy.

'Nothing else on your mind?' Vera inquired.

'Nope.'

'Sure?'

'Yes.'

Sometimes, although she'd never vocalize it, Anna found working with a mental health expert just a bit overbearing. Vera was always watching her, watching everyone, for signs of wobbles. Rather than provide reassurance, the scrutiny made her feel jittery. Anna knew that Vera—like Zoe and her parents—did not consider her hasty decision to marry Nick a sensible one. Knowing Vera disapproved made it impossible to find a way into the conversation about what Nick had said in the pub.

'I think that new woman Mrs Delphine wants to run through her medication needs, so if you don't want to talk about whatever it is that's bothering you, I've plenty to keep me busy.' Vera walked away, with the air of a very industrious woman, only pausing to squeeze Anna's shoulder and add, 'But if you *do* want to talk, I'm all ears.'

Anna should perhaps have taken up the opportunity to confide in Vera. Vera would at least make an effort to be measured in her response. She was trained not to pass judgement or comment; her role was to listen. But Anna stubbornly wanted to keep everything to herself. It was too humiliating. Vera was only human. Would her eyes flicker with something—relief that Anna was prepared to talk about the hasty engagement? Even self-importance that Anna had finally opened up to her? Everyone liked to be needed and be on the receiving end of confidences. Maybe there would even be an element of *I told you so*. Anna wouldn't like that at all.

Nick was just a man that she hardly knew. A man she thought was wonderful.

A man who said he didn't value fidelity. That was only silly banter with his friends!

A man who had broken her trust. A man who had made her feel more whole and fantastic than any other person had in years and years, possibly ever.

The thoughts whipped round and round in her head like clothes in a washing machine: tumbled, intertwined, tangled.

Of course she wasn't able to keep it from Zoe.

'The *bastard*.'

'Well, no.'

'The *fucking* bastard.'

'He hasn't actually done anything wrong.'

'It's only a matter of time.'

'Not necessarily. He said it was a meaningless comment. He was just being silly in front of his friends. He'd had a bit to drink, I really don't think he actually meant what he said.' Anna pleaded, it was what she wanted to believe. It was what she *did* believe. Almost. Not quite.

'So now you can't trust what he says?' Zoe was furious.

'If you knew him like I know him, you'd love him. I promise you would.'

'No, I wouldn't, because we don't think alike.'

That was true. Anna was all about the love, trust and hope. Zoe seemed to feed on hate, mistrust, anger.

'Look, just forget it, please. There's nothing wrong.'

At worst there was something that was just not entirely quite right. It wasn't as though she'd found out he was sleeping with someone else. It was just talk. Not ideal, not perfect, but not the end of the world. So her relationship wasn't entirely perfect. But why should she expect perfect? That wasn't real life, was it?

'Why do you always insist on making out that everything is awful?'

'Anna, I am not the enemy here.'

'Why are you talking about enemies?'

Zoe couldn't resist cranking things up to such an intense emotional level. That had always been her problem. It was unnecessary. If only she could be calmer. More in control.

'I trust him.'

'Do you?' Zoe yelled the question. Spittle escaped from her mouth.

'Yes.'

'Do you? Absolutely? Always and for ever?'

Anna paused. Then, sounding less certain, 'Yes.'

'Well, I don't. The fucker.'

NINETEEN
Zoe

I want, for Anna's sake, to give him the benefit of the doubt, but there is no doubt. Sadly. He is another unreliable bastard. Naturally he is; Anna is inextricably drawn to them. I know there's doubt in her mind. Why else would she have mentioned it to me in the first place? She's asking for my help. She just didn't want to have to spell it out. The truth is Anna wants him to be tested.

Not that it is an actual test. The word 'test' implies uncertainty, an element of experiment. I know, with absolute certainty, how this will play out. He won't pass my test. He will not be faithful. There is no chance of flying colours here, only disappointment. Heartbreak. It's sickening.

Still, it's better that the heartbreak comes before the expense and effort of a wedding, rather than after. Anna would look like a prize twat running headfirst into this silly, unconsidered marriage, only for his infidelities to be exposed within, say, a year. We both know that can happen, you hear of it. I've certainly heard of it. Then the ridiculous bride is left with a poor choice—no choice at all, really. She can either leave the marriage, face public humiliation and ridicule for exercising such dreadful judgement, or shut up and put up, stay with the bastard, wash his socks, cook his meals, bear his kids whilst he pokes every girl he fancies. It happens.

But I am not going to let it happen to Anna. Not again. No way. I can protect Anna. I can save Anna.

And I will.

TWENTY
Nick

Their days, packed with work and wedding planning, flew by, hot and frantic. The longer, early-summer evenings were, by contrast, satisfyingly slow. They took advantage and often chose to walk hand in hand through the streets, rather than simply shifting from stuffy office, to packed tube, to air-conditioned restaurant. Even London streets smelt of flowers occasionally. Roses or lilies in buckets outside attractive market stalls were the most potent; the surprise fragrance banged up against the smell of diesel and sometimes rubbish carts. Odours, like boxers, throwing their weight about, fighting for supremacy. Sometimes Nick felt as though they were waiting for something to happen, then he'd check himself and remember that it had. He'd proposed, there was to be a wedding. Their wedding. That was something. That was happening. Soon. Ten weeks.

This evening they'd chosen to amble along the river. It had been Anna's suggestion; it made Nick smile that she was the sort who believed that good old-fashioned fresh air was beneficial. 'Eases stress,' she insisted. Nick never admitted to, or even acknowledged stress. The belief he peddled was that if you were the sort who was quick and tough enough to do the job he was doing, then you were the sort to shun stress; not just nerves of steel but balls of steel too. It was obvious Anna didn't swallow it.

She said everyone suffered from stress to an extent. 'I accept that there are a rare few who thrive on it. Some confuse adrenalin, dizzy excitement and fear, quite possibly you're one of those, Nick, but I do not accept you're impervious to it. Wedding planning is stressful, your mother is still recuperating, you have a lot on your plate.' She paused before adding, 'Anyway, it isn't just *your* stress levels I am managing.'

'What's wrong?'

'I'll explain when I see you.'

They walked from his office along the river towards the trendy high-rise restaurant where he had a window seat reserved to guarantee a great view of London. Nick threw his arm around Anna's shoulders and pulled her close to him; they walked that way for just a few steps before she said it was uncomfortable and took hold of his hand instead. He noticed that she didn't lace her fingers through his as usual; he wondered why He missed it. It was a bustling evening, scores of people were hanging out. Some were drinking a glass of wine at tables hastily put outside cafes and theatres because summer was here. Others were gathered around the street entertainers; they paused to listen to a young student playing his sax. The notes sauntered into the air, like a soft breeze. Nick threw a few quid into his battered trilby. The student acknowledged the donation with a sharp, precise nod of his head. Nick listened to other people's animated chatter and laughter, a train rattling across a bridge in the distance, the whizz of the wheels of the skateboarders. He noticed Anna's silence.

He sighed; he had often been on the wrong end of the silent treatment. His experience was that women were just as moody and uncommunicative as men when they chose to be, and that was the difference—they *chose* to be. Normally, he rode it out, never acknowledging the atmosphere because if he did ask a woman what was wrong she was likely to tell him, which led to rows, remonstrations or regrets. He didn't care enough to put himself through the aggro. But with Anna? Well, it was different. If something was both-

ering her he wanted to know what, so that he could solve
the matter, even though he feared he might be the problem;
she hadn't quite been herself since the night out with his
friends, last week. He had to face the fact there was a real
chance she'd heard him say that stupid thing to the guys. He
wanted to punch himself in the face. He did not want to nip
out for a burger. It was a crass, ugly thing to say. But then,
she couldn't have heard him because whilst that would explain getting a cold shoulder from a girlfriend, a cold shoulder was not the appropriate response of a fiancée. If she'd
been privy to something so awful, he'd have expected her to
tackle him, ask him if he meant it. He wished she would do
that because then he could tell her, no, of course he hadn't
meant it. He was an immature plonker and he was sorry.

Because he was pretty sure he hadn't meant it.

He knew that the only thing he could do was address the
matter himself, apologize for being a prat and hope she'd
quickly excuse him. He wanted them to get past this misunderstanding. It would be worth the earbashing because he
didn't like this awkward coolness. And besides, he thought
the making-up loving might be delicious. It could possibly
tip them into a new place, somewhere they'd yet to go. Somewhere he was keen to go. Angry, passionate, make-up sex
was different from careful, considerate loving.

He turned to Anna, 'Everything OK?'

'Zoe has been in touch.'

His first reaction was relief. Zoe. Phew. Zoe was bothering Anna, not him. He was off the hook. Wow. Great. His
second reaction was to wrack his brain; he was almost certain that Zoe was her sister. There came a point in a relationship when it wasn't the sort of thing you could ask. Once he'd
proposed, that point had been reached, really. Anna wasn't
one of those women who went on and on about her family.
They clearly weren't particularly close, either physically or
mentally, and to be frank, that was a relief. He was marrying a woman who could stand on her own two feet, not a

girl who referred and deferred to her parents every few minutes. Anna's parents lived in America, not on the doorstep, so naturally their sphere of influence was limited. It came back to him, Anna had mentioned her sister once, when Rachel was being a cow. She'd told him that he didn't have the monopoly on tricky sisters. Oh. He'd dated enough women to know that an overpowering or underwhelming brother could cause trouble, a clinging or jealous sister could be fatal. But he wasn't dating Anna, he was marrying her. This sister was going to be his relative too. He was determined to set off on the right foot. It was important. Feeling guilty about steak-gate made him want to charm the sister, forge a great relationship that would please Anna.

'How is she?' he asked.

'She's got a contact that's going to bring her over here for a while.'

'To London?'

'Yes. It's come out of the blue.'

'That's great,' he said enthusiastically.

'Hmmm.'

'You don't sound so sure.'

'I'm always pleased to see her. You know, she's my sister.' Anna sighed, glanced at him, nervously. 'She's keen to meet you. She's very insistent.'

'Well, I'm looking forward to meeting her too. It'll be lovely.'

'Not necessarily.' Anna moved over to the wall and looked out towards the river, watching the pleasure cruisers move up and down the Thames. 'I mean it may very well be lovely, she can be tremendous fun.'

'But?'

'Well, she's sort of the black sheep of the family. To be honest my parents don't talk to her. They don't even talk *about* her,' Anna said in a speedy, breathless gush.

He got the feeling she was apologizing in advance.

'Because they don't acknowledge Zoe, my relationship

with them is a bit strained. I guess you noticed as much.'
She looked embarrassed and ashamed.

He felt awful for her. He wanted to wrap his arms around
her and fix everything. Even though he wasn't exactly certain what needed fixing. 'Why don't they speak to her? What
did she do?'

'She's an addict.'

Nick tried desperately not to move his face. Not to look
shocked or concerned. He tried not to be thinking, 'God,
what a nightmare. Is that sort of thing genetic?' But, was
it? Was it genetic?

Anna earnestly searched his face. What for? For disgust?
For disappointment? Shock?

He knew that he must not move a muscle. 'What sort of
addict?' he asked carefully.

'Booze, mostly. Drugs too at one point. She's got an addictive personality, or self-esteem issues, or both.' Anna
sighed and looked at her hands. They were tightly clasped.
'She started partying when she was quite young. Partying
hard.' Anna looked crushed by the memory. 'I don't know.'
She shrugged. Her shoulders rose up a fraction and then
down again. She fiddled with her bag strap. Nick felt something in his chest pull. 'I don't know how to explain it. I've
read up on it, attended workshops and talked to endless doctors and psychiatrists but I don't really understand it. How
is it that one person can spend their twenties getting drunk
and hung-over and it can mean nothing, have no long-term
detrimental effects, and yet for another it can be utterly
devastating?'

Slowly, she lifted her eyes to his again. Her face was anxious, pleading. Seemingly, she really wanted an answer; he
felt lacking and hopeless that he couldn't give her one. He
was way out of his depth.

She carried on. If she was disappointed in him she managed not to show it. 'You know the word addiction comes
from a Latin term for 'enslaved by' or 'bound to'?'

'No, I didn't know that.'

'It's so fitting. Anyone who has struggled to overcome an addiction—or has tried to help someone else to do so— would agree with me. Even in high school she was always way more of a party animal than I ever was.'

Nick could well believe this. Snoopy the dog was more of a party animal than Anna was.

'She started to drop grades because she was often hung-over or wrecked. My parents thought—hoped—it was a stage. She managed to get to college, although not an Ivy League one, which was where we all believed she could go if she put the work in. It was crazy to watch her options being closed off so early but she didn't see it that way. She just saw the next party, the next drink. She saw pleas to go to rehab or start on the Twelve-step Program as excessive, insulting. She never really accepted she was an addict. She thought she had everything under control.'

'But it wasn't?'

'No. Things only got worse in college. She was smashed most of the time. There was always someone to drink with, and it didn't matter to her if it was a different someone each time. She'd built up quite a tolerance so she really had to have quite breathtaking quantities to get the high she craved. So then she dabbled with drugs. I guess for her it was the natural next step. That's how people describe it. 'Dabbled', such a homely word. Inaccurate, though. Co-occurring dis-orders aren't uncommon.' Anna's eyes were wet with tears but her irises still flicked from left to right, rapidly scan-ning his face to see what his reaction would be. 'It spiralled into a dark dereliction. She couldn't afford the habit. She did some bad things to pay for it.'

'What do you mean?'

Anna looked pale, uncomfortable. Ironically, Nick wished they both had a drink in their hands to help them through this awkwardness.

'The people who she hung out with. Well, they weren't

very nice at all. They exploited her. When she was drunk or high she was pretty pliable. Couldn't think beyond getting cash for her needs.'

What did that mean, exactly? Did she steal for money? Have sex for money? Nick didn't probe. He wasn't sure how much more he wanted to hear just yet. It was a tragic story. He couldn't imagine it. Naturally, he knew his share of drunks and users, but someone so closely related to Anna— who was the epitome of freshness, purity and happiness— being dragged into such a sleazy mess, seemed incredible.

As if reading his mind, Anna commented, 'I guess you're really shocked.'

He was. 'No, no. I'm not judging. I drank enough to sink a ship in my twenties. Many of my friends and colleagues, even I myself, could perhaps have gone the same way.'

'Except you didn't.'

Shrugging. 'No.'

'No, because most of us just cut back, slow down. Accept that the hangovers aren't worth it. Stop, because there are other things in our lives that we care about more. Our family, our work, our friends. Zoe didn't care about anything else. She got herself into some awful messes. Missed countless lectures and seminars, and when she did turn up she was, often as not, drunk. Inevitably, she got kicked out of university. Dad found her a job with one of his friends but it perhaps wasn't his most considered move.'

'What was the job?'

'She was maître d' at a high-end restaurant, in downtown New York. She looked the part.'

'Let me guess, she drank their stock and got fired.'

'She did drink their stock, yes. The chef caught her doing so, she had sex with him to keep him quiet. Technically, she got fired when they caught her doing that. It was after the lunchtime rush but before the evening diners had arrived. In fact, it was exactly the time schools were breaking up. They didn't stop to drop the blinds. The restaurant manager was alerted when a bunch of school kids began to huddle outside the restaurant to enjoy the free peep show. She was too drunk to even be ashamed.'

'Oh God.' Nick felt a wave of distress sweep over him; second-hand upset that he felt for Anna and her family. If he'd heard this story in a bar or at work he'd have laughed, only seen the funny side, but now he felt nothing other than anguish and worry.

'A classic addict. There you have it, all three manifestations of this enduring and controlling evil, and how it influences the brain. The craving, the loss of control and continuing involvement despite the dreadful consequences.'

This was heavy stuff. He didn't know what to do with it. Anna, his sweet, little eternal sunshine Anna had dealt with all of this for years. It was unbelievably shocking but then it also made absolute sense. This was why she was so good at her job. She didn't just sympathize, she empathized with the vulnerable, the despairing, the carers. This was why she was so efficient and marvellous when dealing with the medical staff that had looked after his mother; she knew hospital procedures; she knew the important questions to ask.

Nick reached for her hand and squeezed it tightly. 'I'm really sorry.'

She squeezed back and then plastered on one of her big, winning smiles. 'But, the good news is she's clean right now. Although breaking an addiction is tough, it can be done. She has completed the Twelve-step Program. She has her four-year chip.'

'That's awesome.' Nick couldn't hide his relief.

'It really is! No drugs in all that time. The sad thing is, my parents haven't forgiven her.' Anna sighed. 'I guess, they daren't love her.'

'Daren't?'

'In case she lets them down again. I think they believe they couldn't go through it again.'

'Is she likely to?'

'I don't know. I mean, they say, once an addict, always an addict. I've heard of people who fall off the wagon after twenty years.'

'Yeah, but you can't punish someone for twenty years, and certainly not for what might happen.'

'Exactly, I have to believe in her, Nick. I have to believe she is better now. I hoped you'd think of it that way. I think my parents were pretty hard on Zoe. Don't get me wrong, I totally love them and completely understand where they are coming from, I just don't agree with them. Besides, it's different for me. Maybe they think they have to do the tough love thing because they're her parents, but I'm her twin.'

'Twin?' Despite listening to the heavy, difficult story Nick could hardly contain his excitement.

'Yes.' Anna smiled. 'Didn't I mention that?'

'No!' Nick was certain he'd have remembered as much.

Laughing now, Anna said, 'I should have mentioned that long ago, shouldn't I? Men love the twin thing. Gets them every time.'

Nick wanted to ask if they were identical but he refrained; he knew if he did so, Anna would (correctly) assume he was imagining two of her crawling all over him. Not for real, just a fleeting fantasy. He pushed the thought away; as transitory as it was, he was ashamed of it. Anna was telling him something really big here, a schoolboy fantasy ought not to interrupt that.

But twins!

'Anyway, she's desperate to meet you and I would like to introduce you. The zig to my zag. I think this is a good time for a fresh start for everyone. If you welcomed Zoe with open arms, it might help to make things easier between her and Mom and Dad.'

'Is she coming to the wedding?'

'Of course I want her there. I want her to be my chief bridesmaid, ideally, but you have to meet her first. You'd have to be totally comfortable with the idea.'

That sounded ominous. How much trouble could she possibly be?

'Is it difficult for her to be around alcohol? Is that what you're worried about?' Nick was thinking about the reception, which would be champagne-fuelled. He hoped that in the evening he'd hire someone from a Hoxton bar who would mix the cocktails; he hoped to hell Anna wasn't going to suggest a dry wedding.

'Oh, she's fine around social drinkers. Well, at least, she has it under control, I'm sure it must still be difficult for her. But she probably will get off with your best man, and most likely a groomsman too.'

'I don't imagine any of them will be worried, no doubt only too happy to oblige,' laughed Nick.

Anna looked concerned. 'No, really, she will. Possibly all the groomsmen. That's the thing with an addictive personality. She's still always looking for hits and highs. She can't get it through booze or drugs anymore, so she gets it through sex.'

'Oh. Well, Darragh is married and his wife is at the wedding, so I think we're pretty safe there. I can't vouch for the others.'

'Darragh is your best man?'

'I thought I'd ask him.'

'We can talk about that.'

He didn't know what she meant, but before he could ask, she'd quickly moved on. 'Her problems are complex. It was the sex which finally finished things between her and Mom and Dad. She slept with one of Mom's colleagues and then tried to blackmail him. And she slept with Dad's best friend, causing his twenty-four-year marriage to collapse.'

'I see.' Nick was trying to process this information. Anna was so shy and reserved, it was hard to imagine her sister, so wildly different.

'It's just another addiction. It makes her behave like she's a total slut.'

He coughed. 'I see.'

'But she's a lovely girl at heart, you know. I don't want you thinking otherwise.'

Nick nodded again, keeping his face neutral. He wasn't the squeamish or judgemental sort. He'd been intimately acquainted with many a slut in his time. He was one himself. Or at least, he had been until very recently. So his sister-in-law-to-be was possibly a sex addict. He could handle that.

'I love her very much. The twin thing. It makes it all the more intense.'

'Right.'

'No matter how epic your fights can be, you always know that your incredible twin bond can't be broken, and you will be best friends for life. I guess that's why I feel I'm to blame.'

'You? How?'

'When we were very young we'd get up to stuff together. You know, mischievous things that kids do, like scooping fish out of ponds to see if they'd survive in the neighbour's pool.'

'I take it they didn't.'

'They didn't even get as far as the pool. We climbed trees to steal fruit and we went further on our bikes than we were supposed to but it didn't matter because we always took these risks together. We had each other's backs and you can bet your bottom dollar that, if we got caught, we never told whose idea it was. Then things changed. She started sneaking out on her own, to meet boys, to drink. She seemed to want a different sort of company before I did.'

'When was this?'

'I don't know. I guess she was about thirteen. We were in the habit of covering for each other by then. I feel I covered for her for too long. I was the ally, then her alibi, and before I knew it I woke up one day and I was her enabler. I blame myself for how far off the rails she went.'

'That's crazy.

'No, it isn't. If I'd said something earlier, when she first started stealing alcohol from my parents, then maybe they could have got help.'

He didn't want to let Anna down, she was looking at him, eyes wide with hope and expectation. 'I'd love to meet her. Obviously. Set it up. I'm sure the three of us will get on famously.'

Anna flung her arms around Nick and kissed him passionately for a good few minutes. She was normally quite reserved when it came to displays of public affection; obviously she was feeling intensely relieved. When she did finally break away she murmured, 'Thank you. I knew you'd understand.'

'When is she arriving in the UK?'

'Next week—Wednesday or Thursday, I think. You can never be sure with Zoe. She's notoriously difficult to pin down.'

'Maybe we should all go out at the weekend.'

'OK, if you're sure.'

'Certain.'

'I'll see if she has plans.' Anna beamed her broad, relaxed smile.

Nick felt a huge sense of relief that he had been able to soothe and calm.

And that Anna hadn't caught wind of his ill-advised talk with Darragh and Cai, after all.

Nice one.

TWENTY-ONE
Alexia

We were so pleased when we came up with their names. Anna and Zoe. A to Zee. Opposite ends of the alphabet to show that they were linked but different. The reverse, as it happened. Opposite ends of the spectrum.

Soon, we started to reap the benefits of doing something so extraordinary as having twins. Becoming a parent. It's a miracle. Every time. No one understands or knows that until they experience it. Becoming a parent to twins is more than that. We felt like celebrities, wherever we went we were stopped in the street. People would say, 'Aren't they cute, aren't they adorable.' The girls loved it, they'd smile on demand, strike a sweet pose, sing, blow kisses, basically perform any which way was requested. Especially Anna, always such a people pleaser. Yes, Zoe liked basking at the centre of attention, however she had other ways of getting there.

It worried me a little. I didn't want to raise the sort of girls who thought looking cute was enough. I did my best to counter the unearned praise that was poured on them for just looking lovely, even doubly lovely. 'Yes, cute and *so kind*,' I'd add, conscientiously. Although this was only ever true of Anna. 'Very academic.' Again Anna. 'They enjoy gymnastics, seem to have a knack.' Zoe probably had the edge there. Anna seemed to hear my message; she liked being recognized as pretty—which little girl wouldn't?—but she seemed to enjoy being thought of as clever and doing well at school, far more. I guess she always had the competitive edge. People often assumed that Zoe must be the more competitive, because she was louder and more confident. People associate those things with winning, yet it's not always the case; in fact, Zoe was a bit lazier than Anna. To be good at anything requires plenty of effort, make no mistake about that. There's a study that claims if you put ten thousand hours of practice into anything you become an expert, even if you don't have an innate talent. You have to put in the hours; even being good at lying takes a certain amount of determination and hard work. Zoe pretty soon realized that she found it harder to accomplish all that Anna did at school. She was slower to learn her letters and to count. She was still above class average, far above it—she could have been quite the scholar too—but she sort of quit before she'd begun. Zoe never liked coming second in any race, she'd rather not get off the blocks.

The differences between them started to widen. They still looked identical genetically but it was far easier to tell them apart. If one of them was misbehaving, it was Zoe; if the two of them were misbehaving, it was Zoe's idea and she was the one out front. Zoe was hard work. She went through all the awful stages, and I mean *all*. She had a scribbling on the wall phase, a biting phase, the endless, mindless stage of repeating the question 'Why?' without listening to the answer, without caring at all really, she just did it to annoy. She took longer to be toilet trained. I always believed she grasped it when Anna did but just sometimes couldn't be bothered to walk to the bathroom. I remember changing her night nappy when she was as old as three, maybe four. She'd eye me lazily. Her look said, 'More fool you for being prepared to clean up my mess.'

Anna also fell into the role of tidying up after Zoe. She never went to bed without putting away all their toys, crayons, books, play dough. Anna thought it was fun to help around the house; she liked to carefully dust, she paired socks and straightened the duvets on hers and Zoe's bed every morning from the age of about four. She liked to run little errands. If ever I flopped down in front of the TV and bemoaned the fact I'd left my glasses upstairs, she'd jump to her feet, 'Please can I get them, Mummy?' As though I was doing her the favour. She never had to be prompted to say her pleases and thank yous, to share or take a turn. As a result, Anna was welcomed into other people's homes, she was the sort of kid people wanted their kids to be friends with. She only ever accepted invites that included Zoe. More fool her. As often as not, they'd be sent home in disgrace because Zoe had lost her temper and scribbled on other kids' books or kicked their chairs out from under them. I found it frustrating, maddening, although mostly it made me sad. I never understood why Zoe wanted to make her life so much harder than it had to be. I was often being called into school. The ticking-offs, the outright roastings were hard enough to endure as a mother, I could only imagine what Zoe made of it, considering teachers invariably ended every meeting with a shake of the head. 'She's nothing like her sister, is she? Anna is such a good girl.'

They rarely dressed alike after the age of about eight. Anna might have gone along with it for longer, but Zoe was determined to be her own person; she just would not put on the clothes I laid out for her, not if they matched Anna's. I think that hurt Anna. Even back then, she thought Zoe was trying to peel away, to separate herself off; Anna was happy for them to be indistinguishable to the point of being seen as one entity, Zoe wasn't. She wanted her individuality, at any cost. I understood. Anna was so good, and helpful, and kind that there was only one place for Zoe to go. Better to be a completely different whole than a bad half. It's more interesting.

We thought going to America would be good for them both. Zoe, if she wanted it, could have the opportunity of reinventing herself, of becoming more palatable to everyone's taste. Anna might shake off a little of her propensity to people please, and learn to please herself a bit. Neither girl changed. Their personalities were set, the yin and the yang, the head and the tail; they were held fast by one another. As they grew up it became obvious that they were different in so many ways, but they were still fiercely close. To her credit Zoe never resented Anna for her success or her sweetness, she wasn't jealous of her; if anything, she was protective of her. Zoe was dark enough to know that Anna's naivety was a risk. Anna thought school was a joy and that she had a lot of friends. Zoe said that it was pitiful that Anna didn't realize they were queuing up to take advantage of her.

'How do you mean?' I asked, concerned.

'She lets people copy her homework.'

'I like helping people,' Anna pointed out calmly.

'Then you should probably teach them the maths, rather than just giving them the answers,' I advised.

'She gives away her cookies.'

'It's good to share,' smiled Anna.

I didn't know what to say. Was it possible to be too good? It wasn't like Anna was going to die of hunger if she sacrificed her break-time snack.

'It's a good job you've got me to look out for you,' said Zoe ominously.

I thought it was a benefit that we had Anna to look out for Zoe. I believed that Zoe mixing with Anna must somehow ultimately do her some good. And she liked being with Anna. I used to worry that it was simply because Anna was a convenient patsy for Zoe's troublemaking, and later because Anna was prepared to cover for her, but I don't think it was just that. I believe, and I have to continue to believe, that Zoe loved her sister. Absolutely. Always and for ever.

That's what they used to say to each other. That was their thing. When they were young one or the other would say, 'I love you.'

The second one would reply, 'Absolutely.'

Then whoever had initiated the loving comment would finish up with, 'Always and for ever.'

It was adorable. Everyone agreed. As the years passed, they stopped saying, 'I love you'. They depended on the shorthand.

'Absolutely.'

'Always and for ever.'

I'd listen carefully and I heard something change. Anna started to have an inflection in her voice that suggested a question. As though she never quite believed it. I worried about that. You worry about a lot of things as a parent, don't you?

TWENTY-TWO
Nick

It took ten days of emailing and planning before Anna and Zoe settled on a date that they were all free to meet up. Nick got the impression that whilst Zoe was keen, she also liked to do things her way. She had insisted on meeting Anna for coffee and then lunch first, just the two of them. He understood that they'd have stuff they wanted to catch up on, sisters and all that; twins, with their special connection, needed time to themselves. He didn't want to intrude. On the other hand, the arrangements seemed to be as complicated as calling a national summit between world leaders. Normally so collected, Anna was obviously in a bit of a state about the whole introduction business; more than once she said, 'Maybe we just shouldn't bother.' Nick had been the one who pushed ahead; he knew that Anna's relationship with Zoe was important to her and therefore his relationship with Zoe was important too. He suggested they meet at the Savoy Grill. It was the sort of place you took someone if you wanted to impress, and Nick did want to impress his future sister-in-law. Although she'd come with dire warnings—basically a walking, talking, ticking time bomb—she was the first family member of Anna's that he was to be introduced to in person; it mattered to him what she thought, he wanted to make a good impression. But Anna had said that the Savoy was too risky.

'What do you mean?' he'd asked.

'Exposed,' she'd muttered, looking sad. 'We need somewhere smaller. Zoe wouldn't be able to resist the urge to show off at the Savoy. It's very open, isn't it? Before you know it, she'll be naked, perched on top of the desert trolley gliding past the other diners' tables.'

Nick had wanted to laugh at the image Anna had conjured up, but the concern in her face stopped him from doing so. Instead, he asked. 'So you've been to the Savoy? Was that one of your dates, before you met me?'

'I wish. No. I've seen pictures online. You know, when you get random emails offering three courses for a set price; but if you take up the offer, then you spend twice as much because you get seduced into buying loads of extras.'

'Extras?'

'Vegetables, coffee.'

'I'd say they were integral.'

'They cost extra.' Anna looked abashed.

They hadn't had a straight conversation about salaries. He didn't know exactly what she earned, and she probably couldn't even imagine exactly what he earned. Safe to say there was a discrepancy. She worked for a registered charity. He worked for an investment bank.

'I'll take you one day.'

'That would be lovely,' she'd said, and then she'd let him kiss her concerns away.

In the end Anna chose and booked the restaurant. He hadn't been expecting great things. He thought she might pick somewhere cheap and cheerful, maybe the sort of place where students paid a cover charge to bring their own alcohol, which they duly brought in copious amounts to mask the terrible food. They probably wouldn't be allowed to bring alcohol, because of Zoe's issues, so they'd have to plough through the awful food without the protection of inebriation. He wasn't looking forward to it; however, he didn't interfere. As it turned out, he needn't have worried. Anna chose an elegant, intimate restaurant in a small boutique town-house hotel, tucked away behind a discrete glossy black door in one of those smart, quiet roads in the West End that tourists never discover.

The London streets were crammed with drinkers and dinners; the hotel lobby offered a calm retreat and air conditioning. It was full of deep leather tub chairs that had been worn just the correct amount, enough to suggest the place had heritage, not so much as to suggest it was suffering cashflow problems. He was shown to a booth that could seat up to six but was set for three. The waiter swiftly removed the 'reservation' sign. The wine and cocktail list was long and complicated, almost a book; just the sort Nick usually enjoyed getting his head around. This evening he snapped it closed after just a cursory glance. He wondered whether or not he should order himself an aperitif; what were the rules around Zoe? In the end he played it safe, ordering a lime soda. He fingered the corner of the heavy, crisp blue-and-white linen napkin, and watched the minute hand on the wall clock slowly edge round. They'd arranged to meet at the restaurant at seven thirty; Nick had come here straight from work, but Anna's plan was to go home and change first.

'No way am I turning up in my work clothes,' she'd said with surprising firmness. 'I promise you, Zoe will be dressed to the nines, she'll look knockout. I'm going to look dowdy by comparison, no matter what I do, but I'm going to at least make an effort.'

He'd thought it was sweet and honest the way she fessed up as much but he also thought she was wrong. He couldn't imagine Zoe would be able to outshine Anna. Even if they were twins. Nick believed people got the face they deserved: Anna's was bright, open, happy, beautiful; he imagined Zoe would wear her hardness and suffering.

He'd arrived ten minutes early; it wasn't like him to have time to spare. Anna and Zoe were now ten minutes late; it wasn't like Anna to leave him hanging. Normally she was pathological about time-keeping. Although he hadn't imagined punctuality would be amongst Zoe's attributes. Of

course, they were still well within the confines of fashion-
ably and acceptably late, but their tardiness was exasperated
by his promptness; he felt silly and self-conscious sitting on
his own. He imagined this must be what it felt like if you
were ever stood up on a date; not that he ever had been. His
phone beeped and he scrambled to pick up. Anna. Thank
God, no doubt she was ringing to say she was just five minutes away. She'd still get here before Zoe. It was crazy, he
was a man who had met heads of commerce and industry
across the world, he'd managed aggressive press confer-
ences, he'd even given a talk to two hundred Year 11s at his
old school—he was not easily phased—but he didn't want
to be alone with Zoe.

'I am so, so sorry, darling. I'm having the worst day at
work.'

He didn't like the word 'having'; he understood that immediately. She sounded breathless and he recognized that
she was anxious. When she felt stressed, Anna didn't yell,
snap or cry, the way so many did, she dealt with it in such
an admirable, mature way, her breathing simply became a
little shallow.

'What's going on?'

'Ivan lost it.'

'The guy with Tourette's.'

'Yes, that's right. He threw chairs and tables. It really
upset the other visitors. You can imagine. We promise them
a calm, safe environment and then Ivan starts to lob furniture left, right and centre.'

'What set him off?'

'Another job rejection. Then Mrs Skarvelis had a little
accident as a consequence.'

'What sort of accident?' Nick imagined cut heads,
bruised knees.

'She wet herself. She didn't dare get past the commotion
although she needed the bathroom. So she just sat in her
chair in the library corner. Naturally, she was mortified.'

Nick shook his head. People thought his job, working with hundreds of thousands of pounds, often millions, was stressful, yet he counted his lucky stars he never had to deal with anything like this.

'A couple of the other oldies left in a huff. I'm not sure when they'll feel comfortable coming back, which is such a shame because, you know, the elderly people are lonely and they do need the company.'

'What's happening now?'

'Well, Ivan is calming down, although he's still pretty prickly. In all the commotion he cut his hand. I'll have to take him to A&E.'

Nick sighed.

'Vera can't do it as it's her youngest son's parents evening at school. Already rearranged from last week.' Almost guiltily she added, 'Also, I said I'd straighten things up, file the report. Everything has to be done tonight. The trustees of the charity are pretty strict about that sort of thing.'

'Oh well, of course I understand.' Nick had the type of job that regularly massacred his free time, he couldn't resent Anna for having the same commitment. 'We'll just cancel dinner. Rearrange things with Zoe.'

'Well, that's what I thought at first but it seems stupid with Zoe just sitting upstairs, all dressed up and nowhere to go. She'd only order room service from the same kitchen. That doesn't make sense.'

'She's upstairs?'

'Yes. She's staying at the hotel. Didn't I tell you that? I thought I had.'

She might have. They both knew she might have.

'I was going to ring her from reception when I arrived. That was the plan.'

Nick could hear the question in her voice before she actually put it out there.

'I wondered whether you'd be OK going ahead without me? I'll join you as soon as I can.'

He knew that wouldn't be anytime soon. A trip to A&E, a report to file.

'Wouldn't you prefer it if I came over to the hospital? I could accompany Ivan while you filed the report. You wouldn't have such a late night then.'

'Soooo tempting! But I've already spoken to Zoe and she says she's happy to have dinner with you. In fact, she sounded crazy keen. I couldn't put her off.'

'Oh.'

'You're OK, with this?'

'Of course, why wouldn't I be?'

'You're the best.'

'Is there, erm, is there anything—?' He didn't know how to phrase it.

'You'll be fine. Don't let her drink.'

He wondered how he was supposed to manage that; take her glass away?

'OK, look, I have to go. Ivan is still very agitated. Zoe said she wouldn't be long. Love you.'

He barely got to say it back to her before Anna had rung off. He sighed, put his phone in his pocket and then glanced around the restaurant.

Bloody hell.

There she was, unquestionably. Not just a twin then, an identical twin. Same height, same weight, same hair and eyes, yet different in every way. Zoe was in heels, a clinging skirt and a top that managed to be flimsy and classy. As she glanced around the restaurant, slowly taking in her surroundings, Nick noted that her gestures were confident, purposeful, designed to draw attention. Their physical similarities were certainly incredible but Zoe's mannerisms were nothing like Anna's. She had none of Anna's desire to ingratiate, to amalgamate. Anna sometimes seemed almost apologetic about her beauty, Zoe clearly revelled in it. Anna was what everyone would consider to be a very pretty woman, but this woman was more vivid. Startling.

She clapped her eyes on him, pinning him to his seat. Then sauntered towards him, hips swaying, hair flicking, breasts—ever so slightly—bouncing. He couldn't look away. Did he want to?

'You must be Nick.' She stood in front of him, straight, stunning, strong. 'And this must be my seat.'

She remained standing until he jumped to his feet, rushed round the table and pulled out the chair for her. She didn't say thank you, she just sat down as though she were a queen taking her throne.

There had been identical twin boys in Nick's class in primary school. He'd schooled with them for about two years before they moved away to Leicester. Like all the kids, he had found the twins fascinating. He had always been enthralled by them and a little envious of them: as a boy he'd thought it must be great to have an on-tap, no-questions-asked buddy; as an adult he'd thought it must be the ultimate gratification for an inflated ego to have a double to study. Not that Anna had an inflated ego, although Zoe may well have. He hadn't been close friends with the boys so he'd never found the knack of telling them apart, which had unnerved him, he liked to know where he stood. Now, he felt momentarily nervous, as he wondered, would he be able to recognize Anna and tell her apart from Zoe if they were both here, side by side? The twin boys at school were obliged to wear the same uniform, which added to the confusion. No surprise that Zoe's fashion style was very different from Anna's; but if they were both naked, would he be able to tell them apart? The thought sent a bolt of fear and excitement shimmying through his body. Why would he think that? He'd never see Zoe naked, obviously. What was he afraid of? What was he excited by? Zoe moved her head a fraction; not her head at all, really, just her eyes. The gesture summoned the waiter; he appeared from nowhere, as though pulled to the table by a Siren call. Anna caught the attention of waiters with her enormous grin and enthusiastic wave. Yes, he'd be able to tell them apart. He felt relieved.

Still, he couldn't tear his eyes away from her. Truthfully, it was like looking at Anna but…more. How Anna might look if she was ever the subject of an extreme makeover, the way women sometimes are for magazine features or on the trashier TV shows. He wasn't saying Zoe was more attractive than Anna, she was just different. It was fascinating. They both had full, pert breasts but Zoe was wearing the sort of top that made breasts into tits. A sheer black shirt, a button too many undone. The low scoop and the sheerness designed to reveal an exciting, lacy, orange bra. Anna wore white or flesh-coloured underwear, in cotton, as a rule. She did own two lacy sets—one in blush pink, the other in baby blue—but he'd never seen either set on; he only knew of their existence because Anna once got him to root through her underwear drawers looking for a pair of trainer socks. He thought it was a shame; she had a great body and ought to feel confident enough to make the most of it, but she didn't, not quite. She dressed well, often beautifully, but mostly her clothes were functional, comfortable, appropriate. Confidence clearly wasn't an issue for Zoe. He could barely imagine anything functional, comfortable or appropriate in her wardrobe, he imagined it to be a mass of silky and translucent fabrics, scarlet reds, animal prints, plunging necklines and short hems. The thought made him reach for his water glass and take a gulp.

Zoe put her elbows on the table, subtly (deliberately?) pushing her tits together, making them swell in front of his very eyes. Zoe was more tanned than Anna. She crossed and uncrossed—and then crossed again—her muscular legs; obviously she was drawing attention to them. Like Anna, she had dark, glossy hair but since their first few dates Nick had rarely seen Anna wear hers loose; usually she scraped it up into a ponytail because it was more sensible for work. He liked ponytails, they made a woman look sporty, energetic.

But long hair, falling in fat glossy curls around a woman's shoulders, well, that was sexy, sultry. And sexy and sultry won over sporty and energetic in most male fantasies. Nick reminded himself that fantasies were for kids, something to wank over, they were not real or important. Anna hardly wore make-up; Nick had always admired that. She was a natural beauty and didn't need to mess about with that sort of thing. Zoe was caked in the stuff. Still, he had to admit she applied it well. It did enhance her features. It was difficult to look away from her lush, long lashes that beat against the air. He imagined them sending a much-needed breeze his way. Her scarlet mouth was mesmerizing. Wet lips. Glistening. A hole in her face. Inviting.

'What are you drinking?' She picked up the wine and cocktail menu and started to slowly flip through it.

He was rapt. He couldn't quite work out why. He'd seen beautiful women before. Had them, plenty of them. Beautiful, sexy, up-for-it women. But Zoe was different from any other woman, ironically because she was so similar. Anna, but not Anna at all.

'Are you sure you want a drink? Wouldn't you prefer something soft?' he asked, forcing himself to remember and try to abide by Anna's instructions. He actually fell over his words, it was humiliating. 'I'm on lime soda.'

Zoe laughed, a hard, challenging bark. 'Boring! Who are you? My mother?'

He shook his head. 'Aren't you on the programme?' he whispered.

'Told you all that shit, has she? Such a blabbermouth.'

Nick felt offended on Anna's behalf. 'She's just concerned for you.'

'Shall I tell you a secret?' Nick felt torn, frozen. He had a feeling being privy to this woman's secrets was a fast track to trouble.

Before he could stop her she said, 'I started drinking again about six months ago. I haven't told Anna because she'd freak, but I'm absolutely fine with it. I have everything under control.'

Nick wanted to reach for his phone and update Anna. This had to be a disaster, right? He didn't know an awful lot about actual alcoholics. Heavy drinkers? Yes. Loads of them. But that wasn't the same. He was pretty sure they weren't meant to drink again, ever. He hesitated. What could Anna do right now? She was at the hospital with Ivan. He'd only upset her.

Zoe interrupted his thoughts. 'They've always made more of my drinking habit than is fair.'

'They?'

'My parents. Anna. I bet she told you I was an alcoholic.'

'Well, yes.'

'I'm not. Do I look like an alcoholic?'

She opened out her arms. He found he was staring at her cleavage. She kept her eyes boring into Nick. She did not look like an alcoholic. She was the picture of health. Alcoholics had ravaged, jaundiced skin or red, itchy skin; hers was smooth and golden. There were no hand tremors, nor were her eyes bloodshot or unfocused. Anna was a worrier; he was inclined to believe she might have unintentionally exaggerated the situation. Zoe was an adult, he couldn't tell her what to drink and what not to drink.

The waiter hovered at the table.

'I'll have a vodka and orange but only if the orange is squeezed in front of me. I can't bear the crap that is passed off as 'freshly squeezed'. The world is so disappointingly full of bullshitters. No ice.'

The waiter nodded, with more enthusiasm than was seemly.

'Make that two,' she instructed him, without consulting Nick further.

TWENTY-THREE

Zoe

I know he will fail my test the moment he claps eyes on me. There's something that states intent in the way he looks at me; long, hard, with some shame and, simultaneously, excitement. I almost turn around right then; I have my answer. But Anna doesn't. She will need undeniable proof. It's pathetic, really; his reaction. Predictable. His tongue is practically on the floor. Men are so stupid and annoying. The biggest annoyance being that they still rule the world we live in when they are so very, very obviously stupid. Yet I stay, I have to. I need to know. Anna needs to know. She always believes the best in people, gives them the benefit of the doubt. There can be no doubt. I move towards him. Throw out my web, insect that he is, he will crawl into it.

I don't even nod towards the concept of subtlety. I can tell at once that's not what he wants from me, and he does want something from me, whether he knows it yet or not, whether he admits it to himself now, or ever. I pull out all the tricks—sashaying hips, playing with my hair, squeezing my breasts together when I lean forward, elbows on the table (no manners!), touching his hand from time to time when I tell a funny story, throwing my head back and laughing with wild abandon when he relays something or other, running my tongue over my teeth, filling up his glass, pushing my knee next to his. All the obvious, tired old tricks. And he laps them up. A parched dog. It is as though he's never before seen a woman in his life.

Depressing, really. Hurtful for Anna.

I was right. He considers the sex he's having with Anna as, shall we say, pleasant? Nice enough? Sufficient? Not exactly adequate. Of course, he doesn't actually confess that to me, I glean as much because he almost comes just talking about sex, and of course that's what I focus on throughout the evening. I want to get him all hot and worked up, I need to see how far he will go. So, despite his feeble efforts to keep the conversation on my work, or even my journey from the States (yawnsville), I quickly, ceaselessly bring it back round to what is important. Sex. Like when he picks up the menu and starts to glance over it.

He asks, 'What do you fancy?'

'An Adonis with a good tongue,' I quip.

He blushes and points to the menu. 'To eat?'

'Oh, I'll have the oysters with the chili salsa.' Everyone knows what is said about oysters so I don't even need mention it. 'What about you?'

He uncomfortably fingers his collar, computing that I've picked the aphrodisiac. 'I'll have the salad,' he says as he takes a gulp of his vodka and orange.

'That salad is designed for women.'

He raises his eyebrow, mock surprised. 'That's a bit of a sexist assumption, isn't it?'

'I'm not thinking about calorie intake or any of that. Look, it's got asparagus and avocados in it. Don't you know that the vitamin E in those greens helps the body churn out oestrogen and progesterone, which circulate in the bloodstream and stimulate sexual responses?' I smile innocently, as though we're discussing nothing more than the inclement weather. 'Specifically, it causes clitoral swelling and vaginal lubrication.'

He actually chokes on his drink.

'Am I the only one who knows these things?' I try to look genuinely confused. Shrugging, 'Maybe I am, maybe that's why I get such good feedback from my lovers.' I wink at him.

What I'm doing isn't flirting. Flirting suggests a level of delicacy.

I order the oysters to start, then steak with a side of the horny salad. He would have to be deaf and blind not to get the message. After my little talk about nutrition he steers clear, ordering sausages, which makes me inwardly giggle. I also order a bottle of wine; when I do so I notice he shifts on his seat but doesn't dare voice any more objections.

'So you're not a vegetarian, like Anna?'

'If I had a choice I'd ask they serve my meat still bleating.' I bite my lip. 'Or talking.'

Whilst we wait for our food he, rather desperately, asks me what I do with my spare time. I mention that Anna and I were both gymnasts when we were children and although she doesn't seem to have time for hobbies now, I value staying flexible. 'I'm a bit of a yoga bunny.'

'Oh really, what type?'

'I'm not too fussy. Ashtanga. Hatha. My favourite sessions are hot yoga.'

'Yes, I've heard of that.'

'It's actually just yoga in a very hot room. Around thirty-seven degrees Celsius. Imagine a tropical island with no breeze.'

'Wow.'

'Working in a heated room raises the heart rate, forcing the body to work harder. It's intense, you know. That said, I love it. It develops strength, flexibility and tone.' I'm sitting ramrod straight. He knows I'm toned. 'Plus, the heat helps the body relax and improves breathing, focuses the mind.'

'All good stuff.'

'Yeah, although it's not for the squeamish. It's pretty undignified. The main point is to sweat out toxins. Within minutes I'm dripping. Sweat running in every crevice, I have to fight the urge to strip.' I pluck at my shirt, as though I'm boiling right now. As though I need to strip right now. I allow a pause in the conversation. People underestimate the importance of what's left unsaid. I find it just as valuable as what is said. I give his mind time to digest and draw the picture. 'You?'

'What?' He looks a little dazed.

'Do you have a sport?'

'I play some rugby.'

'Oh.' Beat. 'Thighs.' I really don't need to say anything more. I let the moment settle. He's imagining a hot, sweating, stripping yoga bunny. I'm pretending to imagine his big, glorious thighs; in fact, just to make things simpler, I do imagine his big, glorious thighs.

We sit in silence until the waiter brings our starters. Silences are powerful. More powerful than screams sometimes.

Nick tries again with a new topic. 'So, Anna tells me you're here for a specific job.' It is sweet the way he keeps bringing Anna into the conversation. Reminding me, reminding himself, of her existence.

'That's right.' I play with my love-knot necklace, drawing attention to my cleavage—as if I need to, he's barely looked anywhere else. It is hilarious, watching him struggle to keep his eyes up.

'And what sort of work do you do?'

'She hasn't told you?'

'Erm, she might have done.' He blushes.

'I see. You don't always listen.'

'Not as well as she deserves, perhaps.' He laughs and looks embarrassed, hoping I'll forgive his foible.

I lie. 'Don't worry, your secret's safe with me, I'm good at keeping schtum. And I know Anna can drone on a bit.'

'Oh no, it's not that. I wouldn't say that. It's just, if we're watching TV and there's sport on or market analysis on the news, I don't concentrate as well as I might, as I ought. It's entirely my fault.'

I wave his protestations and justifications away. They're boring. 'I'm a model.'

'Oh.'

'You seem surprised.'

He watches my lips as I chew. I know he likes my appetite.

'Not at all, you're beautiful. Both of you,' he adds quickly, again stumbling and blushing.

It's almost cute.

'Yet modelling is not what you expected?'

'I just know I would have remembered that, if Anna had mentioned it.' He laughs.

I bet. I decide to let him off the hook. 'Honestly? She probably hasn't. Anna doesn't talk about my modelling often. She doesn't completely approve. Let's just say I'm a bit curvy for the catwalk so a lot of the work I get tends to play to my assets.' I pout, a little. I'm also a little old for the catwalk, I don't see any need to draw attention to that. 'Anyway, I'm over here to do an underwear catalogue.' I name the brand. 'Do you know it?'

He shakes his head.

'It doesn't surprise me. It's pretty slutty stuff, to be honest.'

I can practically see him fight his hard on as he processes this bit of information.

'I've been at it all day, actually.'

'You've been working—modelling—today?'

'It's much more strenuous than people imagine, you know, so much bending and stretching.' I let him think about that for a while too. 'And it's chilly. I mean we're not wearing much, obviously.'

'No.'

'And invariably there's a wind machine, to blow out hair. The art director wants our nipples to ping, you know.' As I say this I touch my nipples with my pointing finger and then do a little action to represent them pinging out towards him. It's hardly subtle.

He almost bites his tongue.

'We girls practically have to cling to one another for body warmth. You can imagine.'

'Yes, I can.' His voice is gravelly with lust. He coughs and then reaches for the wine. He refills both our glasses without hesitating and seems surprised to find that it is the last of the bottle.

I summon the waiter and order another. Nick protests half-heartedly. Once again, I wave away his objections. It's almost too easy. Then I think of his promises to Anna and I feel a swell of irritation. The irritation scratches at my throat and I can't enjoy the oysters.

I continue in much the same vain throughout the main course too. Filling his glass regularly, touching his arm, looking at him from beneath my eyelashes. Luring him in with every syllable I utter, every flick of the head, every sigh. I'm very practised at this. Sometimes, it's actually boring, how easy it is to pick up men. Tonight, at least, is a little bit outside the norm. I have to work at it. And I do. I am like quicksilver: amorphous, shiny, chancy. I can be many things at once and I know he finds all of them interesting and yet alarming.

'So, you're going to marry my sister.' I say.

'That's the plan.'

I reject any semblance of cloaking my feelings with polite small talk. 'Extraordinary.'

He takes a sip of wine. 'Why do you say that?'

'You don't seem the marrying kind.'

'Don't I?'

'No.'

'What kind am I then?'

'You strike me as someone who is very much about the hooking and the fucking.'

He coughs, hearing the word so raw and real in his head and his trousers, no doubt. 'Those days are behind me,' he insists.

I stare at him, as though weighing him up, but I've al-

ready got the measure of him. 'What a bold statement.' I
pick up the bottle and refill both our glasses.

I take care to surprise him; I do none of the sisterly things
he must expect or have previously encountered. I do not
spill any funny, embarrassing and ultimately flattering stories about Anna, the way a best-friend sister might; I do
not point-score or snipe, the way a jealous sister might; I
don't drill him for information on his prospects, the way
a concerned sister might. I barely mention Anna. Will he
forget her?

I wonder how far I'll need to go. At what point do I decide
enough is enough? What is infidelity? Is it talking about sex
with me at this dinner? Is it when he fails to move his foot
when mine 'accidentally' bangs his and then rests there?
Is it him laughing at my dirty jokes? Or is it a kiss? I don't
know. That's a philosophical question of our times. What is
infidelity? I wonder how far I'll have to go to prove to Anna
that this man is untrustworthy, like all the other men she's
dated. I guess if he fucks me from behind whilst we watch
ourselves in a mirror, the case will be pretty open and shut.

TWENTY-FOUR
Nick

Nick had always considered himself quite the accomplished flirt but Zoe was in a different league altogether. He felt like a schoolboy by comparison. She did not behave as though she was Anna's sister, it was almost as though Anna was irrelevant to her. She behaved as though they had just met in a bar or a nightclub, as though he'd bought her a drink and then asked for her number. She behaved as though he was attracted to her and the attraction was unsurprising. A given. She was stunning, undoubtedly. She had to be used to a lot of attention, but there was something horrible, unseemly about her assumption that he, her sister's fiancé, would find her hot.

Unseemly and accurate.

Nick excused himself, dashed to the loo. He wanted to call Anna. Secreting himself in a rather stylish, dark mahogany cubicle, self-conscious yet desperate, he stared at his phone. He hadn't quite thought through what he would say to her. What came to mind was, 'You're right, your sister is a nymphomaniac and is coming on to me. Help!';he supposed he'd have to temper that somewhat. Whilst he did not know what to say, he was sure it was Anna that he needed to call. Anna, who could help. He was out of his depth. He was in trouble. Danger? The word flicked into his head and he shoved it aside. It was a ridiculous thought. He was a grown man; what sort of danger could he be in?

Yet.

Unfortunately, the call went straight through to voice-mail. Of course it did, she'd be at A&E with Ivan now, there would be signs everywhere asking visitors to switch off their phones; Anna always followed the rules. Her cheerful, easy voice rang in his ear, temporarily soothing. 'Hi, I'm so sorry I can't take your call right now. Leave me a message and I promise I'll get right back to you.' She practically sang her instructions.

'Hey, darling, it's me.' He didn't know what to say yet he wanted to say something. Had to. He wanted to strengthen the invisible bonds between the two of them, reiterate prom-ises, murmur gentle thoughts. 'Erm. I've hooked up with Zoe. Met up, I mean.' Oh crap. He paused, that sounded odd. Loaded. But he felt odd, loaded. Zoe's continual innuendo had somehow left him feeling sullied and complicit. It was weird, he'd had countless dates with hot and fast women and he'd never, ever felt intimidated or unsure. Only a few months ago this evening would have counted as a dream date; a beautiful woman practically opening her legs to him over the hors d'oeuvres—breast or leg, sir? Now it was more than a bit of a nightmare. For one thing, this was the first time he'd been tested since he'd met Anna. Tested and—

Tempted.

He knew, of course, that he had to turn away from this temptation. He realized he'd be doing nothing other than turning away from now on. Steak, whenever he wanted it. For the rest of his life. One-woman guy. That's what Anna had been looking for. That's what he had agreed to be.

It was, in all honesty, a faintly depressing thought.

Although Anna was worth it, right? He knew that, ulti-mately, infinite variety did (ironically) cloy, so he'd made a decision. He'd chosen a greater and more profound path. But besides the matter of fidelity, if ever he were to stray (and really he wouldn't, but if he did), then it made no sense for that to be with Zoe who was Anna's *sister*. Twin sister! No, none at all. What was she playing at? He was in no doubt that she was playing; this full-on seductress act couldn't be taken seriously. What exactly was her game? Was it her condition? Her sex addiction? It had to be. As irresistible as he liked to think himself to be, her behaviour was over the top. He had never come across anyone so blatant, so confident, so—

Compelling.

He suddenly became aware that he was still holding the line open to Anna. 'Hey, Anna, get here as soon as you can, will you? We're doing OK but she is quite a handful.' He laughed, unconvincingly. 'You did warn me, right? I'm just not sure I'm managing things properly.' Then, because he meant it, he added, 'I love you.' Nick didn't often say the three little words that were the three biggest words possible. Mostly, he said something like, 'Love ya, babe,' or just, 'You too,' in response to Anna's declarations. Tonight he wanted her to know.

He was just considering whether his message was wise or would cause worry when an automated voice cut in: *If you are happy with your message, then please hang up; if you would like to re-record, press three.* The voice was cool and efficient, a little bit censorial.

Suddenly, Nick felt silly and inadequate. Anna had enough on her plate this evening, she didn't need his flustered ramblings. Zoe was just a bit intense, that was all, he could handle that. There was nothing to be freaked out by. He wasn't thinking clearly. It was the drink. He had been drinking a lot, reasoning that he was saving Zoe from drinking too much. Not that his tactic worked; besides the vodka and orange, they'd seen off the best part of a second bottle of wine already. Panicked, he pressed three. Coughed. 'Hi, Anna, I just wanted you to know that Zoe and I are getting on like a house on fire. She's very entertaining. Hope your evening is sorting out and things are OK now with Ivan. Catch up properly tomorrow. Love ya, babe.'

Then he splashed water on his face before he went back to the table. To Zoe.

He decided the best thing he could do was simply eat as quickly as possible and then pay the bill and get out. He couldn't take the conversation at all seriously, absolutely shouldn't. Anna had explained she was an addict. It was an illness. What sort of man was turned on by illness? Oh no, it was true, he was turned on. How was that possible? Damaged and complicated women had always been a no go area for him. Not interested, life was too short for that sort of aggro. However, Zoe was different. He found it bizarre, looking at her, almost knowing her, not knowing her at all. She looked just like Anna, had her brilliant smile and figure; she showed signs of having her quick brain too, though Zoe chose to think and talk about very different things from Anna. There was no talk of governmental policy on mental health, the artist Delacroix's influence on the rise of Modern Art, or even weddings. She didn't talk about anything serious at all. She was frivolous, fast and fun. She was explicit and extreme; not tethered by social norms or graces. It wasn't anything like the first evening he had spent with Anna. True, he and Zoe were sharing a meal at a decent restaurant, but the similarity stopped there. There were no shy or tentative smiles, there was no baring of souls. Although, he felt stripped. Nor was the dinner anything like the many dates Nick had been on in the past, many of which were boring, predictable and merged into an indistinguishable mass. Tonight he felt as though he was standing, stark bollock naked, on a knife edge. Zoe somehow had the power to slice him open.

'So, tell me a little bit more about yourself,' she instructed, when he returned to the table.

He felt relief sluice through his body. That he could do. That was a normal thing to ask. 'I'm an investment banker. I'm in equity capital markets. I was born and bred in Bath, studied at the London School of Economics.'

'Blah, blah, blah.' She rolled her eyes. 'I know all of that. Anna filled me in with all those details. Give me something important.'

'Aren't those facts important?'

She shrugged. Reducing him. He felt offended and challenged at once. He liked a challenge.

'Tell me something new.' She leaned closer and jokingly whispered, 'Tell me something Anna can't tell me.'

Inwardly Nick winced, he knew where that sort of request led. 'What do you mean?'

Zoe smiled. Her smile started in one corner of the mouth, the other corner behaved as though it was being reluctantly dragged up. There was something very sexy about her unwilling smile. 'You know exactly what I mean. Tell me something you've kept hidden from her.'

'Why would I do that?'

'Keep something hidden from her? Oh, come on, I don't buy this Mr Straightforward Nice Guy act you've got going on. There's more to you than that.'

She'd cut through his bullshit; it was disconcerting and yet strangely flattering. She seemed to see deeper into him than anyone else ever had, or maybe even could. He *was* a nice guy, especially recently, since he'd met Anna, but he was more than that too. He wasn't straightforward. Straightforward was a step away from dull; who wanted to be that? He felt Zoe understood that about him; oddly, he felt known to her. Suddenly and unaccountably, he resented Anna for not peeling him back more thoroughly. Shouldn't she be more interested? He did have secrets. One or two. Of course he did. Nothing life-shattering, nothing criminal. At uni he'd once slept with one of Darragh's girlfriends. A drunken, messy thing. He kept it a secret because telling would cause more trouble than it was worth. It was crap sex and he couldn't even remember the girl's name now. He doubted Darragh could either. They'd both moved on. He lied about his A level results. Not on job applications, that was probably illegal. Just to people he'd met since. He bumped his As up to A*s. He wasn't sure exactly why he did that. Except he supposed he thought he deserved A*s. When he was twenty-one he'd had a married lover. She was a lot older than him. A lot. Just a few years younger than his mother, actually. Although nothing like anyone's mother. It was all very 'Hello, Mrs Robinson'. She was his boss's wife. His boss was a wanker. He wasn't particularly proud of any of these things, although he wasn't entirely ashamed of them either. He would tell Anna, if she asked, but she wouldn't ask. She'd never imagine such things. Why hadn't Anna assumed he was a little more complicated? A little messier? More than just charming and affable. Zoe seemed to see everything brilliant that he presented, and everything torrid that he didn't.

It wasn't right, though. This twin knowing more than the other one. That was the wrong way round. '*If* I had secrets, why would I tell you them instead of her?'

'Because I'm the sort of woman who understands secrets.' She looked directly into his eyes.

Her eyes were the same colour and shape as Anna's but there was nothing of the King Charles spaniel about her. If Zoe were an animal, she'd be a panther, a solitary predator with long claws. She poured them both some more wine. Slowly she played with the stem of her glass; her nails were painted a deep red. Nick took big gulps and laughed, the sort of high, embarrassed laugh that people spill when they are put on the spot.

'She doesn't know where I'm planning to take her on honeymoon.' It was a desperate effort to placate.

'Boring. Tell me why you lied to her about why you were on that dating site in the first place.'

'Sorry?'

'Didn't you give her some horseshit story about your friends worrying about you after a break-up and encouraging you to find true love through the site.'

'Well.' Nick felt hot and cold all at once. He didn't know what to say.

'I looked you up. I know you were registered on Tinder, Zoosk, Match and Elite as well as the site you met Anna on.

What was it? AllThat? That does not strike me as the actions of a shy dumpee hesitantly feeling his way back into the dating world.'

He had been caught out by her clarity of thinking.

'Besides, look at you. The very idea of you needing to look for love on a dating site is preposterous. If you wanted to find it, you could trip over it in the high street.'

He heard the compliment; she meant him to.

'Plus, I know that you didn't remove your profile until after you'd proposed.'

Again, he stumbled. Being with her was like walking up the down escalator. Disconcerting, difficult to stay upright.

'That's not true.'

She cocked her head; it was true, and they both knew it.

'And whilst your proposal was indecently hasty, I'd have thought ten weeks or so would have been enough time to take down your site profiles once you were dating exclusively. If, indeed, you were dating exclusively.'

'Certainly I was. I am,' he stuttered, unsure of which tense to use. 'I proposed, didn't I?'

'Yes, you did.' Zoe looked momentarily perplexed.

'I just never got around to deleting the profiles. Obviously, I wasn't logging in. I forgot all about it.'

'Of course you did.' She laughed suddenly. She sounded harsh, a bit hysterical. 'Don't look so worried. I told you, I'm good at keeping secrets.'

'It's not a secret.' It was a stupid thing for him to say. Absolutely, it was a secret.

'Oh? Anna knows, does she?'

'No, but.' He gave up. He wanted to change the subject. 'Look, this is silly.'

'I'm just trying to get to know you. Really know you. Isn't that what you want too?'

And he did. It was the strangest thing. She was overt and outrageous. She was unswerving, oblique, erudite, blunt to the point of crude, aloof and seductive all at once. He wanted to fascinate her because—Well. She fascinated him.

'Are you into threesomes?' she asked.

'What? No!'

It had been his first thought. When Anna had said she had a twin. Not a fully formed thought, not an intentional thought, just something that had drifted about in his brain for perhaps two seconds. How did Zoe know?

'I'm just checking, because that really wouldn't be Anna's thing.'

'No, no, I'm not. It's not my thing either.'

'Pity.'

What did that mean?

She held his gaze. 'Have you ever had sex with a man?'

'Are you for real?'

'I'm shocking you. That's hilarious. Have you turned all prudish, suddenly? Has Anna's puritanical influence rubbed off? OK, I'll start slowly. Have you ever skinny-dipped?'

'This is a ridiculous conversation. Why can't you talk about something normal?'

'Sex is normal. And abnormal, and glorious and filthy. Have you forgotten all that already?' She started to hum to herself.

He had to lean in closely to catch the tune. It was an old one, something from his childhood. 'Money Makes The World Go Round'. Liza Minnelli, in *Cabaret*. That was it. Now she was singing, a low murmuring tune, but she'd changed the words.

'Sex makes the world go around, the world go around, the world go around. It makes the world go round.' Zoe made her eyes big and wide, she started to bat her eyelashes comically. 'A spark, a screw, a fuck, wouldn't you? A fuck, it's true. A fuck or two. Is all that makes the world go around. That groaning, moaning sound, can make the world go round.'

Alarmed, he looked around the restaurant. Was anyone else within earshot? 'Stop it, people will hear you.'

She laughed at him and he felt stupid, boring.

'Who are you? My father now?'

'You're behaving like a child.'

'I bet you want to put me over your knee.'

He shuddered yet was not repelled, even though he wanted to be, even though he had to be seen to be. 'You're out of your mind.'

'It has been said.'

She was, totally out of her mind. Yes, dangerous after all. Yet, even whilst he was registering this, he was aware that he felt aroused; soused in a giddy, infectious halo of risk and desire. It must be the alcohol. It might be the woman. He sat in a deep, foggy silence. He couldn't think of what to say. Her lips saying the word 'fuck' had wiped his mind clean. The thought of her bent over his knee, buttocks naked perhaps, his hand making contact with her peachy skin. The air was thick with something he could almost taste, touch. Something he wanted to take. A tangible sense of lust. Tangible and suicidal. This woman was trouble. This woman was his fiancée's sister.

This woman was hot.

He felt corralled by her breasts, her brain, her tongue. He felt her throbbing presence as though she was already naked and underneath him. On top of him. Wrapped around him. Somehow she had seeped into his being.

The waiter arrived at the table, brandishing the desert menus. 'Can I offer you desert or a coffee?'

He met her eyes. 'No, just the bill,' he said.

As he made the request he was telling himself that he was cutting the night short because he was going to go home, take a cold shower, sober up, wise up. Maybe call Anna again. Yes, that's what he should do. He should talk to Anna, his fiancée. Quickly. He couldn't afford to waste any time.

Another part of his brain—the part that was programmed by habit, or lust, or maybe challenged by variety or a fear of lost opportunities—knew that he was asking for the bill because yes, indeed, he needed to act quickly. He didn't want to think for a moment more because, if he did think, he'd stop himself doing what he was sure he was going to do. Apparently, Zoe was thinking the same thing.

'Put it on my room. Room 101.'

'You're kidding, right?' Nick felt woozy, drunk, but he could still spot the *1984* reference.

'Not at all. Crazy, huh. It's all very Orwellian, isn't it?'

So, she read. She was not all tits and teeth. Something else. Something deeper and more powerful, or was he just imagining that? Wanting that? Why did he want to believe there was more to her?

'Room 101. The *torture chamber* in the Ministry of Love.' He chuckled over the irony. It was a silly snorting sound, full of nerves and a pinch of self-loathing. Because he knew. He knew where this was leading.

Zoe nodded. 'Where the Party attempts to subject a prisoner to his or her own worst *nightmare*, fear or *phobia*.'

'With the object of breaking down their resistance.' He stopped giggling now. It wasn't attractive. 'Room 101, you say?'

'Fate, don't you think?'

'I don't believe in fate.'

'Don't you? No, nor me. I'm more of a coincidence sort of girl. Anna is the one who believes in fate, destinies and such.'

Yes, yes, and knights in shining armour, love at first sight, everlasting love. Anna. Anna. Her name rang around his head like a bell. Not a clear church bell. An alarm. A screeching, annoying alarm. Zoe smiled. It was nothing like Anna's wide and open beam. The smile offered up not an iota of warmth or amenability. It was the sort of smile that swallowed a man whole.

'What do you believe in, Nick?'

Nick didn't know how to answer. Right then, he didn't believe in anything at all.

TWENTY-FIVE
Zoe

Let me get the excuses out early on. It doesn't matter much anyway. You don't like me. I don't need to be liked. So we're just fine.

Still, I think you might as well know that I was drunk. I didn't expect it to go that far. The whole point of the test was to do Anna a favour. Are we clear on that? I wanted to warn her. Save her making a fool of herself. Save her getting hurt.

Just, save her.

My room was only one floor above the restaurant. We could have walked but we didn't, we waited outside the lift. I don't know why. I guess walking up the stairs would somehow spell out our intentions too definitively; both to each other and to ourselves. Instead, he lingered by the lift in the foyer, not quite making a conclusive choice; at least, not admitting it was a decision, more a culmination of circumstances. There was talk of a nightcap, raiding my minibar, although if it was a drink he wanted we could have got that at the hotel bar. It wasn't a drink he was after. We both knew that.

A kiss. That would be it. Decisive proof for Anna. But.

The lift door slid open, I think he hesitated. For, you know, less than a fraction of a second. A flicker of an eyelid, the start of a beat of a heart. Not long enough. We didn't say a word to each other in the lift. I guess we couldn't risk it. The wrong word might have brought either one of us to our senses; we didn't want that. I kept my eyes down, hunted in my bag for the key card. He kept his eyes on me. I know. I felt them.

I gave him one last chance. I gave Anna one chance. As I slid the card through the lock, half hoping it would fail as they sometimes do and I'd have to go back to reception to get another one, which would give us space and time to reconsider, I turned to him and said, 'You're sure?' He could have backed away, said something about just seeing me to the door, he could have yawned and made an excuse about having to get up early in the morning.

Instead, he said, 'It's just a drink.' Even though we both knew it wasn't.

The little green light flashed. On the door lock. In my head.

My hotel room is fabulous. Lofty ceilings, sash windows, excessive amounts of cushions. The whole thing. I only ever stay in gorgeous hotel rooms; thriftiness is for people with poor money-management abilities or poor self-esteem. I deserve the best and ultimately someone else always foots the bill. It's a mass of dark-grey and copper tones, everything is silky, padded, luxurious, whether that's the walls, the headboard, the bedding. The effect is very up-market harem. I have a balcony, which is useful because it's a non-smoking room. The view isn't great. A tiny backstreet, but hey, that's London. Cheek by jowl.

I'd taken care to leave it tidy, just in case I ended up entertaining. There were no trays of half-eaten room service spreading unsavoury smells. The bed (huge) was still made, although the cushions were in disarray and the top cover somewhat rumpled. I'd staged all of that. I wanted him to know that I'd sat there. Lain there. I wanted him to be thinking about it. Sex ends up in the bed but it starts in the head. Even for men. It's a mistake to think it's all in their trousers. He looked around for somewhere to sit. There was only one chair. Upon which I'd deliberately left a scanty, lacy black bra. I'd made it look as though I'd tossed the bra over the back of the seat, after taking it off. The matching knickers were on the floor; I'd just stepped out of them. He had three choices:

he could move my bra, pretend to ignore it and just sit on it, or sit on the bed. Any which way, I had him. He picked up my lacy bra with his right hand, his thumb moved just a fraction, caressing the fabric. He kept hold of it and then sat down. Legs wide. Balls out. Metaphorically speaking. The toe of his shiny brogue millimetres from my dirty knickers. I knew he wanted to pick those up too. Smell them perhaps. Smell me.

'Drink?'

'Yes.'

'Whisky?'

'Fine.'

His voice was a complex mix, difficult to read. Abrupt yet still inviting. He didn't want to be there. Yet he did.

I opened the minibar, grabbed two Jack Daniel's miniatures and threw one towards him. He effortlessly caught it with his left hand, without having to let go of the black, lacy bra. He spun off the cap with his thumb; a cool, confident move. I had to admit his competency was attractive. I wanted to kick off my ankle boots but decided it was better if I kept them on.

Men. Heels. Yes.

I sat on the bed, arranging myself so that my toned, tanned legs were visible. Stretched. I wrapped my lips around the neck of my miniature and threw it back. Down in one. Look what I can do. He stared at my tanned legs, my red lips, my white throat. I watched him watching me. Here's the thing, I have slept with countless men. Literally, I have lost count. Some of them were poor apologies for men, who smelt of sweat, booze, piss or vomit, any combination of the above. Others were fabulous physical specimens. Muscular, attentive, sexy, beautiful. I've had sex in beds, in cupboards, on chairs, against walls, on floors, I've dressed up, been tied up, played with stuff. I've done it on planes, on trains, standing up, sitting down, bending over, crawling over, I've screamed out their names, I've forgotten their names, I never knew some of the names. The point is.

It's all the same to me. They are all the same to me. Better or worse, they are the same.

Nick is engaged to Anna. That's different.

Anna is in love with his sparkling eyes, his broad shoulders, his blue-black hair, his evident confidence, purpose, humour and intelligence. I'm a tourist, just passing through. Enjoying the view.

Yet, my throat is dry and tight, my hands clammy.

The distance between us was about a metre, maybe a metre and a half, yet the distance suddenly seemed quite insurmountable. How would he get from over there, to over me? Would he ever? For a moment, I thought he would finish his drink and then leave. That he'd pass the test. And I was elated. I promise you, thrilled for Anna. For that small fraction of time I believed it too, all the horseshit about The One, the knights in shining armour, true love, everlasting love. Any sort of fucking love. And it was brilliant. An amazing, startling, hopeful moment. But then, suddenly, he stood up. Six foot one of sex towering above me. Broad, muscular, hot. Then that six foot one was flat on top of me. Lips millimetres from mine. Staring into my eyes, silently asking me how he got there. Like I had all the answers.

I kissed him first. I'll have to live with that. Always and for ever.

He kissed me back. That's his bad.

We started to clutch and pull at each other's clothes, quickly, efficiently undressing one another. We're both practised and so we unbuttoned shirts, skirt, trousers without any awkward banging of hands; bra clasps pinged co-operatively, underwear slithered down thighs. A well-choreographed dance, we seemed to know one another. You know how it goes. Who puts what where. I'm not going to describe the grabbing, grasping and taking. You can imagine the urgent kissing, the shameless licking, the tremendous teasing. The perpetual stroking, sucking and finally seizing. The swift up and down, in and out, over and over. Then, deeper and slower. He moaned, wriggled, slithered over, under, on and in me. I writhed, shook, opened and gasped for him.

It burned, a vivid crimson mix of aching sorrow and in-finite desire.

We didn't speak, not a word. There were sounds. Noise. Animalistic. Bestial moans, groans and roars. But no words.

Finally, we rolled off one another's lithe, sticky bodies, the frenzy abated somewhat, desire satiated momentarily. My hair was damp with sweat and clung to my neck and shoulders. I moved away from him, towards the edge of the bed where the sheets were untouched and cooler. We lay on our backs staring at the ceiling, waiting until our breathing quietened and slackened, inhaling and exhaling in unison. He was lying right next to me but I missed him, already. My body ached for his touch. Bodies can do that. Betray our minds and maybe even our hearts. I think he must have been feeling the same as he reached out to me, lazily land-ing his hand to rest just below my stomach, gently caressing.

I waited for him to tell me it was a mistake. That it must never happen again. I waited for him to tell me that she must never find out. Maybe even threaten me. I waited for him to stand up and leave.

He rolled on to his side, pulled me close to him, his skin melting into mine, fused. He muttered, 'I'm sorry.'

Then he fell asleep. Men can do that. They can screw someone they shouldn't and still sleep. I lay awake, staring at the ceiling. Devastated. Until, that is, I rolled on to my side, pushed my bottom into his crotch, my back into his chest, threaded my legs through his. Then I slept.

Look, I'm never going to say, 'It was different,' or, 'He was different.' That's what every deluded silly cow tells her-self at some point or other, and I know that's not the case, because haven't I *always* known they are all the same.

But.

He was different.

And for all those reasons I haven't got in touch with Anna to tell her exactly how the night went. I'm waiting to see what he will do.

TWENTY-SIX
Nick

He'd woken up at five in the morning. Head pounding, tongue furry, gasping for a glass of water. He'd drunk way too much, and on a week night too. Stupid. His body ached. Overexerted. Like he'd been clubbing. But no, not that. For a moment he'd thought he was holding tight to Anna, a fraction of time when he believed the world was how it should be. Although, why were they in a hotel? Then his mind snapped into shape. Not Anna, Zoe. Fuck.

Asleep, she looked more like Anna than she did awake because her coolness, her need to shock and challenge, were all subdued. If it weren't for her painted nails and the heavy mascara smudged around her eyes, making her look loose and used, he might have been able to kid himself. Her feet stuck out of the bed. My God, she was still in her ankle boots? How had she slept in those? Still, he couldn't help admire her commitment: her legs looked good; toned and sexy. His cock flickered.

He didn't know what to do. His instinct was to carefully crawl out of bed, slowly, so as not to wake her. Get the hell out of there. Go home. Wash it off. Go to work, act as though nothing had happened. Pretend nothing had happened. That sort of louche behaviour wasn't new to him. He knew how to shake off women that he'd done with. But. How would Zoe react to that? Would she call Anna? Yes, of course she would. She'd be angry and vindictive. No doubt she'd go into all sorts of detail. A flashback cast itself into his mind.

It was exhilarating. And shaming. He shook his head trying to dislodge the memory. He couldn't have her tell Anna about last night. It would destroy Anna. He would have to tell her about this himself, wouldn't he? He'd never get away with it. He shouldn't want to.

His mind was a mess; chaos. He couldn't think clearly. Whilst he was wondering whether doing a runner would enrage Zoe, and lead directly to a confrontation with Anna, another part of his mind—a small but persistent, insistent part that he didn't understand or want to listen to—was telling him if he sneaked out now he wouldn't be able to see Zoe again. Well, at least not like this. And the idea blinked in his brain that he did want to see her again. Just like this. They had not swapped numbers; they had not made plans. He didn't know what to do. He was snookered. He dared not move yet somehow his very rigidity disturbed her.

She stirred. 'Morning,' she murmured. Her voice was husky and attractive. She unfurled, stretched her limbs, starlike, across the bed. Invitingly.

He kissed her. Practically pounced on her. He hadn't planned to, but she was delicious. He held her face in his hands and kissed her warm, plump lips. She tasted of drink and smelt of sex. It was dirty and yet somehow clean, a betrayal and yet honest at once. His fingers smelt of her, salty. She kept her limbs star-like and spread, magnificent and naked. She did not embrace him but she did kiss him back. Reluctantly, he broke apart.

'I'd better go.'

'Yes.' She didn't object or urge him to stay a bit longer.

He wished she would. He was glad she didn't. It was complicated. Before Anna he'd been practised at efficient disengagement the morning after the night before, if he ever stayed quite so late. He'd say, 'We're good here, right?' which was an effective dismissal. It was impossible to refute without looking clingy and needy, and no twenty-first-century woman wanted to be either of those things; they always opted to be confused and heartbroken instead. Besides, it was a deliberately vague comment. Whoever said it, or had it said to them, could choose to interpret it in whichever way they wanted. 'Hey, we're good here because you didn't expect anything more than a fast shag.' 'Hey, we're good here because you'll call me and invite me to lunch tomorrow.' Realization of the distance between what was said and meant, and what was heard and understood, was often gradual. Except they weren't good—he and Zoe—far from it. And he didn't dare risk being vague. Slinking away was not possible.

'We need to talk about this,' he offered.

'Yes.'

'On the phone.'

They should not meet up again. He knew how it would go if they did. And yet.

'Fine.'

He picked up his phone. 'Can I have your number?' He felt silly asking for it. But how else could he reach her?

She eyed him. Weighing up his intentions, no doubt.

For one awful moment he thought perhaps she might not agree to give him her number. Not interested in talking to him about this or anything, maybe. He braced himself for the rejection. It already stung.

Then she reached for her phone at the side of her bed.

Relief.

'What's your number? I'll send you a text.'

He told her and then felt his phone throb reassuringly in his hand. He glanced at the screen. She'd texted: Me.

'I'll call you.'

She shrugged, as though she didn't believe him. As though she didn't much care one way or the other.

He hastily dashed around the room, picking through the debris of their illicit night; he scooped up his boxers and socks, retrieved his shirt and trousers. His clothes were entangled with hers, as though their colourful shadows were still having sex. He stepped over the condom packet, almost crushed the empty Jack Daniel's miniatures underfoot, hers tattooed with the imprint of her scarlet lipstick. The room felt sordid, spoilt. Yet exciting, elating.

At the door he paused and turned to her. 'Please don't say anything to Anna, until we've both had time to give this some serious thought and until we've talked this through.'

She didn't look at him. 'What would I say?'

He closed the door firmly behind him. What indeed? As he walked to the lift, the walls seemingly morphing towards him, nothing was steady or how it should be. He felt shaky; he probably needed to eat something, but didn't like the idea. He wondered how he should store her number. He didn't think Anna had ever touched his phone, other than to pick it up and hand it to him. She was not the sort to snoop, search his contacts with paranoia. But if she did? Well, wasn't it the most natural thing in the world that he had her sister's number? Zoe would soon be his sister-in-law. Oh God. Zoe would soon be his sister-in-law.

He stored Zoe's number under 'Joe'.

He took a cab home. The streets were still empty enough for this to be reasonably efficient, still he regretted his choice when the cabby eyed him knowingly and made jokes about it being, 'A good night, eh?' Nick looked out of the window. He didn't know how to answer. He thought of Cai and Darragh's teasing; they'd never believed he could be faithful. It was sex. Just sex. But Nick was honest enough (at least with himself) to know when he was lying. There was no 'just' about it. It was the most incredible sex ever. The feel of her, the feel of him, as he slipped inside her. He shook his head. This wasn't helping. He spent the rest of the cab journey home reading city analysis on his phone.

Nick took a long shower, styled his hair carefully, picked out his newest, most crisply ironed shirt and a freshly dry-cleaned suit. He wanted to look as far away from grubby as he possibly could. He strode into work early, purposefully.

Throughout the morning he kept his eyes on his screen; he was polite although brief when anyone asked him a question or tried to make conversation. He worked consistently, methodically. He watched the markets, replied to emails, filed his time sheets and expenses. He'd drunk three cups of coffee before 11 a.m. He was doing his very best to act as normally as he possibly could.

He thought of nothing other than Zoe. Her lips, her tits, her thighs, her eyes. He tried telling himself he was thinking of Anna—after all, they were so very similar—but he knew he wasn't. Anna would never put her lips there, pose that way, move like that. Zoe practised yoga, she modelled underwear, she liked secrets, she knew some of his. These thoughts were enough to keep his imagination active, he barely thought about how little he actually knew about her. He was swamped with the sensory pleasure he associated with her. He didn't need to know what her favourite movie was, the name of her childhood pet, or if there was a country she'd particularly like to visit.

'So what's up?' asked Hal.

'Nothing.' Nick forced a smile.

His friend wasn't convinced. 'Something so is. Have you and Anna had a row?'

'No, why would you ask that?' Nick was aware he sounded tetchy.

'I just thought, what with you meeting the druggy, drinking sister last night, that something might have gone wrong.'

'No,' Nick snapped.

Hal raised his eyebrows to acknowledge he was taking the brunt of Nick's irritability and whilst he was prepared to work around it he wanted it acknowledged. 'So, are they identical?'

'Yes. At least to look at.'

'Wow. You lucky sod.'

Nick knew which fantasy Hal was accessing; it was filed in all men's minds between being James Bond and playing volleyball with an all-girl team on a beach. Since it was now a reality for Nick, he found he was in no mood to humour his friend.

'Grow up, Hal.'

'What did I say?'

'It was what you were thinking that I was objecting to. Anna is my fiancée, right.' He was such a hypocrite.

'Yeah, yeah. No offence. Although, seriously, what was it like going out with the pair of them? I bet they turned heads.'

'Actually, Anna had to work in the end. I was left with Zoe.'

'Is she as much work as Anna said?'

'More.'

'Will you introduce me?'

'Funny.'

'So could you tell them apart?'

'Yes. They don't act at all alike. And I think Zoe is a fraction taller, maybe. I didn't see them side by side. She seems it.' He wasn't prepared to mention the other differences. Couldn't if he tried. *They move differently, hold themselves differently. Zoe is bolder, brighter. Somehow more.*

At lunchtime Nick sneaked away from his desk without saying anything to Hal or offering to bring back a sandwich for him. He knew that if he explained he wanted some fresh air and to stretch his legs Hal would offer to come with. What he wanted most was to be alone. He needed space to process.

The phone rang three, four, five times. He dreaded the click that would put him through to voicemail. If that happened, he'd have to hang up. He wouldn't leave a message. No footprint. Luckily, she picked up on the sixth ring.

'Hi.'

'Hello.'

He didn't hear so much as a flicker of recognition or pleasure. Embarrassed, he felt forced to say, 'It's Nick here.'

'I'm sorry, who?'

It was excruciating. Nick was never forgotten.

He coughed. 'Nick.'

There was a charged silence.

'Nick Hudson.'

He realized that might not offer the clarity he was searching for—had he even told her his surname? Anna must have. There was still no response. He thought he could almost hear the cogs in her brain whizzing around as she tried to place him.

'Anna's fiancé,' he added at last, exasperated.

'Oh, hello.'

Still, there was no warmth in her voice and yet no anger either. He'd expected one or the other. Something like disappointment skittered across his chest.

'I thought we should talk.'

'Did you?'

'Yes. Don't you?' He subtly changed the tense. She'd put them in the past. He ought to be content to stay there, but he wasn't.

'What would you like to say, Nick?'

He should have found somewhere quieter to make this call. Not that there were quiet streets in the City on a hot, summer lunchtime. Everything and everyone moved at an unstoppable pace. He dodged from left to right, in and out of the shadows of the towering office buildings, avoiding the striding people carrying sandwiches and bottled water in flimsy paper bags.

He cupped his hand around the phone. 'I'm sorry about last night.'

'Which part?'

It was a good question. He'd hoped that his apology, vague and all-encompassing, might do the trick.

'Are you sorry for sleeping with me?'

'Well, yes,' he stuttered.

'How lovely of you to call to say so.' Her voice was icy with sarcasm.

'No, no, that's not what I meant. I'm not sorry I slept with you,' he blurted. It wasn't quite possible to regret it. He wished it was. It was stupid to admit as much, though.

'You're not?' Now she sounded curious.

'Well of course I am. I mean. You're my fiancée's sister. But.' He didn't know how to explain it. It had been the best sex of his life. He'd thought of her all day. But if he admitted as much, then chances were that this whole thing would blow up in his face. Carefully, he said, 'I'm sorry for what I did to Anna.'

'I see. Are you planning on telling her?'

Panicked. 'No, no. Are you?'

She sighed and then slowly said, 'I can't see what it would achieve.'

'Right then.' He tried not to let the relief seep through the phone. It would be somewhat unseemly. Yet it was a relief. He hadn't allowed himself to think about Anna much this morning, his head was too full of Zoe. Besides that, whenever Anna did manage to pick her way through to his conscience, he felt miserable, ashamed, wicked. He did not want to see her hurt, crushed. He did not want to lose her. 'How do you want to progress this?'

'So, we're going to progress this, are we? There is a 'this'?'

He wanted to bite out his tongue. 'I didn't mean that. I don't mean we should continue it or do it again.'

'I see.'

'I meant, how do you want to handle this situation?'

A man on a bike swerved to avoid Nick, who was aimlessly pacing up and down the footpath. The biker almost lost his balance; he didn't fall but he wobbled precariously, and so he turned and flicked the bird. Nick felt a prickle of irritation shimmy through his body. He wanted to yell, 'Get off the bloody pavement, mate,' although he didn't. He had enough to deal with.

'I don't know. Have you any ideas?' Zoe asked. 'Anna

has been ringing me all morning. No doubt she wants to know how we got along.'

'Yes, she's been calling me too.' He'd managed to avoid her calls. He'd got Hal to answer at one point and say he was in an all-day meeting. He hadn't responded to her texts either. Sometimes he cursed the modern world that provided a million ways of communicating with a person. It made it impossible to take any time out to think about anything. Five minutes passing without responding to a happy-faced emoji led to major concern.

'Well? What do I tell her?' persisted Zoe.

'We got on well.' Nerves made him snigger.

'This isn't funny.' Zoe sounded irritated now.

'I never for a moment thought it was,' he admitted more seriously.

'I don't know what to say to her.'

'Oh, come on, Zoe. Don't pretend you're someone who can't tell a lie.'

He didn't want to sound harsh but following the femme fatale act last night, it was hard to imagine she was squeamish about lying to cover up indiscretions. She must be practised in this sort of duplicity. She had done this before, many times. She'd do it again. He was in a line, a long line. The thought should have frightened him, or at least warned him. It didn't.

'You're not asking me to lie to just anyone.'

'No. Of course.'

Well, maybe not *this* sort of duplicity, exactly. This was so much worse. Not anyone. A sister. Her twin sister. His fiancée.

'That's what you want, is it? For me to lie?'

Well, yes, of course. 'It's what's needed,' he said. He couldn't come clean. He just couldn't—Anna would never forgive him.

'At least be honest with *me*, Nick.'

'Yes, it's what I want.'

It was brutal but emancipating. He was being selfish. He was asking Zoe to collude with him to maintain a relationship that he didn't deserve.

She let out another sigh. This one was more accepting, practical. 'So what are you going to say, exactly? We need to get our stories straight.'

'I don't know.' He hadn't thought that far ahead. 'That we had dinner. That we got on well enough.'

'She'll ask you how crazy you found me.'

'She won't ask that.'

'She will.'

He thought he could hear hurt in her voice but that was unlikely, surely. Zoe was tough. Nick read the poster splayed on the side of a big red bus that was passing by. It was advertising the summer blockbuster. He planned to take Anna. With a studied sense of irony, they'd sit in the back row, giggle at the ludicrous plot the superheroes encountered, eat hot dogs and popcorn. He turned his head, and studied the poster on the bus shelter. A beautiful, bikini-clad woman crawled in the sand. She was holding a bottle of perfume; it was irrelevant, gratuitous and yet gorgeous. He imagined Zoe holding the perfume, crawling around in the sand.

'I'll tell her we had a lovely night.'

'Did you?' The tone changed. It was more as it had been last night. Warm, inviting. 'Did you have a lovely night, Nick?'

He decided to be as honest as the situation would allow. 'Excellent, actually.' It was true, and he hoped it was enough; some consolation, because no one liked being undervalued.

'Me too.'

It was just a show of respect because, after all, he had put his mouth between her legs, she'd done the same for him. He couldn't pretend it hadn't happened, that it was nothing. Odd, because he'd always thought it was. Sex. Nothing more than a sport. Until Anna.

And now Zoe.

Yet they were completely different experiences. One was love. The other. What? Not just lust. He'd been there, done that, got the venereal disease. It was more profound than lust. It was imprudent, impressive and unforgettable. He didn't mean to blurt it out, he just couldn't stop himself.

'I'm not sorry for sleeping with you.'

'I see.'

And then. 'What are you doing right now?'

'I'm in Regent Street.'

'Are you working?'

'Not today. I'm heading back to my hotel soon. I'm tired. I need to sleep.'

Without thinking, he said, 'I can be there in fifteen.'

'No.'

'No?'

'No, not now. In three days. If you feel the same in three days, call me then. See Anna first. Talk to Anna, spend the weekend with her.'

Nick felt crushed by the rejection. He was desperate for her, suddenly; like an unruly dog pulling at its lead, he feared he might choke. Yet he admired her restraint. Her sense of fair play. The fact she had a plan. The office workers continued to teem past him, talking into their phones, smoking cigarettes and chatting with their colleagues, oblivious to the road he'd set out on.

Yes, spend the weekend with Anna. Clear his mind. Get his head straight.

Then call Zoe.

Or not.

Probably call.

Probably shouldn't.

TWENTY-SEVEN
Anna

Anna and Nick had plans to have Saturday lunch at his parents' home; Anna had ensured that doing so had become something of a habit since Pamela's fall and their engagement. She wanted the family to be knitted closer together, the yarn intertwined, making a regular, neat pattern that ultimately formed a useful, comforting blanket that any one of them could crawl under for solace and cheer if need be.

She loved going to see the Hudsons: Pamela, kind and interested; George, dour but honest. She had become familiar with the furniture and the knick-knacks, the piles of newspaper and the bookshelves. The Hudsons were not hoarders nonetheless their home was certainly full; every surface housed an ornament, a well-thumbed book or a brimming file. She occasionally came across a small toy that must have belonged to Nick or Rachel, a random piece of Lego or a Barbie doll's handbag, left in a bowl or on a shelf, because no one could stand to throw it out and fully discard their childhood. There were cushions and throws scattered everywhere, suggesting that whilst the house seemed warm at the moment—as the summer sun flooded through open windows—during the winter the family used the throws to stay cosy. The crockery and bed linen were very dated—no doubt bought in the 1980s and now faded through an indeterminable number of washes—but their very unfashionableness seemed to suggest a solidity and safety to Anna. She mistrusted homes that were too tidy or modern, where there were no signs of life. It was clear a family had lived, laughed, squabbled, shouted, cried and celebrated in this house. Sometimes Anna believed she could almost feel the pulse of the place.

Her modest one-bedroom flat that she rented from an anonymous landlord seemed hollow and lacking by comparison. Boxy, unremarkable. The IKEA bookshelves were too neat and nowhere near full, even though she considered herself an avid reader; it took years for one person alone to crowd a bookshelf. Her sofa, bed, chairs, wardrobe were all necessary, practical items that the anonymous landlord had supplied; they lacked charm and style. Like most London flats, there simply wasn't room for clutter or indulgence. She had tried; she'd bought strings of fairy lights and scattered photos about the place, but they did little to counter the overwhelming sense of level-headed necessity. Any one of a vast number of people could live in her flat, probably did live in nearly identical flats. The Hudsons' large, warm, sprawling home seemed specific to them. It was kindly and substantial, big enough to absorb her too. Keep her safe.

Besides, visiting the Hudsons was a delight because Pamela took great interest in the wedding preparations; she absolutely never tired of Anna debating the order of service, the calligraphy on the invitations or the colour theme for the wedding.

The bridesmaids. Anna sighed at the thought. She had been so decisive about all the other aspects of the wedding except that one. She had told Nick that she wanted Zoe to be a bridesmaid but in her heart of hearts she knew that it wasn't ever going to happen, not really. And she supposed she'd have to ask Rachel. It was the polite thing to do. Pamela must be expecting it, honestly,that thought didn't fill her with excitement either. Vera had categorically said she was not the bridesmaid sort. She didn't much like having her photo taken and certainly didn't want to be trussed up in anything that might be peach, pink or lemon with bows or frills. Besides, she had the boys to keep an eye on and wouldn't be able to give Anna her full attention, as was expected, as she deserved. Anna's friends in the States seemed too distant now for her to call on and ask to fulfil this duty. Distant in terms of space, time and emotion. Anna had let those friendships slip. It was a pity—as the neglect of any friendship always is—but inevitable. Besides, many of her American friends were pregnant or breastfeeding; they wouldn't want to run about organizing a bachelorette weekend, or have to stoop to fuss about her train or veil on the day. Anna decided to put the problem out of her mind. She'd think about it later. Sometimes it was important and healthy to just draw a line under an issue. Switch off.

This week, Nick had offered to drive to Bath. She couldn't help but notice that he was being especially nice to her, almost as though he was making a particular effort. He'd arrived at her flat on Friday evening with the most ostentatious display of violet roses, blue hydrangea and lilies. She didn't have a vase big enough and the flowers had to be split into two. They were wonderful. Smelt delicious. It made her sad to have to leave them in the flat—really, she wished he'd waited until after the weekend to buy them.

He said he wanted to take her out to dinner to make up for her missing out the night before. She hadn't been able to decide what to wear (her new pale-pink, floral dress from Zara that was just so pretty or, maybe, simply a pair of trousers and her blue T-shirt with the picture of a pineapple). Whilst he waited for her to make a decision he'd opened windows to let some fresh air into her flat, which had a neglected, stale feel to it. He'd taken her clothes out of the washing machine and put them in the dryer, he'd even thought to lie her much-loved linen trousers flat, as they would have shrunk in the drier. Very thoughtful. He'd taken the time to look at her photos. He picked them up and scrutinized them with an interest he'd never shown before: one of Alexia and David; one of Zoe when she was about twenty-two and, for once, holding a tennis racquet rather than a bottle; a couple of her friends' weddings and children. The usual selection of photos that offered solace and meaning to people living overseas away from their families. Anna came and stood next to him, leaned over his shoulder and looked at the photo that held his attention for the longest. It showed her and Zoe aged about seven at the beach, standing proudly next to the most enormous sandcastle. Both girls were sun-kissed and wore their hair in bunches, sand clung to their wet, skinny legs. Sometimes, when Anna looked at old photos, even she found it difficult to know who she was, who Zoe was.

'I can't think how I missed this one before,' Nick mumbled.

'It's new. It's a gift from Zoe. She brought it with her. I have lots of photos of the two of us but not this one. Zoe has the original. She had it copied and put in a frame. Thoughtful, hey? I was touched. I have a whole album of old photos you can flick through while I get dressed, if you're interested. Then, at dinner, you can tell me all about last night.'

She dug out the album from under her bed. She didn't need to lean over his shoulder to know the contents. She was so familiar with it, she knew exactly which photo followed which as their childhoods were captured, tabulated, remembered. Photo after photo of Anna and Zoe wrapped around one another, intertwined, leaning on one another at a table or near a gatepost, a wall; propping one another up, as though they didn't have the ability, or certainly the inclination, to stand independently. Watching TV, in the bath, on the trampoline. Gappy grins, shiny eyes, blunt-cut fringes. There were numerous photos of both girls asleep, folded into one another, limbs and hair tangled. One where they were sucking each other's pointy fingers. Both the girls identical, impossible to distinguish, except one was often dressed in pink, the other in blue.

'I guess you are the one in pink?' Nick called through just as she was pulling on the Zara dress.

'Yes. Always. They had to find a way of telling us apart, and dressing in different colours was as good as any. Zoe always refused pink. I loved it.'

Anna sighed, trying to shrug off the sense of melancholy that always swamped her when she thought of Zoe as a young child, because whilst everyone else had considered her a total nuisance, Anna remembered that her sister had been great fun, forever playful and, most importantly, Anna's greatest ally. Zoe had always been ferociously protective. Ferociously being the operative word. She'd once pushed a boy backwards over a wall he was sitting on, and he'd landed with a thud and a pool of blood on the concrete road behind, just because he'd said Anna couldn't join in their game—something about her being a slow runner. Luckily, only a couple of stitches were required, still it was a scandal in the neighbourhood for weeks. On another occasion Zoe upended a girl's tray in the school cafeteria because the girl had made some snide comment about Anna's fashion sense, or lack of it. Then there was that time she poured coffee over a teacher's laptop, the day after the teacher had given Anna a B grade; Anna was used to a report card of straight As and had been incredibly upset with the grade, hardly slept all night with worry. They could never prove that Zoe had knocked the drink over on purpose, but after that incident their dad had cautioned Anna to watch what she grumbled about in front of Zoe. 'She no doubt means well, however she has no understanding of the concept of taking things too far,' he'd warned.

Anna decided not to share any of these memories with Nick. It was not the sort of thing people liked to hear about twins. Far safer to stick to the more palatable stories about Anna sitting Zoe's SAT tests to bring up her scores.

And then there were photos of them in their teens. Fewer of those. The colour-coded clothes were abandoned but as the differences became more apparent, it was easier to tell them apart. They had different haircuts, stances, facial expressions. Anna smiled, Zoe scowled. They still had their arms slung around one another, though.

At dinner he asked two or three times how things were at work, how things had panned out with Ivan. When she tried to show the same interest in his day he'd batted away her inquiries, turning the spotlight back on her as though she were a star. Naturally, the conversation she was most interested in was how the evening had gone with Zoe.

'Was it a complete pain?' she asked sympathetically.

He laughed, a little nervous, embarrassed. Anna understood that.

'No, no. She was very—' He searched around for the word.

Anna resisted jumping in, offering one up. Challenging? Inconvenient? Mortifying?

Nick settled on, 'Amusing.'

'Oh.' Anna tried to hide her surprise. Digging, she asked, 'In a good way or a bad way?'

'A good way.' He reached across the table and squeezed Anna's hand tightly, briefly. 'Now, should we go for the shared plate? I always think they are fun, don't you?'

They were in an upmarket Mexican street-food restaurant. Anna had read about it in a Sunday supplement and mentioned to Nick that she'd like to try it out. She loved the fact she was now half of the sort of couple who visited restaurants that were reviewed in glossies. The reviewer had been right, it was vibrant, loud and the margaritas were very drinkable—at least, she thought they were. Nick was nursing his. The fire-eating woman in latex was a bit distracting, though, Anna caught Nick taking sneaky glances in her direction on two or three occasions, although he pretended it was the screen with the Lucha Libre wrestling that had caught his eye. She agreed to the shared plate and tried to decode 'amusing'.

'You're not drinking much.'

'No.'

'Don't you like the margarita?'

'It's fine.'

'You could order a beer.'

'I'm fine.'

'You know, you don't have to drive to Bath tomorrow. We could get the train, then you can relax a bit now, plus have a drink at lunchtime at your parents', if you want one.'

'I don't mind having a day off the booze.' A smile flashed on to his face and he held it there, tautly. 'I'm fine,' he repeated, although she hadn't asked. 'Just a bit tired.'

It was hard to believe he wasn't hung-over. 'Did you drink a lot when you went out with Zoe. Last night?' Anna hoped she didn't sound accusing, although she did feel like reproving him.

'No, not too much.'

Anna watched Nick carefully; he seemed to be deciding whether to tell her something or not. He obviously wasn't comfortable talking about his evening with Zoe. No one ever was. Perhaps a car journey was a good idea, at least then they could have a proper conversation. It might do them good to flee the muggy, boxed heat of the city with all its noise and distractions.

Then he spat it out. 'I thought recovering alcoholics weren't supposed to drink anything at all.'

'They're not.'

'Didn't you say Zoe has her four-year chip?'

'Yes.'

'Have you ever seen it?'

'What?'

'The chip.'

'That's an odd thing to ask. No, I haven't, actually. Did she show it to you?'

'No.'

Anna waited. Wondering what else he had to say, wondering what else he would say.

A slightly manic waitress arrived at their table. She asked

if either of them had ever visited the restaurant before. Then, before they could answer, she began to roll off the complicated names of the specials. Nick tried and failed twice to interrupt.

When she finally paused for breath, he said, 'We'll take the taster menu.'

With a quick nod and smile (it was the most expensive thing he could have ordered, the server was anticipating a healthy tip) she took the menus from them and disappeared.

Nick started to talk, almost as hurriedly as the waitress, about the decor. He asked Anna if she'd ever visited Mexico when she lived in the States. 'It's a popular tourist destination, isn't it?'

'Yes.'

'So did you?'

'Yes, twice.'

'Fascinating.'

He didn't ask her whereabouts, or what she thought of it. Instead, he moved on to wondering aloud whether they would be able to get his parents out for a short walk the next day. It was obvious he regretted cutting the conversation about Mexico short when the one about his parents' stroll dried up quite suddenly. They sat, wrapped in silence, until the food arrived. It was a relief when it did; they both could make comments about how delicious it looked.

'Don't you have any questions about me being a twin?' Anna asked eventually.

Nick looked startled, shocked.

'It's just that people usually do.'

'Do they?'

'Yes. They want to know if we can read each other's minds, or whether we feel each other's pain or like the same foods?'

'I know you like different foods,' noted Nick. 'She's not a vegetarian.'

Anna waited.

Eventually Nick added, 'You look very alike. That surprised me.'

'Twins are technically genetic clones. Freaky word, hey? Very sci-fi, I always think. Did you know that twins are genetically closer to each other than they are to their parents, or even their own children? That's wild, if you think about it. Right?'

'Yes.'

Anna considered what she ought to ask, how much she wanted to really know. It was obvious that Nick was feeling awkward. 'Did Zoe drink when she was with you?' She tried hard not to let a note of accusation taint the question. He'd never be honest with her if he thought he was in for a roasting.

Nick glanced around the room. At first she thought he hadn't heard her above the band playing *ranchera* music; if it hadn't been for the bleak, almost helpless, expression that washed across his face she might have been able to believe that really was the case. She watched him choose.

Choose to tell the truth. Choose to lie.

'No, no, she didn't. I need the bathroom. Excuse me for a minute, will you? If you catch the waitress's eye, shall we ask for the bill?'

Anna looked down at the table; half of the food they'd ordered was still to be eaten. 'Don't you want dessert?'

'No, no, not really.'

'But churros come with the taster menu.'

He patted his flat stomach. 'I'm totally stuffed.' He was already standing up, halfway out of the room. 'You go ahead if you want to. Order what you like.'

Anna hated eating pudding on her own, which she was pretty sure he knew; it made her feel greedy. So she told the waitress they'd skip dessert and that they just needed the bill.

He walked her back to her flat, but then said he wouldn't come up. She was a bit put out, hurt. Naturally, she'd assumed he would be staying over and they'd set off to Bath together from hers in the morning.

'No coffee?'

He was practically a coffee addict. One of the first gifts he'd bought her was a Krups Nespresso machine.

'Better not. Early start tomorrow. I need to get back and get packed.'

'Packed? We're only going for the day.'

'Well, you know, sorted. I want to dig out a book I mentioned to my dad that he's keen to read.' He kissed her on the forehead. Waved, was halfway down the street before she had dug her key out of her bag.

Did he think she was an idiot? He was avoiding her.

It felt like she was wearing cement shoes when she dragged her way back up the stairs to her second-floor flat, each step required a Herculean effort. Once inside, she got herself a glass of tap water. Usually she remembered to refill the Brita filter that she kept in the fridge. But nothing was usual. He wasn't telling her everything. He'd had every opportunity to talk to her tonight, but he was hiding things from her.

Zoe drinking? Zoe making a pass at him?

It was a horrible, nasty, grubby thought although she'd had worse thoughts about Zoe. Thoughts and fears that had proven to be true. Nick had not given her a full account of their evening out together, of that she was certain. She took a couple of paracetamol to try to ease the tension building in her head. There weren't any tablets she could take to numb the pain in her heart.

TWENTY-EIGHT

Nick

Nick couldn't take his eyes off Anna throughout the lunch, he dared not. Odd, because during the car journey, when they were alone together, he'd made a big show of keeping his eyes firmly fixed on the road ahead; then he hadn't wanted to meet her gaze. Pamela noticed him watching his fiancée and made a joke about how besotted he was. Anna had laughed along, but she hadn't tried to find his eyes; she didn't share the moment as he might have expected. Was it his imagination or was she acting peculiarly? Distant. What did she know or suspect? Anything? She looked pale, her eyes were smudged with tiredness. Or sadness. Quite unlike Zoe's, which were bright with mischief and suggestion. Could she know? The thought made his gut freeze. Probably it was him imagining things. Guilt making him wary and suspicious. Part of him believed he deserved to be found out, so he was imagining he had been. He was subconsciously imagining the worst in order to ward it off. Not logical at all—a bit, ridiculously desperate—still, it was how he felt.

He consoled himself, arguing that logically he could not have been caught out, would not be. He believed Zoe when she said she had no intention of telling Anna what had happened. She had as much to lose as he did and, despite her tough-girl act, he was pretty sure she loved Anna, deep down. And down deep, she wouldn't want to see her sister hurt. He didn't dissect that thought too thoroughly. Couldn't, really. Zoe didn't want to hurt Anna. He didn't want to hurt Anna, and yet they'd had sex together, like animals. Why?

He stole another glance at his fiancée; she stubbornly kept her eyes trained on the salmon quiche, as if it could be that interesting. He noticed she hadn't eaten much today, mostly just chased boiled and buttered potatoes around her plate with her fork. She might not know for a fact, but could she somehow sense it? Was it a twin thing? Or was he wearing his betrayal; a mist circling him, perhaps? It sounded insane, yet he felt it might be the case. He didn't quite feel like himself. Not altogether flesh and blood, he was something less substantial, something fleeting. It was absolutely crazy to say so, but he wondered whether Zoe had bewitched him. Mad, right? Obviously. Yet, he couldn't think straight or even see clearly.

He couldn't put her out of his mind.

The drive to Bath had been hell. Instead of the usual chatter filling the time and air between him and Anna, they'd awkwardly swapped pleasantries about the level at which to run the air con. He'd played Radio 1 for the entire journey, letting the DJ take the conversational lead. He had decided not to think about Zoe. Not at all. He would not think of her on her hands and knees in bed, proudly displaying her curvy, sensuous arse. He would not think about her pert nipples, the colour of red wine. Or her crazy, mucky laugh. Or her mouth. He wouldn't think of her mouth at all. He wouldn't allow the thought of her to fill his head or trousers. The problem was when he looked at Anna, he saw Zoe. Zoe's sharp, tapered chin, not Anna's slightly plumper one. Anna's hair was tied back into a neat, almost prim, up-do but he thought of Zoe's hair splaying wild and unkempt across the pillows. They were the same weight, they had very similar figures, although Zoe's limbs were looser; Anna seemed brittle today, tight and closed. Odd, because he hadn't thought of her as closed before, just neat, careful. He'd liked her immaculate, well-ordered ways. What had changed? Had anything changed? He couldn't be sure. He couldn't trust his own judgement. Yet Anna, with whom he had made such a speedy and gratifying connection, must know there was a change.

'How's work?'

His father's question shot through the fog in his brain, not because it was stunningly original but because it was comfortingly familiar. He and his father always talked about work. George, a retired engineer, found Nick's career both obscene and brilliant. Obscene because, well, all that money. So much of it moving about, a fair amount of it landing in his son's pocket. And brilliant, for the very same reasons. George made an effort to understand the markets and keep up with what went on in the City, so their conversations were usually mutually satisfactory and congratulatory. Father and son basking in the son's success. Today Nick's mind refused to respond to the inquiry. Instead of being able to mention his latest client or deal, his brain was devoid of figures, projections, scenarios and even hunches. It was full of—

Her.

'Erm, yes. Fine. Good.'

George waited expectantly. His fork en route to his mouth.

When it became clear that Nick had no intention of adding anything more, Pamela stepped in. 'And how are the wedding preparations coming along?'

Despite his parents being fair-minded, politically correct, all-round good eggs, habit won the day and this question was aimed at Anna. On another Saturday that might have irritated Nick. He might have answered, to demonstrate his interest in the wedding, or he might have talked about Anna's job, to remind his parents that their daughter-in-law-to-be was Yale educated and interested in more than bouquets and seating plans, but today he didn't have the energy. He waited for Anna to pick up the mantel. He needed her to do so.

'Erm, yes. Fine. Good,' she replied.

Pamela looked concerned. In the face of such a blatant lack of enthusiasm his mother was probably drawing the conclusion that they'd had a row. Probably over something silly, like the budget for the stag weekend or who they might ask to do a reading at the ceremony.

With determination, she pushed on. 'We were so excited to receive our invitation.'

'I didn't know what the etiquette was. Whether it was peculiar to send you an actual invite, since obviously you know you're invited, and you know all the timings and details. Still, I thought you'd want a copy to keep,' Anna explained.

'Absolutely,' Pamela replied with enthusiasm. Her eyes slipped to the mantelpiece where, sure enough, the cream card invitation stood proudly.

There it was, in black and white. Well, slate-grey and cream to be precise: Nicholas Angus Hudson and Anna Claire Turner were to be married on August the nineteenth. Just eight weeks from today. Yet Nicholas Angus Hudson had just had sex with Zoe Something Turner (for fuck's sake, he didn't even know if she had a middle name), on Thursday, just the day before yesterday.

And worse, he'd like to do it again.

He wasn't going to, though. No, no way. Zoe had been right to stop him charging over to her hotel on Friday afternoon. She was right to demand this cooling-off period. Not that he was cooling off at all. The truth was, he was finding that far from 'out of sight, out of mind' the old adage 'absence makes the heart grow fonder' was more the case. Or maybe an organ a bit south-west of the heart, to be honest. But absolutely, this was the only answer, he must not see Zoe again. He had to go cold turkey, pray she'd keep her promise to remain quiet about their drunken night together, and move on.

Onwards and upwards. He sneaked another glance at Anna; she chose that moment to lift her head and their eyes collided. For a fraction of a second he felt icicles shoot like bullets. Hell, his conscience was going big on this one. He felt cruel. It had been nearly impossible to look in the mirror this morning when he was getting ready; he'd had to skip his shave. This wasn't right. He loved Anna. He was sure he did. She was beautiful. He appreciated all the obvious things that a man appreciated about a stunning girlfriend— her breasts, her lithe legs, her pert bum—but he adored lots of other things too. She had delicately shaped feet, lovely hands and a cute innie belly button. That was love, wasn't it?

Of course, Zoe had all of this going on too.

He loved how Anna's hair shone, and the way she shook her head when she pulled out the hairband and let it fall loose at the end of the day. It smelt wonderful, her hair. Just shampoo—but her shampoo, a citrus one.

Zoe used a different shampoo. It smelt expensive.

Nick mentally shook his head. This was so wrong. He had to think about Anna, and Anna alone. He loved the gentle jut of Anna's hip bone and the way she almost moaned when he kissed her there.

They both liked to be kissed there. Zoe's appreciation was louder.

Without pulling her eyes away from him, Anna asked, 'Are you managing to complete your physiotherapy exercises every day, Pamela? You know how important they are.'

'I do and I am,' replied Pamela, with a smile that suggested she was rather enjoying being fussed over for a change. 'I'm determined to be as mobile as possible for the wedding. I don't want a stick spoiling the photos.'

He was relieved when Anna finally turned to face his mother, her expression melting into something more relaxed and familiar.

'A stick wouldn't spoil the photos, don't be silly. Just go at the pace the doctors suggest. Your long-term health is worth more to us than the photos,' gushed Anna, reaching out to squeeze his mother's hand. 'We need you to take care of yourself. We all love you, you know.'

Pamela beamed. Anna's years in America had clearly had quite the impact. Nick couldn't remember the 'L' word ever being used at the dining-room table, even though his parents said it to each other, to him and his sister on a fairly regular basis. Pamela looked like a nine-year-old child who had just been given a gold star by the headmaster. Anna did that. She brought happiness. To him, to his parents, to the people she worked with. He didn't deserve her.

George stood up and started to clear the table. Anna jumped up to help and Nick offered too, a fraction too late. 'No, no, you two sit still, stay here and talk to Pamela. I'll take these pots to the kitchen and then get the ice cream out of the fridge. We've cheated and simply opted for some Häagen-Dazs, I'm afraid. Cookies and Cream. I'm not quite up to your mother's standards of home-made apple pie, or even Eton mess.'

'Nothing to apologize for there,' said Anna. 'It was a delicious lunch. Thank you.'

Despite his instructions to the contrary, she gathered the used plates and tureens into piles, picked them up and took them through to the kitchen. Nick listened to her chattering to his father, and to his father's reply; something about what he was planning to plant in the garden. His mother looked at him expectantly. Clearly, he was supposed to kick off a conversation. But he wasn't capable of honest confidences or dusty chit-chat. 'Excuse me for a moment, will you?'

He carefully closed the door to the downstairs loo, which conveniently for him was located at the front of the house, far from the dining room or kitchen. He knew the deal they had made. He was supposed to wait three days. Monday. He couldn't. Just couldn't. He had to pin her down before then. He pressed 'Joe's' number. As before, it rang, three, four, five, six times. He imagined his number flashing up on her phone. Did she recognize it? Had she programmed his name into her phone? Was she deliberately ignoring him or just busy? Busy with whom?

Eventually, she picked up. 'Why are you calling me?'

She had programmed him into her phone!

He didn't hear her irritated tone, he simply felt doused in relief, delirium. 'I need to see you,' he blurted.

'This is not what we agreed.'

'I don't need to wait until Monday to know how I feel about this. I know now.' He was aware that he sounded a bit desperate and that desperation was never an attractive quality. What the hell was wrong with him? He tried to pull it back, say something that he thought she might want to hear. 'We won't hurt Anna. It's just a bit of fun. You did have fun, Zoe, didn't you?'

She was silent. He wondered whether she was going to hang up. Then call Anna. Had he blown it?

'Come to my hotel tomorrow.'

'Sunday?'

She didn't answer, which left him feeling like an idiot. Tomorrow was Sunday, that wasn't up for debate. The bit he couldn't quite compute was that she was asking to see him on a day that she must know belonged to Anna. Mistresses usually implicitly understood that sort of thing.

'Sunday is difficult. Anna.' He couldn't bring himself to be more explicit. Did he need to be?

'Well, if it's simply seeing me that you want, then maybe I should suggest to my lovely sister that we all meet up for the day.' Her teasing tone frightened him.

'No.'

She sighed. 'I'm working on Monday and then flying back on Tuesday.'

'Really?' He was delighted and distraught. It was a good thing that she was leaving the country. This dazzling disruption would disappear then, surely. But he couldn't let her leave without seeing her one last time; he need to be satiated. Somehow, she'd whetted an appetite that he hadn't even known he possessed. Something deeper and darker. 'Yes, yes, OK.'

'My hotel room. Two p.m.' She rang off.

Nick checked his watch. It was two thirty now. Less than twenty-four hours. He couldn't wait.

TWENTY-NINE
Zoe

I didn't plan on doing it again.

But, well, these things happen, don't they?

I tell the concierge that I'm expecting a guest at two. I don't hesitate in doing so, I don't doubt he'll turn up. Then I go straight to my room and wait. I wonder whether I should have suggested a drink in the bar; I didn't, because time in the bar will give him time to think about what he's doing. Inevitably he'll start justifying, apologizing. I don't want to hear his sorry-assed excuses for why he's fooling around; that's just the sort of thing he's bound to offer up over cocktails. Wrong girl, mister. I've noticed before that unfaithful men spend so much time telling their mistress how contrite they are, how they never usually do this sort of thing, how it's out of character and they regret it almost before they've done it, blah, blah, blah. I'm not interested in purging his conscience. The truth is, a drink in the bar would be nothing more than a pretence or a prop. We're past that. We're more than that. Yes, yes, we are. Because this isn't run-of-the-mill stuff for me, either. This is not like when I slept with that tedious excuse for a man that my father likes to call his best friend (or at least, did). I can't even compare it to having sex on my mother's desk, in amongst all her fusty books and papers, with that rather sexy colleague of hers— what was his name? Those affairs were illicit and thrilling, naughty and wrong. True. But nothing like this.

He knocks on the door and I open it. We lock eyes,

searching. I know there's a risk that I might lose him in this moment. He could be stricken and overwhelmed with inconvenient guilt, back away. So I swiftly put my hands on his crotch and lean in to kiss him. Light switch. He pushes me against the wall and kicks the door shut behind him. His urgent kisses rain down on me, hard, insistent, hungry. I wrap my left leg around his legs, my shoe falls off, I wiggle my toes. I find I want to laugh because this is so far from the Cinderella moment, however I'm kissing him too hard to manage a snigger. He grabs my ass and I leap up like a monkey, both legs now tight around him. He holds me as though I weigh nothing. His strength and assurance are impressive. I tug at his T-shirt, pull it over his head, my hands explore his taught, tense body. The wall and his strength prop me up as I pull at his belt, his trousers. It's a relief that there is no hypocritical, bogus demurring.

It's over in minutes. Sated, I slump down the wall. He kneels, then gives in to the fatigue, rolls on to the floor, lies still, holding on to my foot, as though he can't let me go. I listen as his breathing, quick and heavy, slows to something more reasonable. I'm swamped by the sense that everything behind the door is falling away too. As though we're on a raft, drifting, drifting further from the reality. From Anna, the wedding preparations, his parents, our jobs. We're alone. In an endless place without borders or limits, where time doesn't matter. It splinters, unravels and there is only us. This man, with his trousers around his ankles; this woman, with his love slipping out between her thighs. I feel as though I'm drunk or high, although I'm neither. I feel the happiest I have ever been in my life and I feel sick and desperate at the same time as I accept that there's an acute, weighty connection between us. Simultaneously wonderful and destructive. I doubt I'll be able to resist the intensity. I don't think I even want to try. He swoops and kisses my toes, sucks them. His mouth, wet, soft, hot, squashing down.

I know he feels it too.

Later, we do it again, slower this time and on the bed. Later still, he suggests we call for some room service. The air is clammy. Our bodies sticky. Our minds saturated.

'Let's go out to eat,' I propose. 'Get some fresh air.'

He hesitates. 'What if anyone sees us together?'

'They won't, and if they do they'll think I'm Anna.'

He reaches out, tucks some hair behind my ear. Tidy, like Anna wears it. I immediately undo his work, pulling it over my face, wild.

He sort of snorts—a short, embarrassed laugh—as though he understands what he's just subconsciously done and is sorry for it. So he plays with the end of my hair, looks at that, when he says, 'I'll have to go soon. Anna is expecting me.'

I can't pretend it doesn't smart, just a little bit. Pride, I guess. I've always been very competitive. 'Oh yes, of course, you're supposed to be working. She told me. She rang and asked if I wanted to meet up for the afternoon, maybe go to a gallery.'

Nick looks stricken. 'What did you say?'

'I told her I already had plans.'

'What plans?'

I can feel his body go rigid under the sheets, and not in a good way.

'I didn't specify. Thought it best to keep things vague.' I wonder whether he feels bad for Anna, kicking her heels, nothing to do on a Sunday afternoon in this huge city that offers so much. There's nothing lonelier. It's better being in a remote hamlet where your boredom can be blamed on geography. 'She's going to pop over to the shoot tomorrow to say goodbye before I head back to America.'

He rolls on to his side, facing me now. Fingers idly touching my left nipple. My body stirs.

'What time are you leaving?'

'Early flight on Tuesday.'

He looks sad, which is satisfying.

'It's been a great trip,' I say brightly. 'Pretty lucky that the client was prepared to let me stay this weekend. The other models were flown back on Friday.'

'How come you managed that?' He's kissing my shoulder now.

'I'm a special friend of the marketing director. I'm his favourite.' I throw out what I know to be an enticing, intriguing smile.

Nick's a bright man, his eyes flicker, he's wondering exactly what the relationship is between me and the marketing director. How come the budget has been found for my hotel stay for these extra days? Why am I doing a solo shoot on Monday? I let him wonder.

'Then what?'

'Well, I'll check in with my agent on Wednesday. See if she's found me any more work.'

There's no rush. Things are slower than I'd like. I get a steadyish stream of catalogue work but the more lucrative print and TV commercials are rarer. I've never had the big break I so deserve. It's undignified, annoying and I don't like talking about it.

I don't have to, because Nick isn't asking about my career. 'No, I mean then what for us?' He looks at his fingers when he asks this.

I do too. He has neat nails. The white half-moons suggest a wholesomeness that I doubt. It's funny how something as small as fingernails can deceive.

'Us?' I throw out the single syllable doused in incomprehension.

He blushes, actually blushes. It's rather gratifying, if bringing men to their knees is your thing, and I think we know it's mine. Quickly, his embarrassment is cloaked in something approaching anger. Not quick enough for it to go undetected by me, though, a master in deception: specialist subject—people deceiving themselves. I look carefully at his handsome face, so capable of being cruel. It's not his fault. He's just one of those ridiculously attractive men, wealthy and clever enough to get by with unseeing eyes. He's used to always winning the game but he doesn't seem aware that there are rules.

'You're right, there isn't an us,' he snaps, so obviously furious with himself.

'I didn't say that.'

He looks at me, unsure what to say or where to go next. It's always best to keep them in a state of uncertainty. Like lab rats, unsure where the next shock or lump of cheese is coming from. It makes them eager to please.

'We should go out to dinner; come on, get dressed,' he says.

See.

The evening is warm and velvety. People are out on the streets, filling bistro tables or propping up pub walls; the streets smell of beer and cigarette smoke. I like it. Even before I have a glass of anything, I feel a bit drunk.

It's a smart part of town. Nick seems to know where he's heading, he strides purposefully. We eat in the sort of grill restaurant that is hotter than the cooking range they flame the steaks over. It's full of foodie bloggers taking photos of what they've ordered. I imagine the grateful clientele have schlepped from far afield and have waited weeks to secure a table. We get one immediately because we're not the kind of couple anyone turns away. In fact, we're given a window seat; we're the dressing. Predictably, Nick looks uncomfortable. He asks if we can move to a corner booth. I feel he's secreting me away. I should probably mind more but I find I like hiding with him. It's all part of being naughty; the ducking, the diving, the fear of being found out. It's easier for me not to think too carefully or closely about what exactly is going on here. My initial focus was on proving to Anna that Nick is like every other man in the admittedly short but dire line of losers that she's dated in the past. Unreliable, selfish. I think I've proven that, quite categorically. Yet, here I am, still. Spasmodically, I think he too is hit by waves of guilt. I watch him as he checks his phone, plays with cutlery, downs his aperitif a little too quickly. I wonder whether there is a tiny part of me that wants him to suddenly stand up, call a halt, insist that he's going to find Anna, come clean. He doesn't do any of these things. Then I wonder if my only option now is to get him to fall in love with me.

We eat smoked salmon that comes with finely chopped shallots and plump capers, then a mixed grill which includes calf's liver, ox heart and lamb's kidney. I can smell blood in the air.

I ask him about his family but he's reluctant to discuss them. His eyes move to above my head. Anna is very close with his parents; I guess he thinks they're her territory. Or maybe he's thinking about what they'd make of this. Best not dwell. I'm not really interested in his friends, his work or his apartment so I don't bother with any of that. Truthfully, that's all Anna's territory. She's welcome to it. All that dull, domestic day-to-day stuff that we tell ourselves is meaningful, because it's comforting to think so, but is in fact so mind-numbingly dull. Instead, I concentrate on being fun. We talk about music, TV shows and films, I share funny anecdotes about my modelling jobs and famous people I have met through work. Very few of the anecdotes are true but that hardly matters, we're not exactly doing a getting-to-know-you scene here, not for real. We have no future. I might as well be as entertaining as possible in the present.

We talk about sex a lot too—after all, that's what we have in common. We compare numbers and locations, near misses and exhilarating hits. I can tell that he is excited and jealous at the same time. He wants to hear what I've done, who with and where. It turns him on. And off. He is excited by my slutty, careless adventures; he tries to match them with his own. He's also intimidated by them. No doubt I make him feel provincial, tethered. I play with him. Touch his elbow, his knee, his chin. I play with myself. Touch my hair, my neck, my ear. It's tried and tested stuff. It works.

There's one gloomy moment, which I find annoying.

He asks, 'What are we doing? Why are we doing this.'

I choose to answer his question, rather than pretend I don't understand him. 'We're doing this because we can. I can be my complete, fabulous and dreadful self when I'm with you, in total confidence that you'll appreciate me but never expect too much of me. You can be your complete, fabulous and dreadful self with me, knowing I will never expect *anything* of you.'

He nods, relieved, reassured.

That's a mistake, really. I'm annoyed with him for interrupting my funny anecdotes, not keeping his mind in the moment.

I punish him by asking, 'And after the wedding are you planning on being faithful?'

He turns pale. Shocked and gaping, he doesn't know how to respond. Hey, I'm a big fan of Nicholas Hudson but I have to say he looks pretty bloody stupid right now. Making someone confront their own awfulness always has that effect.

'Well, I haven't thought about it.'

'You haven't thought about it?'

'No, not as such.'

'You haven't considered the matter of fidelity yet you're planning on marrying Rose Red.'

He scowls. I'm not sure who he's angry at. Me or himself. Her?

He tries to explain. 'I don't mean it like that. I thought I was going to be faithful. I thought it was going to be easy.' He looks down at his plate. 'Then I met you.'

It's almost touching.

'You can draw a line under this whenever you want,' I point out. 'You called me, remember? I can walk away from this.'

His head snaps up and his eyes plead with mine. He

doesn't want me to walk away. He doesn't want to hear that I can do that.

'And you think that's what I should do? Draw a line under it? Under us?'

There he goes again with the 'us'.

I shrug, indifferently. 'It would seem the sensible thing to do.'

He looks lost. 'When? When do we draw a line under it?'

I'd have preferred it if he'd asked *how*. How has a more tragic ring to it. Star-crossed lovers and all that. How can I possibly walk away from this? Still, you can't have everything.

I pull my face into a brilliant impression of someone who gives a damn. 'Today, right now. We should draw a line under it now. I'm going back to the States the day after tomorrow. I'll return for the wedding. Then we'll just start again, pretend this whole thing never happened.'

I see him taking this in, considering it. Is it viable, possible, probable? I can just about hear the cogs in his brain whirring. I've offered him a Get Out of Jail Free card. I wait, almost breathless. Will he take it?

'Why are you rushing back to the States?'

'That's where I live.'

'I know, but if you haven't got any specific work lined up over the next few weeks, why don't you stay?'

Not taking it then.

I want to punch the air. He's chosen me! Me above Anna. Filthy, sexy, wild, free me.

I want to punch his face. He's chosen me above Anna. Kind, well-meaning, decent, committed Anna.

I do neither.

Instead, I ask, 'Why would I do that?'

'Take a holiday?'

'If I want to holiday, I'll go to Miami or California, get some sun.'

'The weather here has been great this month, and we're set for a scorcher.'

'Whatever.'

I make a big show of stifling a yawn and I let my gaze casually slide around the restaurant. If he thinks he's losing me, he'll work harder.

'Anna would like to have you around.'

'Did you actually just say that?'

We both know that under the best of circumstances I'm a trial to Anna; considering I'm now screwing her fiancé he can't really believe it's in her interests for me to stay.

'Next you'll be suggesting I can help with the wedding preparations.'

He has enough self-awareness to look uncomfortable. He plays with the stem of his wine glass. Takes a couple of big gulps. The Burgundy stains his lips. I want to kiss them.

'I would like you around,' he murmurs.

He looks defeated and hopeful. This Faustian pact is costing him dearly. That's something.

I stare at him, pretending to weigh it up. 'Where would I stay?'

Fast. 'I'll pay for the hotel. You wouldn't even need to pack.'

'So you're saying stay for how long? Maybe another week? What would that achieve?'

'I don't know.'

'I can't stay for ever, Nick.'

'Well, yes, then a week.' Suddenly urgent, he lunges for my hand.

I move it out of his grasp.

'Or maybe a bit longer.'

The wedding is eight weeks away. We both are aware of that. It's as though the number is visible between us, a great big flashing neon sign. I wait. I count to ten. The silence between us screams.

I can't bear it. 'Excuse me, I need to go to the bathroom.'

The bathroom is decorated with iridescent black-and-gold mosaic tiles, floor to ceiling. The cubicle doors are black gloss laminate. There are skinny plastic orchids set near the basins. I suppose the interior decorator was going for East-ern lux, I think it's more post-colonial brothel. I hold my wrists under the cold tap. Cooling water crashes on to my purple veins. My skin looks thin and pale under the harsh light. I think about it. It's risky.

Very risky. Complicated. Cruel.

When I return to the table I catch Nick checking his phone. He hurries to put it away but not before I get a glimpse of the screen.

'Anna?'

'Yes.'

'No doubt she wants to know if she should expect to see you this evening. She must be confused that you're in the office until this hour.'

He looks pained. I one hundred per cent know I've hit the nail on the head.

'Don't do this,' he says.

'What exactly? Don't acknowledge that Anna is your fi-ancée yet you've just tied me to the bed with your belt?' I don't lower my voice.

The couple on the table next to ours are rapt. They haven't said a word to one another but their eyebrows have repeat-edly met their hairlines.

'Zoe. Please.'

He whispers. Presumably hoping I'll be reminded to lower my voice too. He hasn't the nerve to tell me to shush. He swoops down on me, kisses me. Silences me with his mouth, his lips, his tongue. His kisses are strong, deep, fo-cused, probing. He touches my bare arm, strokes me, brushes me. Every millimetre of my body and mind reacts. I want to arch into him; I force myself not to move. Not to respond. I ache for him. I want him. Can I walk away from this? From him? I've threatened as much, but can I? I sigh.

When he breaks away from the kiss, I shrug. 'I suppose a holiday isn't the worst idea.'

But it is the worst idea. His worst idea, ever.

THIRTY
Alexia

We received an invite as though we were nothing more than guests. Not her parents, not important or special in any way. That hurt. Strange, because Anna has never been the one who caused hurt. In a peculiar way I was glad to note that it hurt. Most of the time I doubt that I can feel any more pain. Zoe has numbed me. Gnawed me from the inside, leaving a big hole where maternal love is supposed to be. Seven weeks. She's marrying in seven weeks. This man we know next to nothing about.

David tried to comfort me. 'It's her life, Alexia. She's a grown woman.'

He said the same thing about Zoe when she was drinking herself unconscious, sleeping in places that were practically hovels, mixing with God knows who. I hate him for that. His passivity. His acceptance. I wanted him to rail against the unfairness. Roar at the addiction. Bellow at the loss. Throw stones, throw missiles.

Instead, we visit counsellors and sip tea, talk in quiet voices.

The next time she skypes, she asks if we received the invite and I find myself saying, 'It just seems a little impulsive, my darling. So soon.'

'Don't.' She holds up her hand to the screen. 'I don't want to talk about it. This is not up for discussion.'

Her words are sharp and tight, even though she's smiling. I believe my ears more than my eyes.

'I'm marrying Nick in August. That's happening.'

She sits in front of me, elbows on knees, hands clasped in front of her, nails short and square. Neat. Clear varnish. My daughter. So proper. So correct. So lost. So wrong.

I nudge David in the ribs, but he just looks at his shoes.

She starts talking about the fact that she wants to go wedding-dress shopping soon, that she'd like to have done it with me however she needs to get cracking; time is marching on. I want to take an interest but I also want to tell her this is madness.

Then she asks, 'Have you booked your flights yet?'

And I've no choice.

'We've talked to our family counsellor here and he suggests that by coming to the wedding we are enabling your irrational behaviour.' I sound colder than I mean to be. Having a broken heart does that to a mother.

'I'm sorry, you lost me at 'family counsellor'. I don't live in New York. I live here in the UK, and you don't even so much as mention Zoe's name. How are you entitled to a *family* counsellor?' Anna demands.

'Now, darling, please try to stay calm.'

'What are you saying?'

'We don't think we can come to your wedding.'

'Of course you can!'

'We don't think we should.'

'I want you here. You should be here,' she says tearfully.

I almost cave. I'm her mother. She needs me! How can I not run to her side? But, the words of our counsellor throw themselves around my brain. He says I enabled Zoe's destructive behaviour all her life, ever since she was a child. He didn't need to add the words, 'Look how that's turned out,' they were implicit. As if he needs to lay the guilt at our door, as if we don't already live with that, not at our door but in our kitchen, in our bedroom, in our heads and hearts. Guilt and grief seep everywhere. I squelch about in it, waist deep, every day of my life. I don't say that to our counsellor, he doesn't like that sort of outburst; he doesn't think it helps. I have to keep looking forward. I mustn't keep making the same mistakes. He tells me I have to be brave. Strong. Clear. For Anna. I owe her that much. If we refuse to attend the wedding, maybe she'll pause for thought.

'We can't do it, my darling,' I whisper, my voice drenched in apology.

'We're doing our best,' David adds.

'It's just not good enough, though, is it?' snaps Anna, then she hangs up.

No doubt there's a ball of fury bouncing around her belly. That's what used to happen when she was a little girl; she'd get a stomach pain if she was upset about something. She's always been the sort to internalize. Zoe was much more out-ward-focused when angry. More likely to throw a book or a plate, slam a door. Her tantrums were always fierce, destructive, frightening. I feel like crying, although I never do any more. I'm dried out. I know that the thing Anna will want now, more than anything, is to hear Zoe moan about us. To complain that we don't understand her or support her. That we've let her down. I don't need to be privy to that conversation to be able to guess how it would play out. Zoe would never say anything as tame as we're 'just not good enough'. She'd say our parenting efforts were piss-poor.

And, what I fear most is that she'd be right.

THIRTY-ONE
Anna

Anna waited outside the bridal boutique. The bleaching sunlight hit the pavement in a way which made it appear silver; it was hard to look at without wearing sunglasses. She tapped her foot impatiently; where was Zoe? She really needed to talk to her. It was true that Zoe had not shown much interest in the idea of coming wedding-dress hunting, or in any aspect of the wedding planning at all, yet Anna really hoped she would show up today. Initially, when Zoe had suggested staying in the UK in the run-up to the wedding, Anna had thought maybe she wanted to be involved it soon became apparent that wasn't her intention; the timing of her sister's trip was just coincidental. Anna could understand why Zoe might not be interested in cake sampling (she had more of a savoury palate) and Anna had not invited her on the wine and champagne tasting sessions (for obvious reasons), nevertheless Anna was desperate for Zoe to turn up today. Wedding-dress hunting was not a solitary sport.

Anna was the sort of woman who had dreamed about this moment, choosing *the* dress that said it all, the dress that took your breath away. She wanted to climb into gown after beautiful gown and flounce around in front of a mirror to the appreciative 'ohs' and 'ahs' of her nearest and dearest. Anna knew exactly how this day was supposed to pan out. She should have both her mother and Zoe accompanying her, fulfilling the role of appreciative onlookers, maybe even a friend or two, and all the important female members of the bridal party; but, sadly, that was not to be. Anna swallowed and jutted out her chin. Never mind. It was what it was. Moving abroad obviously had consequences, that couldn't be helped. True, sometimes over the past couple of years, she had felt lonely—expats inevitably did—but now she had Nick, and soon she was to be Mrs Hudson and she'd never feel lonely again. If Pamela had been steadier on her feet Anna would have invited her along; she'd have been delighted, Anna was certain of it. She had to be grateful for what she had.

Anna glanced at her watch again. It was quarter past; Zoe was fifteen minutes late. Anna sighed, she supposed she ought to go in and at least start browsing. It was the sort of store where you had to make an appointment to look at the dresses and she didn't want to inconvenience the bridal stylist.

She pushed open the door and the shop bell sang out, announcing her arrival. It was ridiculously exciting and maybe a bit daunting at the same time. It seemed as though the *tring* had announced Anna's arrival into another world. A magical, forgiving, enchanted world that she hankered after. As her shoes sank into the creamy, thick pile carpet and her eyes took in the endless rows of long, flowing gowns in whites, cream and oyster that symbolized a purity which was apparently still valued (if only as a visual statement), Anna wished more than anything that Zoe was by her side. It seemed that Anna had landed in a place where normally extremely independent women could—without surrendering any dignity—swoosh and swirl, carry flowers and disappear behind pretty lace a place that allowed them to be at once shy and suggestive. The ultimate paradox. It seemed that in here, the bridal boutique, women were given permission to be both feminine and strong, gracious and yet firmly in the spotlight. Wasn't that a Utopia?

Anna stood frozen on the spot, overwhelmed. The air conditioning was quite aggressive yet still welcome; she could feel the hot, sticky street she'd just left falling away. The plush folds of the gowns fluttered. The silks, satins, laces and gossamers moved in a way that reminded her of thick cream being poured over a much-anticipated dessert. A popular 1970s love song was being piped out, declaring that birds would appear, stars would fall from the sky and dreams would come true. Anna, almost woozy with the promise of romance and everlasting hope, tapped her foot and hummed along quietly. She knew all the words. She was happy to sink into the fantasy, leave the real world behind.

She tentatively moved towards the closest dress and was just about to touch the cushioned hanger, when the bridal stylist appeared out of nowhere, like a magician.

'Miss Turner?' she asked.

Anna nodded and didn't bother to point out that she preferred the title Ms; it seemed a little surly to do so. Especially as the stylist had not mentioned she was fifteen minutes late for her appointment, which was kind of her.

The question became moot anyway as the stylist added, 'Can I call you Anna? I know we are going to be great friends.'

The stylist started and finished every sentence with Anna's name; Anna assumed she'd been told to do so in a handbook on customer service. She was about Anna's age, possibly a little younger, neat, trim, wearing a flattering pink bodycon dress. She was immaculately groomed. She wore an engagement ring the size of an egg and it only took a few minutes before it was established that the stylist, Isobel, was to be married in early September the following year, to Adrian. He was, 'Something in the City. Who knows exactly what!'

Anna felt a surge of pleasure when she was able to volley the tennis ball back over the net. Nineteenth of August, Nick, also in the City, 'Equity capital markets.'

Isobel beamed, clearly thrilled they shared common ground.

Anna smiled back. She'd learned to appreciate the kindness of strangers, but inside she felt the familiar numb ache resulting from Zoe's absence; she ought to be here for this momentous occasion.

Isobel began to point out some of her favourite gowns. She had to stretch up to retrieve them. She held them aloft, like trophies, and then if Anna showed any particular interest or fondness she carefully laid them across the back of the blush-pink chaise longue.

'Anna, I'm so pleased you made this initial appointment almost fourteen months before the wedding. So sensible of you, Anna,' Isobel said seriously. She touched Anna's arm gently, a sign that conveyed approval.

Anna appreciated the gesture—she'd been on the outside of the affianced club long enough to value finally being in the inner sanctum—and almost felt bad about admitting, 'Actually, I'm marrying this August.'

Isobel's eyes widened. 'Anna, do you mean in six weeks?'

'Yes, well, six and a half.'

'OMG, Anna!' Isobel looked as though she'd been slapped. Her calm, demure faced fell apart. 'What can you be thinking?' she demanded. 'Anna, why have you left it so late to choose a dress? Are you pregnant? Did you cancel your first-choice gown? Are you marrying in Vegas?' Then, finally, exasperated, 'Don't you know anything about wedding planning, Anna?'

The questions were fired with such rapidity and suspicion Anna didn't think she was really expected to respond and, even if she did, she had a feeling that anything she said would only further infuriate Isobel because, no, she was not pregnant, she had not cancelled her first gown, she was not marrying in Vegas and, yes, she knew everything there was to know about wedding planning.

Eventually, just as Anna was thinking of mumbling something about being sorry for wasting Isobel's time and that she'd leave and look online, Isobel managed to regain some composure. 'Well, Anna, do you see all those delicious gowns?' She swept her right hand around the boutique, taking in ninety-nine per cent of the gowns on display.

'Yes,' Anna let out a breathless sigh. She couldn't wait to start trying them on.

'Well, you can forget about all of those.'

'Oh.' The disappointment was crushing.

'Yes, lead times for the fittings are eight months, minimum.' Isobel shook her head again, sorrowfully.

Tentatively, Anna asked, 'Have you anything I could look at?'

Isobel considered. Besides the commission she made on each sale, she was good at her job and didn't like the idea of failing to answer the needs of any bride, even a chaotically disorganized one who only deigned to grace her boutique a matter of weeks before the big day.

'Well.' She looked Anna up and down. 'You are a perfect size for our samples. I might have something.' She hurriedly disappeared through a door, reminding Anna of the White Rabbit in *Alice's Adventures in Wonderland*. Returning with four gowns, Isabel warned, 'This is absolutely all I can show you, Anna. I'm truly sorry.'

Isobel led the way to the fitting room, where she carefully hung the four gowns. It was an enormous room, almost the size of Anna's bedroom; plenty of space for the dresses, the bride and her interested family and friends. Again Anna fought the huge wave of loneliness. She longed for Zoe's presence. She knew, of course, that Zoe would not be offering girly advice or even pseudo-motherly indulgence; she'd be rolling her eyes, perhaps making scathing or sarcastic comments about the dresses, matrimony and Isobel's fawning manner. But still Anna wanted her sister to be with her, more than anything. Momentarily, feeling a bit sorry for herself, she wanted to shoo Isobel away.

'I'll go and pour you a glass of champagne, if you like, Anna.'

Champagne drinking was mentioned on the boutique's website. It was obviously part of the experience, brought to the twenty-first century through chick flicks which, rather than imitating life, created a world to be imitated. Anna had always imagined she would sip champagne whilst choosing her wedding gown; now she felt concerned that she might look like a bit of a loser, drinking it on her own. But then, would she look more so if she didn't drink champagne at all? She nodded her head; at least it would give Isobel something to do.

Carefully, she stripped to her white cotton pants and plain white bra. The magazines had advised buying new underwear for this trying-on session although Anna couldn't see the point. Unless you knew what sort of dress you were settling on, how would you know what underwear to buy? A strapless bra? One to accommodate a backless dress? It was silly to waste the money. Glancing through the dresses Anna was immediately drawn to an ivory lace, long-sleeved, chapel train gown with a V-neck. Its shape was completely Kate Middleton. In and then out. It was the sort of gown that you had to lay on the floor and step into, like a hula hoop. She had just done so, and was wondering how to fasten it up, when Zoe poked her head through the velvet curtains.

'Looking good, sis.'

'You came!' Delighted, Anna went to pull Zoe into a hug.

Zoe swiftly moved out of reach. 'You don't want to get make-up on the dress.'

Whilst this was the sort of thing Anna worried about all the time, she did not expect such care from Zoe. The surprising show of consideration was touching. Suddenly Anna felt a shift; she felt better, lighter. The experience could now be as she'd hoped and expected. As she'd dreamed. Zoe was here.

'What do you think?' Anna asked. Turning back to her own reflection, she began to swish from left to right.

'Yeah,' Zoe replied in a way that left Anna in no doubt

that she wasn't bowled over. 'I thought you'd go for something like that.'

Undeterred, Anna beamed. 'Well, why wouldn't I? It's gorgeous.'

Zoe moved her head, not a nod, not a shake. 'It's a very safe choice. But long sleeves? You'll bake.'

'They're lace sleeves, and I think it looks refined.'

'I'd say more retiring. Prudish even.'

'It's what I've always wanted.'

'My point is the heat.'

Anna began to feel her own enthusiasm and confidence in the dress seep away. She recognized it was somewhat twisted that she longed for her sister to be part of the process, but she also knew there wasn't a hope that they would agree on which dress was best. She'd dreamed about wearing this sort of gown. Yes, it was true that they were experiencing an especially hot summer. No one wanted to see a sweaty bride. Reluctantly, she began to carefully peel it off. As she replaced it on the cushioned hanger Isobel returned with a champagne bucket, champagne and glasses. Isobel made quite a song and dance about pouring the champers; she insisted on a toast, 'The Happy Couple,' and said that Anna must save the cork, 'For luck.'

Anna wasn't the superstitious kind, and very much doubted that keeping a cork or not might alter anyone's luck, but she appreciated that Isobel wanted to make choosing the dress into an event, an occasion—even if there were only four dresses to try on. However, although it was a celebration, Anna was firm. She didn't let Isobel pour a glass for Zoe; she discreetly shook her head. Undeniably, it would be quite the occasion if Zoe got drunk—memorable no doubt, just not very pleasant.

Zoe shrugged sulkily but didn't insist. 'Oh, I don't care. It's not a brand I recognize,' she muttered.

It was mortifying.

Anna tried on the second dress. It was a perfectly lovely

dress and she was sure it would make many brides happy but it wasn't for her. It was so tightly cinched at the waist, she wouldn't be able to eat and she wanted to enjoy her day, she'd put a lot of thought into the menus. Plus, there weren't any straps; she knew she'd spend the day fighting the urge to hitch up the bodice. So when Zoe loudly barked, 'No, not that one, absolutely not,' Anna didn't argue.

As Anna slowly stepped out of this dress—taking her time—wanting the experience to last, Zoe quietly said, 'You know I won't be coming to the wedding.'

'What?' Anna, standing in her underwear and a pair of high-heeled shoes that Isobel had loaned her, felt vulnerable and not up to having this particular conversation right at this particular moment.

'Oh, come on, Anna. You know it's impossible.' Zoe stared at her sister; far from looking contrite or apologetic she was almost glaring, confrontational, the way she always did, the way she always had, facing down anyone or anything—including inconvenient truths. 'The day would go tits up. Can you even imagine Mum and Dad's reaction? My presence would ruin everything. You know it would.'

Anna did know this but she didn't want it to be the case. She longed to live in a world where her sister coming to her wedding was a possible and marvellous thing; she'd been stubbornly ignoring the fact that her sister's appearance would, without doubt, lead to a terrible head-to-head. It was too painful.

'Mum and Dad aren't coming.'

'What?' Even though Zoe had just excused herself from the occasion she seemed outraged that their parents were ducking out. 'Why? Because of me? Tell them I'm not coming.'

'No, not because of you. At least not directly. They think my marrying Nick, after knowing him such a short time, is a bad decision. They say coming to the wedding is enabling my crazy behaviour.'

'Well, it kills me to say it but they might be right.'

'Do you know, Zoe, I think you'd be surprised to hear that you are the reason I know I can make this marriage work. Why I'm so certain.'

'*I* am?'

'The bit about me which annoys you the most—my ultimate trust in human nature, my need for companionship and exclusive, dedicated loyalty—is actually a result of being a twin. So, de facto, your fault.'

'What do you mean?'

'Well, I'm used to being in a team. I was born into one. I like having a partner, backup. That's why I think marriage is a good idea. I'm used to sharing my space, my life. I like doing so. I need to do so.'

For once, Zoe didn't argue. She stayed silent. After a moment she muttered, 'You want the parents there, right?'

'I want you *all* there,' Anna insisted.

'You know that can't happen.'

'I do,' Anna admitted with a sad sigh.

'Look, if you talk to them, tell them that you can guarantee that I'm not going to make an appearance, then maybe they'll reconsider.'

'Maybe.' Anna didn't feel convinced. Her mother had sounded pretty determined. 'Either way, I'll still miss you. You should be there. You should be by my side.'

Zoe shrugged. 'It's no biggie. I don't even like weddings.'

'I wanted you to meet Nick's family.'

'That is never going to happen,' said Zoe firmly. 'That's your thing. I'm too much of a free spirit to want to make small talk with random pensioners. They won't like me anyway. I won't be able to help myself. I'll shock or offend them in some way. It's what I do.'

The bit about her shocking and causing offence was more than probable, so Anna refuted the only part of the statement she could. 'They're not random. I'm going to be related to them.'

'Yeah, they'll be your family then.' Zoe didn't sound bitter or petulant, as Anna might have expected. She sounded deliberately enigmatic, as though she wanted Anna to probe more, perhaps make pledges that the new family-in-law would never replace her real family. Her real family who had cut her loose.

Anna wasn't in the mood for humouring her sister. 'It's not like I have to choose,' she muttered defiantly.

'I think you do,' said Zoe carefully. Then she did something so out of character that she almost caused Anna to cry. Zoe leaned forward and kissed her sister on the forehead, gently. 'I think we all must make tough choices now. Things can't stay as they are.'

Anna thought she was especially light-headed and emotional because she was still reeling from the fact that now none of her family were coming to her wedding, she'd knocked back the champagne a little too speedily, a little too enthusiastically, plus she was looking for her wedding dress for goodness' sake. The very symbol of her stepping from her old life into a new one. The thick carpet, the sweet music, the sound of silk slipping up and down her body—everything was conspiring to turn her into an emotional wreck!

True to form, Zoe burst her bubble. 'And if you're honest with yourself, you know there's a tiny part of you that's relieved I won't be attending.'

'No, no, there isn't. I'd do anything to have you at my wedding,' Anna whispered.

But Zoe knew her better. In truth she did feel some level of relief, of freedom. Zoe not attending her wedding was, all at once, heartbreaking and liberating. Zoe wrapped her arms around Anna's waist and they stood facing the same direction, looking at one another through the mirror. The two sisters, so alike, yet so dissimilar.

'I'm sorry,' Zoe murmured. 'For everything.'

'I always thought you'd be my bridesmaid.' Anna found she wanted to cry.

'I know you did, baby. But I can't do it.'

'What will I do without you?'

'Why don't you ask Nick's sister?'

'Rachel?'

'Yes.'

'I'm not sure. I have been playing with the idea.'

'It makes sense. You know it does. You should make an effort to get closer. Nick will no doubt be delighted.'

Anna could hardly believe her ears. Zoe never advocated reconciliation, appeasement or pacification. What had come over her?

'Well, if you believe it's for the best. I'll think about it.' Anna didn't know if Rachel would even accept; she'd left it late to ask her.

Anna had recently been feeling desperate enough that she'd briefly considered hiring a professional bridesmaid off the internet. It sounded crazy, yet such a thing existed. They came with hairpins, tissues and a convincing backstory. People did it. Although it seemed extreme. Asking Rachel was probably a better idea.

Anna tried on the third dress. Despite Isobel insisting that Anna was the perfect size for the sample dresses, this one came up a little large, clearly lots of nips and tucks would be required. Isobel insisted that Anna emerge from the changing room and do a twirl. It had a sweetheart neckline and was heavily embellished with pearls. Isobel lavished praise, ohhed and ahhed excessively, still Anna wasn't convinced; even if they could do the work in time, her heart was still with the first dress.

'Do you think I'll be too hot in the lace number?' she asked Isobel, desperately hoping for some support to counter Zoe's negativity about the dress.

'Well, you could have the sleeves altered, Anna. You have time for that. Just. Pop it back on, I'll have a look.'

Excitedly, Anna clambered back into her favourite gown. Zoe pulled faces and said that the fourth and final one, which had yet to be tried on, was clearly the winner. Anna did her best to ignore Zoe's comments and to keep smiling.

Isobel was much more encouraging about the lace gown. 'Anna, I really think we could do something with this. It's just a matter of capping the sleeves. What do you think? Might that be the solution for you?'

'I think it's a brilliant idea!'

'Because you'd have to be sure. It's a sample dress and then once it's altered there is no chance of a return.'

'I couldn't imagine anything more lovely.'

Zoe rolled her eyes. When Isobel was occupied finding a veil to accessorize, Zoe said again, 'I really do think you should try on the fourth dress. Go on, just for fun. Just for me. What's the worst that can happen? If you don't like it, then all you're doing is confirming your choice. And if you do like it, then you've been saved from making a mistake.'

'Oh, I'm not sure.'

Admittedly, Zoe had terrific taste and style; she just didn't have Anna's taste or style.

'Of course you are, just give it a go. That's all I'm saying.' Thankfully, Zoe didn't say anything more as Isobel returned with a veil and accessorized Anna in the dress of her dreams.

Isobel stared at Anna's reflection and then sighed contentedly. 'I'll go and call the seamstress to see when she can come here and pin you. The sooner the better, obviously! As time is of the essence.'

Anna took off the dress, hung it up and was about to pull on her normal clothes when Zoe held up the fourth and final dress. 'Oh, go on, Anna, for me!'

It was actually the idea of having more time to luxuriate in the moment that persuaded Anna to try on the fourth dress. She slipped into it quickly. The fact was the dress did sit well, it did fit well, but it was not her sort of thing, not at all. It had a deep, plunging back and the tiniest barely-there straps. Anna had more modest nightwear! It would be impossible to wear a bra with this dress.

Zoe must have been thinking the same thing at the exact same moment because, in a flash, she unclasped Anna's bra and slipped down the straps. 'Take it off,' she commanded.

Anna was definitely not choosing this dress, but to humour her sister she tugged off her bra; her reflection made her blush. It was too much. Her nipples were quite obvious.

'I think this one is more you than me,' she said.

'A wedding dress that would suit me? There's no such thing,' joked Zoe.

'Why not?'

'Because I think the whole palaver is bollocks.'

'You say that now, but one day you'll fall in love and you'll change your mind,' Anna said giddily.

She wanted to believe this more than she actually did believe it. Would Zoe ever fall in love? To do so you had to be willing to trust, to put someone else's needs ahead of your own, or at least on a par; truthfully, you had to relinquish a part of yourself. Of course it was worth it, because you also grew into something more tremendous when you sincerely loved another person. Love made you more powerful, more passionate and brave. The thought made Anna eye Zoe warily. She was a force to be reckoned with as she was; Anna could only imagine what she might be capable of if she ever allowed herself to love fervently.

'One day I'm sure you'll find your Nick.'

'No, I won't!' Zoe shouted with far more aggression than was appropriate for the playful banter.

'Keep your voice down,' Anna hiss-whispered back at her.

'Why are you whispering?'

'Because we're in a wedding-dress shop.'

'Yes, a wedding-dress shop, not the bloody church. You are allowed to speak at normal volume.'

'Then do, but don't shout. There's no need to get so worked up. I only said you too could fall in love.'

'I'd rather die.'

Anna wished Zoe wouldn't say such terrible things. Why did she always have to be so dramatic? Anna slipped out of the dress and began to carefully put on her own clothes. Isabel popped her head round the curtain and said she had managed to contact the seamstress, and if Anna came back that afternoon at around 5 p.m. they could go through the alterations on the lace dress together.

Zoe tutted. 'You're making a mistake.'

Anna ignored her and, to Isobel's credit, she blanked Zoe's grumbles too; Anna supposed she'd seen worse. Zoe must have been feeling a little contrite because when Anna went to the desk to give Isobel her details and pay a small holding deposit, Zoe helpfully collected up all the dresses and put them back on their hangers.

They left the shop together but were heading in different directions. Anna suggested they go for a coffee however Zoe said she didn't have time, even though she was vague about what it was exactly that so urgently demanded her attention. Before they went their separate ways Zoe grabbed hold of Anna's arm. She held on a little too tightly and with something that Anna might identify as a touch of mania.

'Are you sure about this, Anna?' she demanded.

'The dress? Yes, it's beautiful.'

'No, not the dress. The marriage. The man.'

'Of course I am. What a thing to ask!'

'Because as much as it pains me to say it, Mum and Dad are right. It's been very fast. From winking to walking down the aisle, just six months.'

'I love him.'

'You don't have the best track record in judging men. Do you even know him? I mean really know him?'

'I do. Yes.'

Zoe stared at Anna for a long time. Anna thought perhaps she was going to say something more, and for some unaccountable reason Anna wanted to put her hands over her ears and shout *la, la, la*, like she did when she was a child and wanted to avoid hearing something.

But Zoe didn't say much more, she just shrugged and muttered, 'I guess you do.'

THIRTY-TWO
Nick

Nick didn't understand why he'd asked her to stay. Without question, what was needed was for her to leave. Asap. That was the most rational and reasonable thing. Actually, what he needed was for her never to have arrived in the UK in the first place, but he found that what he needed and what he wanted didn't marry at all. He couldn't stand the idea of her getting on the plane. Leaving England behind. Leaving him behind. How could she say that? So casually, as though it would cost her nothing to walk away. No sacrifice at all. He didn't feel the same. He didn't know what he felt exactly, couldn't bring himself to examine it, but he knew he had to keep her close for a little longer.

When he was with her he found he simultaneously and profoundly experienced two conflicting things. Firstly, with an urgency that was almost fierce, he wanted to get close to her. He wanted to reach her, hold her, gobble her up. He did his best. They had the sort of sex that made him sweat and ache. He got to know every fold and crease of her body. He put his tongue in her mouth, her ears, every hole. His fingers too. He had a need to consume her. Indeed, he felt helpless and frustrated because, even when he was inside her, she held him at arm's length. Somehow separate. Unknown and unknowable.

The equally violent emotion that he entertained at the same time was that he wanted to run away from her. Escape. He didn't trust her. He sometimes didn't even like her.

However, he was fascinated by her. Ensnared. He was not in love with her. He knew he was not because he kept telling himself so. Besides, he was in love with Anna.

But.

It was an affair now. Not a terrible, drunken one-off mistake. It was something that demanded ongoing and elaborate deceit. Lies, plans, excuses, complex arrangements that were awful. And exciting. He told Anna that he was working on a vast, inconceivably important deal and that he had to do many more hours in the office—that old chestnut. She sweetly nodded, murmured endearments and got him to promise not to work too hard, not to stress himself out. She said he wasn't to worry about her, that she had the wedding to plan and plenty, plenty, plenty to fill her days. Besides, Zoe had decided to stay in London for a while, something about the chance of more work—wasn't that exciting? Great news! She beamed as she explained as much, eyes bright and wide. Delightful but somehow a little too accepting. A bit needy.

Zoe stayed in the hotel. Horrifyingly, Anna had giddily offered to share her flat, obviouslyZoe had insisted she needed to stay somewhere more central. It was appalling, if you thought about it. Best not to. Three weeks had passed since he first met her. Time had flown and yet dragged at the same time. He'd told the hotel he needed the room indefinitely. Hang the expense. She hadn't said anything more about when she might leave. It was an unacknowledged agreement that she'd now stay until. Until the wedding? Or something. Just until. She made herself available on most of the occasions that he asked her to. The main complication being that when he was at 'work' Anna often called upon Zoe to fill her time, so Zoe often had to make excuses to her sister. Sometimes in front of him.

'I'm so sorry, darling, I'd love to see you,' she purred down the phone to Anna, 'The thing is, I'm somewhat tied up at the moment. Quite literally.' Zoe caught Nick's eye as he tightened the silk scarves, as she'd requested. She liked being tied down, it was almost as if she feared she might float away. He blushed; ashamed at the lies or excited by the sight of her slim ankles, tethered? Both, he supposed.

There was a glorious and dreadful passion to their bond, one that was so obviously beyond logic or comprehension, rooted in some silent impulse. When he saw her—or better yet, touched her—he felt a punch of pleasure so strong and vivid that he felt sick.

She was dangerous. He knew as much. She was not only aloof, she was insincere. He had the feeling she was always acting when she was with him. There was something unnaturally performative in her manner. He told himself this attitude was because she was a model-slash-actress, not because she was deceptive and untrustworthy, although he knew for a fact she was both things. He had witnessed her easily and casually lie to her nearest and dearest, of course she could—and would—lie to him, if she ever needed to, or even just wanted to. He chose to overlook that. He was deceptive too, he supposed. He ignored that as well. He sometimes felt he was nothing more than her audience. Oddly, he didn't object as much as he should. He found he just wanted to be around her. That more than anything. That obliterated everything else—like the promises he had made to Anna, or the clock ticking down towards his wedding day.

It had been impossible not to confide in Hal. For a start Hal wasn't an idiot. He sat at the workstation next to his own and saw Nick's private phone frequently buzz with texts. Vibrating, insistently, Nick reaching for it immediately, no longer entirely focused on work. Nick had expected his confession to be greeted with laddish whoops and dirty innuendo. A slap on the back, a shake of the hand. Instead, he was greeted by Hal's bewilderment and confusion.

'Why are you doing this, mate? From everything you've said it seems like Anna is a lovely girl.'

The fact that they hadn't actually met was a testament to

the speed with which the relationship and engagement had powered through; what did it say that Nick hadn't found the time to introduce Anna to one of his best mates? Now, he had no inclination to do so. His spare time was eaten up by Zoe. Which woman would he introduce to Hal first?

'I thought you were in love with Anna. That's why you were in such a hurry to pop the question. You said it was unlike anything you'd ever experienced.'

'I was. I am.' Nick stumbled. He felt somewhat thwarted by Hal's obvious disdain; he hadn't realized how much he'd been looking forward to an endorsement. She had been different, until Zoe came along, and Zoe was different again. 'My mother's accident. It was such a peculiar time. Very intense. Maybe I wasn't thinking clearly.'

'So you're in love with Zoe now?'

He tried to explain. 'It's weird. It's as if I've split myself in half and I'm two people. I'm totally content and happy when I'm with Anna—you know, comfortable.'

Hal pulled an expression that said, *So why then?*

'I'm something different with Zoe.' He paused, then took a risk, 'I'm exhilarated.' He'd have been wise to leave it at that, but Nick wasn't acting like a wise man. Besotted, he stumbled on. 'It's like flying through the air. Not comfortable at all, just amazing. Yet, I have to admit, I'm also sort of terrified.'

'Of the crash-landing?'

'I suppose, maybe.' He suddenly felt helpless.

'Then why do it?'

'I can't not.'

Hal picked up his Montblanc ink pen and began to twizzle it, expertly threading it through his fingers; Nick knew this was a subconscious habit that Hal always resorted to when he was wrestling with a problem.

'Did it have to be her sister?'

'I didn't plan it.'

Hal rolled his eyes at the tired cliché.

Nick pressed on with his explanation, hoping to find ratification for actions he knew couldn't be sanctioned. 'I'm very much OK in both separate worlds.'

'They're not separate, though, are they?' said Hal with a sigh, leaning back in his chair.

'I'm not doing anything to Anna.'

'Yeah, you are.'

'She doesn't have a clue.'

'She'll find out. They always do.'

'No, no, she won't.'

'Yeah, she will,' Hal said firmly.

In the deepest crevice of his brain Nick thought that this was quite possible, almost probable; he chose to blank that awful eventuality.

Because they were mates, and there was lad-loyalty, Hal made an effort to be understanding and helpful. 'If you no longer love Anna, then you should call it off, mate. Before the wedding. Do yourself and her a favour.'

'It's not that simple.'

'Why not?'

'I've tried to explain. I need her too. I need them both. They give me different things.'

Nick was exasperated with Hal. The truth was that, recently, everyone irritated him to some degree or other. The security guy at reception who always insisted on seeing his pass, even though they knew each other well enough to forgo the formality; the lethargic young woman who worked behind the counter at the local Starbucks and seemed eternally oblivious to her customers' need for speed; his mother, who started every conversation with an inquiry about the wedding, as though there had never been any other subject between them for the past thirty years; Anna who unquestioningly, trustingly accepted every one of his flimsy excuses for his absence.

Everyone, other than Zoe, seemed lacking.

He could explain that being with her was like climbing

on to a Ferris wheel and being picked up, taken higher and higher. He wasn't an idiot. He knew the moment he reached the pinnacle, he'd descend. He'd possibly crash. He couldn't bring himself to care enough. He was so locked in the moment that the future was inconceivable, irrelevant. Everything after her was somehow less. Everything before her was just before. When he was with her it was as though his life was paused. Yet at the same time, only then was it happening.

'It can't last,' pointed out Hal, matter-of-fact.

'No, it probably can't.'

'You have to choose.'

'I don't know how to.'

Hal looked despairing.

Nick blurted, somewhat inevitably, somewhat pathetically, 'I do love Anna.'

'You're screwing her twin sister,' pointed out Hal flatly. 'That doesn't sound like love to me.'

He loved her in a way. Not in the pure and clear sense he had before. His affair with Zoe had tainted, ruined all that. He grieved for that, but what he felt for Zoe—or rather, what he felt when he was with her—was, he found, compensatory.

'Mate, break it off. It's the only decent thing to do.'

Hal's heavy-handed, pedestrian solution disappointed Nick. He'd hoped his friend would understand the nuances, the difficulties.

'How would that help? Do you think I could ride off into the sunset with Zoe?'

'Is that what you want?'

'Maybe.'

He wanted it more than he didn't want it. Although he couldn't imagine it. Not really, not absolutely. Zoe was not the happily-ever-after, settling-down type and, even if she was, he could hardly swap one twin for the other. What would their family make of that? That wasn't the solution. There was no solution.

When he was with her, he tried to think rationally, logi-cally, critically. He looked for a reason to end it. Not a rea-son, exactly; there were plenty of those. An excuse. A way? An opportunity? But then he would find some new area of her skin that had never been touched, uncharted—around the back of her neck, between her toes, in the crook of her elbow—and then he'd forget to think. He'd just feel. Feel wonderful. More often than not they couldn't afford the luxury of a night or even an afternoon. Then they'd meet up for twenty minutes in his lunch break. They'd bang out their needs in underground car parks, in the toilets in bars, or in back alleys behind theatres and restaurants. Skirt up, knickers pulled aside, zip down, cock out, then in. Then out again. Barely stopping to swap pleasantries.

He just couldn't walk away from her.

THIRTY-THREE
Anna

The moment Anna walked into the bridal shop she could sense a change in the atmosphere. She was pretty attuned to such things, having spent a lifetime watching the nuances of Zoe's moods which, more often than not, impacted all those around them. However, you didn't have to be Sherlock in this case; the atmosphere was akin to a particularly frosty morgue. The *tring* of the bell heralding her entrance was the same, the thick plush carpet, the rows of fluttering silks and satins were just as they had been that morning, but Isobel's smile and ingratiating manner had completely vanished. There was a second woman sitting on the blush-pink chaise longue. She wasn't as groomed as Isobel; she had an earnest, hardworking, hard-done-by look about her., As she wore a tape measure around her neck., Anna guessed she was the seamstress. Anna's wedding gown lay between them. Isobel jumped to her feet the moment Anna set foot in the shop.

'Good evening, Miss Turner.'

Anna wondered what had happened to thrust them back into such formal territory.

'I'm sorry to have to tell you that we will not be able to make the alterations to the lace gown after all. Although, I'm sure that comes as no surprise to you.'

It did come as a great surprise, and Anna's transparent face must have conveyed as much.

'It's damaged,' Isobel added, failing to hide her outrage. 'Ruined, actually.'

Isobel stared at Anna with a blatantly accusatory expression. The seamstress woefully turned the dress over. There was a sizeable piece of fabric, maybe ten centimetres square, missing from one of the back panels of the skirt. Anna couldn't think how the dress could have been accidentally damaged in such a way. It looked as though a piece had been deliberately cut out.

'You must have noticed when you tried it on,' Isobel insisted.

'No, I didn't. It wasn't damaged then,' mumbled Anna.

'Wasn't it? No, I thought as much.'

Anna turned scarlet as she understood what was being insinuated. 'Someone must have tried it on after me,' she offered, searching around for a rational explanation.

The dress had been perfect. Just perfect.

'No one has, I put it in the stockroom right after you left,' said Isobel emphatically.

Anna had no reason to doubt her.

'But—' Anna couldn't think how to finish the sentence. She stood in a pool of frustration and embarrassment. Disappointment and fear ran through her body.

'I thought perhaps you had split it, accidentally of course, when you were taking it off,' offered the seamstress, kindly.

She turned her big brown eyes towards Anna, and Anna knew that whilst the seamstress wished this was the case, she didn't believe it to be true. Anna sometimes looked at those who dropped in at the centre in a similar way when they lied to her about taking their medication, paying their bills or when they'd last got drunk.

The seamstress allowed her gaze to drop back to the ruined gown. 'But…'

The damage was obviously not the result of a careless and unfortunate rip in a seam. The missing section was an almost perfect square; it looked as though someone had taken scissors to the dress.

Anna felt sick. Zoe.

'Perhaps it was damaged when I tried it on after all,' she stuttered. It was impossible to say anything else.

'We thought you might say as much,' said Isobel with a disgruntled sigh. 'We'll never know, will we? We don't have CCTV in the changing rooms, more's the pity.' She was obviously dying to accuse Anna of trashing the gown yet couldn't quite go so far.

Anna's face was scarlet, with difficulty she forced herself to say, 'You can't think I did this.'

'Someone did,' muttered Isobel ominously.

'But what motive would I have for destroying the dress I loved?'

'Maybe you were just planning on putting a small tear in the fabric and then asking for a discount. Stranger things have happened.'

'No!' Anna was horrified and mortified in equal measure. 'This dress will need a new panel; why would I cause so much damage?'

'Perhaps you got carried away.'

Anna never got carried away. Zoe, however, was rarely anything other than impetuous. Anna wondered whether she ought to just offer to buy the dress, damaged and useless as it was. They clearly thought she was responsible for ruining it and, in a way, she was because she had brought Zoe to the shop in the first place.

'Can anything be done?'

'No. We can't match the lace. At least, not in time for your speedy wedding.' Isobel said the words 'speedy wedding' in a tone of voice that others reserved for announcing a paedophile had been hired as the school caretaker.

Sick and lost, Anna realized she had no choice. She didn't want to believe the only thing that could be true. Whilst continuing to tell herself that she had to be wrong, she knew she wasn't, so she felt a moral obligation to fix what Zoe had broken. 'Well, since it seems that the only explanation is that I accidentally ripped the fabric when I was taking the dress off—', it was just a common-or-garden dress now, no longer a gown, 'obviously I'll pay for the replacement lace and the work required to make it as good as new—at least that way it can be returned to the shop floor as a sample.'

Isobel shifted from one foot to another; would she be the sort to accept the pretence, rather than make a fuss and a scene?

'And I'll take one of the other dresses too because, well, obviously I'll need something.'

Isobel beamed at the thought of still receiving her commission.

'Which one, Anna?' Isobel asked in a considerably friendlier tone, all smiles and nods again.

'Well, one was a little tight at the waist and the other drowned me,' Anna admitted. 'I suppose that leaves me with the backless one.'

The one Zoe wanted.

THIRTY-FOUR
Nick

Last night, she'd come to his flat for the first time. It was a risk. There was always the chance Anna would drop by and let herself in—she had a key—but it was a small chance as yesterday he hadn't had to make an excuse to Anna, for once. She told him she was busy and couldn't see him. She was attending a lecture at Conway Hall entitled *Action for Happiness*. Excitedly she told him, 'It's about how to build resilience and boost well-being. I think I'll pick up some brilliant tips to pass on to those who visit Drop In.'

'I'm sure you will.' Oddly, it wasn't difficult to engage with Anna; of course not, she was still delicious and optimistic.

'You could come with me.'

It was, however, difficult to commit to her because Zoe sat firmly, decisively in his consciousness. 'Oh no, I don't think it's my type of thing.'

'I suppose not.' Anna stood on her tiptoes, leaned in and kissed him on the cheek.

An arguably inevitable consequence of his sensual, adventurous relationship with Zoe was that his sexual relationship with Anna—never the most zinging—had become increasingly flat. If she stayed over, they usually just kissed and cuddled, fell asleep in each other's arms. A settled comfortableness that might be more expected of a couple who had been married for a few years and had a clutch of small, exhausting kids to deal with. On the rare occasion that they did make love it was careful, courteous, almost chaste.

'Well, don't be lonely,' Anna added.

'No, no, I won't be.' She smiled at him, waiting for him to elaborate, offer an explanation as to how he might fill his time without her.

'I've a lot of work to get through,' he said lamely.

'Hey, you know what they say? All work and no play makes Jack a dull boy.'

Briefly he wondered, was she complaining? Was he boring her? Saving his best self for Zoe now. He felt a splinter of guilt slice through him.

Then she beamed at him, reassuringly. 'Just don't work too hard, hey? I worry about you. You look shattered.'

It was true, he wasn't getting much sleep.

Zoe had heard that Anna was occupied and had seized the opportunity. She arrived wearing a Burberry trench coat and the strappy open-toed ankle boots that she'd worn the first night they'd met. He opened the door and she held the coat wide. She was stark naked underneath. Breathtaking.

'Did you travel here by tube? Dressed like that? Undressed like that?'

'Yes.' She pushed him in the chest.

He walked backwards in the direction of the bedroom. Hungrily kissing her, grabbing her body. He fell on to the bed and she climbed on top of him. He inched her out of the coat. He could smell her sweat and her sex, it stuck to her. Had she been nervous on the journey over? She must have been. Even Zoe. Yet, she'd done it. For him. It was thrilling. Irresistible. He had the window open because they got hot. The sounds of the street—a wailing ambulance, traffic, laughter—sailed in and cool air licked. He quivered with the thrill of it. He could ask her anything. Ask her to do anything.

Afterwards, spent, sticky and splayed, she dug in her handbag and pulled out some French cigarettes.

'You smoke?' he asked, surprised. Not surprised so much that she smoked—he knew she carefully nurtured as many bad habits as she possibly could—he was more surprised that she hadn't smoked in front of him before. That he hadn't known before. It unnerved him how little he knew about her. Finding out new things about your lover was supposed to be a good thing but with Zoe discovery only made him feel as though he was on thin, cracking ice.

'Sometimes. I have an oral fixation and I can't walk about with your cock in my mouth. Everything else that tastes good is calorific; this is the only alternative.' She shrugged and lit up, without asking whether she could.

He had a no-smoking policy in his flat. He had sometimes caused a flicker of offence when he asked merry dinner guests to go outside to light up. He'd only ever smoked the occasional cigarette back in his university days, before he had the balls to say he didn't care how cool it was, smoking led to a long, slow, painful death and he didn't want that. She offered him the cigarette now and he didn't hesitate, he accepted it, lit it, took a drag. Like a helpless, gormless teen. The nicotine hit the back of his brain, foul. He was licked by inconvenient although, arguably, inevitable qualms—after all, he was marrying this woman's sister in four weeks' time.

'Don't you ever feel bad?' he asked.

'Do you?'

By answering his question with a question she had effectively shifted responsibility. He didn't know what to say. Didn't have the answers. She stared at him. Accusingly. Aware of as much. This thing, how long could it last? How could it end? He couldn't imagine.

Tutting with impatience, she snapped, 'People bury their heads in the sand all the time, Nick. How else would we function?'

'What do you mean?'

'Well, the world is full of horrible truths. None of us can cope with them. A new cancer case is diagnosed every twenty seconds in the United States.' Defiantly she dragged on her cigarette. She grabbed a pillow and propped it behind her back, sitting up, naked but not exposed, just glorious. It was too hot to need the duvet or blanket, they never bothered with sheets either. 'People are dying for the lack of immunization kits that cost a few dollars, but here in the West a modest two-coffees-a-day habit costs seventy-five thousand dollars over the course of your working life. Who thinks about that?' She stared at him, hostility hovering somewhere under her eyes. 'Every two minutes an American is sexually assaulted. Twelve-year-olds are recruited into armies. I could go on.' She rattled out the statistics, barely pausing, allowing no room for compassion or even horror. 'Life isn't fair and we're all going to die, Nick. We can't think about it. We don't think about it. We just have to grab our pleasure where we can. It's pathetic but it's all we have.'

He was surprised, she was more like her sister than he'd ever have imagined. Those were the sort of facts that Anna might splurge. Not ones about cancer and immunization kits, specifically—Anna's concerns were primarily for the homeless, abused wives, people with mental health issues—yet they were both aware. Notably, however, their responses and reactions to the horror were diametrically opposed. Whereas Zoe was happy to bury her head in the sand or pursue a hedonistic lifestyle to salve the terror, Anna tried to help, to ease. It was obvious who was the better woman. The truth was, he was drawn to Zoe because he wasn't a good person either. Not especially. Yeah, he bid extravagantly at charity auctions at corporate dinners and if he was heading to a tube station, pissed, he'd drop a tenner into the paper cup of the random homeless man who slept on his street corner; same one, different one, he wasn't sure. He'd never cheat his taxes or insurance. He often gave other drivers right of way and rarely the finger. Not a bad man.

But not a good man either.

Zoe took a long, slow drag on her cigarette and then casually blew out the smoke in rings. He'd never seen anyone do that in real life, it was like something from a cartoon. It should have been comical; it was mesmerizing. He got out of bed and headed towards the kitchen, intent on making coffee. The evening heat soaked through the walls, the floor, the curtains. He could smell their sex. He'd have to change the sheets when she left. Shower, tidy up so that he could eradicate any sign of her. Was Anna likely to smell the smoke lingering? How would he explain that? Nick sighed. What was he doing?

He didn't ask Zoe, he knew she preferred a double espresso, laden with sugar, so that's what he prepared. They both needed the energy. She padded through to the kitchen behind him, still naked and careless of it. Anna always reached for his towelling bathrobe before getting out of bed; she'd place it within easy reach before they made love.

Zoe opened and closed a couple of cupboards until she found what she was looking for. 'Whisky?' She reached for two glasses, without waiting for his response.

Nick hesitated. He never quite knew how to react when Zoe drank. Anna said she was an alcoholic, yet she seemed to handle her drink with perfect composure. She didn't stumble into unsightly, demeaning stupors, she didn't pick fights with him or strangers. She took risks mostly when drunk. Sexual ones—like giving him a blow job in the cinema—but she took sexual risks when she was sober too. It was her thing. He wondered whether straight-laced Anna had, after all, exaggerated the situation. Not on purpose or through any sense of malice, of course, just because she was so temperate herself. Had she misinterpreted a few heady nights, even years, as alcoholism, when in fact it was simply high spirits and symptomatic of most people in their twenties. Or was it possible that Zoe was, indeed, an alcoholic and whilst currently handling her drink well enough, she'd one day, without warning, tip into something dark and destructive? He didn't know and he didn't know how to ask without talking about Anna, which he preferred not to do.

He accepted the whisky. Sipped it, as did Zoe whilst she mooched around the kitchen, familiarizing herself with his possessions. He tried to shake the feeling that he was a primary school teacher under the dreaded scrutiny of an Ofsted inspector, an anxious, incapacitating feeling that his sister had once described to him. Or, was he more like a teenager whose music collection was being scrutinized by the coolest kid in the year? Did she approve of his tastes or find him lacking? It mattered to him, although he wished it didn't. It shouldn't, because she wasn't supposed to be important to him. Yet, he knew she was.

Her long fingers, tipped with red varnish, reached for the Bagley 'Grantham' art deco green glass vase on the table. 'This is lovely.'

It had to be the twin thing. He watched her stroke the opaque class, practically caress it. 'Made by Bagley. Designed by Alexander Hardie Williamson, I'd say. My money is on this being an early work. 1930s, wouldn't you agree?'

Nick didn't know what to say. He shrugged. The vase was a gift from Anna—his first gift from her, actually. Did Zoe know that? It was possible that Anna had discussed the present with her. Was she waiting for him to admit as much?

It became obvious that she had surmised the source when she added, 'Anna has a near obsession about green glass. I've trailed around endless yard sales and *brocantes* with her in pursuit of some piece or other. This is an especially terrific example.'

'I don't know much about it myself,' he commented, embarrassed.

Embarrassed that Anna's obvious care was standing, visible, between them. Unprotected. Delicate.

'We should all get together, you know,' said Zoe suddenly.

'That's a stupid idea.'

'No, it isn't. I can be careful. She wouldn't guess.'

Nick stared at her in disbelief.

'Look, she thinks it's weird we haven't all met up. She thinks we've only met that first time. She's no doubt assuming I've offended you in some way, that we had a row.'

'Well, let her think that. It's the safest.'

'Has she said anything to you?'

Nick shrugged, uncomfortably. Anna had repeatedly said that she'd like to rearrange the dinner that was supposed to take place between all three of them; he'd gently batted away her comments with the excuse that he was too busy at work.

'Well, she's always nagging me,' continued Zoe. 'We need to be able to all be together.' Zoe examined her nails, as though this conversation only merited half her attention. 'We should do it before the wedding.'

The wedding. He couldn't imagine that day. For a million reasons. 'Why? She told me that you're not coming.' Then, almost accusatory, he said, 'She's really upset about that.'

'Sorry, Nick, would you prefer it if I was there? Took up my duty as bridesmaid?' Zoe's voice dripped with sarcasm.

He couldn't answer her. He didn't need to.

'Thought not. I'm doing you a favour. I didn't want to turn up and distract you.'

His head was spinning. 'We're not meeting up.'

'We have to, eventually. What about after the wedding? We'll have to find a way of getting along then.'

Stonily he said, 'Don't be cruel. She's your sister.'

'And she's your fiancée.'

Zoe sat down on a kitchen stool. Her legs slightly apart, for balance. She sat there like a deity, yet she was flesh and blood; he couldn't help but look between her thighs.

'Well, you'll have to come up with another excuse besides work commitments. She's beginning to be suspicious as to why we can't all get together. No one's diary is this busy.'

'Can't you tell her you have to go back to the States?'

'You want me to go back to the States?'

'No. Just say you are. Pretend you've left the country.'
He knew he sounded desperate.

'Then hide under her nose? Classy.'

'London is a big place.'

'What if she talks to my parents and they say I'm here
and she says I'm in New York?'

'That won't happen. Your parents never talk about you.'
He regretted the words the second they left his mouth.

Zoe immediately looked distraught, displaying a vulnerability he'd never before imagined existed. Unthinking,
she hurled the vase across the kitchen. People say those
moments happen in slow motion but for him it happened
at double speed. One moment the precious gift was being
cradled, the next it was spread in a thousand jagged pieces
on the floor. Instantly, Zoe seemed stricken and regretful.
She flew to the broken glass and started to scoop it up with
her bare hands. Blood spilt through her skin in half a dozen
places, like tiny red flowers pushing through the ground in
springtime.

'I'm sorry, I'm sorry. Anna's vase. Poor Anna's vase.'
Now she was kneeling among the shards, cutting her shins
and knees.

Nick dragged her off the floor, shook her hands free of
glass. Horrified, he held her bleeding hands under the running tap, trying to clear the wounds of glass. With some effort, and after some time, he was able to establish that the
cuts were largely superficial and he reassured himself that
there was no glass stuck in her hands or legs. He fetched
a clean towel and carefully, gently patted her dry. She was
crying quietly now. Not herself at all. Her mascara running
down her face, making her look bruised and used. Her nose
and eyes red. Almost ugly. Suddenly and urgently he wanted
to stem the sense of her susceptibility and weakness. He
grabbed hold of the hair close to the back of her head. He
pushed his lips on to hers and kissed her hard. When she

broke apart, she seemed to have one hundred per cent re-covered her cool.

She whispered. 'We do have to meet up, the three of us. We have to be able to behave normally around her. You may not believe it, but I'm trying to protect her.'

'By sleeping with her fiancé?'

'I'm afraid you don't get to play morally outraged. You, least of all people.'

He shrugged, not indifferently, not apologetically. More resigned. It was too true.

Zoe sighed as though she felt sorry for him. 'Her first husband was just the same.'

'What?' He'd misheard her.

'Larry. That pitiful apology of a husband was just the same. Couldn't keep it in his trousers but swore he didn't want to hurt her. Not that it was me he was sleeping with, I hasten to add. No, it was her supposed best friend.'

'Anna has never been married.'

Zoe smiled, the sort of smile that was never intended to reach the eyes but simply to send a message, a chill. 'Yes, she has. Didn't she tell you? No, it's clear from your face that she didn't.'

'I don't believe you.' A great wave of fear and anger swept through him, from his feet, up his legs, through his back and buttocks, lodging in his head and fists, which he clenched. He glared at Zoe. It had to be another one of her games.

'I don't blame you. But the point is, you're unsure. You don't know for certain. You don't know her. Not at all.'

'I love her.'

'Then why is your sperm dried on my thigh?'

She said this sort of thing and it left him somehow feeling more urgent for her. Feverish, fanatical almost. Untethered. As he looked at his own clenched fist, white and patched red with pressure, he suddenly wanted her out of his sight. She was mad. Dangerous. Trouble. He'd known all of this from the outset. How had he allowed himself to forget? To pretend it was otherwise.

'I think you should go now.' He managed to make his voice sound calm, although his head and heart raced.

'OK,' she nodded, accepting his rejection with a cold unconcern that pained him.

She didn't care. He'd risked so much, and she didn't care. Not at all. He felt like a fool.

'I just need to pee.'

He moved around the bedroom, clearing away their debris, her existence. The cufflink box she'd used as a makeshift ashtray, because neither of them had been inclined to leave the bed to find a more suitable receptacle, the condom packet; he found one of her boots under the bed, another by the window under the chest of drawers. He looked about for her clothes but then remembered she hadn't arrived in any. 'I can give you a shirt and some shorts to travel home in. I'll call you a taxi.'

'I can't hear what you're saying. Come in here.'

Blindly, he followed her instructions and sheepishly pushed the door of the bathroom open. She was wiping herself. He could smell her urine. Sweet, yet vinegary. Contradictory. He should have felt repelled but he was drawn in. He swooped down on to his knees and started to kiss between her thighs. She moaned, allowed it. She placed her cut hand on his head. He looked up to see if he was pleasing her. He wanted to please her. She treated him to one of her slow, private smiles.

All thoughts of the taxi were forgotten.

THIRTY-FIVE
Anna

'What's up with you, girl? You look awful.' Vera, as ever, was straight to the point. 'You look like you've done twelve rounds with Mike Tyson,' she joked.

Anna gave an almost imperceptible shrug of her skinny shoulders. She'd woken in a dreadful mood. She couldn't quite explain it and she couldn't get past it, so it was the worst type of mood. She'd quickly calculated whether her period was due; it wasn't. Yet she had the sort of dull, dragged-down feeling that she often associated with that time. 'I didn't sleep well.'

Vera waved both her hands in the air and shouted, 'No, no, no, no. Don't go showing off. Are you going to tell me it was because you had fantastic sex with your fiancé all night? That is not kind. Remember, some of us have a love life that is so dry, it's a desert.' Vera had been single for four years now. Most of the time this didn't bother her much, her two boys provided all the love and testosterone she needed in one household, thank you very much. Even so, no one in her position wanted to hear the intimate details of other people's sex lives.

'I didn't see Nick last night,' Anna replied.

'So that's why you've a long face. You miss him.' Vera plonked herself down in the other chair on the reception, next to Anna.

It was early. Drop In was open although, except for one or two of their regulars who slept on the street and sometimes came in for an early shower, the majority of people tended not to come by until around ten.

'I'm fine, absolutely so,' Anna lied. She forced one of her bright smiles and looked Vera in the eye; Vera was harder to fool than most, but Anna was keen to manage it. 'I went to a lecture at Conway Hall. It was very thought-provoking; my mind was whirling all night. That's why I didn't sleep. I'm just a tiny bit tired.'

It was more than that, however Anna didn't know how to get into the conversation. Oddly, sadly, Anna had found since she'd got engaged to Nick that she hadn't been quite as honest with Vera as she had beforehand. Even though she'd thought about it a lot over the past couple of weeks, she had not told Vera about the wedding-dress incident. It was too weird. She hadn't told Nick either. No one would understand. Nor had she ever found a way to tell Vera what she'd heard Nick say to his friends in the pub, all that hurtful nonsense about fidelity. There had been so many occasions when she'd just wanted to blurt it out. Maybe she should have said something at the time, instead of bottling it up, trying to deal with it on her own. Looking back now, she realized that Vera would have given her some clear advice and direction, but she hadn't said anything and the moment was long past. It wasn't that she wanted to be secretive, as such, it was as though in order to move closer to Nick she had to put a barrier between her and Vera. It was a shame because, maybe, if she had spoken to Vera she wouldn't have felt a need to unburden herself to Zoe, something she deeply regretted. Zoe had a way of wheedling out every last thought in Anna's head, whether Anna wanted her to or not.

It had been a dreadful mistake confiding in her. She'd gone berserk. Rather than offer any reassurances, as Anna had hoped, Zoe had simply tried to stir up Anna's insecurities by insisting that Nick was bound to prove to be a faithless womanizer and that Anna would sooner or later regret her choice. She'd wanted to hear something soothing like,

'Oh, don't worry, he was probably just behaving laddishly in front of his friends, of course he's trustworthy.' Wearily, Anna admitted to herself that her hope that Zoe might be soothing or calming, rather than disturbing or destructive, was truly a matter of faith over experience. Sometimes it seemed that all she could do in relation to Zoe was ignore her.

Anyway, she had put all that behind her now.

Well, almost.

She hadn't told Vera that neither her parents nor her sister were attending the wedding. It sounded so pathetic. So loserish. Anna felt bitterly disappointed that her parents had decided not to support her decision to marry Nick. She couldn't understand why they didn't just come along, plaster on smiles and suck it up. Plenty of parents disapproved of their children's life choices but managed to show some support. They never had.

Desolate, Anna flicked through the responses to her wedding invitations. Other than Vera, her boys, a few people from the Drop In and a couple of girls she'd done a Spanish evening class with, there would be no one on Anna's side of the church. She didn't have any living grandparents; there were distant relatives back in Manchester but she hadn't seen any of them since she was a young girl and had felt it would be peculiar to send them an invite out of the blue, especially as they were bound to ask why her parents weren't attending. None of her friends in America saw fit to fork out thousands of dollars on air fares just to see her walk down the aisle. She'd received a dozen polite refusals, citing work commitments, previously booked holidays and challenging childcare arrangements.

Vera couldn't know exactly what was getting Anna down but she knew something wasn't right. She patted Anna's hand. 'Wedding planning, lectures, your work here. You're run off your feet, girl.'

Anna stared at her friend's warm, black hand on her own

cool, pale one. It was somewhat reassuring, somehow tempting. The air changed, tightened. She would like to confide in her. Tell her everything.

'I suppose we're both very busy at the moment, we've seen a bit less of each other recently. The wedding planning is a joy but it's time-consuming, and Nick's got some big deal or other going on.'

He hadn't been specific. The part that she just couldn't bring herself to add was that even when they were together she'd started to think he was acting a little cooler with her. Almost distant. That was in her head, right? It had to be. Of course they were fine.

'And how is that sister of yours? When's she going to come and say hello?'

Anna knew that wasn't going to happen. Zoe wouldn't be seen dead in a place like this. Giving back wasn't her thing. She hadn't planned on telling Vera about Zoe at all. As much as Anna loved Zoe, she wasn't fool enough to not realize that Zoe caused complications wherever she went, and Anna had learned through bitter experience it was sometimes better to keep her sister separate from the rest of her life. People had to be pretty tolerant and understanding to accommodate Zoe. Vera was both things. Still, why complicate the life she was building here? Zoe had wrought enough destruction on her in the past. Anna was not in the blame game; she knew her loyalties lay with her sister, but she had lost friends, jobs and even family relationships because of her. It had been such a risk introducing her to Nick, but what else could she do? Zoe was part of Anna. Twins were like that. A particular, unbreakable bond.

Vera only got to hear about Zoe through Nick. A couple of weeks back he'd called to check some arrangement or other, Anna had been on her lunch break and so he'd got chatting to Vera. Nick had mentioned Zoe. Naturally.

Anna shrugged. 'I honestly don't know. She seems to be pretty busy.'

The truth was Zoe was being almost as elusive as Nick at the moment. Other than their trip to the bridal boutique, Anna had hardly seen her and, considering how that had turned out, maybe it was a good thing. Anna had feared that Zoe's temporary move to the UK would result in greater confusion and intrusion. How could it not? She'd expected Zoe to be constantly in her life; nagging, poking fun, criticizing. She'd expected that she'd be called upon to bail her out of tight spots on a more or less continuous basis; the way it had always been, back in the States, when they were in their twenties and Zoe partied hard whilst Anna cleaned up after her. However, Zoe had been distant and uncommunicative since she arrived, which was strangely emancipating and unnerving at the same time. It was peculiar that in the past Anna had sometimes secretly wished for a level of independence from Zoe, and yet she was now surprised to discover that she felt cut adrift when faced with Zoe's relative silence.

It seemed as though it was something to do with her engagement to Nick. Certainly the timing coincided. It was as though they were going their own separate ways; even though Zoe was now here in London, Anna found she couldn't talk to her so easily. Couldn't reach her. Was that coming from Anna herself? Could it possibly be the case that she was subconsciously pushing Zoe away, distancing herself as she moved closer to Nick, a little like she was doing with Vera? If that was the case, her parents would say, 'Not before time.'

Or was it Zoe building walls? Anna remembered when they were kids and Zoe first started dating—if you could call what she did something as homely as dating—Anna had felt lonely, excluded. Maybe Zoe felt the same now. Or maybe it was just that Zoe was settling in quite well here in London; she'd apparently made friends. She must have, because she seemed to have a full social life, she was never available when Anna called on her. Still, Anna knew that something was amiss. Zoe had never made the right sort of friends, the right sort of choices. She feared Zoe was drinking again, possibly doing drugs. When they did talk, Zoe had seemed secretive, deceptive. She was hiding something.

Anna had wanted to confront Zoe about the wedding-dress incident but she found she couldn't. She remembered her blood slowing, her heart pounding as she absorbed Isobel's thinly veiled accusations; the humiliation was immense, the cruel disappointment was breathtaking and she found she couldn't pass it on, didn't want to. She was pretty certain Zoe had been responsible for sabotaging her preferred dress but it was an impossible thing to accuse anyone of. You'd have to be mad to do such a thing. Mad or riddled with jealousy. But the dress wasn't ripped into pieces through rageAnna and Zoe had endured countless difficult conversations and situations in the past. They'd seen one another at their most base and detestable. There had been a number of times when Anna had discovered Zoe lying in her own urine and vomit. One time she'd dragged her, kicking, screaming, swearing and scratching, from her dealer's frankly terrifying house, and she'd sat through endless substance-induced rants in which, uninterrupted, Zoe had poured out ceaseless vile insults and filthy claims and recriminations. But Anna had endured it because Zoe had been there for Anna too. When she'd scurried home from Yale, not much more than a pitiful sack of despair and disillusionment, Zoe had been about the only person Anna could face. Refreshingly, Zoe did not judge or even bother to dis. All she said was that John Jones would eventually get what he deserved.

When everyone else was frustrated and disappointed with them, the twins had each other. Absolutely. Always and for ever.

Things weren't the same any more, though. Anna felt they had entered a new stage in their relationship.

'It's a shame that she didn't want to stay with you,' commented Vera.

'I don't really have the space, she'd have had to sleep on the couch. And her boss is paying for her hotel, so it seemed silly to pass up the chance of all that luxury.'

'Fair enough, I can see that clean sheets and minibar chocolates could replace family,' said Vera, and then she hooted with laughter, thinking of her own much-loved boys and what she wouldn't do for a night alone in a luxury hotel; someone else making breakfast and the bed.

'We'd probably have got on one another's nerves, living in such close proximity again after so much time apart. Funny, though, because we used to be inseparable. When we moved to America our parents put us in the same room, even though there was space for us to have a bedroom each; it was what we wanted. They got us bunk beds. I got the bottom bunk, Zoe bagged the top one. But we soon found out neither of us could sleep that way.'

'Why? You wanted the top bunk?'

'No, we needed to be side by side. When we'd had single beds next to each other we'd slept face to face. In the night we'd reach out a hand to check the other was still there. So every morning my parents would find us curled up in one bunk bed together.'

'Oh, cute! In which bed?'

'That was the funny thing. It didn't matter whose bed. Sometimes it was the top bunk, sometimes it was the bottom. We used to say we were going to get a house together when we got older.'

'You never did?'

'No, we never did.' Anna hoped that she didn't sound as wistful as she felt.

'Maybe, but it might have been nice if she'd given it a go for a night or two.'

'She said she needed to be where things were happening. My apartment is a bit out of the way. Zone three. And she wasn't prepared to be bored by wedding planning details twenty-four/seven. I know I can be a bit boring.' Anna shrugged her shoulders, as if she was trying to dislodge the issue.

Anna spent the rest of the morning filing, essentially

avoiding any more probing questions from Vera. Just before lunch, she received a call.

'Nick!' She was happy and somewhat surprised.

He'd stopped calling to ask her to grab a sandwich with him at lunchtime a few weeks ago—because of all the work he had on his plate, obviously. Her heart plummeted a little when she noted that he didn't return her glee.

He sounded strained. 'Can we meet for lunch? There's something I want to talk to you about.'

She deliberately ignored the ominous tone in his voice. 'Lovely.'

'Villandry, St James's at one p.m.'

That's where they'd had their first date. Was that significant? Or had Nick simply suggested it because it was his favourite place, or was it just because it was more or less equidistant between both of their workplaces and so reasonably accessible for both of them? Following that fabulous first date, Anna had started to think of Villandry as her favourite restaurant too; she couldn't stand the idea of it being tainted, and she suddenly feared Nick's need to talk might ruin everything. The four-word combination, 'We need to talk,' was one of the worst sentences in romantic history, rivalled perhaps only by, 'Let's just be friends.'

'Oh, it's so hot, I can't face sitting in a restaurant.'

'They have air con,' he said with a stoniness that she wasn't used to.

'Even so, wouldn't you like to get some fresh air?' Whatever he had to say would be even more stilted if they were conscious that other dinners were listening. 'I'll put together a picnic,' she added winningly.

'Fine. I'll meet you at Green Park tube. We'll go there.'

The heat was beginning to char her shoulders and arms; strappy dresses, whilst undoubtedly pretty, had this drawback. It was a miserable, excessive sort of heat. Beads of sweat were pooling at the base of her back, under her arms, even on her eyebrows. Maybe they should have gone to the air-conditioned restaurant after all. She sighed heavily; this sort of heat was only fun if you were at the beach and had covered yourself in Factor 30. Her head started to pulse painfully. She feared the veins would burst through her skin. She could step into the shade, but would he still spot her? To distract and cheer, she watched little kids messily eating ice creams; it was adorable. Was she so wrong to want it so badly? A husband and a couple of cheeky, rosy-faced kids? Seemingly everyone else managed it quite easily. Why wasn't she entitled to it too? She noted that some kids sat quietly whilst others tore around their pushchairs and ignored their parents' half-hearted urges to 'play nicely'.

It put her in mind of herself and Zoe when they were kids. She was always careful, thoughtful, considerate and polite. Zoe was a risk taker. Stubborn, selfish and wild. The thing most often said about Anna was, 'She's a good girl.' The thing most often said about Zoe was, 'That one will end badly.' She wondered whether the adult predictions, scattered down on them like liberal handfuls of confetti, had in some way sealed their fates. Did they both simply fulfil other people's expectations? Was it all predestined and unalterable? Rather than find their own paths, were they pushed down certain routes? Anna taking hesitant steps, Zoe charging full pelt, certain to trip up and end up bloodied.

Whilst half dreading it, she also wished Nick would hurry up, but a glance at her watch showed he was just two minutes late. She was always pathologically early. It was a poor life choice; it created the impression that everyone she knew was forever irritatingly late, indicating that they valued her time less than their own, leaving her with a sense of frustration and resentment, even when they were fairly prompt and respectful. The string of the paper bag from the deli dug into her fingers. She'd picked up some delicious treats. Crusty loaf, hummus, pre-chopped carrots to dip, an assortment of spicy meat cuts and ripe cheeses, and a bottle of mineral water. She had considered buying a bottle of chilled wine with a convenient screw top but dismissed the idea. True, big talks were often more palatable when accompanied by a Chardonnay, but they were also often more messy and emotional. Besides, Nick had to get back to work this afternoon and drinking wasn't very sensible. Anna was, above all, beyond anything, sensible.

She saw him walk towards her. Jacketless—left behind, no doubt, tossed over the back of his chair in the office. His sleeves were folded up to reveal his strong forearms however the relaxed, informal sartorial choices were negated by the stormy look on his face.

Anna took a deep breath.

THIRTY-SIX
Nick

He wasn't sure what his intentions were when he called her this morning and insisted on meeting up, he'd acted on impulse—he rarely did anything else nowadays. He knew he had to see her, talk to her, although he suspected a full and frank confession was beyond him; he wasn't up to it. Over many years, he'd noted that in these sorts of situations two-timing women were far more likely than two-timing men ever were to own up to being in love with someone else and no longer able to carry on with the deception. Men never wanted to admit to themselves, or anyone else, how faithless they were. They generally fell back on platitudes. 'It's not you, it's me.' 'I need some space.' 'I love you, I'm just not *in* love with you.' He'd used them all, to his shame. Awkwardly, not especially convincingly, he hadn't really cared. By the time the time came when the phrases were necessary, he just wanted out. As fast and far as possible.

He'd never imagined he'd have to use any one of the inadequate, weary platitudes on Anna.

But then nor could he imagine telling her the truth. God, no. That would be impossible.

The air was clammy and he was as damp as if he'd been caught in rain. He didn't like the feeling. He didn't see himself as a nervous, sweaty man. He spotted her when he was about ten metres away from the park entrance. Slim and graceful, pretty in a summer dress. She looked slightly hot and anxious too. She moved her weight from one foot to the other; possibly her summer sandals had caused a blister, possibly she was worried. Anna was a brilliantly clever woman; he knew that academically she was his superior, but it was a fact that she was more than a little naive. Too trusting, some might say. Even so, she had to know something wasn't right between them. Their sex life had never roared and now it barely spluttered; she must know that wasn't normal for a newly engaged couple. He'd imagined taking his time with her, listening to what she wanted, suggesting things that might please, teaching her, reaching her, but that sort of thing demanded honesty. He'd detonated any chance of that. They weren't even talking to one another properly. Of course not; what could he tell her, other than lies?

He felt dreadful.

The clean and clear division between both women, both lives, was inevitably blurring, smudging, bleeding. He found, to his profound dismay, that he loved them both. Another cliché, one he had never believed in until now. He loved them both, not more or less, just differently. He cared for one, was enthralled by the other. He wanted to cherish Anna, he wanted to devour Zoe. Both women spoke to different parts of his masculinity. It was a depressing thought but it meant he was only half a man, whichever woman he was with.

He didn't fully understand either woman. Intellectually, Anna left him behind. She saw deep and serious meaning in just about everything, whereas sometimes he simply wanted to laugh and call something bollocks. For example, they had gone to an experimental theatre production in Somerset House last week. Throughout the play (and he used that word loosely), the actors spoke in different foreign languages, there was a lot of shouting and then they stripped off their clothes. They just stood about, with their breasts, vaginas and penises on show, arguing in Chinese, Italian and Swedish. It was comical, but Anna looked at him in a slightly pitying way when he struggled to silence a snort of derision.

'It's about the Tower of Babel, right?' he'd asked, trying to recover some ground.

She shook her head in a way that neither confirmed nor denied.

Later, he told Zoe about the experience. By coincidence, she'd been to see the play too. Of course she had, it was getting such widespread reviews, it was that week's hot ticket in London.

'Bollocks, wasn't it? Literally. There's no way I would have gone if I'd known Anna rated it. Her recommendations, other than yourself, are the kiss of death.' She'd shrieked with laughter and then said something complimentary about how favourably he was hung, compared to all the naked men in the play.

It had made him feel a lot better. Zoe seemed to make it her business to shock, surprise, mystify and confound, yet he understood her more than she might imagine; he was more like her than he was like Anna, he supposed. Other times, of course, she was simply aggravating in her unpredictability, frightening. For example, she sometimes insisted on making calls to Anna whilst they were in bed, just after they'd had sex. It left him feeling despicable. He always felt compelled to leave the room. He didn't understand why she did that. To shame him? To scare him? It was risky. It was cruel.

He watched as Anna spotted him; he waved lazily. She turned her smiling face in his direction, stood, ever so slightly, on her tiptoes and leaned towards him for a kiss. So chaste was their relationship becoming, she offered up her cheek. Without thinking, he ducked and gave in to the impulse of kissing her on the lips. Startled, gratified, she kept her eyes open; he did too as he continued kissing her, staring at her. People had to weave around them, and they did so, smiling, because everyone loves a lover.

Anna broke away first. 'I've brought a picnic,' she said, beaming. She held up the brown paper bag, made greasy in patches by something or other.

He took it off her, carried it effortlessly in one hand, and they headed off to hunt down a couple of available deck-chairs. Once settled, Anna delved into the deli bag. He was aware that she'd bought all the things he most liked to eat but, even so, he found it hard to chew and swallow; he looked hopefully for alcohol, unfortunately there wasn't any. She chattered about something or other. The elevating, motiva-tional and interesting tone of yesterday evening's lecture; the problems she was having trying to get a response out of a North London landlord for someone she was representing at the centre; a new and important study that the Government were commissioning about the links between mental health issues and homelessness. Everything she said was valuable, worthy, important. He couldn't hear her.

He was thinking about the fact he hadn't been able to let Zoe walk away last night. She had been perfectly willing and able to leave him. He'd made her stay. The thought that he cared more than she did caused deep panic and anger. His brain was being hijacked as his senses recreated Zoe. Visions of her limbs and his, entangled; the smell of her, warm, musty, heavily perfumed; the salty taste of her—it all tumbled about his head.

He had to let Anna go.

It was a terrible thing, not what anyone would call the honourable thing, but it was the only thing he could do now. He would be with Zoe. Then what? Well, they would not make a life together, as such—as he had been hoping to do with Anna—that wasn't Zoe's thing. He couldn't imagine any sort of longevity with Zoe, but then nor could he manage to call a halt to it. He would burn with her, roll with her, see what happened. It was all he could do, all that was available. It had to be enough. His previous objection—what might Anna's family make of their affair?—was irrelevant. Zoe didn't belong to a world of families. Their approval wasn't necessary. Mr and Mrs Turner, David and Alexia, apparently wanted nothing to do with Zoe—and they had little to do with him or Anna, come to that. He had never met them; he didn't owe them anything. A few, frankly, stiff and formal Skype conversations didn't count for anything.

'I spoke to your mum today,' said Anna.

'Sorry?'

'Hey, daydreamer, what were you thinking about?' Anna asked, with a patient smile.

'Work stuff,' he lied. Oh yes, his mum. Anna did belong to a world of families and she was firmly ensconced within his.

'Oh, you poor love. You're working too hard at the moment.'

He moved his head, not quite a nod, he couldn't bring himself to absolutely hoover up her unwarranted sympathy, but he didn't dare reject it and put her straight either. Hal would probably say he didn't have the balls. 'So, you talked to my mum?'

'Yes, I just wanted to check in with her because I knew she was seeing a new physiotherapist yesterday and she was a tad apprehensive about it.'

'Oh.' He felt a twinge. He'd forgotten. Damn, just another thing to feel guilty about.

'Don't look so worried, it all went brilliantly. They say she's making great progress. Your lovely mum said that was thanks to me arguing for the correct care and asking all the right questions on those early visits. Bless her.'

'She's probably right.'

Anna smiled modestly and demurred, 'Not at all. It's her commitment and the wonderful work of the medical staff that's making a difference.'

Their deckchairs were side by side, they weren't facing one another. Nick was glad. It was easier to busy himself with watching others than face Anna. Mothers with small children and babies had obviously arrived at the park mid-morning and had secured larger areas of space; they'd spread out colourful picnic blankets that were now littered with plastic toys and sippy beakers. The mothers' chatter was, from time to time, interrupted by the demand for an ice cream. He thought of his trips to parks with his mother and Rachel when he was a little boy. Careless, carefree. His mother who loved Anna. There were couples too. Lying on the grass and in each other's arms. He tried not to look at them. Instead, he focused on office workers who scurried by, grabbed a sandwich then found a patch of grass, determined to snatch some sunshine in their lunch breaks. Silently, he and Anna munched their way through the picnic with much less enthusiasm than the goodies deserved.

'Anna—'

'Oh, I've some good news,' she interrupted. 'I know that traditionally the groom sorts out the cars for the wedding.'

'Does he?'

'Yes, I told you so. It's on your list. You remember the list I gave you?'

Vaguely.

'You still have that, don't you?'

Probably, somewhere. Anna had spent a lot of her time over the last few weeks with her nose in various bridal magazines or visiting online sites, all of which offered information on wedding etiquette and seemed to generate endless lists. He'd never imagined he'd be the sort of man who would go along to cake-tasting sessions, but it was more than a bit sad that he now felt nothing other than panic and self-disgust when he thought about the wedding plans.

'Anyway,' continued Anna, seemingly oblivious to his disinterest, 'cars are supposed to be organized by the groom, that saidI know you've been really busy recently so I've sorted them out.'

'Oh.'

'Aren't you excited? Can you guess what I've booked?'

Apollo 13 for all he cared. 'No.'

She playfully took a half-hearted swipe at his arm. 'Well, to take me to the church and then to take us to the reception, would you believe me if I said I'd booked a *1930 Pierce-Arrow white limousine* that was actually used by President Hoover?'

'Lovely.' He forced himself to smile appreciatively.

It was odd this wedding business. Because whilst it was undoubtedly interesting that they were going to sit in a car that a president had once ridden in, he couldn't believe any little girl, even Anna, dreamed that one day they'd drive to church in a car that a president's arse had graced. It just didn't ring true. If he put a halt to this wedding, would he really be crushing dreams? Or just squashing cleverly marketed ideas that had recently been manufactured into something Anna was prepared to mistake for dreams?

'Yes, but wait for it.' She was slightly breathless, gabbling her words. 'It was a bit extravagant but, what the heck, it's our big day.'

Money wasn't really an issue for them. He earned enough to make sure they could guarantee a stylish and memorable day, yet Anna baulked at spending every last penny. She had an admirable social conscience about inequality and privilege, and she had clear views on what was value for money. Therefore, he was all the more surprised when she announced:

'I've booked a Lamborghini Veneno to take us on honeymoon.'

He gasped, 'You're kidding me.'

'I've honestly never seen a less bridal car in my life but, you know.' She shrugged and beamed.

A Lamborghini Veneno, his favourite ever type of car. And yes, he had actually dreamed of owning one, one day. Unlikely, since he wasn't a sheikh. Those things cost a national debt. But it would be amazing just being able to drive one, even for a short time.

'Wow, I don't know what to say.'

'The insurance cost almost as much as my dress,' she laughed. 'Although it's worth it, hey?' Suddenly she looked serious. 'I know that I've made most of the decisions about the wedding, and you've let me have all my own way, I just wanted there to be something special for you too.'

He knew that if everything had been as it was before Zoe had sashayed on to the scene, he would have leapt in and said something like, he had her, that was all that mattered, that he couldn't imagine anything more special, that she could do what she wanted on the day, whatever made her happy. He wanted to say something great like that. After all, she'd rung his mum this morning, she'd booked his dream car, she was special. Just lovely.

He stayed silent.

She let the air beat and then added, 'That is, providing you've booked a honeymoon for us to go on. You have, haven't you, Nick?'

He had not.

'You're running out of time, you know. You've got barely a month to go.'

Now, now he should tell her. Tell her to cancel the venue, the choir, the caterers, the car; to call up their friends and family; to return her dress. There could be no wedding. He was not the man she thought he was. Worse, he was not sure what sort of man he was any more. His head was thick and hazy. The heat pushed its way up his nose and down his throat, choking him. His shirt was wet with sweat at the base of his back. He should tell her now. Had to. Instead, he said, 'Shall we stretch our legs, find an ice-cream van?'

Nick was not one for soul-searching and he felt miserable being in the wrong. He preferred it when he was the hero in his own story, not the villain. As they queued for ice cream he wondered whether Anna was to blame for his predicament; at least in part. After all, she had been the one who rushed to fix their wedding date. Was he, on some subconscious level, reeling against the unnecessary speed and haste with which they were rushing towards this monumental commitment? Plus, she had been the one who pushed for him to meet Zoe in the first place. They should have postponed that first get-together until Anna was available. Then perhaps things would have started differently between him and Zoe, never reached such a complicated place. Anna had known Zoe was trouble, she'd warned him, but she hadn't protected him.

He was being childish; flailing around, looking for someone to blame. He knew as much, and that didn't make him feel any happier either. Just sulky, stuck.

He thought of what Zoe had said last night, that Anna had been married before. Rubbish, of course, but he hadn't been able to cast the thought from his mind, not completely. Because the truth was, he couldn't swear on it. An intrepid gambler by nature, he would not bet his flat on the fact that Anna had never been married before because, as improbable as it was, it was possible. He didn't know her, not completely. The thought bothered him.

Finding himself at the front of the queue, he asked for a Magnum. The vendor said they didn't have any left, sold out, so he was offered an alternative. Nick didn't care, really; he nodded and took something or other. She chose a ninety-nine; her long pointy tongue darted out, neatly scooping up the ice cream. On their very first date Nick had noted that she ate in the same way as she did everything else: carefully, precisely, with purpose. Zoe ate with energy and a show of great appetite. He liked to watch Zoe's lips move and thought of them now. She often let sauce spill down her chin, provoking him, waiting for him to lick it away.

They began to aimlessly stroll, avoiding the skateboarders, the cyclists and the runners. Anna made a joke about it being like attending the Grand Prix in Monaco rather than taking a lunchtime stroll in a park.

'Anna, I have to ask you something. It's probably ridiculous but I have to ask,' he blurted.

She turned to him, eyes wide and expectant. Her expression open and willing.

He felt ludicrous. 'You haven't been married before, have you?'

She froze for a moment.

For an infinitesimal amount of time, he thought panic sluiced across her face. No, no, it couldn't be panic. It had to be confusion. She must be wondering why he'd ask something so crazy.

She continued to lick her ice cream, carefully. 'Did Zoe tell you that?'

'Well, yes.' Why wasn't she denying it?

'When you met up?'

For a second he was freaked, then he realized she meant when they met up for dinner, the dinner date she was supposed to have attended too, the only time Anna was aware of him and Zoe ever having met.

'Yes.'

'That's why you've been behaving so peculiarly of late.'

So she had noticed. Of course she had. She wasn't stupid. He didn't know what to say. He murmured a non-committal, 'Well.' Neither confirming nor denying that he had been behaving peculiarly. It wasn't in his interest to admit anything.

'I've been so worried. I thought you were going off me or having second thoughts.' She giggled, self-consciously. 'I see now you've just been concerned about this. Why didn't you just ask me straight out?'

Her reasonable tone made him feel a bit flighty and daft. More than a bit wrong. He couldn't very well defend himself by saying, *I am asking you straight out, I only found out last night, right after having sex with your twin sister.*

'I thought it was crazy. You did warn me that Zoe can be crazy, say crazy things,' he justified himself.

'I did, didn't I?' Anna looked directly into his eyes.

There was something too searching and intense for him to bear. He looked around for a bin; he wanted to throw away his half-eaten ice cream, he really didn't have an appetite. Anna watched him glance about. Helpfully, she pointed to a bin just peeking out from behind a tree, a few metres away. He didn't know how exactly she'd read his mind, predicted his needs, but he was grateful. It struck him how simple and pleasant his life would be if he spent it with Anna. She'd make a serene and marvellous wife. He imagined she'd be an organized and tender mother, a careful, considerate hostess, a thoughtful and decent daughter-in-law. Again he felt the tide change, as he vacillated. He couldn't let her slip through his fingers. It would be madness. His successful career in the City was based on taking gambles, yes, but only after carefully weighing up all of the pros and cons, all the possible advantages and potential risks. If he weighed up Anna against Zoe, then the choice was a simple one. Zoe would be an irrational and demanding wife, if she ever became anyone's wife. Mother? Hostess? Daughter-in-law? These were not roles he could imagine Zoe ever being interested in playing.

It was Zoe he had to leave, to lose.

The decision made, it ballooned in his head, filling him with temporary optimism and relief. It was still possible: a decent, happy future with this thoughtful, honest woman. He simply had to step away from the giddy excitement, thrills and chaos that Zoe offered. It could still all be OK. He was on terra firma with Anna. Honesty was so important.

'Yes, I was married before.'

The world tilted.

'What?' He saw everything he thought he knew, and could count on, slipping out of place. As though he was living in a doll's house and a child had just upended that house, the furniture—so carefully arranged—was now spilling, sliding, landing in a tangled heap against a make-believe wall or ceiling. A full-on *Inception* movie moment. He'd fully expected her to deny it. No, he didn't need her to deny it, he'd assumed Zoe had made it up. He stood dead still and stared at her but she kept walking, carefully licking her ice cream. 'When? Who? For how long?' he demanded. 'Was it that guy at Yale you told me about?'

She shook her head. 'Nope.'

'Then who? You've never mentioned anyone else that you were serious about.'

'Well, you didn't seem the type who wanted to listen to too many gory details about exes.'

This was true and accurate; oddly Nick felt it was all the more unreasonable for that. Anger simmered in his gut.

He was not going to take the blame for this. 'I'd have listened.'

'No, you'd have run. Imagine on our first date if I'd casually mentioned I was a divorcee.' She stared at him, eyes wide and pleading.

He took a deep breath. 'I'm listening now.'

Calmly, as though it wasn't a big deal, she began to explain. 'I started dating him when I was twenty-three. I should never have agreed to go on a date with him because, actually, I was still in love with John Jones; he was the guy from Yale.' She explained casually, in a tone more befitting a first date. 'I only agreed because, in the end, it was easier than saying no. He was the son of a family friend. A Harvard graduate, my parents loved him. Everyone loved Larry Morgan. Except me.'

'But you married him!'

'Yes. I was working as an admin assistant in a carpet-cleaning company.'

'What?' That wasn't the career of a Yale graduate.

'I'd dropped out so I had limited choices.'

'You dropped out?'

'Didn't I ever tell you that?' she asked breezily. 'My future didn't look exactly sparkling. I guess I saw him as some sort of option.'

'Was it a whirlwind thing?'

He didn't know how he wanted her to answer this question. Part of him wanted to hear her dismiss her marriage as brief, fleeting, insignificant because that might just explain why she'd never mentioned it. But then *they* were a whirlwind thing. Did she have form? Were they brief, fleeting, insignificant?

'No. We dated for a year, got engaged, had an eighteen-month-long engagement. A respectable amount of time, I guess.'

'You were really serious about him.'

She paused, tilted her head. Her eyes swung slowly left to right, as though she was really trying to weigh up the question and answer it as honestly as possible. 'No. Well, yes. He seemed kind. A good man. I thought he was a safe pair of hands. People kept saying I could do worse. Retrospectively, I see that's pretty damning praise,' she shrugged, apologetically. '. I suppose, subconsciously, I believed he was too dull to be cruel.'

It was a lot to take in. Nick looked around him. People were still going about their business: riding bikes, feeding ducks, slouching about in the heat. That seemed odd to him. 'How long were you married?'

'Three years.'

Crap. He was doing the maths. They'd been together five and a half years. That accounted for the huge gap in her dating CV. He'd thought she had just been picky during those years but in fact she had been married.

He forced himself to ask, 'What went wrong?'

'Same old, same old. He had an affair.'

That's what Zoe had said; she'd told him the truth. He noticed that the ice cream had melted down the cone and on to Anna's hand. They both looked at it; she seemed surprised. She didn't like getting into a mess. She walked back to the bin, dropped the sloppy cone and then rooted in her bag for a tissue. Carefully she wiped between her fingers.

'Why didn't you ever tell me?'

'It's complicated,' she sighed.

'No, no, it isn't.'

'There was never a right time.' She stretched out her hand as though she was going to touch his arm but then stopped. He wasn't sure if this was because she was worried about her sticky hands, or because she'd lost confidence in the act.

'And that's it? He had an affair, you left him.'

'More or less.' She shrugged, almost casually.

The woman Nick had fallen in love with, her all-encompassing desire for honesty, sincerity and simplicity, faded before him. He stared at her but couldn't see the detail of her. It was like looking at the photos on his mother's sideboard that had been burnished by years of sun. He forced his head to adjust. A messier Anna was more accessible, right? More real?

He wasn't sure.

'So you divorced just last year? When you were living in the UK?'

'I divorced three years ago. The marriage ended April seventeenth, 2014. Paperwork adds a few more months but that was the day it died.' Her eyes narrowed, breath tightened a fraction.

He was confused. Such a precise reply and yet the maths didn't work. 'But you met him when you were twenty-three, you were together for over five years.'

'Oh,' she nodded briefly. 'I see why you'd think that. I'm not twenty-nine, Nick. I just said that on my profile because Zoe was certain men wouldn't respond if they knew I was thirty-one.'

'You're thirty-one?'

She nodded.

She was thirty-one. That was a year older than he was. It didn't matter, as such; he didn't care what age she was. But it was another lie.

'Thirty-two in September. I'm so glad we've slipped the wedding through before I have to blow any more candles out,' she added cheerfully. 'I'd totally forgotten that I'd fibbed on the profile.'

'I can't believe you did.'

'Really, Gus?' She was laughing now, not meanly, but with great amusement, as though she thought the whole thing was funny, even a bit silly. 'I'm so glad I did. Admit it, Nick, you would not have pressed 'wink', you'd have considered me middle-aged.'

He wanted to deny it, and yet she was right. He'd never

even have met her because he'd set his automatic filter to cut off at thirty.

She took his hand now, hers still sticky with ice cream despite her efforts to clean up; his was sweaty with heat. 'I'm glad that's out in the open. I feel so much better, now that we no longer have any secrets. Don't you?'

His head was about to explode. It was all too much. Too messy. Too irregular. He couldn't process all this cleanly or efficiently. He blurted, 'Is Zoe an alcoholic?'

It was a stupid question to ask. Non-sequential and therefore likely to arouse suspicion, even in trusting, naive Anna. As the thought formed in his head he shoved it away, irritated, because was Anna so trusting? She certainly wasn't as honest as he'd thought. Even if her deception had come from a simple mistrust of internet daters (a justified mistrust, admittedly), it was still a deception. Momentarily, he lost his bearings. The world slowed about him, voices echoed and slurred. He felt he'd dived into an icy pool, plunged too far underwater, and only with effort could he break the surface.

'She certainly likes a drink,' Anna replied. She looked puzzled. 'Why do you ask? Did she get drunk the night you met up? Did she make a show of herself?' Anna's eyes widened with horror and realization. 'She did make a pass at you, didn't she?'

'No, no, of course not. Why would you say that?' Nick batted away her slow-dawning suspicion; he regretted mentioning Zoe at all.

'That would be just like her. To get drunk and then silly.'

'No,' he declared firmly. Was that it? Was that all? Drunk and then silly. He clamoured for some composure. 'I just want to know. You said she was an alcoholic. Now you're saying she likes a drink. There's a big difference.'

'I don't know what to tell you.' Anna's face expressed true regret. 'I'd say Zoe is an alcoholic. A lot of experts would and have agreed with me. She'd say she isn't.'

'You said she was on the steps programme.'

'That's what she told me.'

'I googled it. You're not allowed to drink at all if you're on that programme.'

'No.'

'But she does. She did. That night we were out.' Nick wasn't sure why he was pushing this point. He'd do better to stick to his policy of never mentioning Zoe to Anna at all. This was dangerous territory but he felt he needed to know, and he had no one else to ask. He hadn't met any of Zoe's friends or colleagues. They operated in an isolated pocket, away from the distracting claims of others.

Anna looked heartbroken. Deflated. A little less buoyant and whole.

'I'm really sorry to hear that. I wish you'd told me at the time.' She said it quietly. No roaring recriminations. No anger. Just a quiet disappointment.

He'd let her down. Of course he had. He knew he had. In a far bigger and messier way than she was aware.

'That's important stuff. You should have said something to me. I wonder whether staying on in the UK has anything to do with the fact she's drinking again. I doubt she's going to meetings here. It starts with drink and then next it's…' She trailed off; it was obviously too painful to articulate. 'Poor Zoe.'

And the fact Anna had once been married to a man called Larry Morgan receded. Apparently that wasn't important stuff. Nick felt bitter and wrong-footed. Those emotions sat alongside his now perpetual sense of guilt and confusion. The swell of uncomfortable, difficult feelings festered deep inside him.

Like a poison.

THIRTY-SEVEN
Zoe

He is there when I arrive, of course he is, that's why I forced myself to be late, to walk around the block at least twice so as to make sure he was waiting for me, even though I'm in high heels, even though two separate groups of men called out to me, crudely offering up their services in a way that insulted rather than flattered; how can they think catcalling is ever anything else?

Being late is a subliminal and important message. He waits for me. I wait for no one. The moment I spot him lingering by the bar's entrance, it feels like the world grinds to a halt. He clocks me, grins and then the world shudders on. Keeps turning. How crazy is that? Every time I see him I'm newly shocked by the effect he has on me. I don't like it. The fact he hijacks me in this way. It leaves me feeling exposed. Open. I wonder what this is now. This thing we have going on. I honestly don't know. I don't like that either. Not knowing things. Normally I'm a step ahead. Obviously, I'm no longer seeing him to test him for Anna. That experiment has a conclusive, indisputable result. I should have just got Anna to face this, dump him, move on. I didn't. I thought I wanted him to fall in love with me. I did. I do. Has he? Maybe. Yet, something different has happened here instead. Something much more dangerous and risky. I'm not saying I'm in love with him too. I won't say that. That's not very me. That's Anna's thing. Trusting, doting, etc.

But.

He's delicious to look at, no one would argue with me there, yet it's more than that. He's intelligent enough; interesting—obviously; complicated—undoubtedly. But none of that is as rare as women like to make out; I've had plenty of that sort of men. The difference is I'm drawn closer; I can't walk away. He looks to me for a deeper connection and, despite my better judgement, I find I respond. He wants me to know and accept all his magnificence as well as his shameful secrets. He looks to me for excitement, thrills and then forgiveness. The things Anna can't or won't dole out. I respond. I want to give him this. All this and more. Everything. I want to feed his needs, like sticks feed a fire; I'm prepared to be consumed. It's unhealthy. He's my latest unhealthy addiction; it's what I like most and least about him.

He kisses me on the lips in greeting; a territorial, hungry, almost unseemly kiss. Then he strides inside; I follow, not my normal position in life. He confidently peruses the bar with a professional, demanding eye. Of course the place is sleek, modern, fast and fun. Later it will morph, dissolve into something where the air is stained with hedonism, indulgence, menace and thrill. I know that he takes Anna to country pubs, to art-gallery cafes, and that they have picnics in the park; they sit and eat shepherd's pie amongst hillwalkers, drink tea next to middle-aged ladies with opinions on Annie Leibovitz (which are entirely formed by the Sunday supplements) and eat deli-bought sandwiches alongside young mothers with strollers full of noisy kids. We never consider frequenting such wholesome sorts of places. We go to bars, restaurants and nightclubs. Places populated with those who make deals with the devil. Dark venues where people are high on drugs and wealth, where clubbers dance until they sweat and people drink until they are sick. We find dim and shadowy corners to indulge in our own compulsive craving: each other. I usually like the bars he selects; normally they are upmarket and discreet about their purpose—the provision of sin. Tonight, this bar hits a sour note. There's a little too much gold and leather decor; the laughter isn't flirtatious, it's harsh; and the women are way too skinny, hungry-looking, ill. They parade around and around the room, as though it's a cattle market or they are performers at a circus.

Even so, we find a couple of stools by the bar and perch. I sit with my back ramrod straight, tits proud, legs crossed. He sits legs open, facing me. He is especially handsome—no, exquisite. I notice it, over and over again. Am struck. We're quite the couple. Men chuck discreet but envious glances in our direction, taking in both the quality of Nick's suit and my face and figure, in one efficient look. They try to catch my eye but I steadfastly stare at Nick; if he notices them prowling he doesn't acknowledge as much. Doesn't see a threat. His arrogance excites me. I see other women turn and throw him appreciative or longing glances. I dismiss them with a slow, intimidating flick of my eyelids. The under-confident types sensibly scurry on by; the bolshie bitches flick back—the middle finger—often as not. I show my disdain in a powerful, practised glare. Designed to frighten. It's usually enough.

This evening a skinny, hard-looking woman emboldened by drink has the gall to stand between Nick's open legs, back to me, blocking me. 'When you get sick of her, call me,' she slurs, making an unsuccessful grab for his phone in his pocket, presumably so she can programme her number into it. She narrowly misses snatching at his crotch; I don't believe her grope is altogether accidental. Nick smiles, half-heartedly, good-naturedly. He waits for her to move along.

I see she has no intention of doing so; I lean forward and whisper in her ear.

She turns to me, scared. Weighs up the threat and then scampers away; off to cause trouble elsewhere, I don't doubt.

Nick laughs, 'What did you say?'

'I told her we were engaged,' I reply with a smile.

'Did you really?' He's still laughing but he looks a tad embarrassed too. After all, he is engaged. Just not to me.

'No. I told her I'd smash a glass in her face if she spoke to you again.'

He stares at me, unnerved now, not sure which to believe. Not sure which scenario makes him more uncomfortable.

He orders vodkas. I like it that he's gone straight to the hard stuff, it shows a certain determination to obliterate. In the beginning he demurred about offering me alcohol. Anna's scary stories about my recklessness, my abandon, my dependency had obviously spooked him. I suppose he must have decided that I can manage better than she professes, or perhaps—and this thought pleases me most—he's happy to accept, even embrace, my recklessness, my abandon, my dependency.

Or perhaps he just needs a stiff drink.

'Did you talk to Anna today?' I ask.

He nods stiffly.

'About her marriage?'

Another nod. Small, sad.

I told you so is unnecessary.

'Why didn't she tell me?' he asks.

I shrug. Presumably she never found the correct moment, presumably she was so desperate to impress him and secure him she didn't want anything to muddy the waters, presumably as time passed she didn't know how to drop it into conversation. But it's not up to me to defend her. She can tell him all of that herself if she wants to.

'I'm sorry,' I whisper and then I lean close to him. Kiss his lips, slowly. I allow my left breast to brush up against his arm.

He responds by gently biting my lip.

'How was work today?' I ask brightly as I break away.

He looks surprised; I rarely take an interest.

'Pretty dreadful, if I'm honest. I'm finding it tricky to focus as well as I should recently.'

'Hmmm?' I make a sympathetic, encouraging sound. I wonder how many millions he's let slip through his grasp since he met me. I'm not concerned. They're not real numbers. It's a figure on a screen, a promise, a wish, someone else's plan.

'I can barely keep my mind on my job,' he admits, as he drains his vodka and swiftly signals to the bartender that he'd like another round.

I'm flattered to be so distracting but I don't actually want him to fuck up his career. His success and drive are part of his attraction, both to me and Anna, we have that much in common. He's done well for himself. Not that he's what anyone would call a rank outsider—a white boy with a university education—still he's worked hard to earn his position. Studied as a kid when he could have been getting drunk or stoned, long hours ever since, lots of research, can-do attitude, talks to the right people, shakes hands, kisses ass, never gives up. What's notable is that he doesn't just fit, he's part of the redefinition, and I like that. However, as he is finding work stressful and not especially fulfilling right now, I decide to move the conversation on.

We're never short of things to talk about. Very soon after meeting him I identified the fact that he likes to figuratively kick off his shoes, walk in the sand, fist with his toes. He sees himself as a rebel at heart. Of course he does, otherwise why would I be sitting opposite him? Whilst he's trundling towards wedding vows, a mortgage and presumably a couple of kids and a Labrador, he's glancing back over his shoulder to days that were more carefree and doused with irresponsible optimism. I allow him time to talk about his thoughts, beliefs, notions and experiences; I recognize that they are fresh and loud and now, far from depleted or obsolete.

I expertly turn the conversation and lift the mood by recounting some charged, long-forgotten encounter with some guy or other on holiday in Jamaica. Of course it was a sexual encounter. He likes hearing about my past conquests. He tells me about his sex life too, pre-Anna. It's not as daring as he'd like to think it is. Basically, he's slept with a number of pretty women; a large number, I admit, but there really isn't much novelty in a good-looking, wealthy, funny man pulling pretty, fit, young women. I vacillate between showing interest and boredom, to keep him on his toes. He doesn't know what I want so he lets spill all the stories of the women who had names he never knew, or once knew and has now forgotten. He wants to prove to me that he's careless, exciting, wild, daring. I listen carefully because I find all I want to know is whether there has been a name that has stuck. Is it Anna? Is she truly different? Really, I want to know, am I? He talks about money too. The large amounts he's made for others, for himself. The even greater amounts he plans to earn. I don't comment at all. Too many men think too many women are for sale. No one can buy me. Even if I allow them to buy things for me, like vodka, dinner or even a gift, they can't buy me. Nowhere near. No one ever could. Still, I appreciate that he wants to impress me and is searching around for ways to do that.

He makes me laugh. Have I mentioned that? He's funny, and I like that in a man. Humour demands confidence, and I appreciate all displays of confidence. I'm funny when I'm with him too. We laugh together—and that feels good. I'm attracted to any number of things about him. If I was more fanciful, more like Anna, I might say that I'm losing count of the things that draw me to him. His recklessness is high up there. As are his stereotypical alpha-male displays of masculinity (don't judge, it's Darwinian), his dance moves, his sex moves, the cut of his suits, the smell of his aftershave, even his latent and inconvenient sense of duty. I suppose that's one of the things I find most fascinating; this deception is harder than he imagined. It's a battle. Battles are interesting. I like a battle. But I have to win the war.

I like how he has an effect on me. Not many men ever have. Other than dealers, I suppose, and that was in quite a different way. He excites me. He tries to be original but pretty much everything he can think of to say to me I've heard before. 'You beguile me. You're astounding. You're exquisite.' The difference is that it's the first time I've ever wanted to believe it.

He thinks he gets me. He doesn't know the half.

We drink more than is sensible, which both of us still judge not to be enough. The lights are dimmed and the atmosphere thickens. Nick gets drunker than I've ever seen him. His inebriated state allows him to touch me more than he usually chooses to in public; his hand rests heavily on my thigh. He works it further up my leg, with all the subtlety of a man who has consumed a week's worth of units in one night. I don't move him away immediately, I encourage the overt declarations of affection that pour, unchecked from his mouth. I wonder whether he'll tell me he loves me tonight. It's possible, since he's so shocked and hurt by Anna keeping secrets. He'll feel wrong-footed and wants to even the score. Couples don't often acknowledge it but basically relationships are a long game in accounting. A magnificent and constant tally: adding, subtracting, carrying over. Compliments, chores done willingly, incomes earned, sicknesses nursed are on one side; lies, infidelities, cash blown, expectations dashed are on the other. He said this. She did that. He earned this. She's due the other.

If he tells me he loves me, I wonder whether he'll mean it.

We become taut and jittery as we both feel a need to find a pragmatic way and place to hammer out our needs. Expediency, not discretion, has clearly become more important to him; he grabs my right tit and fondles it in the bar. It's the sort of place where anyone who notices, pretends not to. I'm surprised by his lack of discretion but not perturbed. I don't move his hand. His screamingly careless behaviour makes me wonder whether he is willing to get caught? Whether he wants to be? I'm still aware that we need to achieve some element of privacy; I like being an exhibitionist but I don't want to get arrested for indecent exposure. He's drunk so much that he's becoming reckless; he necks the shots I sip and refuses to hydrate with water in between. If I don't move quickly, I doubt he'll be much use to me tonight. I make the decision to take his hand and boldly lead him to the toilets. I head to a cubicle in the women's; I draw a line at having sex up against a stinky urinal. Two girls are putting on their lipstick. They stare, open-mouthed.

I say, 'You should probably leave, now.'

Shocked, they do as I tell them.

It's hot and quick. He's told me a lot of stories and so I think I can confidently say this is in his top three in terms of craziness. He's game and grateful. Afterwards we hold on to each other, let our breathing slow, listen to the door to the bathroom open and close. Groups of young women enter. We hear them chatter; others we listen to whilst they pee. We stay silent and cling to each other. There's a lull, the place has emptied out. We're alone.

Usually he avoids talking about Anna but tonight it seems he can't get her out of his mind. Who else can he speak to about her, other than me?

'It was awful, having to ask her about the marriage,' he whispers into my ear.

'I can imagine.'

'I should know that much about her.'

'Yes, you should.'

'Yes, I should,' he repeats with the belligerence of a drunk.

I pull apart from him a fraction, make eye contact and ask, 'Did she tell you about her kids?'

'Kids? Fuck me, you're joking.' He turns pale, almost transparent.

I laugh quietly. 'Yes, actually I am. There are no kids.'

He bites his lip. Angry with me and himself. Unfair, it's her he should be angry with. I'm sitting on the lid of the toilet seat now. I want to get out of here. We should go back to the hotel. He needs to sober up. I need to sleep.

Nick shakes his head, perhaps trying to dislodge a thought, perhaps trying to chase one. 'I feel I don't know her.'

Let's face it, he doesn't. The problem is, he wanted steak at home for the rest of his life but he's come to realize he's settled for cold slices—you know, those processed things you buy at the supermarket. He's naturally disappointed. A blast of music blares into the room as someone comes into the restroom again. By their voices, I'd guess it's two or three girls. They talk amongst themselves. Someone rattles on the door of our cubicle. 'I'm in here,' I call. We wait as they use the facilities, reapply make-up, talk about their bosses and boyfriends and then, eventually, go. Another blast of music and then the volume is muffled again.

'I don't trust her,' he mutters woefully.

This is ironic considering our predicament but I pull up my knickers and don't say so. Anna is losing him. I can see him slip from her grasp. I have to clasp ever more tightly now. He must feel the same as he grabs my face in both his hands; erotic and tender. Purposeful and desperate.

'I'm lost, Zoe. So confused.'

'I know, baby.' I kiss his forehead with something that could easily be taken as tenderness.

'The wedding. We're so far along with the planning. She's booked this car, a Lamborghini.'

'Nice.'

'Yes.'

'We could speed away in it, baby. You and I. Head for the hills.'

He stares at me, perplexed. He can't tell if I'm laughing at him or serious. 'Are you asking me to choose?' It's as though the thought has just occurred to him. He might have to choose. Make a decision. This tea party, where he has his cake and eats it, can't last for ever.

I suspect he was hoping he'd never have to make a decisive move, that instead something would happen to him, to us, to them. 'You know you have to, sooner or later,' I whisper.

His face twists; agonized, tortured. 'I can't.' His eyes are wet.

Do I want to see him cry, to watch the tears roll down his cheeks, which are contorted with indecision and shame? Or not?

'Do you want me to make the decision for you?' I ask, gently.

The air between us is hot and used.

He looks relieved, joyful. 'Yes, yes. Will you? I just want it gone.'

Gone. I nod. Just once.

I tell Nick to settle the bar bill and to hail a cab, I say I will meet him on the street. 'I've something I need to take care of.'

By the time I join him he seems a great deal more sober, and there's quite an extortionate tab running on the meter. I don't apologize, he can afford it. I dip my head and climb straight into the back seat.

He clambers in behind me and closes the door.

'My God, you missed a bit of a rumpus,' he says, recovered from the near-hysterics in the restroom; like a child, he's dumped that problem at my feet and is no longer concerned.

'Oh yes?'

'You know that girl who tried to give me her number earlier on this evening?'

I suddenly notice he looks a bit bashful and shaken up. I make a show of trying to recall, and finally murmur, 'Oh yes. I think so.'

'She's just been carried out by a bouncer. He put her in a cab. She was in quite a state.'

'Drunk?'

'No, hurt. Her face was bleeding. Her nose, or maybe her cheek, was split. I guess. She was sobbing. I think she must have got into a fight with someone.' Nick's eyes suddenly drop to my hands.

They are clean.

I'm clutching my bag. 'She must have upset someone,' I say dryly.

Then I give the address of the hotel to the driver and we move on.

THIRTY-EIGHT
Anna

The water mark on the ceiling of Anna's flat, which had started as a small stain in the corner of the kitchen, had elongated. The flat upstairs must have a slow leak of some kind. If that flat was configured like hers, then it was most probably the kitchen sink to blame. She had knocked on the door a few days ago, she'd heard the TV blaring, yet no one had answered. People could be so unfriendly. She'd popped a note under the door but didn't hold out much hope of a response. She should probably call her landlord, let him deal with the matter, but she'd be out of there in a couple of weeks and didn't need the hassle.

She had enough on her plate.

The thought of living with Nick, as his wife, sent a shiver through Anna's body. Excitement. That's what she told herself. Not apprehension. Why would she feel at all apprehensive? This was *it*. She was going to be living her dream. A wife! Nick's wife! They'd share everything, from the bills to the remote control. They'd come home from work and tell one another about their days: the joys, concerns, triumphs, frustrations. They'd build a future; they'd start a family. That's what was next. Only, sometimes, she couldn't imagine it quite so clearly as before he'd proposed. Which was infuriatingly illogical.

Today she had woken up lethargic, sluggish, almost lacklustre. Those were not very bride-to-be feelings; she ought to be feeling vibrant, excited, expectant. She knew that, but knowing it didn't make it so. It was most likely the heat. The flat, relentless heat that weighed down on her shoulders, climbed into her throat. Not enough places in Britain had air conditioning; it was crazy how the Brits didn't seem to expect hot weather, even in August.

That's all it was. The heat.

It was too hot to call the landlord and talk about leaks; it was too hot to eat or sleep. Last night she'd tossed and turned, watched the sun set through her bedroom window, and then, before she knew it, watched it rise again. She felt weary. Her eyes stung. They needed a storm to clear the air. Literally and, Anna couldn't help thinking, metaphorically. Of course Anna was giddy about the thought of the wedding, becoming Nick's wife, living in his beautiful apartment, starting their life together. Deep down. It was just that those emotions had been somewhat smothered by the debilitating heat and, well—

Anna had become pretty accomplished at fooling the people around her; playing the part of the eternally chirpy girl from America, a regular cornucopia of optimism and good cheer. However, she wasn't capable of fooling herself. Not about this. Anna really wanted to simply feel upbeat and concentrate on the lovely things about getting married. Rachel had said yes to being her bridesmaid—that was a good thing. Pamela and Anna talked on the phone practically every day, pinning down the final details as the day loomed ever closer—that was a good thing. Last weekend Anna and Nick had met the vicar, who seemed like a lovely woman—now that was a good thing.

There was a problem between her and Nick. That was not a good thing.

And it was all because of Zoe.

It was not Zoe's fault exactly; Anna really only had herself to blame. She should have been honest and upfront with Nick about Zoe right from the beginning. The problem was that Nick was such a straightforward, straight-up sort of man.

She'd been at a loss as to how to introduce such chaos into his life; she wasn't sure he could manage the craziness of her raucous, overwhelming, party-girl twin. So she'd been untruthful. It was unforgivable. It wasn't what marriages were built upon. She'd thought that drip-feeding details of Zoe's antics, minimizing them, was the best way forward, but it hadn't been. With hindsight Anna could see that she'd just caused confusion; Zoe had become a wedge between them.

That business about Larry! That was just messy. Awful. What had Zoe been thinking? Nick had been just fantastic about the whole thing. He hadn't thrown recriminations at her; he hadn't mentioned the matter again, actually. She'd thought he might. It would have been perfectly understandable if he'd wanted to hear more details. Although she was glad he hadn't probed. It was a terrible time to think about. To talk about. Her past mostly was. Anna was all about the future. Moving on! That's what counted, but she knew the only way that was possible was if everything was as it should be between her and Nick. Anna feared Nick didn't trust her quite so much as he used to; obviously, he felt he didn't know her as well as he should do. And she supposed he was right about that.

She could fix this. She could! Anna knew what had to be done. It wouldn't be easy—frankly, it would be terrifying—opening herself up completely, laying herself bare. She needed to place a huge amount of trust in him and in herself. But it had to be done. Anna looked in the mirror. She looked dreadful—sweaty-faced and frizzy-haired— nothing like a blushing bride-to-be. She'd better fix that too. The heat was like a heavy blanket. It was the kind of day that could only be enjoyed if you were outside, yet she was hanging around the flat, half hoping, although not expecting, that Zoe might show up. She had called her several times, left messages asking her to drop by, but there were no guarantees. Zoe was a law unto herself.

Anna opened a window; the gentle evening breeze was

welcome in the airless room. Then just when she was beginning to think she'd never see or hear from Zoe again, her twin appeared at the door. She was wearing skimpy denim shorts, an enviably beautiful

'Zoe! How fantastic to see you!' Anna went to fling her arms around her sister.

But Zoe stepped away. 'Don't touch me. It's far too hot for any physical contact.'

There was a time, when they were kids, that they'd practically been joined at the hip. Their hair, limbs, thoughts constantly entangled; they didn't care about each other's perspiration then. She didn't want to think about it. Nor did she want to think about the fact that Zoe had been elusive, had refused to come to her wedding and had, no doubt, ruined her wedding dress of choice; she was just so pleased to see her sister on her doorstep.

'You got my messages. Nick is on his stag weekend; I was wondering what to do with myself.'

'Yeah, difficult to know how to fill a day when you live in London. One of the cultural and retail capitals of the world.'

If Anna heard the sarcasm, she chose to ignore it and giggled instead. 'You are so right. Here's me, sat inside contemplating scouring the bathroom. Come on, I'll put the kettle on. Or do you want a cold drink?'

'Tea is fine. Why are you doing housework? Are you expecting guests?'

'No. I just thought I'd make a start on the chores that need doing in order to get my deposit returned.' She said this as she walked the few steps towards the kitchen in order to boil the kettle.

'On a day like this? You sure know how to live.' Zoe plonked herself down at the small kitchen table. Idly, she started flicking through the bridal magazine that lay there. 'Anyway, aren't you having a bachelorette party?'

'Can you imagine me eating chocolate penises and drinking shots with a male stripper on my lap?' Anna laughed as she busied herself preparing the tea tray.

Zoe shook her head. 'No, more's the pity. However I thought maybe you'd do a posh afternoon tea at The Dorchester or something. Pretty dresses, girly chat. All that.'

Anna would have loved an afternoon tea at The Dorchester; most of all she'd have loved it if Zoe had offered to organize it for her. As Zoe hadn't, Anna had never quite got around to sorting anything out for herself.

As ever, Zoe read her mind, she sighed with exasperation. 'Don't pin this on me. You must have known I wasn't going to be planning tea and scones. You could have gone ahead without me.'

'With whom?'

'With Pamela and Rachel, your boss, your friends from your evening class.'

'Pamela still can't get about easily, Rachel lives in Edinburgh, Vera has to oversee the boys' soccer practice and homework at the weekends. I just didn't think I could pull together a robust enough gang to make it fun.'

Zoe rolled her eyes. In the past, they'd discussed Anna's dearth of friends; sometimes their discussions had rolled over into fiery rows. Anna knew how it frustrated Zoe that she didn't have more friends, but she'd never needed them, not really, she'd always had Zoe.

Anna fingered the belt on her cotton robe, she really ought to have got around to getting dressed. 'It wouldn't be the same without you,' she admitted.

'Anna, for God's sake. You can have a good time without me. You just have to try.'

Anna didn't know what to say to that. She wasn't sure if it was true. Anna needed Zoe. She always had. Everyone believed that Zoe was the needy, demanding twin but it was much more of a two-way deal than most imagined. Anna needed Zoe, if only to feed her need to be needed. She depended on Zoe as much as Zoe depended on her. They were intertwined, inseparable. Or at least Anna still liked to think they were. It was hard to believe Zoe did need her now, since she was capable of disappearing out of Anna's life for weeks at a time, even though she was only staying in a hotel a few miles away. Anna had made excuses for her irregular contact when there was an ocean between them, but now it was harder to explain.

Anna tried to hide her hurt; it was never a good idea to show Zoe her softer side, it only irritated. Instead, she commented, 'Anyway, I've done the bachelorette party thing before, as you know.' Streamers, bows, cake, toasts, speeches, the whole nine yards.

'True, and I didn't make it that much fun, did I?' Zoe pointed out.

Dancing on the table, heckling, puking, flashing her boobs from the minibus, redefining the whole nine yards. It had been awkward. When Anna married Larry Morgan, Anna had had six bridesmaids, including Zoe. They'd all sworn they'd be friends for ever, have kids at the same time and watch them grow up together, but it hadn't panned out that way. Her bridesmaids' commitment didn't extend to dealing with Zoe by proxy. She scared people away. It was deeply depressing, if you thought about it. Fractured relationships, broken ties, ardent vows melting into tenuous excuses. Anna decided it was best not to think about it. 'The bachelorette party isn't important anyway.'

'Oh yeah.'

Anna took a deep breath and then, as she pulled cups from the cupboard and poured milk into a jug, declared, 'I'm so sad you're not coming to the wedding, and that mum and dad aren't either but it doesn't matter. It's not about the day. That's not what's important. Not really. It never has been.'

'Oh yeah.'

Anna turned to face Zoe. 'Nick is important. Just Nick. My future with him is all that counts, not my past.'

Zoe stared at her. Incredulous. Mocking.

'I know what you're thinking,' Anna said defensively.
'Do you?'

'You think that I make mistakes when it comes to men.'

The kettle had boiled, she turned back to the tea-making
with relief. The names of her exes began to bounce around
her head. She wished they wouldn't; none of them brought
any joy, just heartbreak, hurt, shame and self-loathing.

John Jones then Larry Morgan. The love of her life and
the supposedly safe rebound. So very different, yet just the
same in the end. The last man that she had allowed into her
bed, before Nick, was called Kelvin Manner. She'd dated
him for just three months when she first arrived in the UK.
If anything, he was the one she least liked thinking about,
because his deception had been perhaps the most despicable.
He was *married*. She didn't know at the time, obviously! He
was one of those who slipped off his wedding ring when he
walked through the pub door. She only found out when they
bumped into a friend of his wife's at a bar. The look that
woman gave Anna! It was horrendous. Who'd have thought
facial expressions could actually say 'Slut!' She thought she
knew Anna, or at least Anna's type. But she didn't, not at all.
That was the most awful, vile thing about him; he turned
her into the other woman. *That* sort of woman. It was humiliating, horrifying.

These thoughts were all ugly and distressing. Infidelity
was so destructive. People didn't understand that. Because
it was so commonplace, people became anaesthetized. But
it was a cancer. John Jones, Larry Morgan, Kelvin Manner. All the same.

Now Nick Hudson.

'I have made mistakes in the past, I admit it. But Nick is
different. I'm marrying him.'

'You've married an asshole before.'

Anna carefully set a tray with a pot of tea down on the
kitchen table and counted to ten. It was important to stay
calm and measured around Zoe, she was volatile and un-

predictable; somebody had to remain reasonable. Yet, Anna thought, even if she counted to a thousand, she'd be compelled to ask.

'Did you have to tell him about Larry?'

'Well, you never would have.'

'Exactly.'

'I did you a favour, Anna. You can't hide a marriage.'

'That's ironic.'

'What is?'

'You telling me that full disclosure is the way to go. You've never been totally honest about anything since you learned to talk.'

'That's a rude thing to say,' muttered Zoe laconically, but she didn't deny it.

Anna poured the tea through an old-fashioned strainer. She liked the ritual of brewing tea leaves, it took a little longer but she'd always believed good things came to those who waited and that patience was a virtue. Zoe's hand hovered near the cup, keenly hoping to seize it.

'Anyway, I wasn't exactly hiding the fact I'd been married before, I just didn't think it was relevant,' Anna explained.

'Yes, you were hiding it,' Zoe said firmly.

'Well, if I was, then that was my decision.'

Zoe looked scathing, contemptuous. 'So, not all sweetness and light then. You like secrets, after all, don't you, Anna?'

Anna swallowed. 'Actually, no, I don't. You're right. It is better that Nick knows about Larry. There should be no secrets between us.'

'Interesting.' Zoe took her tea and spooned four teaspoons of sugar into it.

Anna thought she was most likely hung-over and she wondered where she'd been the night before but didn't ask. Sometimes with Zoe it was best not knowing things.

Anna continued, 'I think I'd better come clean about everything.'

'Do you?'

'Including you.'

'Me?'

The women locked eyes. As they had thousands of times throughout their lives. Staring into one another's souls. It was a peculiar thing, staring at your twin. It was like looking in a mirror, yet not, because you had no control over the expressions that were being pulled.

Anna nodded. She'd given the matter a great deal of thought and she'd decided that she and Zoe and Nick had to reconcile in order for Anna to be able to go forward with Nick. Nick had to know and understand *everything* about Zoe—however surprising or difficult or different he might find her. It was the only way they could work properly as husband and wife. Zoe and all her crazy mess were too big a part of Anna's life to be ignored.

'I've been thinking about it and I really want the three of us to get together. I feel we need to move forward.'

'I don't think I can allow that to happen,' replied Zoe coolly. She was clearly not in a co-operative mood; when was she ever?

'What are you talking about? Of course it's going to happen. We're getting married in just a couple of weeks.'

'That's nothing to do with me. I'm not even coming.'

'And what about after the wedding? You are planning to be in my life after the wedding, I suppose?' said Anna, exasperated.

Zoe shook her head; it wasn't necessarily in answer to Anna's question, but it might well have been. 'I don't like to think too far into the future, you know I don't.'

'Stop being silly, Zoe.'

'I've a really hectic schedule, right now. I don't even know when we can make this happen.'

Aggravated and exasperated, Anna suddenly demanded, 'Why did you destroy the wedding dress?'

'I didn't like your choice.'

'So you're not denying it?'

'Anna, it was almost identical to the dress you wore when you married Larry,' said Zoe.

'No, it wasn't.'

'Yes, it was.'

Anna thought about it. She supposed she could see that there were some similarities. Both dresses were lacy, both had tight waists and wide skirts, the necklines were similar. Defensively, she muttered, 'Well, that style suits me.'

'You look hot in the skimpy one,' Zoe said with a sultry smile.

'No, *you'd* look hot in the skimpy one.'

'That makes no sense. We are identical.'

'It's just not me,' Anna insisted.

'Well, it will have to be now, won't it?'

'I suppose.' Anna wanted to be angry with her sister but Zoe smiled winningly. Maybe she would look...well, hot in the dress. Hot hadn't been the look she'd originally intended but perhaps she could pull it off. If she bought a fake-fur stole to cover her shoulders, she'd feel more comfortable. 'I just want everything to be OK, you know.'

Zoe nodded, her expression shifted to a more serious one. 'Anna, I don't think a big reveal is in anyone's interest.'

'What do you mean?'

'Telling Nick everything is unnecessary. I'm out of here.'

'No! That's so typical of you to storm out of an argument, rather than sort it out like an adult.'

'I hadn't realized we were arguing.'

'Well, disagreeing then. You know what I mean.'

'I'm not storming out of the argument or disagreement. I'm storming out of your life, this country, your mind space.'

'Zoe!'

Zoe stood up. She leaned towards her twin and kissed her on the forehead. A gesture that seemed rich in meaning and symbolism. A blessing, a goodbye. 'Anna, trust me, I'm doing you a favour.' She turned and walked towards the door.

Anna jumped up and grabbed her wrist. 'How can you be doing me a favour if you're leaving me? Abandoning me? I love you. Absolutely.'

Zoe didn't reply.

Anna stood, her mouth gaping, uncomprehending. 'Haven't we always said 'Always and for ever',' she demanded, confused.

'As kids we did, yes. But, Anna, things aren't the same any more.'

Zoe slammed the door behind her.

THIRTY-NINE
Nick

Nick had never seen Anna display such determination and tenacity. He knew that she wasn't lacking in either quality but she'd always diluted her sturdy core with oodles of charm and affability; over this issue she'd definitely been more steely than sweet. 'We're all three going to meet up this week, it's non-negotiable.' Zoe had told Anna that she was going back to the States and Anna wanted to throw a goodbye dinner. 'It's the least we can do.'

But Zoe was not going back to the States, she'd made the whole thing up to avoid the three of them having to meet up. It was ironic that the very thing she was trying to avoid had precipitated the very thing she was avoiding.

He'd tried the old excuse that he was busy at work but Anna was having none of it. She called his PA directly and discovered that he had nothing in his diary on Wednesday evening.

'In fact, she said you has nothing much on at all,' commented Anna.

'Maybe not actually in the diary—no meetings or dinners, as such—although I have a big project, lots of research to do.'

'We're booked for seven p.m., Nick. Be there or the wedding is off.' She laughed when she said it.

He half believed her. He wondered, would that be a solution? If Anna called the wedding off, he wouldn't be blamed for breaking her heart, he wouldn't be the bad guy.

But he wanted to marry Anna.

Whilst sleeping with her sister.

It was complicated.

His best hope was that Zoe would give him a stay of execution by being a no-show. He was pretty certain that if she turned up, the game was over. There would be a scene. He'd hurt Anna, monumentally. His stomach slipped with the thought. Nick did not know how he was managing to place one foot in front of the other and walk towards the restaurant. Anna had booked somewhere just around the corner from Zoe's hotel, for Zoe's convenience. It was a restaurant he and Zoe had visited together on a number of occasions; would they be recognized and treated with the convivial respect of regulars? That would be awkward. If that happened, Nick would just have to bluff, convince Anna that it was the unique friendly vibe of the restaurant, rather than any genuine familiarity. He felt like he was walking far out to sea, acutely aware that there was a very real possibility that a strong current might sweep him away; dangerous, dark, risky. The only strategy that he'd come up with was inviting Rachel; it wasn't exactly clambering into a lifeboat but it was at least a rubber ring. He'd called on her because he hoped her presence would help keep everything in check.

Zoe had assured him that she could pass off the deception right under Anna's nose but he wasn't certain *he* could. Besides, it was a dark promise to make. Nick knew that it was Zoe's hedonism and irresponsibility that he found wildly attractive, irresistible even, yet at the same time those characteristics bothered him, unnerved him. It was galling and contradictory that her cool composure in this situation— whilst utterly essential—almost repulsed him; part of him wanted her to struggle more with what they were doing; did she so much as have the occasional twinge of conscience? They were sisters, after all. That was the thing about Zoe, she set him on fire with clashing, opposing emotions. She was like a rocket going off nowhere near the choreographed firework display—dangerous, thrilling, somehow admirable and breathtaking. He asked himself what sort of woman could deceive her twin so spectacularly? Did he want that sort of woman? But he knew the answer to the questions even as they formed in his head. Zoe was not any 'sort' of woman. She was beyond categorization. She was unique and spectacular and, yes, he did want her, any which way.

Nick had not told Anna that he'd invited Rachel to join them. It was a last-minute plan, only made that afternoon when he rang Rachel and she said she happened to be on the train, on her way to Bath to see their parents. When she mentioned that she would be changing trains in London, he'd seen an opportunity. He persuaded her to break her journey; promising to buy her a new ticket and put her up in a hotel if need be.

'It's OK, I have a flexible ticket. There is a train at ten fifteen and even one as late as eleven thirty; as long as I make that, I'm fine. I suppose I could stop for dinner in London. I don't doubt whatever you're offering is likely to be far tastier than the soggy cheese sandwich that will be available on the train.'

'Thanks, sis, it means a lot to me.'

'This twin must be pretty scary if you feel you need to call in the cavalry,' said Rachel.

He could hear the amusement in her voice. He hadn't told her the half of it. 'She is.'

'OK, well, I'll see you at the restaurant. I haven't got anything fancy to wear, though. I'm just in jeans.'

'That's fine.'

'Yeah, I didn't imagine you'd care.'

He caught her meaning. 'Anna won't mind.'

'What about the terrifying sister? Is she the judgemental clothes-fascist type?'

'I didn't say she was terrifying. I said there were issues.'

'Whatever.'

'But don't be late. Anna *does* have a thing about time-keeping.'

'I'll be sure to tell Virgin trains of the importance of keeping to their schedule so as not to inconvenience your fiancée. I'll go and speak to the guard about it, right now.'

'Funny. Just do your best.'

It was good to hear Rachel's teasing voice, to know that she'd be at the restaurant. It was only when Nick heard her usual jokey tone that he realized how little of his life was usual at the moment. He'd begun to think that nothing he said or did recently seemed at all normal or even real. Zoe's tone was always challenging; either flirtatious, defiant, flattering or puzzling. He rarely knew where he stood with her but, wherever it was, it wasn't anywhere normal. His actions meant that nothing he did with Anna was real any more. Not the visits to his parents, the walks in the park, the time spent in beer gardens. Nearly everything he said to her was a lie. Besides which, Anna had changed too. Since the engagement it was as if she had entered a different world, one where she talked incessantly about their happily-ever-after; he never thought he'd say it, but he was becoming overwhelmed by her constant breeziness. It was impossible to match, therefore irritating. Hadn't she noticed he was weighed down with guilt? Shouldn't she have realized he wasn't the same any more? That there was something wrong with him? He recognized that it was unfair of him to be angry with her for not sniffing out his deception, especially since he was going to great lengths to hide the truth from her. However, being aware of how unfair he was being didn't mean he could change things.

It felt like there was layer upon layer of complexity and duplicity in his world, he sometimes felt he might suffocate under the weight of it. Hal had made his disapproval of Nick's affair very clear, which meant that Nick had been reticent about confiding in Darragh or Cai. They'd only take the mick anyway; they'd be awash with, 'I told you so.' As a consequence, his conversations with his friends were strained, confined to sports and holiday plans. It never crossed his mind that he might confide in his parents—good God, no. He didn't want to be responsible for their simultaneous cardiac arrests. Weird, then, that despite the fact he had a fiancée and a lover, he'd started to feel he was on his own with this. And therefore with everything. Isolated. He wasn't complaining. Just saying. He knew he'd made his bed and had to lie on it.

It was just nice to have Rachel along for the evening, that was all. Normal.

He arrived at the restaurant ten minutes early. Luckily, the maître d' did not appear to recognize him, and Nick didn't spot any other staff that were familiar from his previous visits with Zoe. Temporary contracts and high turnover of staff had worked in his favour tonight. Rachel, to his relief and gratitude, arrived not long after him, making her five minutes ahead of schedule, so when Anna walked in at seven on the dot, he felt he had at least passed that first small test of the evening.

As much was confirmed when she beamed and cried, 'Wow, you're on time! How lovely.'

He kissed her on both cheeks, as though she was a pleasant acquaintance. Rachel glanced at him, no doubt surprised, and then she followed suit.

Turning to Rachel, Anna said, 'I don't want to sound like I'm boringly strict about time-keeping, it's just that of late, Nick has been working so hard, he hasn't managed to arrive at a single one of our dates on time, or anywhere near.'

'I see.'

'I'm just so glad he's managed to take some time off tonight.'

There was a brief kerfuffle as they took their seats, deciding which one to leave for Zoe. Nick didn't want her opposite him, or next to him, for that matter. She was likely to think it funny to covertly place her hand on his crotch;

he wouldn't be able to pull that off whilst dining with Anna and Rachel. He managed to work it so the spare seat was the one diagonally opposite him. He wondered whether he looked as stressed as he felt. His palms were sweaty, he nearly dropped the butter knife. He needed a drink. He'd been drinking quite a lot of late. People did in the summer, right? Hot nights made people thirsty.

Anna was good at wearing her game face pretty much twenty-four/seven; however, he had noticed that when she spotted Rachel something like frustration, or possibly disappointment, momentarily flashed across her face. Nick knew that Anna and Rachel had not entirely bonded but right now that was the least of his problems. At least both women were making an effort. Rachel had been coolly polite when faced with the news of their engagement. She had enough tact and respect for her brother to send a card and even flowers to congratulate them. True, there wasn't a slushy, sentimental message written in the card; in fact, all it said was: *Congratulations on your engagement, Rachel.* Thankfully, Anna was reasonable enough to understand it was something, an olive branch, following their slightly tricky introduction in the hospital. Anna had been gracious about it, she said it was because Rachel was worried about her mother and not thinking straight. 'Stress makes people act out of character.' Subsequently, she'd asked Rachel to be her bridesmaid. Rachel had accepted, although he knew it was hardly her dream to be trussed up in in dusky-pink organza, batting off comments from their rellies that, 'She'll be next!' She was doing it for him, for their parents, for form and, probably, for Anna too. No one could understand why her own twin sister was not only refusing to be a bridesmaid but refusing to come to the wedding, and everyone wanted to make it up to her.

Well, no one could understand it, other than him.

Rachel and Anna might not be besties but everything was as it should be between the two of them.

Nick explained, 'Rachel called, saying she was on her way to Mum and Dad's for a week. I just thought, as she was changing trains in London, it would be silly to miss the opportunity of catching up.'

'I totally agree,' enthused Anna. 'I'm so glad you could join us. I really am.'

Nick noticed that her face didn't match her words. Like him, she appeared nervous and somewhat anxious. She played with her napkin and cutlery. They sat for a moment in silence, someone made a comment about the unusually hot weather they'd been experiencing. Then there was a bit more silence. Rachel excused herself, said she needed to nip to the loo.

As soon as she was out of earshot Nick reached for Anna's hand. 'I'm sorry to spring an extra guest on you.'

'No, no, it's fine. Lovely.' She really would never win an Oscar.

'Come on, tell me. Why is she a problem?'

'She's not.' Anna looked awkward. 'It's just that I'm re-gretting confiding in Zoe that I thought Rachel didn't like me much.'

'Why is it a problem? You're getting along fine now.'

'Well,' Anna hesitated. 'Zoe can be a bit overprotective of me and she might be purposefully rude to Rachel, to show me she's on my side. She's someone who likes to take—no, *make*—sides. To be honest, purposefully rude is the best we can hope for, there might be an out-and-out declaration of war. I just want everyone to get on.' Anna looked crest-fallen. 'Why does everything have to be so complicated?' She sat back in her chair so he couldn't reach her hand, even if he was so inclined. 'I'm not blaming you for inviting Ra-chel but the last thing we need to bring to the table tonight is more complexity and potential hostility.'

'I don't think you have to worry about them.' Nick knew that Zoe had bigger fish to fry this evening and that relations between Anna and Rachel would not feature on Zoe's radar.

Although he couldn't guarantee that hostility was altogether off the menu. 'Oh and by the way, I haven't mentioned to my family about the Larry Morgan business,' he added. He couldn't bring himself to say, 'Your previous husband.'

'Oh, right. You could have. It's not a secret.'

He didn't know what to say to that. It *had* been a secret. 'Well, it's a bit of a shock, at least a surprise, so close to the wedding,' he pointed out. He knew his mother would be disconcerted by the news. She wouldn't care that Anna had been married before but she'd think it ought to have come up in conversation earlier, like on the first date. He didn't want to disappoint or worry her.

'OK. We'll tell them after the wedding, will we?' Anna suggested brightly.

'Yes.' He had no idea. After the wedding was another time dimension, as far as he was concerned.

'That is, unless Zoe tells Rachel tonight,' added Anna.

Oh crap. He hadn't thought of that.

'You see my problem, don't you, Nick? Once something becomes a secret it's so hard to find the right moment to clear everything up.'

Nick hesitated. 'Well, yes.' But it wasn't his secret. That one was hers. But, yes, yes, absolutely, he did see the problem. It was so hard to find the right moment to clear everything up. Impossible.

Rachel returned to the table. She'd obviously splashed water on her face in an attempt to freshen up after her train journey, some drops were still hanging off her chin. Anna leaned forward and dabbed them with her napkin.

'Oh,' said Rachel, startled. Was the action affectionate intimacy or a criticism?

Anna smiled. 'It looked like sweat. I know it wasn't,' she added hurriedly. 'But still.'

The two women smiled at each other, uneasily.

The waiter came to the table and asked if they wanted

to order drinks. Nick explained they were waiting for one more person.

'I'm going to apologize in advance. Zoe is a terrible time-keeper. She's often hours late, sometimes days,' Anna admitted with a faux giggle. 'I think we might as well order drinks. Better to do that without her anyway.' Turning to Rachel, she admitted, 'I don't know if Nick has mentioned it to you but, to be honest, Zoe is quite the hellraiser.'

'I already love her,' said Rachel. Then to the waiter she said, 'Mine's a G&T.'

They all ordered the same, except Nick asked for a double. He wasn't sure it was wise but he was certain it was necessary; he had to get through this evening somehow. No one spoke until the waiter returned with their aperitifs. They clinked glasses and said cheers. Nick's mind was whirling, he thought perhaps the others could hear the cogs, yet he could think of absolutely nothing to say. Normally so amiable and confident in any social situation, here he was, sitting between his nearest and dearest, mute. He wished they hadn't exhausted the topic of the weather so early.

Rachel took a pickaxe to the ice. 'So, in what way is she a hellraiser, this sister of yours? Come on, give me the low-down.'

It was such an ordinary, reasonable thing to ask. It was the first time Rachel had behaved entirely like herself with Anna: interested, gossipy, open. Nick should have been delighted but he actually wished Rachel had alighted on any other subject over which she and Anna might bond. The thought of talking about Zoe horrified him, it seemed weirdly disloyal. Yet, he was also curious. He found he was holding his breath, waiting to hear what Anna might say about Zoe. What drops of insight might he soak up? He didn't know enough. He was thirsty for more. He'd probably never be satiated.

'Well, let's just say, she's a party girl and she's never known when to say when.' Anna let out a deep, regretful sigh. 'I sometimes feel I've spent my life cleaning up after her messes, but you know, she's my sister.' She smiled bravely. 'There's a lot of good in her but you do have to look for it.' Rolling her eyes comically, she added, 'Really hard.'

Nick thought it sounded like something she had practised saying; obviously, she was using humour as a coping strategy. Rachel stayed silent, which encouraged Anna to go on.

'I want you both to like her. I really do. It's just that all our lives our friends, and even our parents, have found reasons to object to Zoe, to take offence.'

'Why?'

Anna glanced between the two of them nervously, she was probably wondering whether he'd be shocked. He thought of the things that Zoe had said and done with him; he doubted he could be shocked.

'It's hard to say, exactly. Things just often go wrong around her. It's frustrating because she has so much going for her, but she always seems to want to push the self-destruct button. It's safe to say she certainly does not always help herself.' Anna caught the waiter's eye. 'Can you bring my fiancé another G&T?'

He was surprised to see his glass was empty, the other two were still nursing theirs.

'Do you want to see the wine menu now?' she asked him.

He did. Very much so. He feigned nonchalance. 'Yes, OK, I'll have a look. Do either of you have a preference?'

'I don't know what I'm eating yet, so no, not really,' replied Rachel. 'You pick.' Then, turning to Anna, 'What do you mean she doesn't help herself?'

'So, we're identical, right?'

'Yes, Nick said.'

'But we're really, really not. She's—' Anna searched for the correct word and then landed on, 'Spellbinding.'

Nick thought Rachel was probably supposed to say something nice about Anna right about now. Or maybe he was. He missed his cue.

As she quickly continued, 'People fall for her. Fall in love with her. Even though she ought to come with a health warning, everyone wants to be her friend, gain her confidence, her trust. Everyone wants to feel they are special to her.'

Nick coughed. It was probably the air con.

'I think it's sort of spoilt her. You see, everyone goes out of their way to help her but she doesn't return the sentiment.' Anna paused in her storytelling and looked Nick in the eye. 'Not ever. She's not ungrateful so much as completely unaware of others.'

'What do you mean? Give me an example.'

Nick was glad Rachel had asked. He pretended not to be listening, to be absorbed in the wine menu, but in fact Anna had all of his attention. Or rather, she had it when she was talking about Zoe.

'So someone will feel they can help by finding her work and then employ her as their house-sitter; she'll throw a party, trash the place. Or they'll give her a loan and whilst they are reaching for their chequebook, she'll steel their silverware. She's stolen from her friends' wallets, from her friends' parents, from our parents. She doesn't ever accept that something might belong to someone else and that she has no right to it.'

That double G&T must have been especially potent. He must be drunk because he had the weird impression that Anna was trying to talk to him in particular. To him, on a different level. But that wasn't Anna's style. She was straightforward; if she had anything to say, she'd simply say it.

Except she hadn't said anything about being married before, had she?

But that was different. No, he was being crazy. Whilst the stuff about Zoe not knowing what did or didn't belong to her seemed oddly pertinent, he had to be imagining things. It was his conscience. Plaguing him. Or the drink. Tricking him. He wasn't seeing things clearly. The waiter poured some wine into his glass for him to taste. Impatiently he swallowed it back in a gulp and indicated he wanted his glass filling. To the top.

Rachel looked a bit surprised. 'Should we order food?'

Anna glanced at her phone, checking the time and her messages. It was already seven twenty-three. 'Maybe some bread and olives. I'm still hoping she might show up—after all, this is supposed to be her goodbye dinner. She's the guest of honour.'

For a while they talked about other things. Inevitably, the wedding was discussed. Anna had ordered Rachel's bridesmaid's dress online and had it sent directly to her in Edinburgh. 'Do you like it?' she asked keenly.

'It's very nice,' Rachel assured her.

Anna's face fell a little. 'Nice?'

Nick watched Rachel try harder.

'It's lovely.'

'How's the fit?'

'Yeah, great.'

He knew his sister well enough to understand that probably meant she hadn't tried it on at all.

'And have you thought about shoes? I was thinking nude shoes.'

'Nude shoes?'

Anna explained, 'The colour. Nude.'

'I see.'

'Do you have any?'

'Erm. I'm not sure. Probably not.'

'Well, if you get a pair I'll reimburse you, obviously. But you will need to try the dress on with shoes.'

'Oh yes.'

Nick admired his sister for faking an interest.

'So you'll need to get shoes asap.'

'Right.'

'Maybe you could look whilst you're in Bath.'

'Sounds like a plan.'

'Should I text Pamela, just so she can remind you?' Anna asked, trying her best not to sound overbearing. Failing.

'If you like, but I'll probably remember.'

'Probably?'

'I'll remember.'

'I'll text anyway, to be on the safe side.'

'If you like.' Rachel needed her glass refilling now.

'If anything needs to be altered on the dress I'll pay for that, obviously, too.'

'Oh, it's fine,' said Rachel. It wasn't clear if she meant that the fit was fine or her bearing the expense of altera- tions was fine.

For a moment there was a lull in the conversation, then they agreed they might as well order and Rachel picked up the mantle by talking about the latest reality TV show that she was gripped by.

Anna asked lots of questions about it although hadn't actually watched it herself. 'I will, though. I'll watch it on catch-up. Promise,' she said.

Anna regularly, anxiously, checked her messages but Zoe hadn't been in touch. Nick pretended to be attending to some work emails but took the opportunity to surrepti- tiously see if she'd sent anything through to him—an ex- cuse, an explanation, an update or an apology? Nothing. He was relieved. She wasn't going to come. She'd done him a favour. The food arrived, Nick asked for a second bottle of wine by way of celebration. It crossed his mind that drink- ing alcohol was a lot like being with Zoe; it created the ef- fect of two things happening simultaneously. Time slowed, he felt sluggish and swollen, yet he could also access clear, precise thoughts. Right then, watching Anna and Rachel negotiate their way towards some sort of understanding, Nick could imagine what things could be like for him in the future. Cheerful family Christmases, a house in a buzzing part of London, kids at a smart day school, Anna doing a lot of stuff for the school's Parents' Association, the children

shining at any number of things—sports, maths, music—
maybe they'd go to Oxbridge, there would be grandchildren.
He and Anna would grow old together.

There would be no confrontation tonight. He'd got away
with it.

The conversation did not exactly flow but it chugged
along pleasantly enough, only interrupted by Anna's regular and anxious scouring of her phone for news from Zoe.
Rachel was on her best behaviour, employing a tone of polite interest most of the time; the tone he suspected she used
when kids in her class told her about their Pokémon Go adventures or similar. For her part, Anna was being the most
ingratiating he had ever seen her; a clear eleven out of ten
in terms of asking interested questions about Rachel's job,
home, friends and even cat. Nick didn't contribute much.
He just drank.

Then sank.

He couldn't find the energy to join in. What was the point
in talking about the wedding? Would, could, should it take
place? Unexpectedly, the cheerful family Christmases he'd
only just imagined, seemed dreadful and claustrophobic.
Sod the day school and the Parents' Association, the shiny
children would be smug and annoying. Undoubtedly, it was
a relief that Zoe hadn't turned up tonight; he'd have hated
a row in such a public place, where the waiters were polished and discreet, the food above par, the decor stunning,
his fiancée beautiful.

But he missed her.

He could taste his food for a second time.

He swallowed it back; he was not the sort of man to throw
up on white linen tablecloths. Yet, the swift clarity of understanding was distressing, because he suddenly understood.
She'd made the choice. Her choice. She'd gone. Left him.
Left the UK. The thing she'd said to Anna wasn't a convenient way to get Anna off their backs; it was for real. He

thought back to the conversation they'd had about him being unable to make a choice. He'd asked her to do it.

And she had.

His innards became loose and useless. Something in his chest hurt. A raw pain, like he'd been winded. He could see it so clearly. She was standing in a queue in check-in. She was in the lounge. She was boarding the plane. She had taken off. She'd moved on. She wasn't coming tonight but it wasn't a stay of execution; it was goodbye. *People fall for her. Fall in love with her but she doesn't return the sentiment. Not ever.* He looked across at Anna. She was talking to Rachel but drumming her fingers on the table at the same time. He felt for her. It was all his fault. Her sister wasn't coming to her wedding; her sister was leaving the country. She must miss her. He understood. Him more than anyone. They had that in common and yet they could never talk about it.

'Hey, you've had your nails done,' he said, suddenly, to Anna. His comment came out a little loudly and unexpectedly. He really needed to drink some water.

The people on the next table glanced at him in the way Londoners did when they wanted to convey disapproval. Anna smiled and waved her manicured fingers at Nick.

'You've had a colour put on,' he observed. Or rather, slurred.

'Just for a change,' smiled Anna. She told Rachel, 'My usual preference is a clear varnish.'

Rachel nodded, appreciatively. 'Oh, I like the blue. It's very modern, summery.'

Anna beamed, happy to receive the compliment. 'It was Zoe's idea. She gets hers done all the time. She persuaded me.'

'Subliminal 'something old, something new, something borrowed, something blue'?' suggested Rachel.

'Maybe.'

Rachel's casual and positive reference to the wedding

made Anna beam. The waiter reappeared and suggested they might all like dessert, or a digestif, maybe a coffee.

Anna glanced at her phone again. 'Oh my goodness. I'd better go. It's nearly twenty to ten.'

'Go? Go where?' Nick asked, confused.

'To check on Zoe, of course.'

'What are you? Her babysitter?' laughed Rachel.

Anna smiled pleasantly. 'I know it probably seems crazy to you but I'm the older twin by five minutes. As the big sister I need to take care of Zoe, even when she doesn't want to be taken care of. Nick, you must get that.'

'Him take care of me? No chance,' laughed Rachel. 'One day, when you have more time, I'll tell you about how he once nearly drowned me in a swimming pool when we were on holiday in Malta.'

'It was an accident!'

'So he says. Or how often he's left me stuck up trees that he's encouraged me to climb.'

'It was character-building.'

Anna smiled politely. 'Those sound like great stories.'

Even through his drunken haze Nick recognized that she wasn't as interested as he might have expected. She was forever pumping his parents for stories of his childhood; now, she wanted to get away. He wondered whether she'd drawn the same conclusion as he had. Did she, too, fear that Zoe had already gone?

'It's just that a no-show, with absolutely no word, usually spells trouble. Who doesn't turn up for their own leaving do?' Anna grabbed her handbag and began rooting around for her purse. It was a bit of a show of politeness for Rachel, really; Anna knew Nick would happily foot the bill as he usually did. She just didn't want to give the impression that she was taking him for granted.

'Just go and put your mind at rest. I'll sort this out.' He didn't dare suggest accompanying her, in case she took him up on the offer. 'Text me, right.'

'OK, I will.' She hugged Rachel and leaned towards him.

He thought she was going to squeeze his hand or give him a peck on the cheek. She didn't, she kissed his lips. In front of Rachel. Unabashed. Out of character. Did he imagine it? He must have, he thought he'd felt the warm wetness of her tongue. Just for a moment, finding its way into his mouth. Fast, discreet. Anna smelt sticky, musky. The heat had overpowered her usual floral fragrance. He liked it but it was disconcerting. Confusing.

Breaking away, she turned to Rachel. 'I hope I haven't given too bad an impression of Zoe, tonight. She really can be very lovely, when she puts her mind to it. Can't she, Nick? What am I saying? You've only met her once. You don't really know. Do you?'

'Oh yes, I'm sure she's lovely,' said Rachel tactfully.

Nick didn't know what to say.

'I firmly believe all she needs is a bit of understanding.'

'Right.'

'It's just that I might go to her hotel and simply have to clean up vomit or—' She broke off. 'I always expect the worst, you see. It's difficult. I've always lived with the feeling that my twin is hurtling towards disaster and I can't help but hold the belief that it is my responsibility to stop that disaster from happening.' She shrugged, somewhat helplessly. 'Goodbye.'

And before Nick could say anything more, Anna had dashed out of the restaurant.

FORTY
Nick

Nick and Rachel watched Anna run out of the restaurant. For a moment there was silence. Nick broke it the only way he knew how. 'Are you having dessert?'

'I need a glass of something strong after that,' Rachel replied.

Nick chose to ignore the inference behind her comment but ordered a couple of whiskys from the hovering waiter.

'Since when have you drunk whisky?' asked Rachel.

'It's a relatively recent thing,' he said with a sigh.

They stayed in their own heads until Rachel said, 'Look, Nick, I don't want us to fall out over what I'm about to say.'

'If you think we might, then don't say it.'

Rachel looked surprised that he'd cut her off so abruptly, but he was serious, he didn't want to hear what she had to say. He didn't need any more aggro. He had more than enough going on in his head.

However, Rachel was not easily silenced. She knew her own mind too well and she loved her brother too dearly. 'I have to.'

They stared at one another. It was uncomfortable. She took a deep breath, her nostrils flaring slightly. It was funny the things you noticed about a person over time, when you were up close and personal. Rachel's nostrils always flared when she was tense.

'Are you sure about this wedding? About marrying Anna?'

'Rachel!'

She rushed on, refusing to be deterred. 'I know Mum and Dad love her and think she's basically Florence Nightingale and Mother Teresa rolled into one cute little package, but I can't help thinking she's batshit crazy.'

Nick laughed despite himself. His sister always said it as she saw it.

'I mean I can't even imagine what her sister is going to be like if Anna is the sane one.'

Nick sighed but didn't know what to say.

'You can't see it, can you?'

'No.'

'She's so ensconced in the fairy tale I keep expecting to see little singing mice and birds appear to make her clothes.'

'Lots of women get carried away with wedding prep. It does not make them crazy.'

'And why does she put up with that crap from her sister?' Rachel waited for him to respond.

He didn't. Couldn't.

In an effort to placate him, or understand him, or something, she added carefully, 'I can see she's a beauty.'

'She's a lovely person,' he clarified.

'Yeah, she seems it.' Rachel's tone was flat and unconvincing.

'She really is,' he insisted.

'Nick, I don't think anyone is that lovely. She's like Mary Poppins on happy pills! There was something off tonight. Something forced. Don't pretend you weren't aware of it. You were super tense. Not yourself at all.'

Nick felt guilt flood through his body. Sloshing and slipping about, weighing him down. Anna was not to blame for the strange atmosphere tonight. He was. It was entirely his fault that things had seemed weird and strained at times because he was betraying her in the worst possible way, by screwing her sister. This was not something he could tell Rachel. They were close, she had a realistic view of him and a reasonably thorough understanding of how he lived his life, but she'd be disgusted if she knew what he'd been up to these past few months. Who wouldn't be? He felt awful that Rachel was blaming Anna for the tension. That she couldn't see how great Anna truly was because he had muddied the waters.

Deceit piled upon deceit.

He felt sick with shame.

Or it could have been the alcohol.

This would not do. He must be resolute. Zoe had probably gone and that was a good thing. She'd made a choice, the right choice, and she'd done it for him and Anna. He could not have continued to live the way he was. Ultimately, it wasn't him. He'd put things right with Anna. He had to. It wouldn't be easy. But he'd work at it. Kind, clever, decent, beautiful Anna was the woman for him. Any man would be lucky to call her his wife. Once more, he brought to mind the imagined cute-looking kids. He put them inside images of wholesome holidays: lazy, barmy days in the garden; informative, inspiring museum visits; splashing about in rock pools and building sandcastles. All that could only happen with Anna. That was not Zoe's scene at all. What was he thinking? That he could hang out in nightclubs with Zoe until they were drawing their pensions? That she'd bend over her Zimmer frame and he'd take her from behind? Stupid! Stupid!

'Rachel, please don't say anything else. I don't want to hear it,' he said firmly. 'Anna is a really lovely person. Wonderful, in fact. The truth is, I don't deserve her.'

Rachel looked suspicious. 'Since when has it ever bothered you that you got more than you deserve? You're the guy who once licked all around his birthday cake to discourage others from having a slice.'

'I was eight, Rachel, let it go.'

'You were eleven and I think secretly you're still a selfish bastard. A nice-looking, rather persuasive one, but one all the same. I don't believe the only thing that's worrying you about this marriage is that you're punching above your weight.' Rachel fell silent; she was clearly hoping he'd confide in her.

He couldn't, just couldn't.

Especially when she added, 'You know I love you, bruv. Right? Everyone does. I don't want to see you making a mistake.'

Too late. He'd made an awful mistake. He'd ruined the purity, innocence and honesty that he and Anna had shared. The heady, swift romance had been blemished by his despicable behaviour and he doubted he'd ever be able to retrieve that original feeling, that sense of certainty, but he knew he had to go ahead with the wedding. It was the nearest thing he had to honourable. Dumping Anna at this late stage, breaking her heart, well, that would be unforgivable. Zoe had loved her enough to give him up; he had to be equally decent.

'I'm marrying Anna. I hope you can respect my decision. I really appreciate that you made an effort with her tonight. I think if you make an effort for long enough it will stop being an effort.' He wasn't sure who he was trying to convince—himself, or his sister—still, he was glad that he sounded more sober than he felt.

'Well,' Rachel shrugged. 'If you're sure, and if you're happy.'

He looked at the table.

'Are you, Nick?'

'What?'

'Happy?'

'Of course I am. I'll get the bill. We're going to need to get a move on if you're to catch the ten-fifteen train.' He looked about for the waiter.

Accepting that he wasn't going to discuss the matter further, but not feeling quite ready to leave him, Rachel said, 'If I promise not to say another word about Anna, am I allowed pudding? I can get the later train.'

Nick grinned. 'You'll be OK catching the very last one? You won't be in Bath until after one in the morning.'

'I'm a big girl and I fancy the baked Alaska. I bet that's quite a show here.'

Nick signalled for the waiter and ordered the baked Alaska, two spoons and another whisky.

'Get your own Alaska,' said Rachel. 'I do not want you licking mine.'

Much later, when the waiter came with the bill, Nick handed over his card, without checking the total. 'My treat,' he told Rachel.

She didn't argue. A school teacher's salary versus a banker's salary, there was no argument.

'OK. Cab or tube?' he asked.

'The tube will be quicker.'

'I'll walk you to the station.'

The weather had changed and the night was abruptly cooler than it had been for weeks. Litter whipped along the road; the sky was a deep, dramatic, sombre blue. The fresh, chilly air did not make him feel sober, just more aware of how drunk he was. He'd drunk far too much. It had been an emotional roller coaster of an evening. It had started full of trepidation, then relief and finally something akin to—what?—a bitter-sweet acceptance, not quite a celebration. Of course he'd drunk too much. It wasn't a way to live. Far from sensible. Things had to change.

'A storm's coming,' said Rachel in a funny pretending-to-be-in-a-horror-movie-type voice.

Nick nodded and was about to fling his arm around her to keep her warm, to show his brotherly affection, when his phone buzzed. He was expecting an update from Anna, letting him know if she was at her flat or his. He doubted she'd have caught up with Zoe; in his mind she was halfway across the Atlantic by now. He hoped Anna had gone home to her flat. He'd join her there. It was a bit further out, but it was one of the few places that he felt remained untarnished. After the wedding he would put his flat on the market. He couldn't walk into the bathroom now without thinking of Zoe: naked, brazen, beautiful. And he shouldn't be thinking about Zoe at all. He allowed himself a moment to imagine slipping between Anna's clean sheets, which always smelt of fabric conditioner. Then he checked the message.

It was a text from 'Joe': It's all over. You'd better come.

What did that mean? Deep and profound panic pricked the base of his neck, then seeped through his body. Had she confessed? Did Anna now know all? Was he being called to account, to arbitrate, to confess, to choose? Or did the message mean something else entirely?

It was all over between him and Zoe.

She wanted him at the hotel because there was some problem with the bill and she wished to check out.

Both scenarios were possible. The panic was shoved out, as frustration slammed into his body. Zoe was being as annoyingly cryptic as ever. He felt as though he'd been thrown down a snake in a game of Snakes and Ladders. Back to square one. It would probably have been better if she'd been on a plane.

Yet, he would go to her. He quickly leaned in and hugged his sister. 'Hug the parents for me. I've got to dash now.' Unceremoniously, he left her at the tube station, staring after him.

'Well, I guess I'll see you at the wedding?' she called.

Her words were picked up only by the wind and buffeted in many directions.

FORTY-ONE
Nick

Nick started running towards the hotel. That's where she must be, right? At the hotel he was paying for. Or was she somewhere else? He couldn't get the image of her at an airport out of his head. He'd conjured it up so often that evening, he now believed it wholeheartedly. But after all, it was only conjecture. It was maddening that he wasn't absolutely sure where he was being summoned to, let alone why. Situation normal with Zoe. He stopped running and stood under the canopy of a late-night convenience store. He called Zoe but it went straight to voicemail. He called Anna; it rang and rang and rang until, on the seventh ring, it went through to voicemail. Zoe often didn't take calls and switched her phone off at her own convenience, but Anna tended to keep hers on in case anyone from the centre felt the need to contact her. Anna was deeply considerate, she never let her phone ring through unless she was totally indisposed. She knew that if someone actually wanted to talk, in this day and age—which was an unusual enough occurrence—then it demanded attention. It had to be a bad sign that she hadn't answered his call. She must know. It was a sickening thought. Listening to her chirpy tones asking him to leave a message reminded him of that time, several weeks back, when he first met Zoe and had called Anna from the loos, confused, overwhelmed. Unlike that time, he did not leave a message. What was the point?

Instead, he sent Zoe a text: Where r u? I need to speak to you.

No sooner had he pressed 'send' than his phone rang.

'What's going on?' he demanded, unable to hide his extreme agitation.

'She knows. We've had a row.'

'What? Fuck!' The worst thing, the inevitable thing. He had expected this and dreaded this, but most of all he'd hoped to avoid this. He was a lucky guy. Usually. Of course he had always thought he'd get away with it. Didn't everyone? 'Where are you now?' he asked.

'On my way to Heathrow. I'm going back to America.'

So he'd been right, she was leaving him.

Then she said something unexpected and wonderful, 'You should come too.'

'What?'

'Get on the tube. I know you always have your passport on you.'

It was true he always did, in case he had to suddenly hop on a flight one afternoon to talk to a client in Europe. It was an occasional thing but not unheard of. He always liked to be prepared.

'What are you waiting for?' she asked.

He was stunned. It was crazy. What a thing to suggest. He'd drunk a lot so it was difficult to know how to respond properly. He started to giggle. A thirty-year-old man giggling was inappropriate at the best of times. 'I can't just fly to America.'

'Why not?' Zoe sounded amused.

About a thousand reasons: Anna, his work, his parents, Rachel, his mates Darragh, Cai, Hal. He'd miss them all. Their names and faces crashed around his head. Each one of them claiming a small part of him. Was she seriously asking him to give up everything and everyone for her? Was he seriously considering it?

'What about my work?' he stuttered. Somehow he felt

that would be the most palatable objection to raise to Zoe. She couldn't be jealous of his work.

'They have banks in America, Nick. Big ones,' she teased, in the way you might tease a very young, uncomprehending child. 'Anyway, we're not going to America tonight. There are no flights this late. We're staying in an airport hotel. We'll head to New York first thing tomorrow morning.'

'That makes no sense. Why are you going to an airport hotel tonight? Why not just stay put for one more night?'

'Believe me, it makes a lot of sense. Now stop talking about it and go and catch the tube,' she said bossily.

He forced himself to say it. He couldn't allow himself to kowtow to her. They'd have no chance if he did. 'What about Anna?'

'You don't want to think about her any more,' she snapped. 'You are not in love with her, Nick. You may be fooling yourself but not me. I'll see you at Heathrow. I've emailed you the details of the hotel we're staying at tonight, the flight details, tickets, etc. You're already checked in.' Zoe's voice had lost all its playfulness.

'What? I'm already checked in?' She'd assumed he'd go with her. Of course. Yet. 'I can't just leave. I have to talk to her first.' Was he thinking of doing this? He didn't know. It was too sudden. Too impossible. Too wild. At least if he went to speak to Anna he'd buy some time. Clear his head.

'That is not an option. This is a now-or-never deal,' replied Zoe stonily.

Big, slow splats of rain began to fall about him. It was as though there was some signal from the universe. He felt the world shift. A cosmic change. 'I have to speak to her,' he stated firmly.

'No, you have to come away with me, right now.'

He stood his ground. He wasn't a man to be pushed around, and he knew that however inconvenient Zoe found this, she was also attracted to it. 'Where did you have your row?'

'At the hotel. She came to find me.'

'Where is she now?'

'I left her there but you don't want to go there, Nick.'

He didn't reply to that because his drunken brain stumbled upon another point. 'How did you buy the tickets?'

'I didn't. Well, at least not technically. You did. I used your computer and credit card for the bookings.'

'What? How? When?'

'A while back, I stole the key to your flat off Anna and had one cut for myself. I knew it would come in useful one day. Two nights ago, when you were staying over at Anna's, I let myself in. I put the flights on your Visa.' She sounded accusing.

It was ridiculous. He had every right to stay at Anna's, didn't he? As it happened, Anna had had to work late and so he'd prepared supper for her at her flat. No doubt Zoe thought they'd had hot sex; in fact, they'd had cold gazpacho soup very late at night. Besides, hadn't she just confessed to breaking and entering and fraud? Surely he was the one entitled to sound accusatory right now.

'It would have been easier if you'd given me a key in the first place,' she pointed out, matter-of-factly. When he remained coolly silent, she laughed. 'Oh, come on, Anna must have given you a rundown of my skill set.'

She doesn't ever accept that something might belong to someone else.

'Nick, come with me now, do not go and try to find her at the hotel. You're opening up a whole can of worms. I'm telling you, you'll regret it. Come to me.'

Nick thought that Anna was unlikely to be at the hotel by now anyway—she'd probably have gone home to her flat— but as the hotel was only a five-minute walk from where he was, it was worth a try. He could only imagine what sort of state she'd be in, betrayed by her sister and fiancé. Would she be devastated, furious, hysterical? A mix of all three, he supposed. He'd behaved despicably over the last few weeks. Of course he had. He knew he had. He didn't like himself much at all. And now Anna knew everything, she wouldn't like him at all either.

He wondered, if it was possible for him to turn back time, would he? He didn't know for certain but he did know what he needed to do next. He owed her an explanation, or an apology. He owed her something. At the very least he had to look her in the eyes and absorb whatever it was she wanted to hurl at him: abuse, accusations, dismay.

'I have to do it, Zoe.'

'Don't.'

He hung up.

FORTY-TWO
Zoe

Stupid, stupid man. Predictable. though. Totally.

I wish he'd just agreed to come straight to the airport. It would have been much more straightforward and some sort of victory for me. A decisive action at last. The path he's chosen is far harder and more complicated. Heartbreaking, actually. He'll be sorry for it. Still, I warned him. He only has himself to blame. I told you I'm a fan of people owning their own mess. I was, of course, prepared for it to go either way. I'm not the one who is going to get burned here. I have it all planned out. I'm one step ahead, always. I know he'll ring me within five minutes, which gives me just enough time to check in at the airport hotel and start Plan B rolling. Obviously, the entire thing has been harrowing and regretful but, that said, I'm almost looking forward to revealing it to him. It's brilliantly clever and final.

Finally final.

He has been unreasonable, he has asked too much of me and Anna. Although, I've limited sympathy there. She has always been so wet about men, overly keen to placate, mollify and pacify. Bloody fool. Made herself into an eternal doormat. Come on in, sir, wipe your feet on me, why don't you? It was always going to end badly. I, however, am not the sort to put up with this kind of vacillation, and Nick needs to understand that.

The lesson is coming to him in high definition, any moment now.

I check in, using Anna's passport as ID. I knew they'd ask for some as the booking was made online and they're a bit more careful about that sort of thing at airport hotels. There is a level of amusement, playing her. It's sort of fun. I haven't done this since I was about seven. When we were very young we used to like to pretend to be each other; it's the perk that every twin has to exploit at some point. However, I got bored of it. I did not like having to be Miss Goody Two Shoes and, frankly, our trick never lasted any length of time because Anna was hopeless at being me. She just didn't have the edge. She didn't know how to be naughty. She gave herself away by picking up litter that someone else had dropped, or holding a door open for a schoolteacher. They'd know it was her in an instant. Idiot. Poor darling idiot.

At the hotel reception, I'm smiley and ingratiating. I start up a conversation with the woman on duty—to make sure she remembers me checking in, if anyone asks. I say she must be tired and she admits she is. I sympathetically comment that working the nightshift must be a terrible drawback, so restrictive on her social life. She notices my (Anna's) engagement ring when I sign for the room (sure she did, I flashed it about so much, I thought I might take out an eye). I giggle and ask if she can keep a secret. She makes a joke about the TV series *The Night Manager* and says it's part of her job description to be discreet. I tell her that my fiancé and I are eloping.

Her eyes widen with excitement. 'Really?'

I do lots of wide-eyed giggling—Anna stuff. I tell her we've just been overwhelmed by all the planning of the big day, and besides, my parents can't attend the wedding in the UK, so we've made a last-minute plan to surprise them, dash back to the States and marry there. 'We're flying out first thing tomorrow. We decided to treat ourselves to a night in the hotel, rather than have to get up at the crack of dawn. I'd hate to miss our flight!'

'Oh my gosh, that's so romantic,' she gushes.

There it is again. That word. Romantic. Like that justifies everything. I wonder how she'd react if I told her Nick actually isn't the romantic sort and the girl who spoke dirty had won the day. Not well, I should imagine.

'But what about your fiancé's parents? Won't they be sad to miss it?'

'That part is actually breaking my heart.' I make a sad face. People use lots of emojis nowadays. I mean *lots*. Anna never texted without using at least two per message. As a result, people aren't particularly attuned to reading real faces. They accept clumsy pantomime to convey emotion. If I stroked my chin, this woman would believe I was genuinely confused. If I stuck out my tongue and winked, she wouldn't bat an eyelid, she'd just look around for the object of my lust. I avoid the use of emojis at all costs, just to make a point of difference. 'They are *such* lovely people. Unfortunately, his mother recently had a hip replacement operation. She can't fly. Nick is making the ultimate sacrifice for me. His parents are missing out so mine can be there on our big day, which is actually going to be quite a small day, as it turns out.' I giggle the way Anna would; ingratiating, a bit desperate.

'Wow. That's so special.' Then the receptionist leans forward conspiratorially and whispers in my ear, 'But after all, we all know it's the bride's day, when it comes down to it.'

Anna is not marrying Nick. I am not marrying Nick. But if I was ever to be tempted, I'd call to mind this ingrained inequality, which would have the same effect on me as a slap in the face on a hysteric or a bucket of cold water on the sexually aroused.

My phone rings. Nick.

I grin at the receptionist. 'This is him now.'

She mouths an offer to find someone to help me with my bag, I shake my head and walk towards the elevator.

'Hello, darling,' I say loudly. This is for the receptionist and must confuse the hell out of Nick, as I never use endearments.

'What the hell happened here?' he demands without preamble.

'I told you we had a fight.'

'You said you had a row.'

'It started as a row. It turned nasty.'

'There's blood everywhere.'

'Yes.'

'In the bathroom. A lot on the marble counter near the basin and on the floor. Smeared *all over* the floor.' He sounds shocked.

Yes, well, it is shocking.

'Whose blood is it, Zoe?'

He knows.

'She fell. She cut her head.' I get in the elevator. 'I'm in an elevator now, I might lose the signal. Hold the line for a minute.'

Unbelievably, he does as I instruct. It pleases me. It's a good sign. I give him a running commentary as to what I'm doing, in the idiotic way people do when they're on the telephone and wanting to offer the other person reassurance that they're still at the end of the line, even though it would be much more elegant to simply stay quiet for a moment or two. Normally I'd remain silent, enigmatic. Nothing is normal tonight.

'Here we are, third floor. I'm just walking along the corridor. Yup, this is mine. Number three hundred and six. Third floor. OK.'

I run the card through the lock, green light. I close the door behind me, push my case against the wall, kick off my shoes. The balls of my feet are aching because I'm wearing Manolo Blahnik; I'm the sort of woman who knows the importance of a fabulous shoe. My temples and back are aching too because it's been a very difficult night. I don't tell him any of this. I need a moment. To breathe. To think.

The room is clean and basic. It lacks all the luxury of the hotels I'm used to, the hotel I've just left, but I'm glad. I didn't want the rooms to be anything alike. I let out a sigh. I hadn't realized I was holding my breath. I sit on the bed. My back bends, I just can't remain ramrod straight. Then I lie down. I can't afford to accommodate any uncertainty. If I pause and doubt, even for a moment, then I'll be overwhelmed. Undone. I—we—must push on.

'OK.'

'Where is Anna now, Zoe?' His voice is shaky.

I can tell it's taking a huge effort for him to stay calm. 'I don't know,' I answer honestly.

'I'm going to her flat.'

'She's not there.'

'How do you know, when you've just said you don't know where she is?'

'She's dead, Nick.'

The words tear from my lips to punch and claw through his consciousness. It's a foul, defining sentence. One that can never be taken back. One that I'll never be able to apologize for. One that he'll never be able to fix, or ignore or walk away from. That's the important thing. He can't walk away from this.

'What the fuck? You're mad.' He starts to laugh, a nasty, sarcastic, disbelieving laugh.

I let him. He's entitled to it.

When I don't respond, he adds, 'What are you saying? What a fucking weird thing to say.'

He's swearing a lot. He sounds drunk. And scared.

I wish I was drunk. 'I'm just telling you the truth.'

'I don't believe you.'

So, I have to explain, as clearly and simply as I possibly can. 'She came to my hotel to find out why I wasn't at the dinner. But I couldn't tell her, could I, Nick? Not really. I was packing my bags and she got worked up. She kept saying that she just couldn't understand why I was leaving so suddenly and secretively. Again, I couldn't offer a decent enough reason, could I? I don't know, Nick. She just guessed. It came out of nowhere. She suddenly accused me of seducing you. Her words.'

'Did you deny it? Why didn't you deny it?'

I don't think he's seeing the big picture yet. Shock, disbelief, denial.

'I was going to but then I thought, what's the point? These things always come out in the end, don't they? You know that. You've always known that. It was a risk we took. It was horrendous. The things she called me. I've been called it all before, but not by her. It was weird, hearing her say that stuff. Sad. She was yelling the abuse. Top volume. Totally out of character yet totally understandable, I suppose.' I sigh. Let out a long breath. But the weight stays on my chest.

He doesn't interrupt again.

'You really got under her skin, I'll say that much. I tried to calm her down, then to ignore her. She started grabbing at me, my arms, my shoulders, following me from the wardrobe to the bed where I had my suitcase almost full, almost ready to go. If only you'd managed to keep her at the restaurant for another twenty minutes or so, Nick.'

I wonder what he's thinking. He's probably not thinking. Just feeling. Feeling scared. Horrified.

'She followed me into the bathroom where I was gathering up my toiletries. Just screaming in my face. *Slut, whore, home breaker.* Over and over again. She'd completely snapped. And then I did it. I pushed her. Just once. She slipped, there must have been water on the floor from my shower. She fell backwards, hit her head on that marble basin unit.' I imagine him turning his head now, looking at the blood. There was a lot of it. On the basin unit, splatters up the mirror, on the floor where she fell down. Mostly there. It's difficult to think about. 'I checked her pulse. She was dead before I left.'

He's silent. I can hear his background noise through the phone: rain, traffic, his breathing.

Eventually, he says, 'I don't believe you. You're just trying to scare me.'

I can hear the terror in his voice. He doesn't quite believe me but nor does he entirely disbelieve me. I wonder whether he's staring at the corner of the unit where her blood and hair are smeared, matted.

'You're making this up. You are fucked up.'

'That's not a very nice thing to say,' I point out.

'If she's dead, why isn't her body here?'

'I know people, who know people, who can deal with this sort of thing. I called someone to come and take her away. It cost a lot of money. I was lucky I had kept your card, I had to withdraw a lot of cash.'

I imagine him scrabbling for his wallet, noticing for the first time that one of his clutch of credit cards is missing. He was once too drunk to enter his pin number when paying for drinks at a club. He told me the combination so that I could punch it in.

'You're talking bollocks. This is ridiculous, Zoe. Stop it.' His voice is raspy, crammed with outrage.

I start to cry. I'm as surprised as he, no doubt, is. This wasn't part of my plan. I wanted to stay utterly in control, eminently cool and collected. Crying has always been more Anna's thing than mine. She could turn on the waterworks whenever they were needed. Happy tears, sad tears. Frankly, it bored me to tears. However, I'm battered by the thought of what I'm doing.

What I've done.

I know it's the only way forward but it's overwhelming. Horrifying. I start to gasp and splutter. 'She's dead, Nick. My sister is dead. There's just me left.' I repeat this, over and over again. It's a pitiful, dreadful sentence to utter. I can't control myself. The thought of her cold and dead is too much to deal with. My hands are shaking. I'm in shock.

It's vile. It's done. I'm crying really hard now. It strikes me that whilst he has heard me in the throes of passion, moaning and orgasmic; and whilst he's heard me laugh and tease and scold, this is the most honest sound he's ever heard from me. Devastation. Unadulterated grief.

'Zoe, Zoe, calm down. You need to say calm.'

Funny, the one thing I didn't plan—the hysterics bubbling up and out—has got to him. Has made him believe me.

'Take a deep breath. We need to stay calm,' he instructs.

He's said 'we.' That helps. I take a deep breath and then another. I stop talking, stay silent. Let him think.

'Hold on a minute, what do you mean you called someone? Paid someone to move her. How would you have had time to do that? Anna only left the restaurant a couple of hours ago.'

I hadn't expected him to be so thorough at this point. I thought the drink and the shock would provide me with enough momentum to get through these first few hours. I'd hoped that he'd go along with all my instructions and I'd explain everything properly at a later date. I sigh and realize I might have to give him more now, but it isn't the time to tell him everything. If I tell him everything, if he guesses this was planned, he won't come with me. He has to come with me. I haven't done all of this to lose him now. I need to lure him in, carefully, like a wary animal. Then bang the cage door behind him.

Through my gasps, I whisper, 'I'm surprised you didn't bump into them. They probably only left just before you arrived. Maybe you disturbed them. Maybe that's why they haven't done a thorough job.'

'I don't believe you. You're talking bullshit. She's not dead. If you paid someone to clean up, why haven't they? There's mess everywhere, blood everywhere.'

The issue is, he doesn't want to believe me.

'They're a couple of cokeheads not members of the Secret Service.' I allow him to see some of my frustration.

'Bastards. Hopeless bastards…' I pause. 'You're going to have to clean up, Nick.'

'What? No!'

'Yes. Yes, you are.'

'But cleaning up means I'm covering up a crime.' He obviously can't process this.

'Cleaning up means there wasn't a crime.' I let that thought take hold. 'How much blood is there? Could it just look like someone's cut themselves shaving, or someone's having a messy period or something?'

'Zoe. Fuck. No, I don't know. No. There's far too much blood for that.'

'Where's the blood, Nick?'

'On the basin unit, and there's a great big smear all the way out of the bathroom. They must have dragged her. Jesus, Zoe.'

It's sinking in.

'Is there any on the carpet in the bedroom?'

That would be impossible to clean up. I wait a second while he checks.

'No.'

'Is there a rug?'

'No, no rug.'

'They must have taken her out in that. Probably via the fire escape. Luckily my room faced on to that back alley.'

'I can't take this in. Is she really dead, Zoe? What have you done?'

FORTY-THREE
Nick

The hairs on his body stood proud. As though they were trying to desert him. He felt sweaty, clammy, yet icy cold. He put his hand out to steady himself. The flat of his palm against the mirror. His hand in her blood. A perfect print. Fuck. He reached for the water glass where not long ago Zoe's toothpaste might have sat. This was surreal. This couldn't be happening. He filled it with water from the tap; it was lukewarm. He swallowed it back but still his throat was dry. Closed. It was like swallowing sand. He sank down on to the bathroom floor; his arse was in Anna's blood.

'She just fell?'

'Awkwardly. Unluckily. These things happen.'

No, no, not to her, she didn't deserve that. Not to him. This sort of thing didn't happen to someone like him. He was a normal bloke: he worked hard, he had his teeth whitened, he enjoyed a few jars with his mates, he was about to get married to a lovely girl next week. He was a good guy. Or at least a good enough guy. That's what he'd always thought.

But he was also the sort of bloke who lied on dating sites to worm his way to a thoughtless shag; he had sex in alleyways and toilets; he tied up his mistress. His fiancée's sister was his mistress. He didn't know what sort of bloke he was. Maybe this kind of thing did happen to guys like him. Not-good-enough guys. They did. You read it in the papers. Sleazy, chaotic people ended up in sleazy, chaotic situations.

'What was I going to do? Call the police and say I killed my sister?' Zoe asked.

'Yes, yes, if that's what happened.'

He still didn't believe it. Not quite. Even though there was so much blood. It was impossible. His thoughts wouldn't sharpen or clarify, they squelched around in his head. He could smell the iron of Anna's blood. He stared at his hand. Covered with it.

Zoe's voice cut through his turmoil. 'You shouldn't have gone there. But since you did, maybe it's a godsend.'

'What?' he spluttered, disbelieving.

'You can clean up, then you need to get out of there quickly, Nick.'

Anna was dead. He believed it now. It wasn't some sick joke of Zoe's. It was real. He knew. Somehow he just knew. He felt it, she'd gone. Her goodness was no longer on the planet.

'No, I'm going to call the police.'

'And tell them what?'

'Tell them everything you've told me. Tell them you pushed her in a temper.'

'Don't be stupid, Nick. I'm not going to jail for this.'

'You wouldn't. Probably not. It was an accident.' His head felt thick and slow, he wished he hadn't drank as much as he had at dinner. He needed to think clearly, never more so in his life than now.

Pause.

'Would anyone believe it was an accident, though?' she asked.

'What do you mean?'

'I mean I did deliberately shove her, and I am sleeping with her fiancé. It wouldn't look good. Not for either of us.'

A death. A motive. They'd think it was murder, not an accident.

He scrambled to his feet, turned to the basin that was smeared with Anna's blood, and threw up. Zoe must have been able to hear him puke and cough and splutter. She continued talking, regardless, and somehow, he wasn't able to put the phone down but held it to his ear all the while he was vomiting.

'You're the one who wanted me to sort out our situation. You said that you just wanted her gone.'

'No, I never said that—'

The trendy little basin with its small plughole wasn't designed for this sort of waste. His vomit settled in the bowl; he could see remnants of the evening's supper. Spinach. Carrots. How could it be that he was still digesting a meal he'd eaten with Anna but she was dead? Not breathing. Not laughing, never going to eat again. He had to push his waste away with his fingers, run the taps. Without thinking about it he started to splash the water around the basin, cleaning away her blood too. As he did so, Zoe kept talking.

'You might have said you just wanted *it* gone, I suppose. Meaning the predicament we found ourselves in. It amounts to the same thing.'

'No, no, it doesn't. And even so, I said gone, not *dead*.'

'Whatever.'

'Stop it, Zoe. Stop this right now.' He was furious and the anger made him spit and weep. Weep, yes. He was crying. Oh God, no, no, this was too awful.

'Pull yourself together. I've thought this all through. You need to clean up. Carefully. Get rid of all the blood, rinse everything away, don't leave a hint that there's been a scene. Then the cleaners will be in tomorrow with bleach. No one will be any the wiser as long as no one raises the alarm in the meantime—and they shouldn't, unless we're very unlucky, and anyone heard her rumpus. Or worse, saw her being taken away.'

'Shit, Zoe.'

'Are you listening to me? Go downstairs and pay the bill. They have your card details already, so they can trace you now. Since there's nothing we can do about that, we need to make the best of it. It will look suspicious if you just leave without settling things properly, better bring the stay to a close respectably. Make small talk with the receptionist. Tell them you and your fiancée have a madcap idea to elope. It might be too late for a tube by then. Take a taxi. Don't waste time going back to your apartment. We're probably going to be fine, unless the dickheads have dumped the body somewhere stupid and it turns up before we're away.'

'Her body.' It was a hideous thought. She was a body now.

'Listen carefully. We are going to catch that flight to New York tomorrow morning. I'm flying out using Anna's passport. In a few days I'll call Veronica.'

'Who?'

'Veronica. The woman Anna worked with in that crappy little mental health centre.'

She'd just spoken of Anna in the past tense. This was real.

'Her name's Vera. It's a centre for the vulnerable and homeless.'

'Right, you can brief me on the details. I'll facetime Vera and resign, say we're loved up and want to stay in the States.'

'What if I don't want to come with you? What if I don't want to follow your plan?'

Zoe paused. It wasn't because she was lost for words; he felt her threat and power in the silence.

'Then I won't pretend to be Anna, alive and well in the USA, and you're up shit creak without the proverbial paddle. It's up to you. You booked the hotel. It's in your name. Your fiancée will be missing. We know she's dead. Maybe they'll find her body sooner or later. Maybe the dickheads I employed won't stay quiet, after all. Your DNA is all over the hotel room.'

He looked at the glass he had held. His print on the mirror.

'No one knows I was ever even here in the UK.'

'Your DNA will be in the room too.'

'It's identical to Anna's.'

The truth of her words burrowed into his skull, like a heat-seeking missile, and then they detonated. She wasn't kidding. She wasn't making this up to teach him a lesson or to scare him.

Yet he was scared. Fucking terrified, actually.

She hung up.

It took a few moments. Just a few moments for him to decide. Zoe's words replayed, over and over in his head. She had thought it all through. She'd bought a ticket for him, on his card, on his computer, a couple of days ago. He was checked in. Presumably she was only planning for them to leave, not to be on the run but he'd look as guilty as sin. He was implicated. Up to his eyes in this. It was *his* fiancée who was missing. No one here knew of Zoe. Anyone who had seen them together would have thought she was Anna. A bartender, a waiter, if asked, they'd identify Anna. Would there be footage of them in back alleys? Sex up against walls. The things he'd done.

He could imagine what the papers would make of it. Champagne-fuelled nights. Sex marathons. *Banker wanker in love triangle*.

He couldn't go to the police. They'd never believe him. If he stayed, he'd be ruined, his family disgraced. What would this do to his parents? To Rachel?

Staying wouldn't bring her back. It was brutal, thinking about Anna. He tried not to do it.

Just in case.

Just in case he discovered how much he loved her, still. Wonderful, beautiful and betrayed, as she no doubt was.

He didn't have any choice. He had to go along with Zoe's plan. He was a man who had swiftly fallen from having too much choice, to no choice at all.

FORTY-FOUR
Zoe

We did not have sex last night, out of respect for my dead sister. I kinda wasn't in the mood. Nor was he, if I'm honest. That's a first for us, spending more than twenty minutes together alone without ripping one another's clothes off our backs. A depressing first, let's face it. Not like the first time you come together or the first time you do it making him wear a fireman's uniform. Sometimes death turns people on. I've had a booty call from a guy who was at his father's funeral; he was literally walking away from the hole in the ground. We hooked up and did it at the wake when other people were downstairs drinking sherry and eating egg sandwiches. He said he needed to feel alive. Death clearly doesn't do it for Nick.

Last night, when he slowly pushed open the door to the room and sneaked in, he looked like he'd been punched, repeatedly. I could instantly see that he'd taken it badly, worse than I imagined. He could barely look at me. When he did, I saw that his eyes were bloodshot and wild. He looked gaunt, haunted. Not just fear, sadness too. Grief. He must have loved Anna more than I knew. More than he knew. It's a shame that she never got to believe that.

He arrived at the airport hotel just before two in the morning. The woman on reception called me.

'Sorry to disturb you, Miss Turner, but I don't think you're going to mind too much. I have a nice surprise for you here at reception.'

I did mind. I'd just fallen asleep—no mean feat, under the circumstances—and I really didn't like the giggly presumption in her voice. Then I reminded myself Anna would be delighted, and so I slipped into role.

'Is it Nick? Is it my fiancé?' I asked breathily, like he had just come back from a war or something.

'Yes, indeed, I have a Mr Nicholas Hudson requesting a room key. Do I have authority to issue him one?' She said this in a falsely coy way.

'Of course,' I giggled. 'Poor man must be exhausted. He's come straight from the office.' It couldn't hurt, offering up an alibi as to where he'd been in the hours between the dinner with his sister and now. I spoke loudly, hoping that he'd overhear and feel grateful towards me. Thinking about him listening in also stirred the mischief maker in me. I couldn't resist adding, 'He's so conscientious, he didn't want to leave everything in a mess for others to deal with.' He'd see the deeper meaning.

'Uh huh.' I could hear the smile in her voice.

She'll be thinking I've netted myself an ambitious but conscientious, dependable sort of guy. She'll be thinking he's just the sort of partner she'd like.

'And can I take this opportunity of congratulating you on your security measures,' I add.

'Just company policy.'

I could tell she was pleased. That was always Anna's way. Sprinkling compliments here and there; making people happy, making people like her.

'Well, I appreciate it. But hell, yeah, let him up here!' I said it in a manner that was heavily laced with nudge, nudge, wink, wink undertones.

We both giggled.

Nick let himself into the room. I stayed in bed. Lying on my side. Watching him, watching me. He eased himself in through the door as though he was getting into a pool with a shark—which, in a way, he is. He kept his back close to the wall, practically clung to it.

'All done?' I asked.

He nodded. 'This won't work,' he said. 'We won't get away with it.'

His voice was low and slow. Could he possibly still be drunk? I'd have thought the vomiting had got most of the alcohol out of his system.

'Yes, we will,' I snapped. I am in no mood for his self-doubt or self-pity.

'No one will believe you are Anna. You don't sound the same. You have a more pronounced American accent. You don't have the same sort of clothes.'

I was irritated that his voice cracked, he was aching for her. Too late.

'For Christ's sake, Nick, I'm a trained actress. Well, not exactly trained, but I can pull off Anna's accent. It's just a slightly more British version of mine, a bit toned down, less swearing. And less saying what she thinks. I'll buy new clothes.'

'But what will I do? What about me?'

I bit my tongue to stop myself mimicking his whiny tone, *what about me*? I thought he was stronger. 'You'll have to resign too—that's if you're not fired.'

'Which I probably will be.'

'You can always get another job, Nick. You have holidays owing to you, right? Take those at first.'

'You have to book holidays, you can't just flit.'

'Let's just hope your boss has a romantic streak.'

'He doesn't.'

'Whatever. It's worth it; we'll be safer in the States if her body turns up.'

He sways, leans against the wall.

'Why?'

'Because I have an American passport. Obviously. We've both lived there since we were nine. Anna and I were naturalized and have citizenship. If the crime comes to light, it will be harder to subpoena me from the States.'

'But I haven't got American citizenship.'

'No. Anyway, none of this matters.' I didn't want him to dwell on this. 'If you don't report her, how will they find out who she is? They won't be looking for her. Or us.'

'There must be records. Dental records or something.'

'Anna was always terrified of the dentist. I don't think she ever registered in the UK. Frankly, if she was going to have dental work done, then she'd have come back to the US, we're light years ahead when it comes to that sort of thing. Once things have died down, I can go back to being me and we can carry on as we were.'

'What about your parents? My parents. They'll miss Anna.'

I was getting tired by then. Must I be the one to think of everything? 'Oh fuck, Nick. I don't know. You can tell your parents you divorced her in the end, that it didn't work out. I'll stage a falling-out with my parents. Anna can just disappear. Whatever. Look, let's just get through this initial crisis, shall we?'

'You'll never be able to go back to being Zoe.'

Was he for real?

'You'll have to stay as Anna for the rest of your life.'

'No fucking way. Can you imagine me playing Little Miss Sunshine for the rest of my days?'

He couldn't.

'You might have to. No one will miss Zoe but—'

'Frankly, that's pretty insulting.'

'You know what I mean.'

'Well, I'll keep her ID and my personality then. How about that, Nick? Best of both worlds, after all?' I snapped.

'She'll never have a funeral. She won't be remembered and honoured. What about Ivan, Vera, Mrs Delphine, Rick?'

'Who?'

'He's a guy who took a bullet for his country, and she's a

woman with kids with osteosarcoma. They're all people at
the centre who loved Anna, had been helped by Anna. They
would want to say goodbye to her, they have the right to.'

'Or maybe they would want to believe she'd never died.
That she was living in America with her husband. Haven't
they all endured enough?'

'I'll sleep on the chair,' was the only answer he gave me.
'Whatever.'

I wasn't going to beg him to get into bed with me, was
I? I've never had to do that. I rolled over and pretended to
quickly fall asleep. Genuine sleep followed pretty swiftly.
It had been a long day.

Things are a bit easier this morning, largely because we
both have so much to do and activity alleviates any need to
talk. We have to be at the airport by six thirty, and although
it's just a five-minute shuttle-bus ride away we're still up
against the clock. I don't know what to wear. I haven't got
any of Anna's clothes with me and Nick's right about one
thing, most of my clothes are a bit too out there for Anna.
In the end I settle on jeans and a baggy T-shirt. Usually I'd
wear these (skin-tight) jeans with a vest top, and I'd wear
the baggy T-shirt with teeny cutaway denim shorts. This
look works, though; I'm happy with it. I finish off my outfit
with trainers, rather than heels, which would be my usual
preference. I tell him he needs a shave and I order him a full
English breakfast. He doesn't touch it.

'Never mind, they'll give you something on the plane,'
I say.

I'm not sure he hears me above the running faucet; he
doesn't respond. I have natural yogurt and a fresh fruit salad.

I understand the importance of playing the part so choose
to behave just as though we're an excited, giddy couple eloping, both when we're in public and when we're alone. It's
too much to constantly dip in and out of Anna's character;
I'd lose the plot. It's safest to just pretend to love life. The

way she does. Did. The thought makes me crumple slightly inside, as though my organs are being twisted or scrunched up, as though they were made of paper that can be rolled into a ball and tossed into a bin. It's a terrible feeling; debilitating. I push it away.

Nick goes through the motions; he doesn't respond to my chatter, it seems to be all he can do to say his name and mutter monosyllabic replies such as 'yes' and 'no'. At security I think he gives the guy the impression that he's packed fireworks, liquid nitrogen and a car battery in his hand luggage, he is behaving so peculiarly. Nick isn't interested in looking around the Duty Free shops, although they are brilliant at Heathrow. I swiftly buy him a clean shirt, underwear and trousers, all from different retail outlets, as that's less likely to draw attention. I insist he goes into the toilets to change.

'Don't throw your clothes away. Put them in this bag. We'll destroy them later. You have blood on your jeans.'

He looks like he might faint when I say that, but he does as I tell him without offering any objections. While he's changing I buy a book from WHSmith, although when I give it to him he doesn't even thank me. When he thinks I'm not looking he keeps his eyes trained on me, wary, defensive. He's studying me, like an opponent at a chess match. He's trying to piece it all together, predict my next move. When I turn to him he swiftly looks away. He won't meet my gaze. We can't look one another in the eye any more. We're both scared of what we might see.

I'd booked us Premium Economy seats. Initially, I had wanted to splash out and get Club but decided against it because if Nick does lose his job, we might have a few tight months before he secures another one. Economies must be made. Now I'm glad that we're booked into the busier section of the plane because there's some comfort in having more people around us. They provide a distraction. Watching other people go about their normal lives—squabble over seats, huff and puff about cabin space, noisily order drinks—

helps tether us. Nick is still being deathly quiet. I don't think anyone watching us at all carefully would believe we are love's young dream; I can only hope no one *is* watching us too closely. It's not until we're in our seats, the engines are running and the flight attendant is vainly trying to keep everyone's attention focused on the safety video that Nick leans towards me. He puts his mouth very close to my ear, so that I can feel his breath tickle and no one else can hear what he's saying.

He whispers, 'Was it your plan all along to kill her?' It's a brave question. I didn't think he'd go there. 'You booked the tickets and airport hotel in advance. You found someone to take her body away with remarkable swiftness.' His voice cracked. 'Did you plan it, Zoe?'

I turn to him, wide-eyed. 'Nick, how could you think such a thing? I thought there would be a fight at the restaurant. I thought it was a good idea for us to have these flights booked so we could have a place to retreat to.'

For a moment he looks relieved. He needed to hear as much. He had to have it said. A tragic and terrible accident he'll learn to live with. Anything more would be inconceivable, unforgivable. The crease on his forehead between his eyes softens. He sits back in his seat and reaches for his headphones but then he freezes. I watch as the colour drains from his face. He was grey to start with today, now he looks blue—no, colourless. Like a winter sky. His jaw goes slack, yett his hands grip the arms of the seat.

He opens his eyes and stares at me. 'But you booked the flight under her name. You knew you were going to use her passport.'

I suppose it was only a matter of time. I'd hoped his hangover, the guilt and shock might have kept this at bay longer. I try to bluff.

'If you'd chosen her, I thought it would be a good idea for you two to take a break. For you to fly out and meet Mom and Dad,' I say hurriedly.

He's shaking his head. I think he's going to be ill again.

'You expect me to believe you'd be gracious in defeat. No way, Zoe, no way. You'd have expected to win all along if there was a showdown. Losing is not an option for you. Losing me, or whatever it is you'd set your mind to. You'd always have the confidence to believe you'd be the one picked, if it came to it. You told her you were leaving; you always knew it would be you on this flight.'

He's right. I had no idea he knew me so well.

'Yet, you booked it in her name.'

What can I say? After a moment I decide that all I can do is tell the truth. It isn't very me, but what the hell? I turn to him. Lean close so that our lips are just centimetres apart. If I put out my tongue, stretched it, it would be inside his mouth. I wonder, would he let me? Would he like that.

Instead, I say, 'Everything I've done, I've done for you.'

FORTY-FIVE
Nick

Fuck, fuck, fuck. He didn't know what to do. Where was the handbook on this? Fuck. He wished that word didn't keep spiralling around his head. It wasn't helping. He knew it was pretty Neanderthal but he really couldn't think of any other word that would do. Repeating it had the effect of stunning him. Not calming him, exactly—he couldn't imagine anything could do that—but lulling him into a sort of transcendental state. He had no idea how he would manage to sit through an eight-hour flight. Next to her. A murderer.

It was surreal. From the moment she told him about the fall he'd doubted her. The story didn't quite hang together because it actually was *too* neat. Last night, he hadn't been able to take it all in, piece it together, in order to take it apart. It was only at the moment when she handed over her passport that it struck him. It made sense to leave the country as Anna if she was covering up Anna's death, Bbut how could she have known that when she booked the ticket? Zoe had planned it. She'd planned to kill her sister. For him.

The thought made him shake and quake. He imagined the scene. He didn't want to; it was the last thing he wanted, yet he couldn't not. Violent images hijacked him. If it was deliberate, then it was unlikely that Anna's death was the result of a single shove. That would be too unpredictable. Maybe Zoe had used an instrument, a weapon. She must have clubbed Anna with something to be sure she'd go down. Not one blow and a fatal slip, more likely a beating, over and over again. A sustained attack. He closed his eyes, nonethe-lesshe could still see it. Blood up the mirror, blood on the basin and floor. Blood on his hands.

He wasn't in the slightest bit flattered by her 'I did it for you' routine. Did she think he might be? He was disgusted, despairing. Doomed. He sat absolutely still for the entire flight. He wanted to be away from her. He wanted to scramble out of his seat and push towards the exit, fling open the door and plunge thousands of feet, just to be away from her, but he couldn't do that. The only way he could escape her was by being absolutely and utterly still, turning in on himself, sinking inside himself and not acknowledging his physical needs. He didn't eat, or sleep, or speak or even visit the toilet. Instead, he thought about what he should do next.

His initial thought was to simply call over a flight at-tendant and explain the situation, confess to his part in it. Complete and unequivocal. How could he find the words? What was his part in it? He'd covered up a murder. He was the motive for a murder. It was his fault someone was dead. The thought punched him in the gut. Anna was dead be-cause of him.

He'd only ever got into a fight once in his life. Aged six-teen, walking home from the cinema with three of his mates. They'd bumped into a gang of older, harder boys that they knew by reputation. One of his mates was the lippy sort. He had some long-standing wrangle going on with these older boys; Nick couldn't remember what it was about, if he ever knew. His mate said something to the wrong guy, the next thing he knew there were punches flying. He took three quite serious blows: two in his stomach and one in his shoulder. The pain of it was breathtaking. It wasn't fast and glamorous, like he'd always imagined. Being in a fight was brutal, messy, undignified. He'd thought he'd be the sort to fight back—one, two, take that.He didn't, he cowered. There were two of them on him, both bigger, older, stron-ger. He couldn't do anything. He tried to curl himself into a ball. He remembered it clearly, each punch being landed, even though it was half a lifetime ago. He remembered being outraged and impotent.

Like now.

Humiliated, outfoxed and full of horror.

Like now.

Two of his friends had fared much worse, and the third had run, screaming, for help. Wise move, as he'd managed to avoid any blows and his actions broke up the violence sharpish. His mother had wanted them to go to the police, press charges. His father was old-school. He'd said that these things happened to boys and that now Nick would know better than to mix with trouble-seeking, lippy sorts in the future. Learned his lesson.

He hadn't, though, had he?

He eyed the button that would call the flight attendant but did not push it. What would that achieve? He'd scare those around him; cause further panic and horror. They'd have to land the plane, maybe turn around. He'd be disrupting the day of hundreds of people. People going to weddings or funerals, important business meetings, much-needed holidays. No, he would wait until he was in America and then he'd hand himself in to the authorities there. The thought sent huge waves of terror through his body. American police officers carried guns, and they had the death penalty in some states. Not New York, he was pretty sure of that, but years of American TV and movies had convinced Nick that American cops were tough. He didn't know anything about the law out there. What would they do to him? Would they lock him up until UK policemen could pick him up, or would he be tried and imprisoned in America?

Just moving his eyes, Nick stole a glance at Zoe. She was sleeping. Unbelievable. How could she sleep? Didn't she have a heart or a conscience? Anna had had so much of both that Zoe's lack was all the more notable. Anna had once said that Zoe was the zig to her zag. He thought of her proud display of childhood photos in her flat, the stories about Anna's loyalty to Zoe. Anna had loved her sister so much. She'd sworn that it was a two-way thing. But it obviously wasn't. She'd misjudged that. Badly. Zoe was insane, it was the only explanation. The drugs she'd taken when she was young, they must have had some effect on her. He couldn't believe that twins who had once lulled themselves to sleep by sucking one another's fingers would end up this way. One killing the other.

She was unpredictable. Selfish. He'd always known that. What if she carried out her threat of insisting that she'd had nothing to do with it? That he'd killed Anna, cleaned it up, booked the escape route. What would happen then? He would be sent to jail for Anna's murder. For a very long time.

Or she might even stick to her story that she was Anna. How would he prove any of it had happened? There was no body. It would sound like the ravings of a madman. He wouldn't go to prison but he'd be offered psychiatric help. He'd go to his grave sharing this secret with Zoe. He'd be in her debt. Not hell but purgatory then. Was that her plan?

It was too complicated. Too much. He had no idea what to do.

Zoe's face was beautiful, still and so like Anna's. The similarity was more striking when she was resting, he'd always thought that. Poor, poor Anna. God, he missed her. He should have grabbed her hand and not let go. What could have been simpler? He felt a wave of sorrow and longing wash over him. He missed her. Her optimism, her belief in a good and happy world, her prattle about wedding cakes; he thought of her singing hip hop karaoke on one of their early dates, self-conscious yet enthralled; he remembered her kitten pyjamas and the gentle way she put socks on his mother's feet in the hospital. Such artless, easy company.

Although, even as he had these thoughts, he knew he was kidding himself. Anna was not as straightforward as she'd wanted him to believe—as he'd wanted to believe.

Who was? Everyone had secrets, told lies, did their best to
cover up their weaknesses, highlight their strengths. She
hadn't wanted to tell him about Zoe at first, because Zoe
was trouble. She'd lied about her age, because she'd been
concerned that he wouldn't have been interested in her if
he'd known she was that bit older. She hadn't quite trusted
him enough to confide in him about her miserable first marriage. These things had left him feeling outraged. He'd used
them to vindicate his own lies and deceitful behaviour but
now—thinking about it coolly, without the sting of resentment or the throb of self-justification—he saw that, funnily
enough, Anna's deceptions did nothing to detract from her.
They made her more human, more accessible. At least, they
could have done. If they'd had time. He saw that most of the
issues were because she lacked confidence in him.

Rightly so, as it happened.

What had he done to her? Why had he started the affair
in the first place? He couldn't remember. It was just sex.
People said that all the time, didn't they? *Just sex.* There
was no 'just' about the sex he and Zoe had. Their sex reminded him that sex was life; literally, sex was where life
started. At its best, sex is compelling, enthralling, forceful
and urgent. He regretted it now, though, with every fibre in
his body. Why hadn't he found just one of them enough?

Well, because neither of them on their own *were* enough
for him. Simply that, he supposed. He needed different
things from each woman, and only together did they form
a whole for him.

Then he noticed it, a fat tear running down Zoe's face.
Was she awake or crying in her sleep? He didn't know. He
didn't know anything any more. The tear clung to her chin.
He should hate her. What she'd done was disgusting, devastating. He did hate her.

And at the same time he did not. Not really. Not entirely.

FORTY-SIX
Zoe

Poor Anna. I do feel absolutely dreadful thinking about her. It's not that I feel guilty about how this whole mess ended. Not exactly. I think I've done her a favour in many ways. Offered relief. A way out. No, I feel dreadful thinking about her because I think she's wasted her entire bloody life. Her unremitting faith in Prince Charming and the happily ever after has been incredibly draining. If only she'd chosen to focus elsewhere.

It's funny, if you think about it, we're not so very dissimilar. Everyone has always thought we were chalk and cheese, that our personality types were completely opposed, the truth is, we're the same. Not funny, actually. More like sickening, when you consider the way my parents have always treated me because I'm keen on partying; or, to use their words, I'm *addicted* to partying. I'm an addict. OK, so I like to have a good time. Shoot me. Anna, however, has always been considered the little darling, their little darling. Eternally needy and wounded Anna, the one deserving their pity, affection and understanding. Lovely, lovely Anna. Really! Really? The brutal truth is she was an addict too, addicted to the fairy-tale myth. The countless times I've said to her, 'Woman, get a grip! Help yourself. Find some perspective.' But she wouldn't.

I mean people fall in love at university and they get jilted. Newsflash, it happens. It hurts but you're meant to be able to get over it. Pick yourself up, dust yourself down and start all over again. It's a life lesson. Why did she feel she had to be John Jones's sacrificial lamb, the eternal victim? So he slept with someone else when she thought they were exclusive. Yada, yada, yada. Did she have to have a breakdown? Couldn't she have just flipped the finger? Leaving Yale, giving up all those opportunities, that really pissed me off. She'd worked her ass off at school, everyone had great hopes for her. We were so proud of her. *I* was so proud of her. And she chucked it all away because of a man. She let us down.

Next, to plunge herself into that dreadful marriage with that boring, arrogant man just so she could keep up with her girlfriends who were all tripping down the aisle with their college sweethearts. To hear her tell it, everyone loved Larry Morgan. Even if they did, no one loved him quite as much as he loved himself. We certainly never saw eye to eye. He hated the relationship between Anna and me. Resented our closeness. He was always like, 'Why is she around here again?' 'Why is it always you who has to bail her out?' He was pretty much a stuck record, demanding, 'Choose me, choose me.' I think he had an affair to get her attention. Loser.

Yet, she did choose him. That night. April seventeenth, 2014. And that changed everything between us. We never came back from that. If you knew more about that night, you'd understand me way better, maybe even hate me a little less.

We never talked of it, Anna and I. Just didn't. Just couldn't.

A lesser person than myself would blame our parents. I mean, looking at it from an outsiders' point of view, it might be noted that we've both ended up more than a bit screwed-up, and, in our very own ways, more than a bit needy. She's always needed a Prince Charming. I needed a drink, or some pills. And now Nick.

I need Nick.

Sad, in the end, what I've discovered. The fact is, it's the worst thing, needing a person. Worse than needing any number of stimulants because you can't buy a person, you can't get someone to deal you a few grammes of a person. You have to win them, then keep them, and it's hard. Almost impossibly hard. It's exhausting. I guess discovering as much gave me a level of understanding of Anna's personality that I hadn't been able to access in the past.

I see now that, in many ways, her cravings are harder to satiate. People are complex, unreliable, mercurial. It's funny, the moment in my life when I understood Anna the best was the moment I stopped protecting her, and I betrayed her.

Utterly.

I had been protecting her up until that point. It might not have looked that way, because she was the one who would clean up my messes, but it was a lot more of a two-way thing than people imagined. She knew that. She'd be the first to admit it. She'd possibly be the only one to admit it. She has always needed me as much as I needed her. She needed to be needed. If I hadn't been so bad, she couldn't have been so good. The problems started when we found common ground. Nick. That's when everything became unsustainable. We were knocked out of balance.

There's only ever been room for two.

I have not turned into her, get that thought right out of your head. No one could call Nick my Prince Charming. I am not pursuing that fantasy. But I do want him. More than anything.

More than Anna.

By which I mean I want him more than Anna does, and I love him more than I love Anna.

It's just the way it is.

FORTY-SEVEN
Nick

Finally, they pushed through the clouds,; the grey tarmac loomed up to meet them. The wheels banged on the runway and, despite instructions to the contrary, people immediately started to loosen their seat belts and reach for their hand luggage. Focused, Nick and Zoe were amongst the first to disembark.

He walked as quickly as he possibly could through the airport; Zoe matched his step but she didn't speak to him, nor he to her. Their heels clicked and clacked on the polished floors, echoing, even though the terminal was heaving. He felt singled out. Conspicuous. He imagined a spotlight shining on them. No, not a spotlight, a search beam. He expected that, any moment now, a hand would land heavily on his shoulder, that he'd be cuffed and dragged away. His eyes stung with lack of sleep and trauma. He could smell his own body, and it disgusted him. He kept his eyes ahead and maintained his pace.

For the bulk of the eight-hour flight Nick had grappled with thoughts of what would come next. His imagination, stretched and limited by popular culture rather than any real experience, took him to an interrogation room, to a cell, to a dock, to a cell again. He imagined his parents' horror and profound disillusionment; would they ever be able to forgive him? He imagined his friends' and Rachel's shock and silence; would they stand by him? Yet, for the first time in months, he had found some clarity.

He deserved to be punished.

He was appalled at the thought of it. Terrified. Sickened. But there was no other way. He couldn't fix this but he wouldn't dodge it. He would hand himself in. His account may or may not be believed. It didn't matter to him at that moment; all that mattered was that he confessed, that he repented. He couldn't live with himself otherwise. However, before he went to the police, he had to find Alexia and David. They deserved to know the truth. The facts. Stiff and formal as they were, he hadn't especially warmed to them, but no parents should have to live through this nightmare. News that one of their children had murdered the other was incomprehensibly vicious; it was enough to send someone mad.

He'd caused this. He hadn't beaten or pushed Anna but maybe he'd pushed Zoe.

He remembered Anna telling him that they were a special sort of twin: monochorionic, monoamniotic twins. The sort that had shared everything from before they were born. He shouldn't have expected them to share him. He'd taken advantage of Zoe. He should have been stronger and turned her away that first night when she was flirting. He knew she was ill, vulnerable. Anna had warned him but he'd been drunk, flattered, intrigued, drawn in. He had to go to her parents, explain as much as he could. It would be a vile and dreadful story to tell and the most awful one for them to hear, but he had a duty to set the record straight. If he didn't, they would only ever hear sensationalized titbits as the press reported his arrest and subsequent court case. They'd have to wade through the facts, the speculation, the allegations, the lies. And that would be unbearable. He'd caused so much pain. He would face them, as he'd never faced Anna. Tell the murky, horrific story and then they could call the police to arrest him.

Besides believing that they were owed the truth, or as much of it as he could deliver, Nick had another motive for visiting the Turners. Whilst he was resolute that he had to be punished, he was not certain Zoe ought to be too. Surely, it would be punishment enough to wake up, day after day, for the rest of her life, and for her first thought to be, *I killed my sister*. And certainly this must be her first thought. Every time she looked in a mirror, she'd see Anna; there would be no escaping.

Zoe was obviously out of her mind, and it terrified him. The shaming fact was he'd known as much within minutes of meeting her but he'd chosen not to confront it. There were grey mists and he'd hidden in them, although he knew that respectable eccentricity bordered on dangerous insanity. He'd hidden from the facts because it had suited him; he'd gained from it. Zoe needed help. If he turned himself in, thereby turning her in, would she get it? The Turners were pretty wealthy, he thought that they probably could get a decent lawyer if they wanted. A lawyer who could explain her addictions, who would ask for some leniency. Some clemency. But might their awful relationship with Zoe, their frustration with her past behaviour, be a barrier to doing that? They might not recognize that she needed help. They might just hate her for taking Anna.

He didn't know, but he had to try. He owed it to Anna to do the right thing. He owed it to Zoe too. He had finally worked out what sort of a man he was. A man who made mistakes. Terrible, unforgivable mistakes, but a man who could at least take responsibility for them.

Nick and Anna were directed to different queues to pass through security. Hers was for nationals, and therefore considerably shorter and more efficient. She brightly told him she'd meet him at the carousel, as she needed to collect luggage, but he only had a carry-on case.

'I'll be through in a jiffy. You'll be ages, but it will even out,' she said brightly as she stood on her tiptoes and kissed him on the cheek.

Playing Anna.

He felt a wave of pain, grief and love. But he didn't know who for.

* * *

As soon as he'd cleared passport control, Nick took his chance. He dashed towards the exit. Mercifully, he was near the front of the taxi queue and he'd lost her in the labyrinth of the airport. He didn't doubt she'd call him as soon as she realized; she'd track him down, corner him once again. However, for now he was free of her. For the first time since he met her, he was his own man. He didn't turn around and check over his shoulder. He didn't want to risk catching a glimpse of her.

Just in case.

Just in case he discovered that he loved her, still. Mad, bad and lethal to know, as she no doubt was, he knew it was a possibility.

'Where you heading, sir?' the cabby asked.

Nick checked his phone and found Alexia and David's address.

'Bridgeport is a long drive. Way out the city. It's gonna cost.'

Nick nodded.

It didn't matter. Nothing did.

FORTY-EIGHT
Pamela

Rachel enjoyed a long lie-in and emerged from her room just in time for an early lunch. Although, in theory, she was there to look out for her parents, no one objected to her lazy start. Unfortunately, although she caught the last train out of London, it had been delayed and she hadn't made it home until nearer 2 a.m. Her parents had both lain awake, waiting to hear her let herself in, although they'd both pretended to be asleep. It was one thing worrying about your twenty-seven-year-old child; it was another letting her know.

Together, they ate scrambled eggs and smoked salmon on toast. The conversation gently drifted; Pamela and George were thrilled to hear Rachel had received a late callback to interview for a position as deputy head.

'Usually these things are settled before now, but apparently the person they offered the job to is suddenly moving to Aberdeen and so they're recruiting again. I think I stand a decent chance.'

They were also excited to hear that she'd broken her journey to spend the evening with Anna and Nick in London. They loved to hear that their adult children socialized with one another; it somehow reminded them of times gone by when the children played Monopoly together.

'Smart restaurant, was it?' asked George.

'Desperately.'

'What did you eat?'

George liked to hear if anything was especially delicious

or disappointing. Rachel obliged. Once he was vicariously satiated and had also finished his actual lunch, he retired to the sunroom to read the *Telegraph*. Rachel and Pamela lingered at the table, sipping coffee and dunking a constant stream of biscuits.

'Anna's twin was supposed to come along to dinner but she was a no-show,' commented Rachel.

'That's a shame. I get the impression that Anna finds Zoe a challenge.'

Rachel nodded. 'Don't you think it's odd that her sister and parents are refusing to come to the wedding?'

'Families are odd, darling.'

'We're not,' Rachel insisted defensively.

'Well, not to ourselves, no, but we no doubt are to others.'

'How?'

'Your father and I enjoy jigsaws.'

'That's hardly odd.'

'I knit toilet-roll covers in the shape of cupcakes.'

'That's creative.'

Pamela smiled. She was trying to avoid gossiping. Her daughter was her daughter. Nothing could or would change that intense, tight, beautiful relationship, but they had to find room for Anna now, a daughter-in-law. It didn't seem especially kind, sitting around speculating as to why her family had decided not to attend the wedding.

'Why do you think they're refusing to come?' Rachel obviously disagreed; she thought a good gossip was lifeblood.

'Well, Anna said it was a matter of finances for her parents.'

'But they're quite well off, aren't they? And anyway, Nick would've paid,' Rachel said through a mouthful of biscuit.

Pamela wanted to remind her daughter not to speak with her mouth full, but didn't; she hadn't had that right for years. 'Maybe it was workload, I forget.'

'And don't you think it's odd that her sister is leaving the country just a week before the wedding? Why wouldn't she stay, since she's been here for ages?'

'I'm not sure it's any of our business.'

'Of course it's our business,' Rachel gasped. 'Nick is marrying into that family. We've a right to know what's going on.'

Pamela was from a different generation. One where she only expected to know what she was told, and she didn't expect to be told anything much. In an effort to turn the conversation she said, 'Did you all have fun together last night?'

'It was OK. Although as Zoe didn't show, Anna went into freaked-out mode.' Rachel fell silent.

Pamela had hoped her daughter would embrace the idea of Nick marrying and see it as gaining a sister, not losing a brother; this didn't appear to be the case. Rachel looked genuinely concerned about something. Something bigger than having to wear a bridesmaid's dress.

'Nick didn't seem himself yesterday.'

'In what way?'

'He was distracted, agitated.'

'Wedding nerves, I should think.'

'You think he's having second thoughts?' Rachel sounded almost pleased.

'No! I never said that, Rachel. I meant he may be subject to the usual and expected nerves that a person might have before they embark on something so momentous as marrying. Or he might just be excited.'

'He didn't look as though he was excited.'

'How did he look?'

'Scared.'

Pamela didn't know how to respond. What could Nick be scared of? He was a grown man. A particularly successful one, who was about to marry a very lovely young woman. He had the world at his feet.

'Could it be a work matter? He does carry a lot of responsibility.'

'I don't think so.' Rachel let the silence settle between them, but she couldn't hold it back in the end. 'Don't you think it's all a bit fast, Mum?'

'Well…' Pamela didn't know how to answer.

She hadn't in all honesty expected things to move quite so quickly as they had, after she'd dropped her hint that he should think about relationships more seriously. Just five hours from the telephone conversation to the proposal. She had no idea she wielded such power. She used to have to ask him at least thirty times before he tidied up his bedroom. He never learned not to throw damp towels on the bed, and she must have mentioned that a thousand times. Not that Pamela had a problem with Nick proposing to Anna. Far from it. Yet, well, the speed of the commitment was startling. She was just a little dizzy with it. She thought perhaps they all were.

'I trust Nick to do the right thing, darling. I always have, and he always does. I don't think there's anything to worry about.'

FORTY-NINE
Nick

Nick stumbled out of the taxi. He could smell the aeroplane on his clothes, he could smell the fallibility of his own body, his breath, his sweat. There was nothing he could do about it. He handed over his credit card as it hadn't crossed his mind to pick up currency at the airport. He stood on the pavement and looked towards the house; the home where Anna and Zoe had grown up together. Anna had told him all about it. She'd loved it. Nick shook his head. He couldn't get used to thinking about her in the past tense. What had Zoe done? What was he a part of? Anna had described the mature trees they'd climbed, and how one of them—an elm at the back of the house—had the twins' initials carved into the trunk. There, he would also find the pool they'd dipped in and the two swings that they'd been given when they turned ten. Zoe had apparently said they were too old for swings but in fact they'd both played on them for hours throughout the long hot summer days and even into the chilly winter evenings. The house was as he'd imagined from her descriptions: large, white, wooden with a picket fence and a porch. Modest Anna hadn't hinted at how prestigious her childhood home was but Nick guessed that it had been built when the city was founded. He glanced up at the windows and wondered which bedroom they'd slept in when they were girls. Then he remembered, it was one at the back of the house; Zoe had taken advantage of the fact, shimmying down the drainpipe to escape to parties as a young teen. This was the only thing Zoe had ever told him about her home.

The lawn was closely cut, although the woodwork was flaking and there was moss on the roof; the place had a neglected air about it. He walked up the path, the front door loomed. He rang the bell, which chimed through the waiting house.

'I'll get it.' A man's voice.

The door was flung wide open with an energy that bordered on a sense of challenge; it seemed that David and Alexia were not used to visitors.

'I'm Nick.'

'Yes. I know. I recognize you from Skype' David said abruptly. He peered over Nick's shoulder, looking for Anna.

Nick wanted to cry. If only she were with him, right by his side. If only they were here to persuade her parents to come to their wedding. Why hadn't he ever suggested they do that? Fly over here and talk to her parents. He knew why. He had been too tied up with Zoe, he hadn't given the matter his attention. He regretted that. That and so much more. He could feel his heart beating through his chest, feel it actually vibrate through his entire body, causing his teeth to chatter. He wondered if David could see as much. Maybe he would have, but the father was looking for his daughter.

The taxi pulled away and she hadn't emerged.

'Is there something wrong?' he asked.

'Can I come in?'

They stood in the hallway. Alexia appeared from somewhere, he wasn't sure where. There were a number of doors leading off to other rooms, pictures on the walls, photos on a console, a vase but no flowers, a mat. He wiped his feet. Slowly. Carefully. He couldn't take in anything more. He just had to get the words out but it was impossible to know where to start. No one hugged him or shook his hand. That struck him as odd. They knew, he thought. They must know. Alexia had one arm folded across her body, the other hand at her throat. David's forehead was creased, his eyes angry. Angry at what he was about to hear. They knew something.

'Anna's dead,' he said.

Because there was nothing else to say.

'No, no, no.' Alexia's knees buckled.

David moved with unbelievable speed, caught her elbow. Both men led her, dragged her through to a room where she could collapse on to a sofa. She sat on the edge and rocked backwards and forwards, her hands clasped to her head, her fingers wrenching her hair.

'No, no, no.' It was a moan, a howl. Primitive.

'How?' asked David.

'Zoe killed her. She pushed her, I think. She told me it was an accident but now I believe that maybe it was planned.' He spat the words out in a hurry, there was no other way.

Alexia stopped howling, she fastened her eyes on to Nick. Her mouth hanging open in astonishment, shock. David looked confused, stunned. Nick pushed on. He didn't want to—he wanted to run from their shock and pain, their broken faces—but if he didn't speak now, then he'd never manage to.

He spluttered, 'It's all my fault. I was having an affair with Zoe. I think she did it for me, at least that's what she said. I'm sorry. I'm so sorry.'

The words were pitiful. Nothing, nothing he could say would stem the flow of agony that must be coursing through their veins right now. He started to cry, heavy tears ran down his face. He didn't dare move to rub them away, it would seem somehow indulgent.

'It's my fault. I realize what has to be done. I know you need to call the police but I came to you because Zoe needs your understanding.'

'No, not Zoe. Anna,' said David.

'It's too late for Anna.' Nick realized David was in shock. Uncomprehending. Nick had to brutally hammer home the facts. 'I'm sorry. I know this is a staggering, horrendous thing to hear, I realize that. And part of you must hate Zoe right now. I know part of me does but—'

'What you're telling us is impossible.'

'Of course, of course you would want to think that, but it *is* true.'

David put his hand on Nick's shoulder.

Nick wanted to scream. It burned him. The shame. The burden of bearing this man's comfort.

'Nick, son, Zoe couldn't have killed Anna. Zoe died three years ago.'

FIFTY
Alexia

Somehow you know you've lost your child before you're told. You feel it in your gut, or your heart or your subconscious, somewhere. At least, I did. Again, science can't explain that. You don't feel it in your soul, though, because in the moment you lose a child, you doubt the existence of a soul, or a god, or justice, or peace. Yet at the same time you're making bargains, asking for time to be reversed, offering up yourself rather than your baby. Your fully grown, adult baby. Your baby still.

When I heard the facts I roared. I screamed so ferociously for so long that my throat ached for a week afterwards. I was flaying, kicking and screaming in the hospital corridor. They tried to hold on to me. Hold me tight. Hold me down. So I didn't damage anything. Didn't damage myself. David and a nurse held me but I fought and struggled. I just wanted to lie on the floor and pound it with my fists, or kick walls or smash windows. I hated them for restraining me. I roared because I'd failed. I'd failed at the one thing that matters as a mother. I hadn't kept her safe. I wanted to die. I wanted that for many months afterwards. They had to sedate me, drug me. Ironic, as my daughter's cold body was lying on a slab in the morgue, in the hospital basement, because she'd taken too many drugs. We'd always feared it. From the first time we found dope in her bedroom when she was fourteen. It is what you fear with a kid like Zoe—that they'll end up dead.

Zoe was never destined to live a long life. I roared, because what was the point of me? A mother who had lost her child.

No mother, no parent, should ever have to receive news like that. It's unnatural. A mother is not supposed to outlive her child. Abhorrent. Twisted. My life shattered. The pain tore at me. Many women know the pain of giving birth. Flesh rips. But the pain of hearing your child has gone—well, that's one hundred times, one thousand million times, worse. The grief was so profound it was disabling.

But there was Anna. She's the reason I carried on.

In the beginning people said it would get easier, that time would heal, at least to an extent. They lied. It never gets easier. Fragments of pain hang around like shadows. And even now, I can't piece myself back together. I can't be whole again. So I understand Anna and what she did.

For a moment there I thought I was going to have to go through it all again. Nick said Anna was dead. Zoe first, now Anna. I know I wouldn't be able to go through it again. I wouldn't have to, no one could expect that of me. No one would expect me to get up every day if they'd both gone.

But he had it wrong.

It's hard to call who is the most confused. Nick looks at us as though we are mad.

'Zoe isn't dead,' he insists.

'She is,' I sigh.

'Overdose. April seventeenth, 2014,' states David.

He looks at his hands. It will never be an easy thing to say.

'But, but I've been—I've—'

I watch him sway, blanch, stagger backwards and fold into a seat.

David and I piece it together quite quickly. We exchange looks. He said he was having an affair with Zoe. Poor Anna. I am angry with this man slumped in front of me. I don't like him for what he's just told me, but I pity him. It seems he's been well and truly hoaxed. Anna has been playing with him.

Before I can even try to explain it I need to be absolutely sure for myself. 'You've seen one of our girls recently?' I demand, desperate for confirmation that everything isn't over. 'One of our girls is alive?'

He nods mutely, stupidly. Coughs, and eventually manages, 'I left her at the airport. Just a couple of hours ago. Zoe.'

'Anna is alive,' I say firmly.

'But I saw the blood. There was blood and I cleaned it up,' he stutters.

'Was she cut?'

'What?' He gazes at me, unable to focus, unable to think.

'Zoe died at her boyfriend's flat, if you could call him her boyfriend—her dealer, really,' clarifies David.

I've heard him say this dozens of times. He has a way of doing so that suggests a dignified acceptance. It isn't real. I know he rages, underneath. Thunders.

'Disgusting man,' I force the words out. 'When he found her, his first thought wasn't calling an ambulance, it was saving himself.'

She lay on the cold tiles, while her heart struggled to pump blood around her body and instead backed up into her veins and lungs, causing a heart attack.

'He lost time, clearing the house of the other crackheads and then hiding his gear.'

Nick blinks slowly. Trying to follow me.

'Only then did he bother to get help. Too late. For her. It worked perfectly for him, though. The police were hardly able to pin a thing on him. The evidence they did find meant he was given three months' community service. That's all. Three months, an hour a week, picking up litter. For my daughter's life.'

'I don't understand,' mutters Nick. 'I know Zoe. I've met her.'

I shake my head. I didn't take in any of that at the time, the detail about the useless boyfriend who let her die. It took months for me to grasp that because, at first, I was too beaten to give a damn. Nothing could bring her back so nothing mattered. For me, the fog has never quite cleared. But I do know one thing.

'Zoe's dead,' I reiterate.

Nick looks terrified, mystified.

I start to explain. 'Anna took it very hard, as you can imagine. Grief is extremely profound for twins. After Zoe died, she was so lonely. Her grief was relentless. She turned up in court desperate to hear that the dealer would go down, be made to pay. Even though she knew he could never pay enough. Her grief and anger only intensified after the court case. She felt let down by the police and the judicial system—although, in truth, they'd done their best with what they had to work with. She made a tally of how many people had let Zoe down. The scumbag, using boyfriend who'd supplied the filthy, fatal dose, but didn't call an ambulance. The pathetic crowd she ran around with who she thought were her friends but had only been concerned with saving their own skinny asses. David and me for—oh—so many reasons—' I break off, lost in the memory.

The thing is, however many reasons Anna came up with, I've thought of more. Guilt and grief are cannibalistic bedfellows; they feed off one another. Grow fat on one another. I feel guilty for punishing Zoe too severely when she first started running about doing stupid things. And for not punishing her enough, because maybe I could have stopped it getting out of hand. I feel guilty for imposing curfews and for not managing to get her to abide by them, for taking her to doctors and support groups and for trusting her to continue to attend, when she wasn't. Ultimately, I feel guilty for treating the symptoms of her addictions and not ever knowing the cause.

I sigh and get to the crux. 'Anna blamed herself for not picking up her phone.'

In the three years before Zoe died, she'd been admitted

to hospital five times because of drugs or drink. I remember all of those times; running through the corridors breathless, helpless, hopeless. Anna was always already at her side. *Always*. Next of kin, first to be informed, she'd move mountains to be there, to help her sister, to soothe her, if she could.

Except that last time.

'Anna had ignored the call. She'd just found the texts from her husband to his PA. Pictures, explicit, shocking. Irrefutable. Another betrayal. It was unlike her but that evening she was caught up in her own world and didn't have time for Zoe. She saw Zoe's number on her screen and just didn't have the energy to pick up. She switched off her phone.'

She couldn't face being needed. That one time. Zoe was forever calling her as though she was nothing more than a taxi service. If Zoe was stuck, paralytic somewhere in town, no cabbie would give her a lift so she'd call Anna. If she needed a lift home from the police station, same thing.

'Larry, Anna's husband—'

Nick nodded. He knew who Larry was, evidently. That was something.

'Well, he was always complaining about it, saying Zoe took advantage. The truth was, he was jealous. Their relationship was so intense, so exclusive and excluding. Maybe he got sick of playing second fiddle, maybe that's why he had his affair. The timing of the discovery of the affair couldn't have been worse.'

No one could blame Anna. No one did, except she blamed herself. When they picked up Zoe's body, she was clutching her phone. She'd pressed redial on Anna's number seven times. She should have called 911…

I pause in telling the tale. It's too much to speak of, it's too much to listen to, without a breather. I listen to the wall clock ticking. I hate a ticking clock, counting down, but David's mother bought it for us for our wedding and David is attached to it; he doesn't understand why I want to get rid of it and all the other clocks. Clocks and calendars and sunsets and sunrises. Anything that takes me further away from when I had two daughters.

'I need some water.' I feel light-headed and heavy-hearted.

David stands up, walks to the kitchen and returns with a glass. He hasn't thought to offer Nick. There's no ice or lemon; it's a functional glass of water. So much of what we do now is simply serviceable. We don't light scented candles, or put bows on gifts we wrap. We don't live life, we get through, we get by. But it's not just Zoe who we are grieving for.

David takes up the story, and I'm grateful.

'You see, however devastating it was for us, it was worse for her. Our twinless twin. Psychologists agree that there is no comparable grief. When Zoe died, Anna seemed to start to disappear. They'd always been as one. Without her, Anna felt she wasn't quite whole. She felt half of herself was missing. As though she'd been sliced right down the centre.'

Cleaved. That's how she described it. She missed her so much she just wanted to keep a piece of her, if she could.

'She felt such guilt. Firstly, because she hadn't answered the call, and more profoundly, because she was alive when Zoe was not,' adds David sadly. 'She went beyond grieving.'

Nick is shaking. The room is warm but he's shivering. It's shock, I suppose. What we're telling him is unbelievable. I glance at David. We've done well, David and I, considering. It's tough, pitiless, trying to keep a marriage going after something like this, but we've clung to one another. We both knew we had one duty: to shore up Anna. And we've tried. We've tried so hard.

Failed, it seems.

David puts his hand on my lower back and makes a small, circular motion. He knows my back always aches when I speak of Zoe. The doctors can't find anything medically wrong with me.

'The psychologists said that, following Zoe's death, Anna obviously felt a need to live for two and do the things her twin could not do any more but had once enjoyed. This is not an uncommon response to a twin's death. In Zoe's case that meant drugs, drink and sex. But Anna, so strict and straight-laced, couldn't bring herself to do those things. At least, not as Anna. She had to actually *be* Zoe.'

Nick turns pale. 'What do you mean?'

'I think you know,' says David steadily.

'What? Is she bipolar? Schizophrenic, or what?'

'She's sad, Nick.'

'But there must be a name for it.'

He wants a name, so then he could look for a cure. We understand. David tries to explain in a careful, measured way.

'You know, those labels, more often than not, are used incorrectly. People have such a poor understanding of what it means to be schizophrenic. Largely because of how it's presented in movies and such. It's safest to say she has a disorder. Identity confusion. And she suffers from bouts of psychotic episodes—you know, delusions.'

'Can they do anything?'

'She's seen doctors and counsellors. There are pills. She doesn't like taking them. Did you see her taking pills regularly?'

David always prefers to concentrate on the medical side of things. He finds it somehow reassuring and more accountable.

Nick shakes his head. 'Why wouldn't she take her pills, if they help her? That's crazy.' He hears himself and turns red.

I don't know him well enough to know if it's embarrassment or frustration.

'She's traumatized,' I confirm. 'She very much wants Zoe to be alive.-She makes it so, the only way she can.'

'The psychologists said that after Zoe's death she felt displaced. Not really here any more, because her twin had gone.'

Naturally, this is something I feel guilty about. Another thing. I'm drenched in it. Wading through it. I've always wondered, was it was our fault? Had we placed too much emphasis on the fact that they were twins?

Nick glances around the room, uncertain he's understood. 'She pretends to be Zoe.'

'Almost, not quite. She thinks she *is* Zoe and she thinks she *is* Anna.'

So here we are. One daughter dead, the other destroyed.

She was grief-stricken and guilt-stricken. Always extreme and sensitive, she just couldn't get on with it or get over it. She believed she could have changed things, if only she'd picked up the phone. She insisted that Zoe's death was her fault. It wasn't. Zoe was way down her path of self-destruction by then; if it hadn't been that night, it would have been another. Anna could never have dragged her back. Anna couldn't have saved her.

But Anna couldn't let her die either.

And she was the only one who could keep her alive.

FIFTY-ONE
Nick

His mind was bleached. He didn't know what or *how* to think.

'It started with her wanting to sleep at Zoe's apartment, crawl into her bed. She'd just left her husband, she needed to stay somewhere, we didn't think it was odd. Then, when she didn't appear bothered about colleting her own clothes for ever such a long time, she wore Zoe's. We still thought that it was a reasonable response to grief. It was a way to be closer to her sister and a way to avoid further confrontation with Larry. It was a very painful time. Next, she started wearing make-up in much the way Zoe had, which is—'

'Very different to the way Anna does,' Nick interrupted Alexia.

'Exactly,' she confirmed.

David coughed and continued with the explanation; it was like a finely choreographed relay race. The husband and wife knew how much the other could bear before they took up the baton.

'It's actually quite a common occurrence amongst twins. When one dies the other takes on some of their habits or characteristics. It's a way of holding on. I once read about a twin who completed his dead brother's bucket list. People called it a tribute. They were proud of him.'

When does tribute slip into a disorder? A mental health problem? Nick wasn't sure. He thought that it was possibly when you and your dead twin were both sleeping with your fiancé.

'Three or four months after Zoe had died, Anna signed up to a modelling agency. Something Zoe had always talked about doing but had never had the discipline or drive to get around to. We didn't think it was a problem until we discovered she was working under Zoe's name. That was the beginning of the blurring.'

'She started going to the bars Zoe had visited, hanging out with the sort of people Zoe would have befriended. Not Zoe's actual friends, you understand—they knew she was dead—but those sorts.'

'Did she drink like Zoe? Do drugs?' Nick asked.

'No, that was the only thing that gave us any comfort. She was sort of living Zoe's life but a better version of it. No drugs, drink at a manageable level, and a job.' Alexia sounded almost hopeful, as though she too wanted to buy into the fantasy. 'It was almost as though she was trying to show what could have been. She was more confident, more sassy. At first, we told ourselves there was no real harm, maybe it would even be good for her.'

David sighed. 'But then she started talking to Zoe.'

'Many grieving people do that,' Nick pointed out. 'I imagine it's comforting.'

'And then she started talking *about* Zoe, in the present tense. 'Zoe wants a salad for supper, she needs to lose a few pounds for her next job,' or, 'Zoe told me to paint the flat grey, she hates the blue I've picked out.' That sort of thing.'

'Oh.'

'It was complete denial. That's when we took her to see some experts.'

Nick stared at these two earnest middle-aged people who were greying, sober, seemingly genuine and intelligent. However, he didn't know how to believe them. He'd met Zoe. He'd had sex with Zoe. She was a completely different woman from Anna. He knew, because he'd been engaged to Anna. And all that went with that statement. He'd know if they were the same woman. He would.

But.

He was struggling with understanding that he'd never met Zoe, just an imitation. He was baffled by the fact that he'd an affair with the woman he was cheating on. He wondered, how was Anna capable of such enormous duplicity? Then he squirmed with shame as he admitted to himself that he was the last one to talk about duplicity. He let his head fall into his hands. He fought an urge to give up completely, just slide on to the floor, through the cracks in the floorboards, let the earth below the house swallow him up. This seemed preferable to pushing through the consequences of what they'd just told him. How could she have fooled him? He thought of the yelps of delight he'd elicited from Zoe as she crashed through orgasm, and the shy blushes Anna used to bestow when she felt comfortable in bed. How?

There had been blood. It had smelt like blood. He'd cleaned it up. It had made him vomit. That was all real.

David and Alexia wanted to understand everything they could about Anna's recent state of mind and so they insisted Nick tell them all that had happened in the past six months. He owed them the truth, but the words choked him. He slowly ploughed through the story; he didn't come out of it well. They hung on his every word. Alexia bit her bottom lip, and David commented that, 'Things seem worse than ever.' Neither of them said so but Nick felt it; it was obviously his fault that Anna had been pushed to this extreme. No one needed to tell him. So many thoughts were charging through his head, fighting to find order. He recalled particular evenings when Zoe pretended to be talking to Anna on the phone and teased him by offering to put her on speaker phone. He'd always recoiled, his brashness never quite spilling over into that level of cruelty. What might have happened if he'd said yes? How would she have played that? The fact they had never met up as a threesome

made sense now, as did the fact that Anna was always occupied with something else when Nick was sneaking about
with Zoe. He imagined the lengths Anna must have gone to,
changing her clothes, her shoes, the colour of her nails. The
logistics of this deceit were interesting, fascinating. Almost
admirable, he thought. When he said as much to David and
Alexia, David looked furious.

'Don't you understand? This isn't about her deceiving
you, she's deceiving herself. She thinks she is two people,
and now she thinks she's killed her other self and become
Zoe. She's seriously ill.'

Maybe, or maybe she was brilliant. Nick wasn't sure.

One thought banged against his temples repeatedly,
drowning out everything else. *Anna is not dead.* Not dead,
after all. Although Zoe was, but not the Zoe he loved. Both
his Anna and his Zoe were alive. That was something. He
had to cling on to that.

They were good people, these people who would have
been Nick's in-laws, he could see that. He didn't know what
they were to him now but, considering all he had told them,
he thought that they'd be within their rights to throw him out
of their house, to hurl abuse if not actual stones at his head.
But they had been through a lot, seen a lot. Alexia, in particular, didn't want to judge him. She knew everyone was weak.

Eventually, David and Alexia left Nick to his thoughts.
They busied themselves in the kitchen, hiding behind the
excuse of making a cup of coffee. They just wanted to talk
about him. Naturally.

Nick listened to them hiss-whispering. Words tore between them.

David said, 'He's an opportunistic bastard. He was engaged to Anna and thought he was screwing Zoe.'

'I know, I know. It's complicated,' replied Alexia. 'But
what isn't, when it comes to Anna and Zoe? And look at him.'

Nick didn't know what they saw, but he didn't imagine
it was good. Eventually, to his relief, they asked him to stay

for something to eat. He wasn't hungry, but nor was he ready to leave them. Where would he go now? He was unclear whether he was being offered late lunch or early dinner. He'd lost track of time. He checked his watch. It was 4 p.m. locally, 9 p.m. at home. They'd been AWOL for a day. He should call someone. Work, or maybe Rachel. He couldn't. He didn't know what to say.

Nick ate their soup and accepted their hospitality as his mind slowly processed what they'd told him. He found it difficult to swallow. No one had much of an appetite.

He said, 'I need to find Anna. Do you have any idea where she might be? She's not answering either her number or the number she gave me for Zoe's phone. I have to see her.'

David tutted with impatience. 'You'd better get a plane home. Get on with your life. We'll sort this out. We can call you a cab to take you to the airport.'

'I'm so relieved that she's not dead.'

'Yes, you won't be going to prison,' pointed out David. He put down his soup spoon, stared out of the window. Nick knew he'd like to leave the table but was staying put for his wife.

Nick turn to Alexia and appealed, 'I need to find her. Will you help me?'

FIFTY-TWO
Anna/Zoe

'Anna?'

I swing around on my bar stool to face him. 'I'm sorry, you have me confused with my twin, it happens all the time. I'm Zoe.' I look him up and down, cool and blank.

He seems shocked at my rebuttal.

Of course I recognize him. Of course I know who he is, I'm not totally mad; I'm just giving him the old-fashioned cold shoulder. The way he dumped me at the airport. Shocking. After all I've done for him.

Frankly, I didn't really expect to see him again. I thought he'd be on the first plane back to England. I'm staggered by this show of balls. I didn't expect him to pursue me; he hasn't shown an ability to be single-minded thus far. People say better late than never, but I don't know, some things are just too late.

He throws a nervous look around the dark, heaving bar. Other than myself, I don't know why people are hiding in here. It's a beautiful evening outside; it deserves to be enjoyed.

'Anna, there are some things I need to say to you.'

I stare coldly.

'I know you're Anna. Not Zoe playing Anna.'

How irritating.

'Do *you* know it?'

I can hear the hesitancy and confusion in his question. 'Don't be so bloody prosaic, Nick,' I snap.

He runs his hand through his hair. 'I've talked to your parents.'

Oh, great. I feel a ball of fury swirl around in my gut. My parents have never done anything other than nag and interfere, although Anna would say that they are only doing their best and they mean well, that they must be worried sick. I try to push that thought aside; I haven't got room in my head to think about what Anna would say.

I look at Nick and take him in properly. He looks dreadful. It's not just the shaving shadow, the blue bags under his eyes, the sweat above his lips; he's grey, he's aged. There's nothing boyish about him any more. We've bashed that out of him. If he'd looked like this when Anna initially met him, I doubt he'd have pulled either of us. What am I saying? More likely, Anna *would* still have been interested, what with her desperate desire to fix everything and everyone the entire time. She'd have wanted to fold her arms around him, pull him into a big hug and promise him everything was going to be OK. She can't help herself. She's just so *nice*.

'What are you drinking?' he asks.

I let him buy me a vodka and tonic. He picks up our drinks and nods towards a quiet table in the corner. Part of me wants to make him squirm, say what he has to say here within earshot of the bar tender, but I follow him, weave my way through the crowds, to the quieter spot.

'How did you find me?' I ask.

'Your parents gave me the addresses of some of Zoe's old haunts. This is the ninth bar I've looked in.

I raise my eyebrows sceptically. 'Nine, you say?'

'Yes.'

'How many might you have visited before you gave up?'

'As many as it took to find you.'

I doubt that, I know this man has limits, and so I push for specifics. 'Twenty, thirty?'

'I'd have just kept looking,' he says smoothly.

'Careful, Nick, you're in danger of sounding a little mad.'

He doesn't comment on that but asks, 'Have you been in here all afternoon?'

'I went to my apartment first but the asshole landlord has rented it out to a new tenant. I walked in on this middle-aged woman doing Pilates with her personal trainer. It was quite the confusion. I've only been away a couple of months. I'm still paying rent.'

'You mean your place in the West Village?'

I nod. Good old Ma and Pa really have been spilling the beans.

'You know you haven't rented that apartment for over two years, right, Anna? And Zoe hasn't been there for three years,' he says carefully.

To refute this, I hold up the keys and dangle them so they clink together like bells.

'You should have handed those over, Anna,' he says primly.

'Anna is dead.'

'No, Zoe is dead.'

I turn away from him. This is not useful. We're going backwards now.

'I'm sorry,' he adds gently. 'It must have been horrific, losing her like that. Your parents explained how brutal it was for you. How much you missed her.'

'You've got it wrong.'

'No, I haven't.'

'Zoe was dead,' I admit with a sigh. 'But now Anna is.'

He stares at me, concern bleeding all over the table. This is not new for me. Doctors, counsellors, my parents have all worn similar expressions that show varying degrees of unease, alarm, distress. It's not as helpful as they'd like to think; it's pretty boring, actually. But then Nick surprises me and I get a tiny hint of the mind I fell in love with months ago, when he asks something unexpected.

'Why does Anna have to go?'

There's no point in pretending. 'You like Zoe better.'

'No, I—It wasn't—'

We stare at one another. What can he say?

'You wanted her more, so Anna had to go. But Anna had paperwork, a national insurance number, a passport and a driver's licence. All Zoe had was a death certificate.'

'Wow.' He swallows back his drink.

I do too.

'Do you want another?'

I say yes because my legs suddenly feel too heavy to move. And besides, he looks like he needs company. It's a warm summer evening, couples all over the word are enjoying a glass together. Why shouldn't we? 'I'll have a lemonade.' Vodka is Zoe's poison. I'm not sure either of us has ever ordered a lemonade since we were about ten, it just seems a sensible choice. I need the sugar and I don't need to be any drunker.

He comes back from the bar with two lemonades; very wise, quite the adult.

As he puts them on the table he asks, 'Why did you do it this time? I understand about how it came about in the first place—the profound grief, the shock, the response to Zoe's death—but why did you bring Zoe to London to meet me? We were so happy.'

'Were we?'

'Yes!'

I glare at him. 'I heard you.'

'Heard me when?'

'With Cai and Darragh, in the pub, just two weeks after we got engaged.'

He lurches, ever so slightly. Any residue of colour he carried now drains away. I see that he's in pain. He's mopping up the fault and blame, absorbing it. If I'm being fair, I'd say he is sixty per cent to blame for Zoe's reappearance. There are other contributing factors. I was lonely in London, friends are hard to come by—that had an effect of, say, ten per cent. I'd stopped taking my tablets regularly—maybe another ten per cent. I was still pretty bashed up emotion-ally—the vulnerability I felt following my relationships with John, Larry and Kelvin accounted for the remaining twenty per cent of blame.

Zoe would say the whole thing was one hundred per cent mine.

It was one of her most admirable qualities, that she be-lieved people ought to own their own mess. That was ac-tually the thing she first came back to tell me. When I was blaming myself for her passing, she wanted me to know that she didn't blame me, she took responsibility. She kept say-ing, 'I made my own choices, Anna.'

I wish I could have believed her.

Nick is gasping air like a fish that's just jumped out of its bowl. 'I was only joking,' he says.

I must look sceptical.

'Sort of joking. Certainly not serious. I just said that stuff to the lads to shut them up.'

'Yet, you did sleep with Zoe. Repeatedly.'

He looks irritated to have that pointed out. Annoyed with himself or me? I'm not sure.

'But you presented Zoe to me. And she was you but more than you.'

'More?' I ask sharply.

'Well, different. No one else could have tempted me.'

'You see, you do like Zoe the best.'

'No, if I'd met Zoe first and then you, I'd've—'

'What? You'd have had an affair with me?'

'No, that's not what I mean.'

It sort of is.

He admits as much when he says, 'I was in love with you both.'

I tut at him. Zoe would have thrown a drink. Neither of us were enough.

We sit in the centre of this mess and don't know how to plough our way out.

Eventually, Nick says, 'You could have just said something. Tackled me. Called me to account. That would have been the ordinary, normal thing to do.'

'I *never* claimed to be normal.'

He blanches, responding to the sliver of anger that I could not keep in check.

Men have called me a lot of things in my time. Zoe has had all the usual ones thrown at her: slut, whore, bitch. She's also been labelled a troublemaker, a freeloader, a junkie, and many other things. Anna has been called frigid, cold and a prick-tease, as well as a starry-eyed, overly romantic pushover. And then, finally, clinically insane. None of it is nice but, right now, I think calling me ordinary is the worst thing he could ever call me. I'm a twin, I've never been normal. I've always been special; *we've* always been special. He must understand that much. Being a twin is like being a celebrity. It gives you an inflated sense of your own importance. It's like everything we did as a twin was more than twice as important and so, maths being complex and tricky to understand, when she died I was less than half a being. It was devastating. I missed her so much. I miss her, still.

'So you're admitting you're Anna, we're agreed on that now?'

I shrug. 'I'm not sure.' I have been Anna and Zoe. I have been Anna being Zoe and then Zoe playing Anna. I'm in a unique position, I can be either, and I find I'm not ready to pick.

He sighs.

I would feel sorry for him but, hey, I don't owe him any favours. I rather admire his next comment, though, it's a careful way around what is, let's face it, an awkward situation.

'Why didn't you just tell me you had a twin who had died?'

A million reasons.

Because I didn't want her to be dead. Even three years

after she had gone the words ripped at my heart and lodged like splinters in my throat. Because admitting she was dead would inevitably have led to a conversation about how I handled my grieving. I'm not sure at which stage mental health is OK to discuss when dating. Second date? Third? Before or after sex? Tricky, huh? I glance around the bar; it's awash with embryonic flirtations, exciting first dates, miserable break-ups and tentative reconciliations. They're all brewing here, right now. People will be talking about the number of sexual partners they've had, their first fling with drugs, the last time they got paralytic drunk; I don't imagine many are sharing details about when they were committed to a mental hospital. The last taboo.

'And how were you going to explain the absence of a sister to me after telling me she was alive and in London?'

I meet his challenging tone. 'Well, if you'd passed the test, I would have revealed myself, told you about the whole set-up. It could have just been a sexy joke. We could have just laughed about the entire thing. But you didn't pass the test. You had an affair, Nick.'

'With you,' he argues defensively.

'No, with *her*,' I insist.

'What's the difference?'

I don't know, so I just glare at him.

His face collapses into a look of regret. 'I'm sorry, Anna, I really am.'

I know what he's thinking. He's thinking about the sex. Oh yes, Zoe and Nick's sex. Mind-blowing. Literally.

'And then I began to enjoy it.' I shrug. I mostly mean the sex here too, but the other bits—being careless and carefree, being challenging and cheeky—these are not things that sit easily with my personality. 'I'm able to be someone I'm not when I'm her. Look, it's complicated. I guess you think I'm insane.' I say it before he has to.

'No. I don't.'

'No?'

'You're imaginative. Everyone likes a little variety now and then, we like to escape ourselves, that's why we buy new clothes or go on holiday.'

I was not expecting that, a level of understanding, empathy. I'm so shocked, all I can do is refute his tolerance and perception. 'It's not the same,' I insist.

'In many ways it is,' he replies soothingly.

'She's not variety. Zoe. She's dead. She's my dead sister.'

He looks pleased with himself. I suppose he sees the fact I've admitted Zoe is my dead sister as progress.

'People talk to the dead people they miss. It's very normal.'

'Will you stop calling me normal!' I bang my hand down on the little wooden table between us. Our drinks quiver. 'I didn't just talk to Zoe. I *became* Zoe.'

'Well, maybe you're extraordinarily normal.' He grins winningly.

I almost believe he gets me. That he understands that I'm not insane. Not exactly. I'm fluid. It's beguiling, believing I'm understood—by him, especially. But it's too good to be true.

I remind him how extreme I am. 'I told you I'd murdered her.'

'Ah, technically, you told me she'd murdered you,' he grins.

Can he think this is amusing?

'How did you do that trick with the blood anyway? I've been wondering.'

I suppose it's quite fun being able to reveal it all. I mean I have been brilliant, and what's the point of brilliance, if no one else sees it?

'I got it on the internet. It's not real blood. They use it on TV.'

'But it smelt like blood.'

'I added liquid iron. You can buy that in Boots. I thinned

it down a bit, but I was depending on you not having that much experience with real blood.'

'Nice,' he nods admiringly.

I can't help but grin. 'Thanks.'

'I guess I was served, well and truly.'

'I guess you were.'

I don't quite know what is happening here. We're almost flirting, let's be honest, we are flirting. It's a little bit like that first night when we met in Villandry and it's a little bit like that other first night when we met in the boutique hotel restaurant. But better. Better than either of those dates. This feels more truthful. Messy, embarrassing but real.

'I'm sorry, Anna, that I betrayed you. I'm sorry that I wasn't a better man. I know there's no reason why you should believe me, or even care, but I'd never, ever do anything like that again. Never.'

I search his face and it is oozing sincerity. The sort neither Zoe nor I have seen from him since he met her. I guess I cured him of that at least; cleaning up after your fiancée's murder probably makes you doubt your right to fool around.

He plays with his glass, drawing his finger through the condensation that is bubbling there. Quietly, he says, 'Perhaps you can let her go now.'

'Please don't say anything crass like she had a good life, or she burned bright, or whilst she was only on this planet for a few years she lived a bigger life than some people who get to a ripe old age.'

'Why can't I say those things, aren't they true?'

'No, I don't think so. Her adult life wasn't very happy. I mean it couldn't have been, could it? If she needed all those drugs and men and the drink. I think my version of her life was better than the reality. That's what kills me, Nick—the futility.'

Nick looks at his fingers—the neat, clean fingernails that I loved—and asks, 'How much of her life did you take on?'

'A lot. She's slept with about twenty men since she died.'

'Fuck.'

'Don't you dare judge. You're in no position to judge.'

'No. No, I won't,' he says quickly.

'She didn't sleep with anyone since I met you, if that's what you were wondering.'

'No, I wasn't.'

I can see he was. For a moment I feel it again. The grief washes through me. 'I can't explain how much I missed her. There was a hole in my soul; a great big gaping nothingness. I was so lonely. Those men she was with, after she died I mean, they were me trying to plug the gap. I know everyone else thought she was a pain in the ass. I thought she was spectacular.'

'I see that,' he says gently.

'Do you?'

'Yes. You made her spectacular for me. You showed me that.' He reaches forward and touches my face.

I'm stunned to realize that it's wet with tears.

He blots one with his fingertip and then puts it to his lips. 'But you also showed me she was a pain in the ass.'

'I did, didn't I?' I try to smile.

A hush settles on our table. He leans close to me, his forehead almost touching mine. As he speaks I feel the warmth of his breath on my face.

'I understand. I wanted to split myself in half too. It was dreadful. Frightening. I didn't feel in control of myself.'

I stare into his eyes. Is it possible? Does he understand?

He pulls back. Sits at a distance from me.

I imagine that is it now. He's got the answers he needs so that he can sleep easily at night. He's been pretty graceful about it, and now he can slink back to the UK and carry on with his life of meaningless shags and shallow relationships. Nick will be fine. No damage done, after all.

'I love you,' he says.

'You're in love with a dead girl,' I say sadly.

'I'm in love with *you*.'

'Me, playing a dead girl.'

'Yes, and you being yourself. Aren't you perhaps both?'

'I don't know. I suppose I am.'

'You were really good at being bad,' he smiles. 'Maybe, just hear me out, maybe you don't have to be quite as sweet and good as you always thought you had to be. Maybe, that was something you did as a reaction to Zoe's personality and you did it from such an early age you never got the chance to explore an alternative. Perhaps you can relax a little, breathe out now. Be your sweet self but with a bit of an edge too.'

I want it to be so. Me, but looser, freer. Me, having learned from Zoe but not having to *be* Zoe. 'Do you think that could be true?'

'I don't know. Maybe. Why not?'

'And is that what you want?'

He stretches across the table and tentatively puts his hand on mine. 'I want you, whoever you are.'

'And you'd cope with that?'

'I don't know, but I'd like to have the chance to try. I want you to be healthy and happy. You'll have a greater chance of being those things if you let me support you.'

'No one knows me better,' I concede. 'I want to be healthy and happy too, Nick. I hid a lot from you. I didn't dare show you who I was because I thought it would scare you off, but you know me now and you're still here.'

'Sure am, sitting opposite you, nursing a glass of lemonade,' he says goofily.

I feel the loneliness that has perpetually surrounded me since Zoe's death slip slightly, like a slow thaw. The huge well of solitude does not seem so wide or deep. I want to fold my arms around him, this faulty, sorry man who loves me and has hurt me, who I loved and hurt, who says he loves me still. Who, in a way, I love still. I think of the beautiful wedding I have planned and all the people who are expecting to attend on Saturday. They will have bought new clothes and gifts, booked hotels and taxis. I would never want to inconvenience them. I want to waltz down the aisle in a cloud of bliss, I want a happily ever after.

That, more than anything.

So, I have no choice.

I scrape back my chair and I stand up tall. 'Thank you, Nick, for everything. But it would never work out with us. It's time I stopped looking back. I need to move forward.'

He looks stunned, shocked. 'But I thought we were getting somewhere,' he stutters.

'When Zoe died I didn't want to accept the reality. That was a damaging mistake. I should have just found a way to grieve for her and then to let her go. It would be a mistake now to kid myself and think of you as anything other than a man who betrayed me within a month of proposing. I deserve better. I deserve more.'

The word 'more' must echo through his head. I was not enough. He needed both of us. John, Larry and Kelvin had wanted more too. I was not enough for them. But this isn't my fault. This is theirs. I *am* enough and someone, somewhere will see that. Some day.

'Anna—' He grabs my hand.

I'm not going to lie, his touch sends sparks all over my body. I close my eyes to stop the tears coming.

'You've just said, people make mistakes. I made one. Can't you forgive me?'

'No, Nick. I'm sorry. I can't. I wish you well. I hope you find someone lovely, and I hope the next time you'll value her.' I shake my hand loose and walk away.

Leaving behind a man I know I will grieve for but a man I will let go.

EPILOGUE

'I don't want to go,' Anna groaned.

Vera nodded sympathetically. 'I understand, honey, of course you don't. But you sort of have to,' she added with her usual punch of good sense. 'It's such a big deal for the centre. Our first ever corporate donation and such a *huge* one. I've rung the organizers, and they've assured me that there is no Nick Hudson on the guest list. It's an enormous bank, they didn't even seem to know his name.'

It could not be a coincidence. From the moment Anna had picked up the phone to the polite, efficient woman who told her Herrill Tanley was looking for small charities to support, through their local and global corporate responsibilities investment programme, Anna had suspected Nick was behind the call. He must have joined the charitable committee and suggested Drop In as a worthy cause, otherwise how would such a huge bank ever have heard of their existence? It was probably a strategy to atone, possibly a way to make contact with her again. The woman with the crisp voice had said that there would be some paperwork and then her colleagues would need to assess the centre itself. On the day of the assessment Anna had barely been able to eat with stress. She'd wanted to take the day off but her counsellor had advised her not too. Rather, she had to face her fears. Anna had been seeing her counsellor regularly and knew the value of her advice. In the end, it was two women who did the assessment. Throughout the process there had been no sign of Nick.

One hundred thousand pounds.

It was a massive amount of money. Life changing. For so many. A miracle. The things that they could do with that. Still, Anna did not want to see Nick. Ever again. You can't go backwards. Time blunders on. However, she could hardly pull out of the event now. They were going to be presented with one of those enormous photo-worthy cheques. Vera and Anna were taking along six of the centre's visitors. Names had been drawn from a hat because pretty much everyone fancied eating canapés and drinking champagne in the City at someone else's expense. Vera couldn't be expected to keep an eye out for everyone as well as take receipt of the cheque.

It had been a long, hard six months since she'd walked out of that bar in New York. Since she had left part of her heart behind. There'd been times when she was riddled with familiar, dreadful feelings of sadness or loneliness. Sometimes it felt even worse than before; now she missed Zoe *and* Nick. She had, from time to time, questioned whether she'd made the right decision by walking away from him. Should she have clung to him? Maybe they could have managed to forgive one another. To bear it. Her counsellor talked a lot about healthy, honest relationships and, somewhat confusingly, she talked about realistic expectations too. Anna was still wading her way through it all. Her counsellor wasn't as much fun to talk to as Zoe, but she had the advantage of being alive.

Anna had been tempted to exclusively throw herself into her work. She was safe and secure at the centre; vital, valued. However, she had forced herself to recognize that she needed more in her life than work. She'd joined a support network for bereaved twins, she'd signed up for the evening class in advanced Spanish and had persuaded some of the other students to do the same. Now, instead of scuttling home after the class, they usual went to get tapas. Once they went to a salsa club; there was even talk of a weekend break to Barcelona this coming spring. She'd also somehow found the nerve to knock on the door across her corridor and invite her neighbours around for supper. It was embarrassing, explaining that it wasn't exactly a dinner party she was inviting them to, because there were no other guests. However, they'd been incredibly nice about it and, in the end, they'd just eaten a takeaway in front of the TV; in fact, it had become their thing on a Thursday evening. Relaxed, casual, friendly. They'd watched the entire series of *The Apprentice* together. Serena and Kit had asked her to one of their proper dinner parties, where she met five more new people. One of them had asked her for a coffee, and another had persuaded her to join their local gym; she was enjoying the Zumba and kickboxing classes and she'd met more people there too. Making new friends felt like a slow, laborious process—except when it didn't. Sometimes it felt fun and free and possible. Besides, she found she had plenty of extra time to invest in these embryonic friendships because she hadn't bothered to re-subscribe to any online dating sites. That wasn't where she was going to find the happily ever after she craved.

She finally understood the wisdom you so frequently found splattered across greetings cards, sewn on cushions in craft shops and popping up on Facebook feeds. You had to learn to love yourself before you could expect anyone else to do so.

'He has to be behind this,' muttered Anna for about the fiftieth time. 'The donation and Ivan's new job.'

Whilst doing their assessment of the centre the women at Herrill Tanley had also explained to Vera and Anna that there was an outreach programme where the bank tried to employ a quota of people associated with the charities they supported. As a result, Ivan was now employed as a cleaner at Herrill Tanley. He mostly worked the night shift so didn't run into too many people and even when he did, a few more expletives were barely noticed in a bank. Anna was almost as delighted as Ivan that he'd finally found regular, paid employment; she couldn't resent it—in fact, she was grateful for it—but she wished it had come about independently of Nick.

'Well, maybe he is involved,' admitted Vera. 'But so what? He seems to want to keep his involvement quiet. You haven't heard from him directly, have you?'

'No.' That was part of the reason for Anna's infuriation.

If he'd done something traditional like call her, she'd have had the satisfaction of hanging up on him. If he'd sent flowers, she could have watched them wither and dry to a crisp. His good deeds were anonymous but weighty and heavily stamped. He knew her well enough to guess that the way to her heart was through those she cared for. It was hard to refuse what others needed. He was making her beholden, and she didn't want that at all. She almost hated him for it.

'I hope he knows he can't buy his way into my good books.'

'He might be just trying to make amends,' pointed out Vera sagely.

Vera knew the whole story. Anna had decided to tell her the truth when she returned from New York. She'd wanted to keep her job at the centre and needed to explain her sudden, unexpected absence. The truth seemed the only way forward, partly because she was too exhausted to think of one more lie, one more deception, and partly because Anna knew that if she was ever going to be truly well she needed some support around her. Who better qualified to help than Vera?

Vera had accepted the situation with her usual equanimity. She'd passed tissues but no comments, other than small encouraging sounds such as 'uh huh' and 'OK', whilst Anna spluttered and blushed and wept her way through her story.

'Can I still work here?' Anna had begged.

The truth was, her wage from Drop In barely covered her bills; she made more money from Zoe's modelling. Of course she realized that she could do catalogue work as Anna too, but it wasn't what she wanted. She wanted to work here at Drop In, alongside Mrs Delphine, Rick and all the other people she cared about, but she realized that her poor mental health was an issue.

Vera had hugged her, laughed and commented, 'Like I'd dare cross you, after hearing all that.' She was the one who put Anna in touch with the counsellor.

Vera had remained loyal, understanding and sensible. Right now, she reached across the reception desk and squeezed Anna's fingers. 'Hey, remember, it's not his money. Even if he is on the committee that decides these things, you don't owe him a thing. These big banks give away tons of cash. So, we're the lucky recipients this time. Let's just enjoy it.'

They took a tube and then scurried through the City streets, arriving wide-eyed at the imposing building that was the bank's head office. Their gang made a crazy and colourful contrast to those around them. For a start, they were not dressed in dark designer suits, they were not striding purposefully, oblivious to the stupendous grandeur of the building, but rather gawping carelessly. And besides, they were laughing and chatting rather than scowling or trying to look sophisticated.

'Wow, this place is stunning, if not a bit intimidating,' said Vera. She gazed up at floor after floor of glass and marble. 'Imagine working here.'

Anna had been there before. Well, technically, Nick had brought Zoe; they'd had sex on his desk. Neither incarnation had ever been introduced to his colleagues; there hadn't been either the time or the occasion. The whole episode had been a whirlwind—or, more accurately, a tornado.

They took the elevator to the nineteenth floor, where the lift doors parted; they followed the noise of laughter and clinking glasses and the heady perfume of fat waxy lilies. Someone offered to take their coats and, in exchange, someone else proffered a tray of champagne. Everyone took a glass; a few with grateful shyness, others with bold entitlement. The room was crowded and noisy. They'd been told it was to be an intimate gathering, which apparently in Herrill Tanley translated into at least a hundred people.

Anna had assumed their gang would all stay close to one another but, within minutes of their arrival, Vera and two of the others were whisked away by the bank's publicist who wanted to introduce them to someone or other, a journalist or the boss, maybe an influential client. Mrs Skarvelis pushed Mrs Delphine towards the food table. And Rick and Ahmed moved towards the window because they wanted to check out the view. Anna was left alone. She didn't mind. She wanted to stay at the back of the room, cling to the wall. Just in case. It was a lovely party; she couldn't fail to be impressed. Everyone looked elegant, pleased or proud. The champagne was copious, the canapés delicious, yet she couldn't relax. She nervously scanned the room and avoided small talk being forced upon her by engaging with the waiters and talking about the cute little savouries that they were offering. She found she had a particular fondness for the crab cocktail with tomato tartare, in fact she had one in her hand when—

She saw him.

Then he saw her.

Eyes across a crowded room. Bang. Their gazes locked. Tall, handsome, notable.

He weaved determinedly through the crowds, expertly dodging pleas for him to join small clusters of people who so obviously wanted to detain him. She quickly swallowed the remaining mouthful of crab, dabbed her lips with a napkin.

She couldn't take her eyes off him. Nor he, off her.

'Hello.'

'Hello.'

'Nice dress.'

'Thank you.'

'Beautiful colour.'

It was raspberry pink. Over the past six months Anna had tried to dress more boldly. She didn't want to wear invisible blacks and greys all winter; she no longer wanted to vanish. Anna had known since the moment that Pamela had told her about wearing a raspberry-coloured jumpsuit the night she'd met George, that she'd secretly craved owning something that colour. Something vibrant, luxurious and cheerful. Something full of life. She'd spotted this raspberry dress in Whistles and although it cost more than she usually spent on clothes, she hadn't been able to resist it. Now she was glad. From the way he was looking at her, it was worth every penny.

'It's what caught my eye. It's quite the statement. But you carry it off.'

It wasn't the smoothest compliment, but she believed it was well intentioned.

'Thank you.' She thought she sounded calmer than she felt. She hoped so.

'Is it velvet?'

'Yes.'

'I want to touch it.' He looked surprised that he'd actually said so.

Anna felt like giggling. There was something attractive about a person inadvertently blurting out exactly what they were thinking. It was refreshing, most people tried so hard to be cool.

'Velvet has that effect,' she told him.

'No, *you* have that effect.'

'Cheesy line,' she smiled.

He laughed and blushed. 'Sounded a lot like one, right? But honestly, I meant it.'

For a second she closed her eyes. Remembered to breathe. Felt the moment. Then slowly she opened them again. He was still there.

'Can I get you a drink?' he asked.

She nodded at the glass of champagne she was holding. 'I have one. The nice man on the door gives them out for free.'

'Oh yes, of course. Sorry.' He looked awkward but determined. 'Look, I'm not doing very well here. I'm normally considerably more impressive,' he managed to muster a grin.

'I bet you are,' she replied, laughing gently.

'Shall we start again? Pretend we've just met.'

She considered it. He seemed well intentioned, clever, pleasant, he was certainly handsome. There were worse ways to pass an evening. 'If you like.'

With an obvious sigh of relief, he asked, 'So where do you fit in? How come you're here?'

'I work for one of the charities that are benefiting. We're picking up a big cheque tonight.'

'Ha! Well, you have me to thank for that,' he said, looking pleased with himself for the first time.

'Really?'

'Well, not entirely. Although, I am on the charity committee. I've had some influence on picking a longlist of worthy charities.'

'How did you choose?'

'A bit randomly, really. I just picked ones I'd heard of. Ones my friends, or friends of friends, had an interest in. It's as good a place as any to start for a longlist.'

He held out his hand and she shook it.

'Sorry, I should have introduced myself. I'm Hal Douglas. I'm in equity capital markets.'

'Oh.' Anna blanched. 'I'm Anna Turner.'

He swayed. 'Nick's fiancée?'

'Well, no, not for six months. But well, yes.'

'I'm—'

'His friend, I know.' She dropped her eyes to their hands.

He was still clasping hers. He ought to let go now. He didn't. He just moved his thumb a fraction, like an inadvertent caress.

Then he coughed. 'More of a colleague, I'd say, than friend; we didn't have all that much in common in the end. Ex-colleague, actually. He left the bank after, well—' Hal looked away from her for a second.

It was only then that she realized it was the first time he'd broken his gaze since they set eyes on each other. She found she wanted him to look at her again.

'He's taken a year's sabbatical. Did you know?'

'I didn't. I actually thought he was behind Drop In receiving the cheque.'

'No, sorry. That was—'

'You.'

'Well, yes. I guess. I'd heard him talk about your good work. Did you want it to be him?'

'No.'

Hal looked relieved.

It was true that she hadn't wanted to be beholden to Nick, but now, somewhat annoyingly, she realized that she did want to think he was repentant, or at least aware.

With a smidge of irritation she asked, 'Where is he spending his sabbatical? LA? Monaco? Barbados?' Anna threw out the names of the most glamorous places she could imagine.

'He's actually doing voluntary work in El Salvador, building orphanages, I think.'

'Wow.'

Hal smiled. 'A pretty impressive way to find yourself, you'd have to agree.'

'Is that what he's doing? Finding himself?'

'I suppose so. He never discussed it with me. I always believed we were quite close but I suppose we were boy-close, if you know what I mean. After he left I realized we didn't talk about the big stuff as much as we perhaps should have.' Hal shrugged. 'It's not what happens here, not usually. His move was sudden, unexpected. I just assumed you must be at the root of it.'

Anna coloured. She took a sip of her champagne. They were still holding hands. No longer as though they were shaking hands, but something closer and more familiar. Tender. She should break away. She didn't. And it didn't feel as weird as it should have done.

'Did he tell you why we split up?'

Hal shook his head. 'Just cleared his desk over one weekend.'

Someone offered them a canapé. They shook their heads; neither wanted to be interrupted.

With some reluctance, trepidation, Hal asked, 'Would you like to talk about it?'

'It was complicated. My sister died.'

'Oh my God, the one he was having an affair with?' Hal looked shocked, saddened.

Anna could only imagine all sorts of horrors that he was trying to process and order. She quickly dived in. 'Before he had an affair. Technically, he was having an affair with me.'

'What?'

'It's a long and boring story.'

'It really doesn't sound boring!' Hal's eyes were wide; it was almost funny.

'No,' she admitted. 'Complicated then.'

'I have time, if you want to talk about it.'

Anna glanced around the noisy room. This was not the time or the place.

Reading her, Hal said, 'Maybe it would be better if you told me in a quiet bar.'

She looked hesitant.

'Or over a cup of coffee,' he added.

She did not get the chance to answer because at that moment they were interrupted by the distinctive tapping of a microphone being brought to life. They listened to the rather wordy speeches and clapped when the cheques were bestowed. Vera's acceptance speech was tight, polite and upbeat; Anna felt enormously proud.

Suddenly it was time to go. People were collecting up empty glasses; there were no more canapés being passed around. The ordeal was over and it hadn't been an ordeal at all. Anna let out a breath that she hadn't been aware she was holding on to. She, Vera and the Drop In gang started to gather up their belongings and amble towards the door. Unexpectedly, Anna realized Hal was by her side.

He quietly slipped his hand into hers. 'So do you have time for that coffee?' he asked.

She glanced down at their hands.

Hal followed her gaze and grinned. 'Look, I know I shouldn't be holding your hand,' he admitted.

'No,' she agreed.

'It doesn't make any sense.'

'No.'

'It's really presumptuous. Nick always said I was a bit of a romantic idiot,' he mumbled, then added, 'I probably shouldn't be talking about Nick.'

'No.'

Hal shrugged, seemed to wonder what to say next. 'The thing is, it just feels OK. I just saw you across the room and something drew me to you.' Almost apologetically, he admitted, 'I don't want to let go. Not yet—'

Not ever?

'Is there any possibility that you know what I'm talking about?'

There was.

Anna nodded.

And so he led her through the throbbing crowd towards the exit.

Towards possibility. Towards a new beginning.

* * * * *